A Man
from the
North East

Beatrice Holloway

TSL Publications

First published in Great Britain in 2011 by Beatrice Holloway

Revised edition 2018
By TSL Publications, Rickmansworth

ISBN / 978-1-912416-32-5

Acknowledgements

I would like to take this opportunity to thank everybody who has helped with their time and shared their memories with me.

Special thanks go to:

George Temperley C of W, 1907-1974

Anne Samson
for encouragement and patience

My sons, Derek and Ray
for their continuing support

Kath Lewis and Brian Temperley
for their humorous contributions

Jenny Hunt and many other good friends
– you know who you are.

CHAPTER ONE

The steel, folding gates of the lift cage clanged shut behind George, Joseph his father, his cousin, Thomas and other members of the crew. As it began its journey downwards with a jolt, George felt the usual frisson of fear. As the lift settled and dropped more smoothly down the shaft he spoke quietly to Joseph standing beside him, hoping not to be overheard by the others. 'I'm packing it in on Friday, da. Giving in me notice.'

Joseph turned sharply towards him, and peering up at his son in the gloomy light afforded by their Davey lamps, asked, 'What's that you said, son?'

George knew his father had understood what he had said, but he'd made up his mind. 'I've had enough. I'm finishing on Friday I'm thinking.'

'Thou'll do nowt of the kind,' Joseph snapped back.

The lift stopped and as the gates opened to release the miners, George blurted out 'I'm twenty-one today, da. Thou can say what thou likes but you've no longer a say in my affairs.' George stumbled behind his father along the narrow, uneven tunnel towards the coalface. 'I'm away to London. Our Jessie will see me right. Wrote and told me plenty of jobs going down there.'

Joseph stopped dead in his tracks, almost causing a domino effect on the men behind. 'You leave our Jessie out of this. Shut your trap for now, lad. We'll discuss this at home. No need to air our differences down here.'

George sighed. Jessie had been Joseph's favourite daughter, and George knew her absence had made the old fellow crotchety, even though he'd acknowledged that girls had to work until they wed. George knew Joseph missed her, and the other sisters in service, and complained that the house was too quiet after they'd left, often saying, 'Me family's breaking up around me.'

The gang began to move forward again. George clenched his jaw and answered, 'I've made up me mind da, and nothing you say or do will stop me.'

Today was his twenty-first birthday, twenty-seventh of April nineteen thirty-one and no matter what, he was off to the Inn tonight for his first legal pint. Aye, he thought, there'll be lasses, and I'll play me fiddle for a dance. Tommy would play the drums and Freddie the piano, and he hoped that a good time was in store for them all. Maybe even a kiss or two, maybe more, who knows if he walked Pat home afterwards. It was rumoured that Pat was a little too free with her favours with the lads of the village.

Tommy had said only yesterday, 'I tell you our Joe, I saw her with me own eyes with that Sammy fella. He had his arm tight around her waist and she were giggling fit to bust.'

George had tried to laugh this off, and had lit up a cigarette before answering, 'It's alright. She's nothing special. Folk got nowt to do but gossip. No daft promises between us or owt like that,' but the news had niggled George. They had after all, an arrangement so it shouldn't bother him, but somehow it did. George liked the smell and feel of girls. Holding them in his arms as they danced the foxtrot, was warm and comfortable and gave him a feeling of needing more. However, he was deeply uneasy when he thought of his friends thinking likewise about his four teenage sisters.

The gang were working together, George and Joseph side by side, speaking only about the tasks in hand. George was aware, from the monosyllable grunts from his father that a row was brewing between them but his mind was made up.

What's more, Thomas had agreed with him. 'By lad, wished I could come with you,' he said. Tommy was the life and soul of the party when on the surface. 'Aye, but going down the pit,' he confided in George, 'well, man it's like dying. I hate the smell of coal, and the taste of the bloody stuff everywhere. Everything covered in black dust. Why even the beach at Seaton Carew is edged with the stuff. I can't stand the darkness knowing the sun's out up there. It's hell on earth as far as I'm concerned. I tell you our Joe the pit'll be the death of me.'

'You've a job, lad,' his uncle growled. 'There's many in this village'd change places with you. Think yerself lucky with a bob or two in your pocket.'

Every member of the crew heard the ominous crack. They all stopped working, backed up a little along the passage, and held their breath. Then Joseph said to George, 'Go back a bit son, and take a look.'

George had crawled carefully backwards, looking all the while at the roof. Then he saw it. A huge bulge in the roof, the wooden pit props straining to hold it. He turned, and called out a warning. 'Run! By God! The roof's about to go. Run! Quick, run for it.' Suddenly the roof caved in on either side of him.

George spat the dust out of his mouth. His lamp gave only an eerie glow on the rich coal seam ahead of him. Rolling over onto his side, he gazed at a now unfamiliar workplace. There was no one, no familiar voices, just the grating of rock and coal settling. 'Da! Da, where are you?' he called out. He heard nothing and his panic began to mount. Fearing that his father was dead, he wished that he had said nothing about London. The disagreement between them would never be resolved now. His last words to his father had been of defiance. Could it be that all the gang, his friends, were dead too? Crushed or suffocated? Thinking of Thomas's prediction, just wondering about their fate, made him want to cry. How could he tell his Aunt May that her only son, her only child was dead?

Slowly he began to realise his own precarious situation. He was alone, destined to die alone, and he felt deep sobs gathering in his chest. Surely, he thought, the rescue lads will be out by now. The rumbling would've been felt throughout the mine, bringing dread to everyone below ground, and to those, above once the warning hooter blared out across the fields and village. Someone must have alerted them by now, he told himself. He knew he could be in for a long wait, but the thought of rescue settled his uneasy thoughts a little. They might even get to da and the others first and find them in fine fettle with a bit of luck, he told himself.

George ran his hand over his face, and felt the grit sticking to his skin. Carefully, he felt slowly over his body for any injuries, and hesitated as his hands stretched down towards his legs. His legs! His life outside of work revolved around dancing, music and tennis. After all, he was the overall champion of the village tennis club and had won all the matches against their opponents last season. 'Please God,' he whispered, 'let me legs be.' A satisfactory sigh left him as he discovered no apparent injuries.

Still thinking of the evening ahead, he knew his mother would have the tin bath ready and his white shirt freshly laundered. The collar had been turned and the cuffs were frayed but he had to pay for his keep, that was fair enough, and he wanted, needed, he wasn't sure, cigarettes every day. A night out with the lads on a Saturday too. Consequently there was little left for new clothes. He would wear the fashionable dark blue, pin striped suit with very wide legs at least twenty-three inches at the turn-ups, second hand, of course, but who's to know. He would try on some ties to see which one he fancied from his meagre collection of two. As usual he would have to slick down his fair, curly hair, so like his father's, with an unruly cluster of curls right in the front, which made a parting difficult. Hetti, one of his sisters, if he asked her nicely, would mix up some sugar with hot water, and when the sugar had dissolved he would comb the sticky solution into his hair so that when it dried, the hair would be fixed tidily in place.

The dust was settling around him and disturbing thoughts again entered his mind. Firstly, where was his father, and secondly, looking around again, he thought how on earth can I claw myself out of this small tomb? Since he was fourteen years old, Joseph, known as Joe to everyone, had always been at his side in the mine. When they stood shoulder to shoulder, Joseph was a good four inches shorter than George's six foot two, but it was Joe who guided and protected his eldest son in the pit. Working conditions for both were cramped, and almost impossible at times, but they knew they were lucky, unlike some of their neighbours, still finding it difficult to find work after the 1926 strike, and who were endlessly struggling to make ends meet. Even now, those in work were still bitter, as their wages had been reduced from seven shillings and sixpence a shift before the strike, to six shillings and nine pence. The men's tempers were not improved by knowing that the wages they did earn, went straight back into the pocket of the mine owner, who also owned the two village shops.

Carefully, George sat up, his hard hat just scraping the top of the passage he'd been working in. He adjusted his lamp, and moved his head slowly around him. There were large boulders blocking each end of the shortened passage, and he could hear a trickle of water. Not given to swearing as a rule, he muttered out loud all the expletives miners old and young alike used, when not in the company of their womenfolk. Even knowing himself to be strong, he realised that there was no way he could shift any of the imprisoning boulders. Angrily, he flopped back against the coalface.

That's it, he thought, this is definitely my last day down this God awful pit. I'm twenty-one, and I'm away to London to make me fortune as soon as I get out of this hell hole. No one can stop me, everyone knows at twenty-one, a fellow becomes a man, and makes his own decisions. Yes, and while I'm settling my future, I shall insist on being called George from now on. Everyone, including mother, calls me Joe despite the fact that the last baby had been called Joseph, after his father. Three Joes in one house was too much he told himself. Even when he won the county's handwriting competition, he remembered, the newspaper reported him as Joe, his teacher was responsible for that. Miss Simmons, who advised him to keep his temper under control by putting his hands in his pockets should he feel the urge to punch anyone. His handwriting was considered so neat that he was allowed to make the last entry in the family bible: Eleanor Jane Carr 1911 to 1924, the death of his favourite sister, who had died of peritonitis. It was then he knew that his mother had turned against God. Yes, he thought, George it will be. George Carr- The Herald reporter, or The George Carr Trio, who will perform at the Ritz – yes George Carr sounded just grand.

Resignedly he leaned against the wall. There was nothing he could do to ease the situation. His bait tin, pickaxe and bottle of water were on the other side of the roof fall. Longing for a cigarette, he felt in his trouser pocket for the twist of tobacco he could chew. He always blessed the person who had thought of this. It kept the need for a fag at bay, kept his mouth moist, and made him breathe through his nose when the dust got too much. A really damned good idea by some clever fellow, he thought. Although he was hot, he knew that the air shaft was allowing some air to enter. This ensured there was oxygen to keep his Davey lamp alight. There was only a limited amount of oil in the lamp, enough for a shift. George knew that to be in total darkness would unnerve him, especially as his only company would probably be rats. He was not worried about the water. There was always some water trickling along the colliery floor. From his bedroom window he could see the reservoir which held the water pumped up from the mine that overflowed into a gully, before running down into a ditch alongside the railway track.

The roof cave-in had been unexpected, but he knew the drill. The older miners he worked alongside, had told him time and time again, 'Any trouble lad, try not to move, stay quiet and listen for the rescuers. As soon as there's bother, they'll be out. When you hear anything, shout to let them know where you are. They'll soon have you out.' Well, George was quiet, he couldn't be quieter – he was alone. Ruefully, he admitted to himself that he could hear nothing, except, of course, the soft trickle of water and the creaking, groaning of the pit props straining to hold the buckling roof. Looking up he could see that the fall had partly dislodged them, but they were holding, and for the moment he was safe. If there should be another fall? He let the thought hang.

Sighing, George thought about his mother. Must be in her early forties he surmised, but she looked nearer her mid fifties. Ten children in eighteen years had taken their toll. Hannah Jane was a tall upright woman, an inch or two shorter than her husband. George pictured her bending over the range, a spotless apron over her long grey skirt tied around her ample waist, her greying hair escaping from the tight bun at the back of her head. He could almost see her wiping her brow with her forearm, or scolding a child too near the heat, something he had witnessed all his life. She was severe, practical was a fairer word, thought George, but firm with her children. Only the youngest got an occasional kiss or cuddle from her. George was the eldest, and it was many years since such affection had come his way. It was obvious to all that she loved her brood. She saw to it that they were clean, well fed, well mannered and God fearing.

She was also fiercely defensive of any criticism of them, as if anyone would dare, thought George. She was well liked and was respected among the village people, and he was proud of her. It was obvious that she and Joseph had a special bond. Nothing was too much trouble for her as far as her Joe was concerned, and George was often amused to see and hear how his father teased her, inviting a sharp reprimand which never left her lips.

It always surprised George when he saw his parents together. Hannah was so well-rounded, due, no doubt, to the daily pork chop for breakfast. He could never bring himself to say fat. His father far too thin. Joseph was in his fifties. He could be identified always by his cloth cap tipped to the back of his head, and the pipe clamped between his teeth, not always alight.

Wriggling to try to get more comfortable, George began to wonder what the time was. The rescuers seemed to be a long time coming, and he thought, if they don't come soon there'll be no celebrations tonight. There was a tune he was going to try out, made a good foxtrot dance. He hummed the refrain to himself. Laughing quietly, he remembered coaxing Nancy, one of his sisters who had just had her eleventh birthday, 'Go on Nance, copy out the manuscript for us pet,' he'd begged, 'and I'll give you a penny bit on pay day. There's a good lass.' Pleased to have an extra copper she agreed, and had very carefully copied out the words and music twice, so that the three musicians each had a copy. George was a good singer, and clearing his voice, in a rich tenor began to sing. He sang Hoagy Carmichael's haunting tune, 'Sometimes I wonder why I spend the lonely night dreaming…' Suddenly he stopped. Was he mistaken? Did he hear something – a muffled voice? Yes, there it was again. Not from the rocky side leading to the main passage, but the other side, where he presumed the rest of the gang were buried. Thankfully, then some were still alive.

'Who's there?' he shouted. He rested his ear on one of the larger rocks and listened for a reply. Faintly he could hear someone shouting back.

He could barely make out what was being said but heard, 'Is that you Joe?' No time like the present, start right now on your future, he told himself.

'It's George, George Carr,' he bellowed back.

'Joe? Joe Carr's lad?' George gave in and sighed.

'Aye, that's me.'

'Your da's here with us.'

'Who else?' George yelled.

'No need to fret son, everyone's safe, but…'

George's heart sank, there was always a 'but' he thought, and felt himself tense up with apprehension as he called, 'Aye, go on, what's the bother?'

'Joe?' the strained voice called, 'Joe, it's your da, his leg's taken a beating, a bit crushed you might say. We're doing our best for him. Don't you worry.'

George was dismayed – his father injured, how badly? Was he hurting? Would he walk again? It was too difficult and unfair to keep asking, and trying not to show his concern, he shouted back, 'He's a tough ol' bugger. He'll do.'

'You stay still lad, won't be long now, only shout if you're in trouble,' the voice called back.

Boredom brought on an uneasy sleep, and in his dreams George saw his youngest brother, Joseph with the family hair inheritance – wayward blond curls mid-temple. Staggering, tumbling, dribbling and laughing, full of mischief, everyone's pet. There was always someone there to play with him, but he loved George the best. He followed George around, trying to stride manlike, and mimicking all that his hero did. George laughed out loud in his sleep, as he dreamed of the wee lad trying to comb his own unruly hair, and both of them stealing titbits from the table when mam wasn't looking. When George wasn't around, Joe followed his father and with his set of play tools, hammered away at a piece of wood. Tap, tap, tap. On and on, he never seemed to tire of playing grown-up. Tap, tap, tap.

George woke with a start. The tapping was repeated, and George realised he was no longer dreaming – the noise was real. Could that be the rescue team making their way towards him? He picked up a piece of rock, waited until the tapping sound stopped so that all was quiet and any signal would be heard. He banged against the unforgiving rocks, three times as was the arrangement. The answering taps came back. Relief flooded through him, now all he had to do was wait. Excitedly, he banged on the rock to the trapped men on the other side, 'They're here boys. The rescue team. I've heard them.'

The answering, raised voice, hollered, 'Ye bloody woke me up! But thank God for your news, lad. I'll sleep better for knowing!' George grinned to himself as he thought, trust someone to keep the lads' spirits up.

It wasn't long after this he watched, with dread, his lamp flicker then go out. The oil in his lamp was gone. This is what he had feared the most. He was in total darkness and he gave a little whimper. His heart began to race, he strained his eyes in the blackness and he knew what it was to be blind. Now that he knew the rescuers were on their way, every minute seemed like an hour. The kerchief around his neck seemed too tight and he loosened it with his finger. He heard a whisper of a sound. Surely that was the squeaking of rats. By now he was hungry and was convinced that he would starve to death. The rats must have sensed this and were getting near to their anticipated meal of his body he reasoned, and he quickly drew his legs up to his chest. People can go days without food, he'd heard, but it was lack of water that brought about death. As he had plenty of water, he could still hear trickling somewhere, he felt a little better.

His only consolation in this thought of death, was that he would be reunited with his playmate, Eleanor in Heaven. In his short life, he reasoned, he had done nothing sinful, so Heaven it would be. He thought then of his injured father. What if he died of his wounds before the rescuers got to him? Would the rescuers be in time he wondered, for both of them. George fought down the urge to thrash about and scream like a babby, then reminded himself again that today was his first day of manhood. Grown men would not be so scared he guessed. The dread returned when he thought he felt the brush of soft fur against his hands, and he shoved them quickly in his pocket. The blackness engulfed him and he began to sweat. The constant creaking pit props added to his fear, and he held his breath when he heard small, loose debris skitter down the rock face. Although he could hear the tapping as the rescuers worked, he thought no man should ever have to endure loneliness like this. What about those poor blighters who had died in the pit, hungry, lonely and in darkness? It didn't bear thinking about. Please be to God, he whispered, get me father out too.

Three hours later, the rescuers had created a tiny gap and, much relieved, George could just see a wink of light from a lamp fastened to one of the rescuer's helmet. He didn't have long to wait. Within a short time a larger gap had been hewn out, big enough for George to crawl through. The rescue team shook his hand and slapped him on the back joyfully.

George thanked them over and over again, then said, 'There's others behind that lot,' he said pointing to the forbidding rock-fall. 'Me da and his gang. Give them a bang so they know you're here.' Just as he was leaving he added, 'My da's legs are done for. I reckon you'll need to stretcher him out I'm thinking,' and after a last handshake, the men set about the task of securing the roof and rescuing the others.

George with hope for the gang, made his way to the lift. As he got nearer to it could hear the winding mechanism and saw two others who had been saved. Samuel, who had just left school and only fourteen, with tears running down his young, frightened face. The other man was Henry who had a family and George was glad his wife was spared the agony of grief for a lost man. They entered the lift, the banksman gave them a grin, pounded their backs and started the upward journey. All sighed with relief as its monotonous whirring sound took them to the surface.

It was dark outside, a more friendly darkness, and the lanterns, held by the waiting women, gave a welcoming glow. In just a few brief seconds George watched as Sam's mother rushed forward, arms outstretched and gathered her son close to her. Her tears mingled with his, and George heard her say, 'You'll not be going back down my pet. Never!'

He saw Henry's wife and mother fold him into their arms. 'Thank God you're safe,' said his heavily pregnant wife as she held on to Henry's arm.

George looked for his mother. There she was, he went towards her, his heart full of love, but then his heart sank as the smile left her face. All she said was, 'Oh! It's you. They told me Joe Carr was coming up. I thought it was your father.'

Longing for her to show she was pleased he, her son, was alive, he choked back his misery and muttered no more than, 'Aye, but he's not coming up whole.' As the colour drained from her face he wished he'd not been quite so blunt.

'What...what do you mean our Joe?'

Without thinking, he brushed her aside as he said, 'I'm away to me home.' George wept the whole way, his tears making white streaks through his coal dusted face. He feared for his father and had hurt his mother badly. As he put the latch up on the gate and entered the yard, his brothers and sisters tumbled out of the house shouting and laughing to greet him. Their warm, unconditional love cheered him a little, and he cuddled them all in turn. Naturally, duty bound, his mother had left a hot pot simmering and chunks of homemade bread for his and his father's supper, and the girls had kept the bath topped up with hot water, but something that night had died in his heart.

CHAPTER TWO

It was Monday a few weeks later and, at last, the letter, post marked London, George had been waiting for arrived. Emily, two years younger than George, was already in service in London as was seventeen years old Jessie. Hetti, a year younger than Jessie, was employed as a scullery maid locally, and visited at weekends. He had written to Jessie, and he had thought to write to Emily, but she was as stern as their mother, and probably wouldn't have helped him. No doubt, George thought, she would harp on and on about his duties to the family. But Jessie, so full of life, always cheerful and hardworking, and looking so like Eleanor, he knew, would do her best.

There was a hushed sadness about the house. Very much like the time Eleanor had died. This subdued air was due, mainly, to worry about Joseph. He had spent two weeks in the infirmary and was now home. His wounded leg was healing, but it was obvious, like so many other colliers in the village, that he was crippled. However, George realised, God was back in favour with his mother, as she was often heard saying, 'Praise be to God,' and 'Thank God, Joe, you're still with us.' The vicar resumed his weekly visits, and Hannah was safely back in the parish flock and attending church. A penny-a-week insurance for such an accident, now doled out a meagre sum that barely kept them fed and the rent paid.

George's determination to seek work in London also added to the unhappy atmosphere. His father's accident had not changed his mind. Hannah made it clear she did not want him to go.

'You can't leave us and the bairns, our Joe,' she said, 'You can see for yourself your da's not able to work. God alone knows if he's going to be able to walk let alone work.'

'I bloody well will,' her husband growled from the sofa.

George answered her patiently. 'There's little work here ma, and there's no way I'm putting myself down that hellhole again.' Almost too soft to be heard he added. 'Not for anyone or anything. Never. That's an end to it.'

Hannah went across to the oven and took out a loaf, 'I'm your mother. Don't you dare speak back to me like that.' Angry tears filled her eyes. 'How am I expected to manage, tell me that laddo? Tell me that,' and after placing another loaf in the oven to bake, she slammed the iron door shut, and began muttering, 'Just selfish like most men. Thinking only of yourself, never mind your brothers and sisters, and I might add, your parents who brought you up. Gave up our dreams to raise you. Made our sacrifices too. You don't think about that do you?'

George could feel his temper rising. 'What sacrifices for God's sake?' he demanded. 'I don't recall any sacrifices being made when I passed the eleven plus. Oh, no. Gone was my chance of a good education to get out of this place once and for all.' He paused for a second then said, 'So now, mother I'm not going to miss another chance to make something of meself. I'm away, I tell you, as soon as I hear from our Jessie.'

Hannah bristled at his remarks. 'There was nay money for your scholarship, you knew that. You was eleven, old enough to under-stand.' Pausing for a moment she then went on. 'And that Jessie will get a piece of my mind too, when I see her again, I can tell you. What can she be thinking of, knowing there's little money coming in?' Turning on her husband, she demanded, 'Well, say something our Joe. He's away if you don't stop him.'

'Lass, lass. Don't go on so. Let the lad be. His mind's made up.' Then groaning a little as he stretched his shattered leg, added, 'Dost thou want another cripple to tend? Let him go I say. We'll manage.'

Eagerly, knowing that his da was siding with him, George said, 'Aye, mother and I'll see to it that you get part of me wages every week once I've got a job and settled somewhere.' Then mischievously he added, 'Just think, one mouth less to feed.'

His father gave out a quiet chuckle and puffed on his pipe. 'There hinney, didn't I say he was a good lad? We're going to be fine. Now stop fretting and get us a cup o' tea, pet.'

As George waited for the reply from Jessie, and determined never to enter the mine again, he went out daily to find some sort of work to bring in a few shillings. Some days he was lucky, a farmer or builder wanting a day's labour, other days he helped load trucks with coal destined for the Yorkshire factories. There were days when there was no work to be had.

George didn't open the letter at once. All eyes were on him in anticipation of news, but he felt he wanted to be alone to read it thoroughly before sharing any good or bad messages with his family. He chose the long front garden, where the vegetables and prize chrysanthemums were grown, and sat on the weathered, wobbly seat and leaned back against the wall. He read,

Hi there our Joe, so you've seen sense at last. Of course the bairns will miss you, as will mam and da, but you've got to make something of yourself. You'd best catch a train to Kings Cross and I'll meet you and take you on to some digs I've found near my place. There seems to be plenty of work about, lots of good looking fellows like yourself working on the roads, pickaxes and all. In fact, although don't tell on me, I'm walking out with someone now. He's called Ron. I haven't told our Emily either, such a prune! Come soon, then you can take me dancing, I'm getting really good. Give my love to the family. Jessie.

George smiled as he thought, plenty of work, a place to sleep and girls and dancing. Without a second thought, he sold his fiddle, and the money he got for it just covered his fare, and, he hoped, a week's lodging. Ruefully, he admitted to himself, that was probably the end of one of his ambitions, though to be honest he hadn't held out much hope of ever performing in the Ritz.

In a battered cardboard suitcase, he packed his suit, his best and only shirt, the one with frayed cuffs, his ties, his dancing shoes and shaving brush. At four-thirty on Thursday morning he left home for Darlington station, dressed in his work clothes, that he had brushed, sponged and brushed again, and his sturdy boots. He had written back to Jessie telling her the time the train would be arriving, and added that if he came on a Thursday he could spend Friday and Saturday looking for work. It surprised and pleased him to see that his mother had prepared some sandwiches for his journey, even though she had not given him her blessing. He was disappointed that she had not got up to see him off. The station was some six miles away and for the first mile he strolled along with Jane Ann, the herdsmaid, patting the rumps of the wandering cows as they plodded stoically to the milking sheds. It was market day in Darlington, and after he left Jane Ann, he soon caught a ride on a cart, laden with local vegetables, to the quiet country town just waking up its drowsy inhabitants.

It was a long and monotonous journey to London and he wished he could have afforded a newspaper. The hefty sandwiches and fruit supplied by Hannah made a welcome break. A light sleep and some seven or eight cigarettes later, he realised the train was on the outskirts of London, and his excitement grew. Carefully he lifted down the old suitcase that had served his parents when they went on their honeymoon, (three days in Scarborough he'd been told) some twenty-two years ago. Patting his pockets as he searched for his ticket, he realised he was quite nervous. The palms of his hands were sweaty and his head had begun to throb. Right lad, he said to himself, no going back now. You're here in London.

Stepping off the train, he was immediately overwhelmed by the noise echoing in the cathedral built station of Kings Cross. It bewildered him, and it was some minutes before he located Jessie. Rather she located him and she rushed to him with outstretched arms, laughing as she called out, 'Our Joe, our Joe. You've made it then.'

Relieved, he laughed along with her, and looking around apprehensively at the crowds, constantly on the move, said, 'Aye, I'm here, but I'm thinking I mebbe made a mistake.' He could see she was happy and well and he was pleased for her.

'Right, now,' she said, 'A cup of tea in Lyons corner house first, then I'll take you to your lodgings.' They found an empty seat and after the neatly dressed 'nippy' served them their tea and toast, George asked Jessie about her position in the large house she was employed in.

Jessie took the cigarette he offered, and said, 'Well Joe, I get up at six o'clock, but that's no hardship as I was always up at six at home helping mam. That's when I clear the grates, no big range in this house. I lay and light the fires, then dust around a bit as the ash flies about, and the Missus is fussy about that.' She drew on the cigarette and coughed a little.

'You shouldna take the ciggie if you're not used to them,' George scolded.

'Give over our Joe, you're just as bad as Emily,' and successfully drew on the cigarette again. 'I was telling you, after the dusting I get some breakfast, leftovers fried up with an egg, and a cup of tea usually. Then her ladyship...'

'You didn't say she was a lady,' George gasped.

'No silly, that's what me and the housekeeper call her, she does all the cooking. Sometimes the missus has such airs and graces. Still, I'd better not go on. She is good to me sometimes. She gave me a jumper and a skirt this last week.'

'Going all posh now is it?' he teased.

'Wait till you see me in my uniform when madam's got guests! Got to look the part of maid to a rich family but, between you and me, there's a lot of shabby darned linen and threadbare carpets about the place. Stuff our mam wouldna give houseroom.' She looked anxiously at the big clock on the wall, and said, 'I have to be back by six o'clock Joe, to serve dinner. I'd best not be late, as she did give me a couple of hours off this afternoon to meet you.'

He swallowed the remains of his tea quickly. 'What other time do you get off?' he asked as he stood up ready to make a move.

'Oh, as soon as I've finished my chores of an evening around eight or nine, and Sunday mornings.' She gave a little giggle and went on, 'She thinks we go to church. I get every other Saturday from three o'clock. Can't grumble at that can I? More than some of the other lasses get, I can tell you.'

They made their way out into the street and the noise, although different, took George unawares for the second time. There were drivers of horse drawn carts shouting abuse at noisy motor vehicles whose horns were constantly being hooted, newspaper vendors yelling out the latest, and all in a tongue that seemed foreign to him. Added to the noise was a mixture of smells, few pleasant. The scent of a well dressed lady, a rich smell of food cooking from a nearby hotel mingled with the stench of unwashed bodies, droppings of horses and inefficient drains. For a brief moment he thought he preferred the familiar smell of coal, that invaded every home surrounding the colliery. Would he ever get used to London he wondered.

It was wonderful, he thought, how confident Jessie was, wending herself through the throngs of people. She coped with buying tickets for the underground railway, elbowed her way, and dragged him by his arm, onto a train, bound for God knows where. Been here five months, he thought, and already knew the strange talk and her way about. They stood for the journey to Baker Street, swaying and unable to talk to or hear each other above the chatter of others, and the rattling of the carriage. At last they arrived, and George was relieved to be out in the air again and into a less noisy, bustling thoroughfare. Jessie took him down a variety of side streets, each one becoming quieter as they hurried along.

'Here we are,' she exclaimed, and knocked at the door of a terraced house. George surveyed the house carefully. The windows were sparkling, and white nets hung within. The paintwork looked fresh, gutters and down pipes seemed as new, the brass knocker and letter-box shone, and the doorstep had been whitened. Our Jessie's not daft, he thought, looks as if she's found me somewhere decent.

The door was opened by a woman about fifty years of age who recognised Jessie, and then turned to George. 'You'll be George Carr then. Her brother that's right?'

George recognised a few words, 'Carr', 'sister', 'right.' He nodded.

'Come along in. Let's get to know each other. Your room's all ready for you.'

George could see Jessie was agitated. 'I got to go, our Joe, they'll be looking for me shortly.' There must have been a fleeting look of panic on George's face, as very hurriedly, she added, 'I'll be round later this evening about half past eight. See how you're getting on like. Alright?'

He watched her walk hurriedly down the road, and then turned to follow the ramrod back of his landlady. As he entered the house he was relieved to see it was clean and uncluttered, but there seemed to be something cold about the place.

'My name is Mrs Harper,' she said carefully, as if speaking to a child. George was amused, but grateful for this. It made understanding of this southern tongue a little easier. She sat down at a desk, in what she called her office. 'There are a few rules I should like you to observe. Letting my rooms is a business.' George's spirits sank as he thought, My God, she's going to be a tartar, and as she reeled off her rules this thought was confirmed. 'Breakfast is at six-thirty sharp. If you are late you will find the table cleared. Supper is at seven. I trust you finish your work at six like my other boarder?'

George didn't answer. He didn't dare tell her that, at present, he had no job.

'I will not tolerate any drunkenness or indeed any alcohol on the premises. It goes without my saying, definitely no females are permitted into the house. Have you understood all that young man?'

He patted his pockets for his faithful cigarettes, drew one out of the packet and searched for the matches.

'And absolutely no smoking on the premises.' Resignedly he put everything back in his pocket. 'Thank you. Now I will take you to your room. It is at the back of the house. The sheets are changed every two weeks without charge. There is a small fee for personal washing. You may bathe once a week, hot water is provided by payment in a slot meter in the bathroom.' She led him into the room, soon to be his. 'You provide your own soap and towel of course.'

The walls were whitewashed, clean but so cold looking and uninviting. The bed was a single and George looked and wondered at its length, thinking he might have to curl his legs. On the wall over the headboard was a temperance notice. He read:

'Happy is the home where sobriety dwells. There abides the blessing of God.'

On the opposite wall yet another text,

'Drunkards shall not inherit the Kingdom of God'.

George began to feel more and more depressed.

'You have one blanket and the bedspread. In winter I provide an extra blanket.'

He looked around. There was a single wardrobe, a chest of drawers, linoleum floor covering, and a patterned rug at the side of the bed. There was also a small gas fire, beside which was a meter.

'My terms are twelve shillings a week, or part of week, payable on Friday evenings.' She stopped and took a deep breath. 'Payable in advance. This being Thursday, you will need to pay me tomorrow.'

George's eyes widened, his mouth opened and closed in disbelief. At that rate his few shillings would soon be gone. George clamped his lips tightly together, then in a voice he hardly recognised a his own said, 'Now just a minute lady, Mrs Harper,' he corrected, 'there's no way I'm paying you for a full week's board and receiving only one day's!'

'We shall see,' she said smugly. 'Where else do you think you can get clean accommodation at this time of day, and so close to facilities in London?'

'I may be new to this part of the world, woman, but I'm not green behind the ears,' he retorted, patting his pockets for the comfort of his cigarettes.

'Wet behind the ears,' she corrected tartly.

They glared at each other for a moment or two, 'I'll pay you two shillings and thruppence for tonight's bed and breakfast the morrow,' he said. 'If that's not satisfactory to you, I shall sleep on your door-step, and when the coppers come I'll explain the meanness of some London landladies.' He watched her face as conflicting thoughts crossed her mind.

Although her hands were tightly clenched together, after a moment she seemed to relax slightly, then through pursed lips, said, 'You put me in a very awkward position, but I think it for the best if I accept your payment offer. I should not like the police visiting my premises. It would please my neighbours greatly, I feel.'

'Right that's settled then. Now if you don't mind, I'd like to unpack my belongings and have a wash before the supper I can smell cook-ing.' He picked up his suitcase and placed it on the bed.

'Not on the bed if you please,' she said as she left the room, then called back. 'If you need a towel it'll be three pence for the week.' Cheeky cow, he thought and fumbled for the coins, felt the cardboard packet of his cigarettes, then remembered the rules.

The supper of boiled potatoes, two small lamb chops and peas, followed by stewed prunes and custard was adequate he thought, but if second helpings had been offered he would not have refused. Not as tasty as his mother's cooking, well it wouldn't be would it he sur-mised, as it had been cooked on a Regulo gas cooker he'd noticed when he looked into the kitchen. For a moment he thought of home, the long, black-leaded range that was constantly glowing with heat, with a boiler for hot water at one side, provided someone, usually one of the girls, kept filling it. On the other side was the oven. There was nothing better than the smell of his mother's bread baking or the enormous beef joint on Sundays, a feast day. Although mam said it was a rest day, anyone not in church gave a hand with the vegetables and pastries. As a child, he remembered, the best part of the dinner was before, when tea-plate size Yorkshire puddings soaked in the juices of the joint were given to the children to stave off their hunger. The remainder of the joint kept them all fed for a number of days, he recalled. Shepherd's pie was his favourite, but cold meat was grand as well, with pickles and spuds. The other boarder did not appear for his supper, and George assumed he was late back from his work.

Jessie came as promised and as they sat on the wall outside the house she sympathised, 'It'll do for now our Joe, till you find yourself a job, then you can look around for something else. I did me best at short notice tha knows.'

'Aye lass I know, and I thank you from the bottom of my heart. I couldn't stay in Durham a minute longer.' He shook his head. 'Just seeing the lads going down pit every day, and wondering if they'll ever come up again.'

They were quiet for a minute or two until Jessie jumped up, adjusted her hat and said, 'Come on, walk back with me and I'll show you where I'm working.' The large house wasn't too far away and as they strolled along, George gave her all the latest news from home.

When they arrived, he said, 'Shall we meet up then on Saturday? You can take me to a dance. Let me see if you have improved!'

Jessie shoved her elbow into his side, 'Better than you think our Joe. Ron will be there too so you can meet him. You'll like him for sure. I think he's rather special.'

'What do you mean special? He hasn't er...?' Embarrassed, he stopped for a moment, and looked at Jessie's grinning face, 'Well, I trust he's a gentleman, has proper respect for you an all,' he muttered uncomfortably.

'You daft bugger. What do you think I'm like!' Jessie laughed. 'Now then, I'll come by tomorrow evening if you like to see if you've found any work.'

George took her hand, 'I'd like that and Jessie pet,' he hesitated for a moment before saying, 'Could you call me George from now on our Jess?'

Surprised, she answered, 'Why, of course, if that's what you want.' She paused, 'Why?'

'It's like this. I just feel I'm starting a new life, in a new place, here in London, and, after all, it is my proper name.'

'I see, but don't you dare go calling me my proper name, Jessica Joanne will you?' They smiled at each other then laughed.

'Goodnight our Jessica Joanne.'

'Goodnight our Joe George. See yer tomorrow.'

Despite the bed being too short, too narrow and too hard, George slept well. As he wriggled himself into some semblance of comfort, he was already missing the soft down of the mattress, and pillows of the double bed he shared with Robert, his thirteen year old brother. As he drifted off to sleep he said to himself, 'By God if I have anything to do with it, I'll see the lad never sees the inside of the pit.'

Sighing, he knew it had been a long day, he was tired, and tomorrow, Friday, he must set out to find work. His very last thought was of his mother, and tomorrow he would find the time to write to her. She'd recognised his disappointment on that fateful day, and had done her best to explain. Joe was her husband, her friend, her breadwinner and the father of their children who would be penniless without his wages, she'd told him. Well it wasn't quite as bad as that George thought, and knowing that she'd regretted the words spoken thoughtlessly out of anxiety, he'd put his arms around her. Although there was no hint of a true apology or a returned hug, he had forgiven her, but knew in his heart he would never forget.

CHAPTER THREE

The familiar sound of the clip clop of a horse's hooves, coupled with the unfamiliar rattle of glass, awakened George on the following morning. Looking at the watch his father had given him for his birthday, he saw that it was just past six o'clock. He wandered over to the window and was intrigued as he watched a milkman collect empty bottles, and deliver full bottles to every door within his view. At home his mother would rush out, with her jug, twice a day for fresh milk. Everything was so different here in London. He'd heard of milk bottle deliveries, of course, but the practice had not yet reached the village, and why should it he thought, milk straight from the cows, of the local farm, could only be better.

After a cold water wash, he dressed in his work clothes and went for breakfast. Again the table was laid for two, but the other lodger did not appear. The breakfast was not the hearty meal he was used too. A bowl of porridge, not at all creamy and, he suspected, water had been added, one boiled egg and two slices of toast. However, there was a large, full teapot, and he was able to help himself to as many cups as he liked. It didn't take long to clear his dish and plate, and, after nodding to Mrs Harper and giving his thanks, he took his leave, and collected his waistcoat and cap from his room.

The first thing he did on leaving the house, was to locate his tabs and matches, light up and draw the smoke in deeply, then he heaved a sigh of satisfaction. The sky, when he looked up between the houses, was blue and clear, and the temperature was already rising. For a moment he regretted bringing his waistcoat and cap, but there was no way he was going back with them. The longer he was away from that cold atmosphere the better.

His plan was to walk the streets and approach anywhere, just anywhere, there might be some work. Cheerfully, he strode briskly along the quiet street, but as he neared Marylebone Road, the noise began to increase. He told himself he was in the open air, not en-tombed below ground, that work was just around the corner, that he had coppers in his pocket, that he was healthy and young and starting out on a new adventure. But all these thoughts could not erase the unease he was suffering whilst walking through the unremitting noise and the hurry-scurry of passers-by. Reaching a road junction, he glanced down a side street, and in the distance, he could see workmen rolling up their sleeves. He heard their bantering as they lifted their tools, and he watched as they began digging up the road.

Here goes, he told himself, and boldly approached the man who looked to be in charge.

'Any jobs going, sir?' he asked as he raised his finger to his cap.

The foreman gave a wry smile. 'What's your trade, sonny?' he replied.

George didn't hesitate. 'Carpenter.' The man gave a shake of his head.

'Stone cutter?' Another shake.

'Labourer then, anything at all? Tea boy if you like?' The crew of three men laughed.

'There's nothing here lad. Try Tylers, two roads on. They might have something.'

George couldn't hide his delight at this news and said, 'Thanks. Thanks a lot. Sorry to have troubled you.'

As he strode away, he heard one of the workers say, 'Another bloody miner from the north trying to steal our jobs.'

Thinking about the remark, George told himself, that any good boss would take on a willing worker never mind where they came from, and by God, no one worked harder than miners! He didn't care, and whistled as he made his way to Tyler's Yard.

He stood for a moment in the yard to light a cigarette. He saw timber drying, properly stacked he noticed, similar to the pit props which were stored horizontally with wedges to stop them rolling and allow the air to circulate to aid drying. Curled shavings and sawdust blew gently around his feet as he began walking to the Office, with its door open, at the far side of the yard.

'Put that bloody fag out now,' a voice roared. 'You want to set the whole bloody place afire?'

Hastily George nipped the glowing end between his fingers, and put it in his pocket for later.

'Whatcha want?' George walked nearer to the Office and called out, 'Looking for a job, sir.'

A bulky body with a bulging belly, and straining braces filled the open doorway. A man with a red sweaty face topped with a bowler hat, asked belligerently, 'What sort of job? Not in this yard if you're a smoker lad you can bet on that.'

'Carpenter?'

The man, Mr Tyler himself, dried his greasy face with a grubby cloth.

'Well, there's not much work here for a carpenter, or any other sod, so good day to you.'

George was not surprised or disheartened by the reply, and politely gave his thanks. Once outside the yard he relit his cigarette, and set out again to find work. There seemed to be plenty of road works in most of the streets, labourers digging, pipe laying, refilling holes or asphalt spreading. Buoyantly, he approached another three such sites, and each rejected him without malice and with the usual choice of swear words.

It was nearly noon and, in the airless heat, George found himself flagging. As he passed a baker's shop, he bought himself two buns for a penny and, by luck, found himself in Regent's park. After taking a long cold drink from the public fountain, he gratefully sat down on a bench, shaded by a tree, to eat his buns. It was so peaceful away from the streaming traffic, and for nearly an hour he watched the world go by. Sitting there, he realised that he no longer had a big problem with the London speech. True it was the swear words he understood first, but the rest was now easier. As someone sat down beside him, he turned and his smile faltered as he looked at a woman whose face was pancaked with garish, cheap-smelling make-up. She smiled in return.

'Hello,' she said.

George barely returned her greeting, inched himself away from her along the bench, and turned away. She touched his arm.

'You from the north?' she asked. He nodded. 'I can give you a good time if you're lonely,' she whined.

George looked up, and saw a matronly woman passing, who stared at him with a sour look of disapproval on her face. George felt himself reddening, and shook his head. The awful woman beside him laughed at his discomfort. Her open mouth revealed gaps and black teeth, and George leant back further away from her.

'Another time, maybe?' she hinted, as she stood up and sauntered away, swinging her hips. The encounter left George wondering if he looked as ignorant as he felt, and yet a little flattered, that possibly she fancied him a bit. Common sense told him she was more interested in his meagre wallet than his body.

Taking another drink from the fountain and now fully refreshed, and full of optimism, he set off again to find work. He was rebuffed time and time again, mostly accompanied with a swear word or two and he understood that there was no animosity behind them.

As he passed a Woolworth's store, he saw an advertisement for a warehouse man, and decided to try his luck. The manager was glad to see him and showed him into a small, airless storeroom, with one electric bulb giving a meagre light, to interview him. Repeatedly a bell kept ringing and the flustered manager not only answered it, but located the stock being called for. In order to get it to the counter, he had to leave George again and again. The demands were relentless.

'You see the problem?' the manager asked, 'plenty to keep you busy.' He paused, 'Well young man, what do you think? Is this the job for you? I could certainly do with another pair of hands.'

By now, in the airless room George longed to be outside and didn't hesitate with his answer. 'No, sir. Not for me. I need to be more in the open like. Thanks all the same.' Might as well be honest he thought.

'You could make a career of working for this company you know. Work your way up to manager in a few years. Pension as well. Think about it.'

George shook his head.

Disappointed, the manager said, 'You'll regret it son. Good, clean jobs not that easy to get these days. You look like a good worker, the sort the company is looking for.'

'I am that,' said George, 'but I'm sorry sir, it's not what I'm really looking for.'

The manager rubbed his forehead, as he went to answer yet another call, and sighed as he said, 'The best of luck young man,' and shook George's hand.

Another job, written in pencil and pinned to a fence outside a coal yard, was for a deliveryman. No thanks he said to himself, I know too much about mining the damn stuff, and how hard the hewers work and their sufferings, to want to have anything more to do with coal.

Late in the afternoon, hot, weary and worried now about his lack of finding work, he decided to make his way back to his lodgings and have a cooling wash. Tomorrow he would try again, perhaps going further afield, even venture onto the underground if he must. Not quite sure which way back to Baker Street Station, from where he knew he could find his way to Mrs Harper's, he wandered down another street where yet another gang was working. As he got nearer he heard an angry voice yell, 'Clear off. We don't 'ave thieves in our crew. Go on, bugger off, now!' George watched as a young boy slunk away. He looked as if he could do with a square meal, perhaps that's what made him steal, thought George. As he approached the workmen he decided to try just once more. The men, who had been resting on their pickaxe handles to enjoy the lad's dismissal, began working again. George was amazed to see how slowly they wielded their tools, three or four strikes at the hardened asphalt and they seem to rest again. Hesitatingly, he asked one of them for the foreman who pointed him out. Half heartedly, George approached him, 'Any work going, sir?'

The man looked at him for a moment or two then asked, 'What's your trade?'

'Carpenter.' George replied hopefully.

The man laughed. 'Not yet lad. Another year or two maybe. Anyway, where're your tools?'

George thought fast, he wasn't given to lying, but this one time he allowed himself to stretch the truth. 'Sold everything to come down here to London,' he replied.

'From the north is it? A miner I guess. Used to wielding a pickaxe boy?'

Carefully, George replied, 'Yes sir. Yes, to everything.'

The man stroked his chin, turned to the rest of the men, and said, 'What say you lads, shall we give this young shaver a try?' There were three men, all resting on their shovel handles again, and all nodded as they gave various answers.

'Give him a go, Charlie.' And,

'He can start by cleaning me boots!'

'Can 'e make a decent brew?'

Charlie pursed his lips, and thought for a moment, then said, 'Tell you what. You can go along with Bert there, the one with the tattoo on his arm and give him a hand. It's all digging, mind, to start with. Bert is a stone mason and will need a labourer shortly. In the meantime, both of you'll be digging.'

George was delighted and couldn't hide his relief. 'That'll be great. I'll not let any of you down. You'll see.'

'Well now, seven thirty sharp, Monday. There's at least two weeks work here and I reckon about six bob a day. We usually finish at six. Suit you?' George was hoping for more, it was less than what he was earning as a miner. The dismay must have shown on his face, as Charlie asked, 'What's the problem lad?'

Taking a deep breath, George answered, 'I was hoping there might be a bit more cash than that.'

'Well, let's see what happens in six weeks time. Maybe then I can find a bit more.'

George spluttered. 'You said there was only two weeks work here, so how come you're talking about six weeks on?' Everyone laughed.

'You're a sharp one.' Charlie said joining in the laughter. 'Go on, on yer way. See you Monday if you're still interested.'

'I'll be there don't you fret,' George answered, 'and you won't regret it, I promise.'

With his spirits high, he lit up a cigarette as he strode, almost cockily, away. Good news to tell Jess tonight, he told himself. He found that the site was only two streets away from Baker Street station, and quite close to his lodgings, so he knew he had no excuse to be late. As soon as I get in now, he decided, I'll have a good wash down, and write to mother and tell her the news. I'll tell her about Mrs Harper and her rules. Mam will be pleased to think someone is keeping a strict eye on me. Ruefully, he decided not to tell of his encounter with a certain woman in the park. Maybe I'll write to Pat and tell her, should give her a good laugh. He grinned as he remembered how passionate Pat had been the night before he left home.

After supper, set for two but only George present, Jessica came as promised and he told her his news. He wasn't sure how she'd react about the woman in the park but he told her anyway.

But Jessica roared with laughter and teased him. 'I'll have to tell Ron. He'll laugh too. Mind you, he'll not be surprised. Those sort of women are hanging about everywhere these days. They got to eat same as the rest of us I suppose.' Plans were made to meet up the next day at seven, and they would make their way to the Hammersmith Palais for the dancing, and where they would meet up with Ron.

CHAPTER FOUR

Together Jessie and George set out for Hammersmith Palais for the dancing that began at eight o'clock. They took the underground train, and Jessie carefully pointed out to him how he could get back to Baker Street after the dance, if they should want to go their separate ways. There was a queue to enter when they arrived, made up mostly of young working girls and boys, but George was amazed to see there were also groups of young men, known as toffs. They were dressed in evening suits and white flowing silk scarves among the waiting crowd. Like him, they all acknowledged Saturday night was fun night and dancing, along with the cinema, was the best of entertainment.

Ron was already at the head of the queue and had got their tickets, two tickets each. This puzzled George for a moment until Ron explained that one was a pass out ticket that could be used in the interval if he wanted to go outside for some fresh air or anything else he fancied. As he told George this, he winked suggestively, and it took George some moments to understand the significance of it. He was not pleased at what Ron was hinting.

The price of the ticket surprised him, but once inside he knew he had got his money's worth. For a moment he stood transfixed in the entrance until Jessie nudged him in the back and said grumpily, 'Get a move on our Joe.'

George was astounded at the sheer size of the room. Far larger than the Assembly rooms or the village school or church halls he was more used to that held no more than a hundred and fifty people. Here the room was large enough to accommodate up to a thousand. A good dance band, made up of seven musicians already playing, was located on a stage at one end of the room. The dancers, he noted, were orderly as they quickstepped around the spacious ballroom. There was a cafeteria and a restaurant, also tables and gilt chairs covered in red velveteen on the balcony above the floor, for those not dancing, to sit and enjoy the music and movement of those below. There were couples and mixed groups of people. Groups of girls ranged along one side of the hall, and close by, gangs of boys eyeing the girls. The toffs were mostly without a female partner. George queried this with Jessie, and she replied, 'Well I heard these rich boys preferred to dance with working class girls as they were the better dancers.'

George grinned. 'You can say that again.'

'I've been told that girls are expected to glide by just raising their feet off the floor. That little trick makes them appear to dance more gracefully,' Jessie told him.

The girls were dressed in every colour and texture he could summon up. Their outfits were, in the main, replicas of film stars' waist hugging outfits and reminded him of Nancy. Shy, little Nancy who like their mother, was a seamstress and was working from home. He pictured her sitting over her work by the window, her long fair hair hiding her freckly face. All his sisters had freckles, but Nancy's crop was the bane of her life. She tried desperately to brave the teasing of her siblings and friends. The local cinema was her delight, and, along with her best friend Ann, they declared their love for Ronald Coleman and Al Jolson. Nancy too, like the girls on the dance floor, carefully copied the fashion ideas from the costumes, portrayed in the films, for herself and her friends. George knew she would dearly love to own a lipstick and some powder, but along with his parents, he agreed she was too young for such flighty aids to beauty. Besides in his eyes, she was beautiful.

Again Jessie nudged him, 'Stop daydreaming will you?' she said irritably. 'We're here to dance.'

Coming out of his reverie he noticed nearly all the girls wore white gloves. From the ceiling hung giant, brightly lit chandeliers and, a feature of all modern ballrooms, a glass globe that twisted slowly scattering starlight medallions on the dancers. It was a warm evening, and he could already smell the sweat from some energetic bodies. This was mingled with the scent of blue smoke given off by cigarettes, men's hair oil, eau de cologne and the favourite heady perfume of his sisters, L'Aimant.

The quickstep ended and there was a smattering of hand clapping as the men escorted their partners back to their places. He watched as one girl limped off, scolding her partner who had obviously trodden on her foot. Another girl was discussing the merits of her partner which seemed to cause much merriment to her friends. Such a melody of laughter and girlish chatter surrounded him. Everyone seemed in high spirits.

The band shuffled their music sheets and chose a popular piece, and as they struck up the opening bars to a foxtrot one or two girls dusted their shoes with French chalk. The floor was quickly filled. George smoothed his wayward curls, tugged at his jacket and made his way over to the waiting girls, and asked his first partner of the evening for a dance. After a few steps he realised that the sprung maple floor seemed to give lightness to his feet. It was to his mind the best experience of dancing in his whole life. Without favouring any one particular girl, he danced time away, even his want of a cigarette was forgotten as he did the waltz, tango and foxtrot until the interval.

As he was making his way towards the exit in order to have a cigarette and some air before joining Jessie and Ron for a welcome drink of tea, a group of girls called him over. Grinning, he approached them, and they began to ask him question after question.

'Where are you from?'

'How long have you been in London?'

'Where do you work?'

He was, to them, a new face and a gift of a partner. The northern accent intrigued them and they teased him unmercifully. Although George wasn't aware of it, the girls said they would call him 'preacher' because he spoke in the local idiom of his village. Words like, thee, thine and thou coloured his conversation. When this was brought to his attention, he realised that indeed, Jessie, whilst still speaking with a northern intonation, had dropped the use of such words.

George learned that the lasses were from all over London and even further, some coming as far as the underground trains went into the suburbs. There was too, a girl from Ireland and another from south Wales. Some were shop assistants for the big Departmental Stores, and were chaperoned more severely than they might have been if they were still at home. Others were seamstresses, laundresses and, some like Jessie, in service.

He was enjoying himself immensely, and began to show-off trying to teach two of them some fancy steps, all laughing together as deliberate mistakes were made and he was obliged to catch and steady them. Something made him glance up, and he was shocked to see three young men about his age standing close by. It was obvious from their scowling, hostile faces, inflated chests, menacing stance and more than one clenched fist that he was somehow in the wrong. He saw the girls nudge each other and discreetly step away from him and seemingly huddle together. He sensed he was in some sort of danger and the girls' apprehension. As calmly as he could, he raised his hand to his forehead, flicked his finger, and said, 'See you later girls,' lit up a cigarette and sauntered over to his sister. Leaving the ballroom might just invite a confrontation, he thought. A fight was the last thing he wanted, and remembering the advice of his teacher many years ago, kept his cigarette in his mouth and put his hands in his pockets.

When he reached Jessie and Ron he saw one of the lads wave to Ron. 'Not your friends are they by any chance?' he asked Ron.

Ron waved back, and turned to him, 'Well, I know them by sight. They're alright.'

George drew on his cigarette and answered, 'You could have fooled me.'

'You're a stranger to them don't forget. On their territory, chatting to their girls, or so they like to think. Get my meaning?'

'Got their meaning more like.'

Ron laughed, 'Don't worry, they'll leave you alone now they realise you're with me and Jess.'

'They know Jess?' he was horrified at the thought. Ron leaned towards him.

'They're alright I tell you. Best mates you could have in a fight.' Fight! George did not like what he was hearing.

Jessie spoke up, 'They're darned good dancers our Joe, trust me, they're good lads, all working too. They would lose their jobs if they got into any trouble. They're just fussy about who the girls dance with, that's all. Now they know you're with us, everything'll be fine.' She stood up, kissed George's cheek and told him to 'cheer up,' then said she was off to powder her nose.

As soon as she was out of sight, George bunched up Ron's jacket and pulled him forwards until they were face to face, 'Let's get one thing straight, now,' he growled. 'You lay one finger on our Jessie and you will never know what hit you. Understand?' Ron was wide eyed and said nothing. George shook him, 'Do you understand? She's not like your interval dalliances. She's from a respectable home and only sixteen. Touch her, and I'll swing for you.' George was surprised at his own vehemence.

Ron pulled himself away. 'Listen mate, I respect her greatly. What sort of person do you think I am? I promise you I'll look after her,' he paused then added almost under his breath. 'Especially after we wed.'

George couldn't believe what he was hearing. 'Wed? Our lass? That's years off. Do you think you'll hang around patiently all that time? I mean it. Hurt her and you'll pay.'

'She's my girl now and forever, whatever you say, and that's an end to it,' snapped Ron. They were both a little out of breath, scowling and red in the face when Jessie returned.

'You two all right?' she asked.

'Fine,' they answered together. A little embarrassed, they grinned, and Ron offered George a peace offering cigarette.

The music started up again, and George formally asked his sister for a dance. It was a quickstep, and George deliberately included quite intricate steps and was pleasantly surprised that Jessie could follow him. When it had finished, he told her she wasn't as bad as he'd expected, although she did seem to stumble once.

'Cheeky blighter!' she retorted, 'that was because you trod on my toe.'

'I never did. I've never trod on anyone's foot in my life!' She laughed at his indignant expression and she playfully slapped him on the arm as he led her back to Ron.

Dancing was what he was here for, and so George warily approached another group of girls. No way was he going to invite trouble, and decided to avoid the earlier group. There were few tall girls, and really they suited him best, and no doubt, they appreciated his height. For the shorter girls, he lowered his arm and adjusted his footwork, neither of which seemed to interfere with his steps. After a few more turns around the room, he was surprised and pleased that one of the girls he had been dancing with earlier, called out, 'Hey preacher! You forgotten me already?' He glanced around, two of the boys who had seemed so threatening earlier, had their arms around girls, and the other was dancing. Holding out his arm to the girl, George quickly escorted her onto the dance floor.

As they passed the lad he'd recognised, there was a half hearted slap on his back and the earlier aggressor shouted above the music and chatter, 'All right, mate?' George grinned, nodded and relaxed. Seems Ron was right after all, and he felt more comfortable now that he had been accepted.

All too soon the evening ended. Everyone stood quietly as the National Anthem was played. George couldn't believe how fast the time had gone as he had been enjoying himself immensely, and was pleasantly surprised at the expertise of the girls.

On the way home, Jessie, between Ron and George with her arms linked into theirs, told George that dancing at the Palais was a treat. Next time if he wanted, she would take him to a local, smaller hall in Baker Street.

'We could go to the Palais if you like, say once a month, but me and Ron are saving up.' For a moment George said nothing. The savings remark informed him that a proposal had already been made and accepted. There was much he would like to say to her, but said only with cheerfulness, that as long as he could dance it didn't matter where.

As they parted at the station, George took Ron aside and said, 'Take great care of her.' There was no mistaking the tone of his voice.

CHAPTER FIVE

After yet another lonely breakfast on Monday morning, no one had appeared at either meal on Sunday, George made his way to the site to begin working in London. It gave him a thrill to think that. He imagined himself at home in Chilton saying to his family and friends, as nonchalantly as possible, 'Oh yes, I work in London.'

When he arrived Bert had already put the large kettle, in which they brewed their tea, onto the well alight brazier. As George approached him he put out his hand and gave a friendly shake.

'Well lad, ready to work 'til you drop. Looks like it's going to be a proper scorcher today.' Just on eight o'clock, Charlie along with two other men joined them. 'Here comes the gaffer. We call him Charlie, Charlie Drew.'

Charlie introduced the two men as Steve and Phil. Both grunted an early morning greeting, but George soon found that, after they had drunk copious mugs of tea, they were just as friendly as Bert and Charlie. They all had London accents, but Bert told him that he was the only true cockney.

'Born in the East End of London,' he said proudly, 'Wiffin the sarnd of St Mary's Bells, in Bow that is.'

'So watch out for his rhyming tricks. He'll catch you out you'll see,' laughed Charlie, then added, 'Right lads, let's get started,' and handed George a pickaxe.

What surprised George was how easy it was to break into the road surface compared to coal. He swung the pickaxe, getting into a regular rhythm, only resting to get his breath back now and again. What astonished him, was how slow the others were. They had begun shovelling up the broken cobbles and asphalt behind him, ready to dig the trench for the new sewer. Pacing themselves, he thought, that's what the older miners used to do, finished up doing a fair day's work, but at a slower rate. It seemed to George that there was a brew-up every hour or so, and this suited him as he was able to light up a cigarette and rest for a few minutes.

Charlie called a break for lunch. The men had sandwiches of cheese or beef and washed down with more tea. George took himself off to the baker's for two large, penny buns.

'You can't do a day's work on those,' Charlie exclaimed when he returned. George was dismayed, 'You'll never last the day.'

George took a mouthful of bun and was shocked when Bert snatched the remainder from him. ''ere, lad 'ave one o' me doorsteps,' and when George protested Bert replied, 'Call it a swap. My missus won't never know. Got a bit tired of cheese meself.' Gratefully, the exchange was made.

'You in decent digs?' queried Steve. With his mouth full, George nodded.

'Feed you well does she?'

'Well,' George swallowed quickly and answered cautiously, 'I'm neither hungry nor full.' Everyone laughed.

Charlie left the men to inspect the progress of the trench, and, when he was out of earshot, the men closed in round George.

'Now listen Geordie – we calls you that. We got to ask you to slow down a bit,' said Bert.

'What can't keep up with a miner,' joked George.

'We aint joking.' George heard a slight menace in Steve's voice and was upset, that after only half a day's work, it looked like he was to be ousted by the gang. The anxiety must have shown on his face as Bert quickly added,

'It's like this. The speed at which you was digging, could mean the trench will be finished in a week. We slow down a bit like, to hang out the job for a couple weeks. Take my meaning? We all got kids to feed and there is never a guarantee a job will follow on.'

George breathed a sigh of relief. So it wasn't only miners who played off the governors, he thought. 'Does Charlie know?' he asked.

The men looked at each other. 'We're not sure. We think he does. Better to say nuffin. If he guesses and lets us get away wiff it, he'll be out o' work afore us. So keep yer mouf shut,' snapped Phil.

'Oh, I'll do that, don't you worry,' he answered. 'And by the way I'm not a Geordie, they're Newcastle folk. I'm from Durham meself like.'

'Makes no odds mate, you sound like one of 'em so Geordie you'll be!' replied Bert as he stood up to begin work again.

Every day George bought his two buns and every day one of the men exchanged a sandwich for one of them. In return he complied with their scheme of stretching the work out. As the days passed, the trench got deeper and deeper and wooden shuttering had to be placed to keep the sides from collapsing in on the men.

One afternoon, deep in the trench with their heads just above the road surface, a youngster driving a horse and cart pulled up beside them. 'Christ,' yelled Phil. 'Oi! You prat, move your bleeding 'orse. He's level wiff me face and if he pisses on me, you'll wish you'd never been born.' Charlie, Bert and Steve grinned but George doubled up, and couldn't stop laughing. The tears rolled down his face and he held his sides. He did his best to control himself, but try as he might, every time he saw Phil's indignant face and the look of consternation on the driver's, he burst out laughing all over again. The others joined in and Phil laughed along with them.

Friday came at last, and George got his wages at lunch time. Looking in the little brown envelope and doing a bit of mental arithmetic he was pleased to see he had enough to pay Mrs Harper, get sensible lunches for the week and go dancing. He could send a bob or two home to mother and thankfully, have some left over for cigarettes to last the week, instead of eking out the few he had only afforded this week.

George was surprised when Steve and Phil, both family men they had told him, invited him to join them at the local pub. Charlie shook his head rapidly and frowned at him. George hesitated, he knew that it would not end at one drink. The wage packet, tucked into his trouser pocket, made him feel proud of himself. Then he remembered his father.

George knew his father was not without fault as he was regularly to be found in the local tavern with workmates after work. They spent their time arguing over politics, the hardship of the lives of the colliers and any current issue that took their fancy. The Saturday before the roof fall in the mine they had discussed the philosophy of Freud. Words like psychoanalysis, ego, dream interpretations and gender identity were bandied about, and, as far as George could make out, Freud's ideas according to the men were ludicrous. These debates were lengthy and needless to say, thirsty work. Consequently, the beer and wages flowed, round after round, and Joseph too often arrived home happy, and singing at the top of his voice. It was obvious Hannah did not approve, but George reckoned she was lucky not to be beaten like Alice next door, who lived with her in-laws, and who gave her no protection whatsoever, from their bullying son.

'Another time,' he said to the two men, and they sauntered away accepting his answer.

'Ah,' said Charlie, 'sensible lad. If they come back unable to finish today's work, they know what'll happen. Besides you need to think of the times you may not find work and still have to pay for your lodgings. Best save a little while you've got some money in yer pocket.'

That was something George had overlooked, and thanked Charlie for his advice. 'There'll be work here for another week I reckon, if you want to stay on?' George definitely wanted to stay on.

The following week was the same, the weather held fine and the work was nearly finished by mid-week when Charlie told him about another contract they were all due to go to next week. He asked George if he would like to go with them.

'Aye I would that. Save me looking around and having to get meself into another gang. Thanks a lot, Charlie.'

'It would mean finding new lodgings, I'm afraid. The job's across the river.'

'I'll take a look round on Saturday afternoon if you tell me where.' A promise of a job next week and new lodgings, life was just fine. First though, he must write to Jessie and tell her what was happening and that he could not meet her on Saturday, as they had planned. The letter was posted early on Friday morning and he knew she would get it by the evening post.

Why have I not yet met Mrs Harper's other lodger he mused, and made up his mind to ask her more about him. On Friday evening after his dinner, eaten alone as usual, he went to pay Mrs Harper and give her notice of his leaving.

'Well, that'll certainly make things hard for me. Where will I get another lodger at short notice, I ask you? Tell me that?'

'But you have another lodger you said, even though he never appears for any of the meals. That should help tide you over a bit,' he said. He could see by her face that he had embarrassed her. 'You do have another lodger don't you? I mean I never hear him about nor have I ever seen him. What's his name by the way?'

Mrs Harper's hands fluttered in her lap and she was quite red in the face. 'It's like this Mr Carr,' she finally said, 'I invented him.' She took out her handkerchief and wiped her eyes. 'I'm a widow lady as you know and to protect myself, just us two in the house you understand, I pretend to my lodgers that there is someone else about, er… just in case they think to, well you know what I 'm saying?'

Solemnly George answered that he quite understood, excused himself and rushed outside before bursting out with laughter. He lit up a cigarette, Christ, he thought, she should be so lucky. Fifty at least, and she's leaner than a rasher of bacon and me just twenty-one! Grinning to himself, he thought of her seduction. By heck, it'd take a month of Sundays to get her corset off, never mind anything else, and chortled at the very idea. I think I'd rather have ingrowing toenails he told himself.

The next day he took his packed suitcase to work with him. They were to finish at one o'clock, but as the job was almost complete, Charlie told Bert to take George off to Lewisham, so that he could look for lodgings near the new job. Bert and George travelled by bus and when they arrived at Lewisham Bert took him to the site then told him to look in newsagent shops as they usually had a board displaying things for sale and lodgings in the area.

'Good luck Geordie. See you sharp on Monday then,' he called out as he left George to go to his own home.

There were a number of advertisements for a variety of accommodation including, bed and breakfast, suite of furnished rooms and paying guests. George rather liked the idea of being a paying guest, sounded so businesslike and probably in a respectable area he surmised. He asked a passing boy the way to the address shown on the scrap of paper in the window, and was told it was only two streets away.

George was a little dismayed to find himself walking along a shabby street of terraced houses. Not feeling very sure, he knocked on number twenty-one, and waited a few minutes before knocking again. The door was opened by a middle-aged man in his shirt sleeves and braces. His hair was tousled and a cigarette hung from the corner of his mouth.

'What ya want,' he growled. George, a little unnerved by this reception, hesitated.'Well?' demanded the man.

Nervously George enquired, 'The advert. The advert for a guest? I was wondering if it had been taken?'

There was an instant change in the man. He wiped his hands down his trousers, held one out, and firmly shook hands.

'Come in. Flo,' he yelled, 'some bloke 'ere for the room. Look sharp.' He turned to George, 'Step inside mate,' he said.

A short plump woman bustled towards him, wiping floury hands on her apron, and a warm smile on her face. 'Blimey!' she exclaimed. 'You're a skinny lad. What you needs is some of Flo's dumplings. They'll fatten you up a bit.' She laughed and George relaxed and laughed along with her.

'Come on into the kitchen ducks, and I'll make us fresh brew, then we can 'ave a chat. Suit you? Sit yerself down somewhere.' The kettle was hissing steam on the gas cooker, and in no time at all she handed George an enamel mug of sweet tea. While he waited for her to get her own and sit herself down, he looked about him. He saw a large saucepan simmering on the stove and by the smell of it he recognised a stew of some sort. On the table was a large basin, and he realised that the woman had, indeed, been making dumplings.

'So,' she said sipping her tea, 'Got a name?'

'Yes, I'm George Carr.'

'Crikey a foreigner. I never takes in foreigners for lodgers!'

'But…but…' George spluttered, 'I'm…'

'Gawd lad, don't take on so, I was only kidding. Where you from?'

George grinned, he knew it was his accent again that always had people wondering. 'I'm from the north. A little village called Chilton Buildings in county Durham.'

She nodded, 'Fort so. Now then, I'm Mrs Stokes. Flo. I've got two rooms. You can choose. The one at the back overlooks the gas works and the one in front overlooks Ada's house across the road. No sharing rooms in this house not like her next door but one, Mrs Askew,' she sniffed. 'Well, she calls herself that. Missus my eye!' Already George liked Flo and her easy way of talking to him. She stood up and yelled out, 'Alf, Alf Stokes come here now.' She smiled at George, 'Treat 'em rough I says.'

The man who had answered the door entered the kitchen. The waistcoat he had put on barely reached across his middle, and he had tidied his hair.

'This is Alf, me husband. Been married twenty-one years we 'ave, aint we?' Alf nodded. 'Well now me old darling, show George Carr the rooms will you, while I get these dumplings in the pot.'

George decided on the front room. Both rooms were freshly deco-rated with clean bedding and a towel, but the front room, with a larger window and facing south, gave better light. On the dresser was a water jug and matching bowl, and under the bed was a white chamber pot. Returning to the kitchen he said to Flo, 'I'd like the front room please Mrs Stokes just so's I can keep an eye on Ada for you.'

Shaking all over with laughter she replied, 'You cheeky bugger! Call me Flo ducks. Now, we only have a privy in the back yard, and no water at all upstairs, but I promise you, Alf will bring you hot water 'alf six every morning for your wash and again when you gets back in the evening.'

'No bath then? Not even a tin one in the kitchen?' asked George.

'No love, but there is some slipper barfs just round the corner. Only a penny or two, and as much hot water as you like, and lovely soft, fluffy towels. That's what we do every week. Suits us fine.'

'What about washing?'

'No problem. Winnie takes in washing just a couple of doors down. Everyfink, even yer cap it you wants. All for a tanner, sixpence.'

George was more than satisfied, but had one more problem, an important one to him. 'Before we agree anything at all Mrs Stokes, I need to know what the house rules are.'

'Rules! Rules! No rules 'ere lad.' George could see she was outraged at the idea. Then she began to laugh a little sheepishly, 'Well, we make them up as we go along, 'cos you can't go upsetting everybody can you? You do as you please and see what 'appens. All right?'

George nodded, made up his mind and asked what the weekly rate was.

'Now let me fink abart this,' she said eyeing him up and down. 'Looks to me, as if you're just setting out down 'ere in London, so how about eleven and six?' George was delighted,

'Fine, just fine,' he agreed. Alf spat on his hand and held it out to George to seal the deal. George was amazed at this, but hid his dismay and shook Alf's hand.

'Right,' said Flo, 'supper in 'alf an hour. Time enough for you to have a wash. Alf see to the water. Then George Carr, come down here and have your supper with us and the family.'

As well as Flo and Alf, there were twin boys, Bobbie and Robbie aged around nine, George guessed, and their sister Rosina.

'This is Mr Carr, he's stopping with us for a bit. You all just mind yer manners around him.'

George learned more about the children during the meal. The twins were in grey flannel knee length trousers, short sleeved shirts and without socks, They had obviously been washed and their blond hair wetted and slicked down for his benefit. All through the meal they chattered away telling everyone about their game of cricket in the park. When the meal was nearly finished, the boys turned their attention on Rosina. George noted that everyone called her Rosie. Rosie, about to have her sixteenth birthday, was a miniature of her mother, but not yet as plump.

'Our Rosie works in Woolwerfs,' Robbie informed him proudly. 'On the broken biscuit counter,'

Bobbie chimed in. 'Yer, and she told us that when the crumbs fall on the floor, a mouse pops out and gobbles them up!'

'Shut up you two,' Rosie said, 'you'll get me in trouble with the manager if he hears I've been telling tales. People won't come in and buy anyfing.'

George, chewing on a tasty piece of tender beef, watched as Robbie nudged Bobbie and nodded to him to speak up.

'Help yerself to more spuds George if you wants,' encouraged Flo. George did so as the food was well cooked and plentiful.

'Da...aad,' there was a sly note in Bobbie's voice.

Sighing, Alf said, 'What now?' The boys grinned at each other.

'We saw Rosie with a feller in the park.' Bobbie smirked. 'Holding hands they was.'

George thought, poor Rosie, at the mercy of these two little monsters, but his pity was short lived. Rosie got up from her chair, raced round to the boys, and boxed their ears soundly, her eyes flashing and her cheeks reddened with anger.

'Stop,' whack, 'telling,' whack, 'tales,' she screeched at them.

Sharply Alf said, 'That's enough Rosina,' then added, 'Is it true? Were you with a lad?'

Rosie, not yet fully recovered from her show of temper her blue eyes flashing, snapped back, 'Yes. Someone I knew at school. You know him. Freddie Smith. We was only talking.'

Flo beamed, 'I know 'im and 'is mother. No harm in him Alf, he's a good lad. Got himself a job with the 'orses down the railway yard.' Alf huffed, the boys, with reddened ears, grinned, and Rosie gave her mother a grateful look.

When everyone had finished the meal and expressed their thanks, Flo turned to George and told him to join Alf in the yard for a smoke while she and Rosie did the washing up. 'He'll like the company before he goes to work. He's the night watchman at the goods yard. Don't have to do much, what suits him, as he was wounded in the war and sometimes it plays him up,' she explained.

George enjoyed his stay with the Stokes family. He joined in with the bantering and bickering, and helped Alf with chores around the house and garden. On Sunday mornings he went with them to the end of the road to enjoy the singing and tambourine bashing, as they called it, with the Salvation Army. In the afternoon they sometimes walked or played cricket with the twins in the park. On Saturday afternoons George routinely took a trip to the baths, before going to the local dance in the evening. Once, just once, he took Rosie to the pictures. Alf and Flo were more than pleased to see them together, and the twins made sly remarks. Next time George suggested another visit to the flicks, Rosie said quite bluntly, 'Forget it!' which, when he thought about it, was probably for the best.

Being so far away from Jessie, they were unable to meet up very often but he wrote to her and their mother every week. The letters he received back from his mother told him that she was relieved he was in a good, family home. George also kept in touch with Pat.

CHAPTER SIX

It was during the work on the new housing estate, that Bert began to train George in the art of stonemasonry. Loaning the tools, mallet, chisels and a metal straight edge from Bert, he learned the basics of the trade. He mixed mortar, and using the borrowed trowel, was quick to learn. He was proud of the neat finishes he was soon able to apply between, and around bricks, by levelling, spreading and smoothing the cement. Although too old to be considered an apprentice, Bert saw to it that George thoroughly learned the trade. As Bert put it, 'Geordie, you might be the labourer on this site, but believe, me any apprentice would have to make the tea, run the errands, do the dirty jobs like the lavvy, but they're mighty glad at the end of their term.' He added, 'Well, I was anyway. Seven years it was, though now it's only about three.'

George loved to hear Bert telling titbits of information regarding the trade. He told him about the skill of men, hundreds of years ago, who built cathedrals using tools similar to the ones they were using. That masons in the past were architects, designers and engineers and that each had a personal symbol, which was carved discreetly on the building, emphasising their pride and that the work was of lasting quality. 'Cos proof of this is in the buildings, bridges and houses still standing. You look out for them next time you go to church. Why even today,' Bert said, 'some architects and masons leave their signature. Some arrange a block of bricks into a pattern or use a different coloured brick, their signature for as long as the building lasts. You'll see.'

Bert told George it would be a good idea if he went to Petticoat Lane on Sunday to pick up some second hand tools which would not be too pricey in the market. 'Just the basics, 'cos at the moment our work will be laying granite kerbs or brick building. I'll make you a list. Be sure you get the best. Just two or three good tools to start wif.' Watching George light up a cigarette, he added, 'If you gave up yer fags for a day or two you'd have a bit more to spend. Think abart it lad.'

On Saturday lunchtime, as they were about to leave, George asked Bert for directions to the market. 'You gets a train to Liverpool Street Station and it's a five minute walk thereabouts. Opens abart ten o'clock.' He stroked his chin for a few seconds, then said, 'I think I'd best come with you. Missus won't mind.' George thanked him, and said really he could find his own way there.

Bert grinned. 'It's yer gob lad. As soon as you open yer marf they'll try it on. Charge you the earth.' He began collecting up his tools as he added, 'and another fing, watch out for pickpockets, thieving little buggers! Have yer wallet afore you can blink if you don't watch out!'

Even though the word 'underground' still unnerved him, after only a few weeks he couldn't believe that now, he could find his way around the London tube and buses. Also he could almost understand the variety of accents and intonations of the English language, especially the quick fire words and dropped aitches of the cockneys.

On Sunday morning, he made an early start from the Stokes household, and found his way to Liverpool Street Station. At first he couldn't see Bert among the milling crowds, then, with a sigh of relief, saw him making his way through the barrier. George was surprised to see how turned out Bert was. Jacket and waistcoat, sporting a spotted kerchief around his neck, and a new flat cap covered his greying hair. They shook hands and chatted about tools and work as they made their way to the market. When they arrived, George could not believe his eyes. In his mind he had conjured up the weekly market held in Darlington town square. The stalls there were mostly of dairy produce – cheese, eggs, butter, although there were also an equal number of stalls selling seasonal farm vegetables. Sometimes, there would be a ladies' dresses, 'bazaar', as the owner used to call out.

Petticoat Lane market was an entirely different scene hemmed in by tall buildings. The sun, slanting through the gaps between them, blinded everyone momentarily. The stalls had wooden poles holding up colourful overhead covers that sheltered the goods displayed below. It seemed to George that these stalls stretched along both sides of the street for miles. Bert made his way directly to a booth, where he knew he could get George some second hand bargains. Many sounds caught George's attention, and smells and colours tantalised him, but Bert hustled him along.

Leaning close to George, he whispered, 'How much you gotta spend?'

'I've about eleven shillings in all,' he answered. Bert winked at him told him to keep his mouth shut tight. He began to rummage among the tools on display, discarding this and that, until he found something suitable.

'Try that lad,' he said as he handed George a trowel. 'Like the feel of the 'andle? Reckon that's beech. Last a life time.' He gathered together a couple of chisels and a mallet. 'That should see you through for a while.'

The stallholder had said nothing until, 'Five bob for the lot,' Bert told him.

'Wot? You trying to put me outta business mate? Eight shillings is me best price.'

'Six,' countered Bert.

'Seven and six,' that's me final offer.'

'Six bob and a tanner?'

The man shook his head as if in despair and took out a pencil and began adding up on a scrap piece of paper. 'Make it seven and that's a bargain. Have me missus in the workhouse you will.'

'Tell you what. Six and nine pence, if you throw in that sorry looking tool bag, and you've got a deal,' Bert countered.

The man smiled as he grumbled about being really generous this fine morning, and Bert promptly shook the man's hand as they laughed together, both having enjoyed the bartering and banter.

Turning to George, Bert said, 'Right that's me done. I'm orf now to me family. See yer Monday lad.' George thanked him for his help and replied that he was going to wander around for a while.

Lifting his new tool bag and belongings to his shoulder, he stood for a moment and looked about him. The bargain hunters were mainly men, nearly all wore cloth caps and were smoking. One or two had a child on his shoulders and others had a woman linked on their arm. None were in a hurry, laughing, shouting and bartering. There were barefooted children dodging in between the legs of the crowd, play-ing a game of their own making, or, he thought, perhaps helping themselves to something or other off the counters. George lit up a cigarette and headed towards the centre of the market his head swivelling from side to side as vendors called out their entertaining patter to passers-by.

George had a weakness for sweets. At home he had a reputation of meanness for not sharing his weekly bag of 'bullets' as they were known, and it was not unusual for him to scoff them, one after the other, until they were all gone in one sitting. On reaching such a stall, he could not believe his eyes, the colours, shapes and tastes on offer excited him. He took his time choosing, mostly hard boiled and toffee ones, he thought they might last longer, but knew he would crunch down on them almost at once. Tucking the screw of paper holding the sweets into his pocket, his attention was drawn to a trader selling crockery. George watched as he piled an entire setting onto a large plate and then sent the lot up into the air and catching all the crockery on the way down. This, the showman told his audience, confirmed the 'robustness of the china'. George thought, it also allowed the vendor to show off his skills. At a ridiculously high price, he offered the artfully named fine porcelain set, rapidly coming down in price, then as the crowds began to drift away, called out, 'Now then, now then. 'ow about I frow in this matching teapot. The lot ladies and gents for ten bob. Can't say fairer than that, can I?' As George watched one or two purchases were made.

A man on stilts, his long legs hidden under wide striped trousers sauntered by and bending down extended his hat to the crowd for coppers. George walked on. There were cages holding puppies or kittens for sale. There were women selling salted herrings and others selling second hand clothes. He passed fruit and vegetable stalls, fruit cut open, melons, oranges, pineapples so that their smell and colour might entice the crowd. He spotted a gang of small boys fascinated by a man beside an upturned beer barrel. For a moment or two, he watched the man taking bets from onlookers, who were sure they knew where the hidden lady was – a small button hidden under one of three split walnut shells. The man's hands were so fast that it was impossible to make a guess and the losing crowd sportingly acknowledged the man's dexterity. George sauntered on, his hand straying to his twist of sweets. As he finished one, he popped another into his mouth. He smiled as he heard, was it the third or fourth, organ grinder? He stopped for a while to listen to a couple of the tunes as the elderly, bearded man, with a leather strap slung over his shoulders, that held the barrel organ in front of him, steadily turned the handle.

Suddenly as if from nowhere, there was pandemonium. In the distance George could hear the clanging of bells, and people scattered hither and thither to get out of the way of a speeding fire engine. As it raced past he could see the gleaming brass fitments, and the firemen clinging precariously to its sides. Ladders were dangerously bouncing, as the vehicle sped over the uneven road. As children rushed behind desperate to keep up with it, the stallholders began to tidy up their goods that had been disturbed, either by the draught the engine caused, or people jostling to get out of the way. And then indignant voices chorused around him.

'Don't you fret, darling. They'll never shut us down.'

'That's a trick they tries every Sunday.'

'Our religion lets us trade on Sundays. We ain't Gentiles.'

'Been 'ere over free 'undred years this market.'

'They can try, but I'm staying put.' George approached one of the quieter men.

'What's the problem? What's this all about?' he enquired, and offered the man a cigarette then a light. Both drew the smoke deep into their lungs.

'Well it's like this guv. The authorities 'ave been trying to close the market for years but we all stands our ground. Me father and grand-father always had a stall here, like Bill over there, and Isaac and Johnny and…well nearly all of us. We ain't gonna let them have their way though. We have fire engines or police cars chasing through every Sunday, trying to disrupt our honest business. Tell you mate, we ain't having it.'

George sympathised, 'I've never been here before, but I think it's one of the best places I've ever been to. Good luck to you.'

George moved on, and was nearly at the end of the Lane when he came across a stall that caught his attention. It was tucked away forlornly between two towering buildings. A blind man with a tradi-tional black, Jewish skull cap sat on a stool and beside him was a boy, about nine years of age, drawing a bow across a fiddle. The sound was awful.

'Go away young one. You're driving me customers away with that row.'

'Oh! Grandda! let me stay.'

'People will think the instrument's no good if they hear what you're doing with it. I got to sell something today boy.' George smiled at the child and put his fingers to his lips. Gently he placed the lad's fingers in position then indicated that he should lightly draw the bow across. The sweet note echoed between the buildings.

The old man, was startled. 'That you boy? That you playing?'

'Yes sir,' the boy replied.

'Don't believe yer. Who's there?' George tapped the man's shoulder.

'I used to play not so long ago,' he said and picking up the fiddle began to play a popular tune. Then another and another until there was quite a crowd around them.

Pennies fell into the old man's empty tin. It was time for George to make his way home and he put the fiddle into the man's hands.

'I suppose you couldn't come back next week could yer?'

George laughed, and as he moved away said, 'Teach the youngster to play, that's your best ticket.'

CHAPTER SEVEN

Three weeks later, the crew were on the move again. Steve and Phil found work locally, but Charlie, Bert and George went further out to Croydon. Charlie and Bert, both family men made an early start from their homes in south London, but George decided it would be more economical to, once again, change his lodgings. The Stokes were sorry to see him go. Flo cooked him a special supper on his last night, and Alf invited him to come and visit anytime.

So began a new search for lodgings. George realised that he had been so lucky to have found the Stokes, and hoped his luck would hold. A postcard wedged in a shop window offered a 'bedsit' at a reasonable price and although he wasn't sure what that meant he went along to investigate. An extremely young woman, her hair in curlers, a wrap-round overall almost completely covering her short frame and a toddler in her arms, answered the door.

'I'd like to see the bedsit if it hasn't been taken?' said George doffing his cap, and releasing his springy hair in need of a cut.

'Yer, come in. This way,' was the cockney reply, and shifting the child onto her hip, shuffled her way up an uncarpeted, creaking staircase. The handrail was missing, he noticed. The wall was grubby where the hands of other residents who, on the upward climb, had pressed against it, in order to keep their balance. There was a lock on the door of the room, which pleased George. The room itself was in the attic and contained an armchair, a rickety table, a bed with a mattress, pillow and a couple of once white sheets. A wooden orange box had been roughly painted, and held a few well worn books. Also in the room were two wardrobes, the smaller he was told was for whatever food he bought.

'You 'ave to see for yerself, you understand that don't yer?' she asked. George nodded. There was a limited supply of crockery and a saucepan in the cupboard. 'So you can keep yer own bits and pieces as you want,' she explained. The second cupboard was extremely large and for his personal belongings. 'Share the kitchen and bathroom,' she told him, 'with three others. That suit you?'

'Could I see the kitchen please?' he asked.

For a moment she hesitated, then sighed. 'This way, if you must.'

The first things to catch his eye when he entered the kitchen were the stacks of dirty dishes, pots and pans. The table still had bread-crumbs and a jar of marmalade left over from breakfast. George was surprised and disheartened at the untidiness of it all.

'Don't worry love,' said the young landlady when she realised his dismay, 'they'll clear all this up when they gets in.' George raised his eyebrows as if disbelieving her. 'Honest mate. They will.'

'Well, I hope so. I couldn't live with that clutter. I'll be over Monday evening after work. Oh, and if you've got the key to the room…'

'Don't worry abart that. Key got lost years ago. Nobody ever asked for it since, so I haven't bovered. But 'ere, I'll get you the front door key. Let yerself in when you's like.' The woman, Clara she called herself, wasn't wearing a wedding ring. George somehow felt uncomfortable with the fact, especially as the child clung to her, and he surmised Clara was its mother. He sighed and decided to make the best of it for now. See how things went.

Letting himself into his new lodgings on Monday evening, he was surprised to hear chatter and laughter coming from the kitchen and went to investigate. The small room seemed full of young women, and, counting up quickly, George saw there were four, including Clara. Two were drinking tea, one was stirring a pot on the cooker, and Clara was feeding the child. All stopped chattering when he opened the door. George politely raised his cap.

'Good evening,' he said.

'Oh blimey! I forgot abart you coming!' said Clara. 'Girls this is…this is…What did you say your name was ducks?'

'George, George Carr.'

'Ah, George! Well, meet the girls. This is Alice. Likes cooking as you can see.'

'You can say that again. Evidence is all on her hips.'

Alice turned sharply to a dark haired girl sipping tea. 'Shut up Ruby. You're to damn lazy to cook yourself so watch yer mouth.' She sniffed, 'Anyways, fellers like me rounded. You ask my Tommy.'

Clara laughed. 'Well, now George, that's Ruby so the only one left is Mildred. We calls her Milly.'

Milly turned her head towards him, 'How'd you do, love. Blimey aint he gorgeous! You can put your boots under my bed any time you like.' On seeing him turn red with embarrassment, she laughed, a coarse, vulgar laugh.

'Now then, I saw 'im first. Hands off you lot,' said Clara.

'I'd thought you'd had enough of men, seeing as you've got landed with little Jack,' Milly jeered, and an argument broke out between them.

'Excuse me ladies,' he said, 'Afraid I'm spoken for.' Well, he thought to himself, he could always talk about Pat if he had too.

'That makes no odds, if a little bit of fancy takes yer, lad,' said Alice. George shook his head, bewildered by the forwardness of the women.

'Oh, blimey, forgot me manners. Have you eaten George?' George was edging towards the door. Thankfully he'd bought a hot dinner earlier in the day, and he had rolls and a couple of slices of ham in his pocket, so there was no need for him to stay in the room any longer.

'I'm fine thank you. I'm away to my room.'

Milly winked at him, 'My room's nearest to yours George. You know if you fancy a bit of how's yer father...? George couldn't leave fast enough, and cringed as shrieks of laughter echoed behind him as he closed the door.

There seemed to be no end to the lewd suggestive behaviour of the women, although George acknowledged to himself that Ruby was, perhaps, a little less vulgar.

Milly and Alice worked in the local factory and Ruby in a bakery. It seemed Clara's father owned the property and, as Clara put it, 'Made me caretaker so I was out of the way wiv the baby. He was ashamed of me or at least me muvver was, so I was got rid of. If you understands me meaning.'

Daily he came across one or more of the girls walking around in their underwear. George did his utmost to avoid them. He ate a hot meal away from the house, got up early and breakfasted on his way to work and managed with rolls or pasties for his supper. The bathroom seemed always to be festooned with lisle stockings hung up to dry. On Friday evenings there were cami-knickers and slips dripping from an overhead wooden dryer, and the women were oblivious to his discomfort. Every evening there was bickering between them, but George was pleased to sometimes hear a radio playing and if a big band was being broadcast the volume was usually turned up. He wasn't so pleased when the various noises continued well after midnight. Returning from work one evening, he found a pink garter pinned to his door. He quickly snatched it off and flushed it down the lavatory, hoping that someone had wasted their money.

What upset him most was that one evening when he opened the door to his room, he knew someone had been in. There was no telltale smell of cheap perfume, nothing seemed to have been moved or taken, but George sensed the intrusion and although he was angry he had no proof to confront the women with.

Arriving at his bedsit on Saturday afternoon, there was a letter from Jessie. The news it contained upset and saddened him, but there was little he could do about it. He'd planned to go dancing although truth to tell, he was not really in the mood but thought, knew in fact, that the music and dancing would cheer him up. Fighting his way through the forest of washing, he gave himself a good wash, when out of the blue Clara called up to him,

'George, George you there?'

He opened the bathroom door his face lathered ready for a shave, 'Aye, in the bathroom.'

'Oh, good. George, the girls are taking me down the pub. They say I need cheering up a bit. So we're just off. Listen out for Jack will you. Ta everso,' and then he heard them all giggling as the front door slammed behind them.

Never in this world would he leave such a young child alone, but, by God, he would tell her tomorrow that he was not ever looking after her baby again, that it was her duty to care for the child, that she was, in fact, a slut. He was so angry, and consoled himself with a cigarette.

It was gone midnight before they returned. Their noisy singing woke him up and he looked out of the window. All were drunk. Milly and Alice, their clothes hanging untidily about them, each had a man's arm around their waists. Ruby was tripping over her feet trying to walk steadily up the path, and not succeeding as she was hindered by Clara, who had to be dragged along.

Every day he was certain that someone had entered his room and he decided to trap them. He began by leaving a thruppenny bit on the mock bookcase, and when he returned in the evening it had gone. Next day he hid another under a cup on the table, it too disappeared, as did one more. On Sunday morning, determined to catch the unwelcome visitor, he went halfway down the creaking stairs, then returned to his room, so that the combined up and down noise would, hopefully, fool the thief into believing he had gone out. It worked. About ten minutes later, he heard the telltale footfall as someone climbed the stairs. He hid in the large cupboard and through the gap between the doors, saw Ruby come in. Astounded he watched as first she laid herself down on his bed, and then she took up his pillow which, as she cuddled it, kissed it again and again. Sighing happily, she began searching the room, and soon found the coin hidden in his tool bag.

As soon as it was in her hand, George leapt out from the wardrobe, 'You thieving little cow!' he bellowed at her. 'That's a shilling you've stolen off me this week. Hand it back now.'

Ruby jumped, and gave a little scream in fright, then burst into tears.

'Shut that row. It won't work on me.' He wandered angrily about the room. 'Hussies the lot of you. Throwing yourselves at me half dressed. Cheap and common all of you. I'm more than fussy about who I mix with, you bitch. But thieving! I've a damn good mind to call the police!' He was beside himself with anger. Exasperated, he threw his hands in the air then dropped them in disgust, and his words as they left his mouth, mixed with spittle. 'If you were a man I'd give you a bloody good hiding! Bugger off. Get out of my sight. If you ever come in here again, I will, as God is my witness, I'll thrash you so hard you'll never forget George Carr!' He took a deep breath.

Ruby's face was white and she hung her head down. 'I'm so sorry,' she whispered.

'Give me back my money and get out of my room and keep out of my way in future.' She held out her hand with the thruppence in it and he snatched it back. 'Leave the rest on the landing ledge, now,' he said. Almost pushing her out of the room he added, 'And another thing, tell that bloody awful woman, an excuse for a mother if ever there was one, that she can look after her own brat in future, or I live here for free. That'll make her think twice. Now get out!' Slamming the door after her, he sat on his bed and was shocked and now angry with himself. He had broken the unwritten rule of his peers, he had sworn profoundly at a woman and hated himself for it. My life's being made a misery, he thought as he reached for his cigarettes.

Relaying all this to Bert and Charlie on Monday morning, they promised to look out for somewhere decent for him, but they all knew there were few lodgings to be had in the area. He got little sympathy from other men on the site who told him if he played his cards right, he would be in paradise.

'I like to do the chasing, persuading, not have girls like that pushing themselves on to me. Got to be on my terms,' he said.

'But I tell you what mate,' one of them said, 'when you leave, you want to…' and he lowered his voice. George gave a quiet chortle and replied that he could never be that mean.

When he arrived back at the bedsit that evening, he was surprised at how quiet the house was. He entered the kitchen to make himself a cup of tea, and found only three women, all properly dressed and the room spick and span. Ever polite, he said, 'Good evening.'

They all chorused back. 'Good evening.'

Clara, rather hesitantly, said, 'We've give Ruby the push. Told her to go. She packed her bags and left this afternoon.'

George looked unsmilingly at each of the women in turn. 'That was hardly fair was it? You're all as bad as each other. You have no respect for anyone or yourselves.'

'Well, fings will change from now on George, we promise,' said Alice.

The kettle boiled and George poured boiling water onto a spoonful of tea leaves.

Turning round to face them with a mug of tea in his hand, he said, 'I'm not a churchgoer, but I know right from wrong. Oh yes, I'm not perfect, but by God I've got some standards to live by. But you lot…words fail me. Just let me be,' and marched off to his room.

Some of the lads he was working with invited him out for a drink. Feeling lonely he'd joined them, but as it turned out the evening was no fun. It was better being out with his mates at home. With them he'd talk about the local football team, mostly the merits of the players and the blindness of the referee in particular. Here, he knew little of the local team. The entrance of three girls had stopped the boys talking. These girls were well-dressed and chatty. They were not like the girls he knew in Chilton, who were softer in tone and manner. Not like these girls, who flirted meaningfully with the group he was with, and in his opinion, were only just a fraction better than those in his lodgings. He left the group early, overwhelmed with feelings he'd never experienced before.

The following day, George felt just a fleeting flicker of the feeling again. Come and gone in the few strides it took to pass a particular house. It all began with the smell of frying bacon. Each day he'd heard the chatter of children, a boy and a girl. He was able to confirm this as their toys, a tin doll's pram and cricket stumps lay by the door and the early morning wash was blowing on the line. Every day on reaching the gate a friendly dog rushed up to him and barked out a greeting. Just like the dog next door at home. Today, the dog had escaped, and rushed up to him wagging its tail, its tongue was lolling out and its eyes bright. George knew it wanted to play. He felt his stomach turn. Then a lump rose through his chest and into his throat. He knew he wasn't ill when the moment passed so quickly, but he felt a twinge of sadness.

'Hi fella,' he said as he bent down to pat the dog. 'Got out to see me today have you?' He led the dog back into the garden and closed the gate. Without thinking then feeling foolish, he waved goodbye. He grinned to himself knowing there'd be no waving back.

Later the same day, the desperate feeling suddenly overwhelmed him again. It was when he spotted a matronly woman with her greying hair twisted up behind her head with pins that had worked loose. This time the oddness was accompanied by a pricking sensation of tears under his eyelids. Quickly he got himself under control. Out of the blue, it occurred to him exactly what these crazy feelings were. Homesickness. That's what's wrong with me he realised. A grown lad like me. Succumbing to an age old problem and suffered by most people at some time in their lives. He couldn't believe it. He felt his sister's latest letter in his pocket, the nearest he could get to his family. At the end of the day, he'd made up his mind. He told Charlie, 'I'm going home,' then added hastily, 'missing my mam and family.'

Charlie nodded. 'Yes lad, it'll do you good. You've been down a bit of late. Get in touch if you ever comes back to this part of the world.' After shaking hands with most of the lads, and thanking Bert and Charlie for all their help and support over the last few months, he took up his tool bag and left.

On the way home he stopped at a corner shop and bought an orange, a baby's potty, it was cheaper than a chamber pot, and a couple of kippers. He said nothing to the women about his leaving. He decided that he could, after all be as mean as the workmate had suggested, and set about the surprises he intended to leave. No one remarked on his not going to work the next morning. When the two women left for the factory and Clara was away to the shops, he filled the baby's potty almost overflowing with water, and added the juice from the orange so that it looked like pee, and placed the pot under the bed. That'll set them off screaming blue murder when they come to clean the room for the next unsuspecting idiot, he thought. It took him some time to find suitable hiding places for the kippers. In the end, he settled for the top of the toilet cistern fitted high up on the bathroom wall. The dust he disturbed confirmed that it rarely, if ever, got a clean. The other he put in a jug at the top of the kitchen dresser, a jug he had never seen used. 'That'll keep the buggers busy for a few days, maybe weeks with a bit of luck,' he thought.

Leaving part of the week's rent on the kitchen table, he picked up his tools and suitcase, now held together with cord, and made his way to King's Cross station for the one-thirty train to Darlington.

CHAPTER EIGHT

There was only one other passenger in the carriage, a gentleman hidden behind a newspaper. The man had not acknowledged George's entrance, so he took a window seat. George surmised he was a gentleman, as a bowler hat and umbrella were in the luggage rack above the man's head. He wondered why a toff, as Bert would have said, had decided to travel in a third class carriage. He thought the man was probably a detective in disguise, or maybe he was hiding from an irate husband or a bad tempered wife, or could the man have fallen on hard times and was saving his money. George shrugged his shoulders, he didn't really care.

Slowly, the train eased its way out of the terminus. On the way to London earlier in the year, he had been too excited and nervous to notice the size or bustle of the sidings, where smaller engines, with plumes of black smoke and white steam, fussily shunted miles of full and empty trucks. George's eyes were drawn to men with leather headgear, from which a protective cape hung down their backs, who were shovelling coal from trucks into bunkers. Others filled sacks from the bunkers and hoisted them onto their shoulders to take them to a variety of horse drawn wagons, ready to hawk around the streets.

Slowly passing a signal box, he saw a signalman leaning out of the window enjoying a pipe as he observed the moving trains, his polished levers glinting behind him. Nor had he observed the ugly, tall, smoke blackened buildings, huddled together, along the embankments on either side of the railway tracks. Some, he noticed, had optimistic washing hanging from them defying the airborne soot. Small sash attic windows in higher buildings, reflected the meagre sunshine. All this gave way shortly when the train gathered speed and the suburbs were reached. George could see new housing estates, offices and roads being built. Every time the train stopped at, or passed through a town, the pattern was the same.

Listening to the rhythmic clackity-clack of the train's wheels passing over the rails, George thought the sound matched a phrase going round and round in his head – going home, going home, going home.' He couldn't be sure of the reason he was making this journey, he only knew that he missed his family. He thought he could have got over that if his last lodgings had been, well, just ordinary he supposed. He also wanted to get to the bottom of Jessie's letter, and took it out of his pocket to read yet again.

Dear Joe,

Just a few lines to let you know that our cousin, Thomas, has died. It seems like an accident, as he was found at the bottom of the mine shaft. Will let you know more after the inquest. Poor aunt May, mother says she is beside herself with grief. All for now. How are the lodgings and the job?

Love Jessie.

George frowned as he thought about the safety rules for using the lift. He recalled that before the lift could descend, the outer gate had to be closed, then the lift door. True, there was a gap between the ceiling and the top of the gate, but it would be more than difficult to climb over, and surely our Tommy wouldn't be so daft as to try and if he did, why? That was one of the questions he was going to seek out an answer to. Lighting up a cigarette, he leaned against the plush upholstered back of his seat and, smiling to himself, admitted he was looking forward to meeting up with Pat again.

Before long, George was fascinated to watch the newspaper his co-traveller was reading, begin to slowly descend, which revealed a round plump face, eyes tightly closed and mouth wide open. Within a short time, there was a snuffle of a snore, and with legs wide apart supporting an ample stomach, the man, who had loosened his tie, wriggled into a more slumped, comfortable position. George grinned, and stubbed out his cigarette in the dull brass ashtray fixed on the door frame, tugged at the leather strap and located the punched hole in it and fixed it securely over the little brass peg. This ensured that the window remained slightly open, then, tipping his cap over his eyes, soon joined his fellow passenger in sleep.

When George woke up, the train had stopped at York Station. The man had gone, but had left his crumpled newspaper. George stood up, stretched then leaned out of the window where he saw porters, lads and guards scurrying about, checking and loading mail bags, parcels and even a greyhound. He also saw a refreshment cart manned by a smart attendant and a young boy. Quickly he jumped down from the train, fished in his pockets for some coins and bought a slice of fruit cake and a cup of tea. A stream of steaming golden liquid was poured from a large pot into a white, chunky cup. Sugar and milk were added and was so strong that George suspected it had been made a good while, but he was glad of something to drink.

Returning to his empty carriage, he picked up the discarded paper as the train resumed its journey north. Settling into his seat again George alternated between gazing out of the window as it sped past fields dotted with sheep, or ripened corn ready for harvesting, and reading the newspaper. Much of the news was of little interest, but the German election stating that Adolf Hitler was now leader of the second party in the Reichstag caught his interest. Germany was experiencing a crippling depression, and George read that, aided by Joseph Goebbels, Hitler's campaign had gathered many supporters, especially as his speeches promised work for all, a united Germany, profits for industries, expanding the army and ending the payment of war reparations. Hitler also promised to deal severely with the Jews. George found himself disturbed by the report. Army? Surely not another war, his early childhood had been touched by war, and what did Hitler mean when he promised to deal severely with the Jews? George didn't like what he was reading at all.

He glanced out of the window for a few moments. At a road crossing he saw three or four children who had climbed onto the safety gates waving wildly, he waved back, but the moment had gone. He saw a man with a gun strolling across a field, a dog foraging ahead of him. Once, George had been told that so many telegraph poles equalled a mile so he began counting but realised he didn't know how many. He turned back to the paper, and was amused when his eye caught a cartoon of Betty Boop's scantily clad body, with her legs in the air one of which had a garter on. The picture was illustrating the film *Barnacle Bill, The Sailor*. One to go and see perhaps, with Pat he thought, she'd like that. He read of the Stromboli volcano eruption which had taken the lives of six people, and of Richard Drew an American engineer who had invented a cellophane adhesive tape which the motor industry was finding useful when painting cars. What surprised George, though he couldn't explain why, was that Drew was a keen banjo player.

At last, the train arrived in Darlington. George gathered his belongings, found his ticket tucked into his waistcoat pocket, and made for the exit. The collector wished him a 'Good evening' and George was delighted to recognise his own local dialect, he was on familiar ground at last. The local bus dawdled its way to his village. By now he was hungry, tired and impatient to be home. He was deposited at his stop, now there was but one mile more on foot to go. He looked into the terraced houses where the lights were being turned on and curtains drawn. Nearly every house had someone he knew well living there.

At last he reached the house next door to his home. The neighbour Mr Greene, was leaning over his gate smoking his pipe and the dog at his feet, welcomed George with a friendly bark, and thumped its tail lazily on the ground. He lifted the latch to open the wooden gate of his own yard, and stood for a moment. The tiny cobbled yard housed the flush lavatory called the netty, and a long cool pantry lined the opposite shady side. Nothing had changed. He could see clearly through the window overlooking the yard, that the fire was low in the blackened range next to which was his father's carver chair, where he sat and invited the younger bairns onto his knees. Close by was a jam pot filled with newspaper spills, twisted by the youngsters, ready for him to light his pipe. Along one wall, just for da's use, there was a horse hair filled chaise lounge that creaked, whenever he moved, as he rested on it. Everyone, George remembered, had to keep quiet for half an hour or so while da dozed. And there was mam, sitting in her chair, hooking pieces of rags into a rug and Nancy sat at her feet, doing the same. That was typical of mother, he thought. What spare time she ever had was spent peacefully hooking mats, always encouraging her children to help. The mats were sold to neighbours, but without fail, there was always a new one for Christmas to go in front of their own fire. He remembered going with her once by bus to the Yorkshire mill where she could buy up rags cheaply. Robert was at the table writing, no doubt doing his homework thought George, and his heart swelled with happiness to see them all.

He crossed over the yard and stood in the open doorway for a moment blocking out the fading daylight. All three turned towards him and then Nancy jumped and squealed, 'It's our Joe!'

Robert grinned shyly at him, and his mother stood up, almost held out her arms but smoothed her apron instead. George knew his mother well-reserved all her life and would never alter. He crossed the room to her quickly put his arms around her and held her close for a moment. She smiled, and stroked his face. 'Eh lad, it's right champion to see you,' she said softly. She turned to the fire and stirred it into a life, 'soon have the kettle boiling. You must be starved.'

Turning to Nancy she said, 'Get that pie from the pantry and some pickles, while I get the lad some supper. Be sharp now.'

'A cup of tea and the pie will do nicely mam,' he said. 'Don't go on so. I'm staying a while, and will eat you out of house and home before I'm done. Then you'll be sorry.'

Sitting in his father's chair, he gave a sigh of satisfaction after his feast. Not content with giving him the pie his mother also insisted he had a large slice of her pound cake.

All three began to question him on his stay in London, but George protested. 'I'm fair dead on me feet. Wait till the morrow and I'll tell you all then.' Sleeping arrangements were hastily made. Baby Joe, without waking was moved out of the bed he now shared with his brother and was laid on the sacred horsehair sofa, and then George crept in beside Robert, who had been sent off to bed earlier.

George didn't rise until after Robert and Mary had gone to school, and when he entered the kitchen there was Nancy sitting in the window at the well scrubbed table, already stitching away at a customer's order. His father was beside the fire reading a paper with baby Joe on his knee. George was surprised and a little hurt when Joe ran and hid shyly behind his mother. 'What! Forgotten me already have you, you little rascal. Come on, come over here and give your big brother a cuddle.' Joe clung to Hannah refusing to look at George.

'You'll need a good breakfast I warrant,' said his mother. 'By lad, ye look healthy enough I must say. Filled out somehow, and all that fresh air has browned you up a treat.'

Nancy looked up from her sewing, 'I'd best not ask me friends round for a while then, eh mam? They're sure to take a fancy to our Joe and he's only just got back.'

'That's enough from you young lady. Get on with Mrs Fraser's blouse, she wants it this afternoon, and watch those buttonholes.' Turning to George she asked, 'Fried bread as usual is it and how many eggs? Two, three maybe?' George tucked into his favourite breakfast and for the moment ignored baby Joe, watching him out of the corner of his eye and saw that the child was observing him just as closely.

It was later in the morning after mam, Nancy and baby Joe left to visit aunt May in the next village, that George's cousin Harry arrived. Harry was nineteen and a collier, who was bursting with energy, even after a double shift. He entered the kitchen at high speed, saw George and rushed across the room to shake his hand, thump him on the back and asked how long he intended to stay. George laughed at Harry's exuberance then put the kettle on.

'Tea for you da? You Harry?' Both men were more than surprised at this. This was women's work and George was offering!

They looked at each other, Harry put his finger to his forehead to indicate that he thought George must be mad, then da said sharply, 'What's up with you lad?' George knew what they were thinking – women's work.

'I've had to look out for meself in London, tea making is nowt to what I've learned down there I can tell you. Now, how much sugar?' His father grunted, and Harry asked if he could knit.

'No, by God, but I can cook a bit now and again!' replied George with a laugh.

After acknowledging that the tea George dished up was nearly as good as his mother's, Joseph settled back in his chair with the paper, and Harry began telling George news of their friends in the village.

'I tell you something though our George, the tennis club will be glad to see you this Saturday. They haven't won a match since you went, and this weekend they're up against Bishop Auckland and you know how good they are.'

George nodded and was pleased to think he had been missed by others, then wondered about Pat. 'Have you seen owt of Pat? Thou knows, Pat Smithson?

Harry grinned at him knowingly and answered mockingly, 'Dost thou mean that plump lass always with a fella on her arm?'

George bristled, slightly clenched his jaw and hoped he hadn't given away his feelings. 'Aye, could be her,' he answered. 'Not married or anything is she? She'd make a fine wife for someone.'

'Depends what you want out of your marriage doesn't it,' laughed Harry.

George rose to the bait, 'Watch your mouth our Harry. That's how girls' reputations get ruined and you've got five sisters. How would you like anyone to talk about them like that? Pat's alright.'

Harry, bubbling with laughter confessed he was only joshing and that indeed Pat had asked after him a few times. 'Although she did say she'd had a few letters from you. Smitten are you, with her?'

Joseph's newspaper rustled, and George whispered back, 'Mind your own bloody business!'

George took out his packet of Woodbines, offered one to Harry and took one himself. After they had lit up and inhaled, George, glanced across to his father then in a hushed voice said, 'Harry lad, tell me what you know about our Tommy's fall.'

In a sombre tone Harry answered, 'He didn't fall. How could he?' He got to his feet and paced about the room, drawing deeply on his cigarette. Then leaning over George, he murmured, 'He was tipped over the guard rail.' George was shocked, and yet not surprised. He, like Harry knew it was impossible to just fall down a mineshaft.

George looked into Harry's eyes, then said, 'Aw lad, come on. You can't be sure of that can you? I mean, who? And more to the point, why? Our Tommy was as gentle as a kitten, what could he have possibly done to deserve such a...an awful ending?' The paper rustled agitatedly, and the lads looked across to da who seemed to be reading. 'Come on now Harry, what's the crack about this affair?'

Stubbing out his cigarette, Harry sat down opposite George clasped his hands together then leaned forward. 'Mind now, it is only gossip amongst the lads, but it seems early in June Sir John went on his jaunt to the Med. Gone for a month as usual and while he was away, a gang broke into the Manor House and stole...' he stopped for a moment to think, 'Ah, yes, pictures, silver, tons of it I heard.' He looked at his cousin who had half smiled, disbelieving the amount. 'Well, that's what I was told,' Harry sheepishly retorted.

George lit up another cigarette, and Harry refused an offer of one. 'Go on, I'll not interrupt again.'

'Anyway, loads of stuff was taken, but not content with that the buggers set fire to the place.'

George sucked in his breath in disbelief, 'Set fire to the place? Whatever for? They'd surely got what they wanted?'

Harry shrugged his shoulders. 'Rumour has it that some of the men had been put off from pit and this was their revenge.'

George frowned,' I just can't understand how Tommy could be involved in this. I mean, for God's sake he was holier than me mam!' The newspaper was shaken as if in warning again.

Harry stood up and paced the room, then sharply turned back and said, 'No he wasn't, but it seems one of his friends might have been.

You remember Andrew? A spineless creep I always reckoned, but he looked up to our Tom.'

'How sure are you about all this? I mean I still don't know how our lad could be part of this.'

'Seems Joe, the housekeeper was still in the manor, and was overcome by smoke before she could get out, and well…she died.' There was silence for a moment and then Harry went on, 'Andrew was so upset by her death. Remember, it's a case of murder now as far as the law is concerned, so it says in the newspapers, and so we think he confessed to Tommy.'

'Did Thomas tell you this?'

'No, but they were seen talking together in the rec. and Andrew kept looking around to make sure they were alone.'

George snorted. 'Could've been anything. Nay, nay laddo, he would-na have been so daft to tell if it were true.'

'I told you it is all hearsay. But if our Tommy knew, and him being so honest, the best the sods could do, was to shut him up for good. Follow what I'm saying?'

George sat for moment thinking about what Harry was hinting at, then got up quickly and picked up his jacket, his face ugly with anger. 'I'll kill every one of the buggers!' he shouted, 'Come on, you know who don't you? Tell me their names, NOW!'

Harry put out his arm to stop him rushing out in haste. 'Steady on George, like I tell you, it's all just gossip at the moment. The inquest is on Friday, we might learn more then.' Then looking straight at George, he said, 'And I don't know any names except Andrew's and how true it all is I can't be sure.'

'Well, let's go and have a word with him shall we. Get something out of the little weasel.'

Neither of them had noticed Joseph crossing the room until he banged his fist on the table and roared, 'Ye'll keep yer bloody gobs shut. Mind your business. If, and I say if, any of what's been said here this day 'appens to be true, then believe me, Tommy won't be the only one to come to a nasty end. You might well find yourselves keeping him company.' He limped breathlessly back to his chair, his hand shaking as he took out a spill to light his pipe. He looked over to the two men, still boys in his eyes, 'I mean it lads. You might be placing yourselves in great danger. I can't stop you going to the inquest, your aunts and mothers will need your support. That's all I want you to do, be united as a family, but no deliberate looking for suspects. If, and I say if, they're there and catches your eye, believe me, they'll know what you're thinking.' Puffing on his pipe he added, 'You might well be wrong anyhows.' He fished in his pocket and handed over a coin, 'Go on down road, and get yourselves some chips to tide you over 'til your mam gets back. Let the matter rest.' He leaned back in his chair, closed his eyes and said, 'Aye, I just fancy some chips,' then smiled and pointed the stem of his pipe at them. 'Remember now, keep yer mouths closed – tight and as you were told as wee lads, keep your hands in yer pocket when you feel like knocking the block off someone. Understood?' Both nodded.

They left the house and began to walk towards the chippie when Harry said, 'I still think there might be some tru…'

'Da has said to keep our gobs shut,' snapped George. They walked along in an uneasy silence for a short while and then found a stone which they kicked aimlessly to each other, but when they reached Mrs Taylor's cottage just past the farm, Harry gave a quiet chuckle.

'Did you ever hear about old Frank Taylor's cabbages?'

'Cabbages? No, what about them?'

Still quietly laughing, Harry said, 'Seems he was mighty proud of them. Told everyone how it was his good compost heap made them hearty. Anyhow, everyday afore he went to work he'd cut one for the old lady for dinner, and every day after dinner he used to say there was never a better cabbage in the whole of England.' He began laughing his earlier spirits now revived.

'And, so…? What's the joke?' asked George.

'Well when he died, God rest his soul, Mrs Taylor told her neighbour, Lily Parker, that every day the cabbage would appear and it was full of caterpillars which crept out all over her table. She couldn't bear the little devils. So…,' he laughed out loud again, and wiping his eyes, said, 'so she used to shove his cabbage into the bottom of his compost heap and go down yonder and buy a cabbage for their dinner.'

Both chuckled all the way to the chip shop where Harry left George who said he could never look at a cabbage again without laughing.

More sombrely he added that he would meet up with Harry on Friday for the inquest. Being on night shift, Joseph had gone to his bed by the time George returned with the now cold chips. Oh well, thought George, no use wasting them and tucked into his father's portion.

It was dismal and wet on the day of Tommy's inquest. George stood in the quiet oak panelled room beside his mother who was wearing her long black coat and black felt hat that she wore throughout the year. He looked around the room. There were no strangers present, only his mother's three sisters dressed in similar clothes and sur- rounded by their men folk. All the women were clutching a white handkerchief to wipe away their tears. It seemed only close family were in attendance. Even the police officer, John, giving his report was a relative.

There was little evidence and certainly no witnesses to Tommy's demise. The coroner, in his summing up, said he was sorry that there was no conclusive reason as to what had happened, that he was certain, given the facts, that it was not the intention of the deceased to take his own life, that it was difficult to believe it was an accident, and that the only course open to him was to return a verdict of 'Misadventure'. There were growls of discontent from some of the men. They wanted to hear 'Death by person or persons unknown' so that someone could be blamed, but along with George and Harry, no one voiced their conviction of murder.

Meeting up outside, the two cousins exchanged their views on the verdict. They walked away and lit up cigarettes. Harry paused for moment then said, 'Hang on a minute, Joe. There's something else you might like to think on.' He looked around and lowered his voice, 'Andrew has been sent to somewhere in Kent.'

This news heightened their suspicions and George shook his head as if he found it hard to believe, 'Silly sod. He must know it confirms what everyone's thinking!' In fear of their own lives, and heeding da's warning, they agreed to say no more for the time being.

During the days of the first week home George slept. Much to the unspoken disapproval of his mother, he spent most evenings in the Dog and Gun, the local inn, with his friends. It took baby Joe another day before he was happy in George's company, a penn'orth of jelly babies did the trick, but he had to share them with Mary. It was

Friday before George finally met up with Pat. Both were more than pleased to see each other, although they were careful not to display too much affection in public, both knew how tongues would wag, and put two and two together to make five in the village they had both been born into.

'How's things hinney?' asked George, offering her a cigarette. She shook her head.

'No thanks. I'm fine really Joe. Thanks for your letters. They were welcome.'

George cleared his throat uncertain how to ask, 'Seeing anyone special yet?' She tossed her head and laughed. 'What do mean, seeing anyone? Course I am. Always got someone to walk out with,' she answered, hoping this would bait him.

Slightly miffed he asked, 'Anyone I know?'

She tapped her lips with her finger. 'Let me think now. There's Dave, and Mike and Mick and John and…'

'Give over you daft cow. I mean anyone really serious about you. You know, courting like?' They stood looking at each other, anxiety on his face, and a flicker of indecision on hers. 'Howay, the truth now hinney, I don't want to cause any bother. To be honest I'm a bit of a coward, hate fighting.'

She gave him a push in the stomach and raised her voice, 'Are you saying that I'm not worth fighting over Joe Carr!'

George exaggerated a stumble, 'Steady on lass, you'll have me over. Come on,' he coaxed, 'put me out of me misery.'

She rocked on her feet making interesting parts of her body sway provocatively, thinking how to answer. 'It's like this Joe, Sammy has been walking me out since you left.' She saw George's face cloud over in disappointment. 'But he hasn't said anything serious…yet. Like engagements or such.'

Miserably, George said, 'He's a good man. He'll settle you down alright.'

'Like hell! Anyway man, he's on the nightshift the morrow, so if you're going to ask me to the dance, I'll say yes!' She giggled, and George laughed with relief.

'Right, I'll meet you at the door around eight.'

'Does the agreement still stand?'

'You can bet your life on it pet,' he answered. With that they parted, he home to his supper and she to, he couldn't be sure.

During the final waltz on Saturday Pat whispered to George, 'I'm that starved.' He flashed a smile as he knew what she was hinting at.

'Supper it is then for my lady, fish and chips as in the 'agreement' then your part of the deal. Right?' He winked at her and she gave a wide grin and nodded.

They ate their supper as they walked to a secluded part of the copse adjoining the manor, their special place, where they went for the privacy of their love making. Lying on his back afterwards and blissfully smoking a cigarette, he smiled as he watched Pat sit up and pull her skirt down over her knees. She leant over him and kissed him lightly. In the stillness they heard the sharp snap of a twig and looking at each other, both froze. It surprised George to see a look of consternation on Pat's face replaced by something that looked like guilt.

'Don't take on so lass,' he whispered, ''tis nothing but a fox or badger. Nothing for us to worry about.'

'Why are you whispering then?' He laughed out loud and she thumped him. 'Shut up, you idiot,' she hissed, 'it could be the game-keeper.'

'We're not in the sacred grounds lass, he can't touch us. Any road it's none of his business.'

'Aye, but what if he takes tales back to the village, and, and...' Pat moved away from him, and sat quiet for a moment, then said, 'Do you remember Joe, the pact we made when we were bairns in the Elementary school?'

'Most of it.' He paused for a moment before saying, 'If I remember, we said we would try out everything new together. Remember we built that raft to go over the weir, and the trouble we got into for that?'

'I mean when we first got together like this. There was no one else, but you I wanted to find out about... I suppose you'd call it lovemaking.'

'And you were my first too.' He pulled her down towards him, but she wriggled out of his arms and looked into his eyes.

'I never noticed. In this light your eyes look grey I always thought they were blue. Funny that.' As she turned away from him and in the dimming light she saw out of the corner of her eye a fox, head held high proudly, carrying in its mouth an unlucky rabbit. She laughed softly, 'You were right Joe, it was a fox. See him over there?'

George nodded then said, 'There's something amiss here. You're not usually so, I don't know, so, I think sad almost,' and noticing the tears in her eyes, said gently, 'Aw hinney. Tell me what's wrong.'

Giving a little sniff then wiping her eyes with the back of her hand, she took a deep breath. 'Joe do you remember we agreed that we would only ever be friends?' She hesitated, 'You haven't fallen for me have you Joe? I couldn't bear to hurt you.'

'Nay lass, I'm mighty fond of you like, but love? What the devil is that?'

'Thank goodness. I'm happy with the arrangement we've had these last few years. Since we were fourteen they've been the best years of my life really, and I will always be your best friend.' George sat up and almost forcefully pulled her into his arms.

'What's up lass? What are you trying to tell me?' She turned towards him and he saw another tear trickling down her face. 'Aw don't take on so, tell me.'

She brushed the tear away, and swallowed, 'It's like this Joe, I've lied to you. I'm truly sorry. I like you a lot, but you asked about love. I love Sammy, Joe, with all my heart, and I feel so bad about us tonight.' Surprised, George loosened his hold on her. 'He loves me, he said so. He wants to marry me and I want to be with him for the rest of my life. Oh I know I've got a reputation, but only by flirting mind, you know that, and he understands.' She snuggled into George's arms, and quietly said, 'I made him a promise Joe. He doesn't know about us so this will be the last time for our arrangement. I'll always love you, but in a different way to how I love Sammy.' George said nothing.

'Speak to me Joe.'

'So be it lass, but if there's any bother you come to me first. All right?' They made their way back to the village, both deep in thought, knowing their long understanding had come to an end.

CHAPTER NINE

During the third week home, George was aware of two things. The first was, that he would forever be called Joe within the family, and by the people of his village. Try as he might, he could not persuade anyone to call him George. The second thing that perturbed him, was he felt as if he were on holiday as he seemed to be treated as a guest by his mother. He tried to resolve this by seeking work. Work in the area was getting really scarce, and he felt he was lucky to be taken on for various harvest jobs. This enabled him to contribute towards his keep, show his mam that he was still one of the family. He realised that they had all readjusted their lives when he left, but now it was almost as if he was outside their new cohesive bond. He recalled this happened each time one of his sisters left home, and wondered if they had the same feeling of almost desolation he was experiencing. Following constantly behind his mother around the house, he realised, that perhaps, he was seeking reassurance from her and recognised this had always been so since childhood. On the other hand, he told himself, he had flown the nest, and the family had understood this at last, and needing to make his own way. There was a warm enough welcome but...By the weekend dancing, tennis and meeting up with the lads during the evenings began to pall. Everything was too slow and too peaceful.

It was just by chance that he met Doris. Doris was in Ma Robinson's back room which served as a shop. A plump, but shapely girl about twenty, and as she talked to Ma Robinson, she swayed a little and swung her long untidy hair from her face. As George entered the room she turned and her face lit up.

'By, lad it's some time since I saw you. Where've you been? You're looking that bonnie. Come home to stay?'

George laughed, 'You're asking a lot of questions missy.'

'That'll be a shilling if you please, Doris.' Mrs Robinson said sharply.

Doris fished in her purse and passed the money over. 'Well, good seeing you Joe,' said Doris as she turned to leave.

'Hang on. If you wait outside a minute, I'll walk back with you a way. I'm just getting my ma some fresh yeast, and some sweeties for the bairns.' Doris beamed her answer and George could see her leaning against the yard wall waiting.

As Mrs Robinson handed over his change he was surprised when she said, 'Best stay away from her lad. She's bad news.'

George raised his eyebrows, then frowned, 'What do you mean Miss Robinson?'

Pursing her lips and shaking her head, she answered, 'A bit too free with her favours if you ask me,' she wagged her forefinger at him, 'Mark my words young man, before you know it, she'll have your money and your good name if you're not careful.' She began to fold some sugar paper into cones then added, 'And I'll tell you something else, your mother would not approve, definitely not I'd say.'

George smiled, lifted his hand, and as he walked out of the parlour shop answered, 'I'm only walking her back to the end of the row Mrs R. No need to worry. Good day to you.'

The chat between them as they made their way along the lane was friendly. Doris asked him about his stay and work in London. 'Is it true, Joe, that there's work on every corner?'

'There's men working on every corner,' he laughed, 'but you have to find the work like everyone else.'

'What about the girls? Are they working on every corner?' and roared with laughter as she watched him slowly understand her meaning.

'By, you're a saucy wench,' he retorted.

She danced a few steps away from him then falling into step beside him, asked, 'You going to the dance this Saturday?'

'I am that. Can't miss the dance.'

'Yes, I noticed you there last week. Didn't have your girl with you, though.' Then looking at him with partly closed eyes, she added, 'I wonder why?'

Thoughts of Pat flooded his mind. Despite the fact that he and Pat had agreed there was no more than friendly affection between them, he knew he was hurting and he also knew he shouldn't be. Funny, he thought, that I should miss her more now than I ever did in London.

He looked down at Doris's upturned face, 'There's nowt between us. Doesn't mean a thing. We're just friends.' After they'd walked on a few yards on, he added, 'Besides, she's walking out with Sam, and it could be serious.'

Doris beamed up at him. 'That means you're free then, and linked her arm through his. 'Shall I see you at the dance, Joe? We could have a bit of fun if you like.'

'Aye, lass I'll be there. I'll see you inside.'

Frowning at first then brightening up she said, 'I'll wait for you outside Joe then we can go in together. All right?'

George sighed, if he agreed he would have to pay for her entrance, but he thought, she is a lively little thing, should brighten up the evening. He took out his packet of five woodbine cigarettes and lit one up.

'Oh, Joe, can you spare one of those? I've not had a ciggie since last Saturday.' He offered her the packet and she said, 'You light it Joe, like they do on the pictures. Looks so romantic I think.'

'You daft woman.' he said as he lit her cigarette. 'Alright, so I'll see you about eight on Saturday. Suit you?'

She nodded, and as they began to make their separate ways home she giggled, 'Well, that will certainly give the old biddies like Mrs Robinson something to gossip about, won't it? Bye for now Joe. See you Saturday.'

As he walked away he ruefully thought, dance ticket and a fag already and a hint of being together. Well seems old Mrs R has a point. I'd better watch meself. Hearing running steps behind him he turned and saw Doris and waited for her to catch up. Clutching her chest she panted, 'Wait, wait. Oh, I'm that out of breath.'

'What is it lass? What's up?'

'I was thinking Joe, what are you doing tomorrow?'

George shrugged his shoulders,' What I do most days. Look for work. Why?' She twisted her body from side to side and toed the dust at her feet.

'I was wondering if you'd like to come to Darlington with me 'morrow?'

'I can't. I'm up at five trying my luck down the farm, then on to sidings to see if there's any coal wants shifting. If I'm lucky I should get half a day's work, maybe more. Can't miss out on that can I?'

He watched her pouting her lips as she thought about his answer. 'If you don't get anything, we could get the two o'clock bus. I got to see my auntie, she's poorly, I go to see her every Thursday. Then, tomorrow I thought I'd get some new shoes, for the dance like. What do you think? You could come couldn't you?' she wheedled.

George scratched his head, as he thought for a moment. It would make a change from sitting around bored to death at home. 'Aye, I'll come but if I'm not at the bus stop go on your own as I'll probably have got something with a bit of luck.'

Doris lifted herself on to her tiptoes, and kissed him lightly on the cheek. 'Aw, Joe! That'll be great. See you tomorrow. Bye.' George gently rubbed where the kiss had been planted, and grinned.

They met up at the bus stop. Doris laughed and clapped her hands when she saw him, saying, 'I was hoping you'd come.'

George smiled down at her, 'Aye well, I was hoping for a bit of work, hinney but…well we'll see what tomorrow brings. Here's the bus.' Stepping aside to let her on first, she promptly sat down and left George to pay for their return fares.

The aunt's furniture was large, dark and seemed to dwarf everything. The room was cluttered, and Doris roamed around the room, touching the odds and ends of ornaments, framed sepia photographs and knick knacks lurking in dusty bowls and saucers. They didn't stay long, Doris, anxious to be shopping, said to her aunt, 'We got to go now, auntie. We got to get the next bus home. I'll see you next week. Take care now, pet,' and as she opened the door turned to George, and said, 'Come on. Don't hang about.'

Puzzled by Doris's lies and haste, he said polite goodbyes to the old lady and followed her down the path.' What's the haste, lass? You could have spent a little more time with that lonely old soul.'

'There's others that never come, just me and me mother sometimes,' she snapped back. Then slipping her arm through his, she added, 'Well, let's away to the shops now. I'm that parched. We'll have a cup of tea in Fraser's café first, then I'll look for me shoes.'

'You change your moods like a tap on and off. I can't make head nay tail of yer.'

Sitting in Fraser's, George ordered tea for two and, knowing he would be paying the bill, was a little vexed when Doris added, 'Aye and two buttered teacakes please.'

In the shoe shop, George lit a cigarette and prowled around, as Doris tried on endless pairs of shoes, and calling to him for his opinion time and time again. To be honest, he was more than fed up with the whole procedure. Once again, he heard his name being called, 'Joe, Joe. Look at these. Aren't they just perfect?'

As far as he was concerned anything would do, but he nodded, and said, 'Aye, they're just dandy, lass.'

She twisted her feet round and round then went to look in the mirror. When she sat down again she patted the stool beside her, 'Sit by me a minute, Joe.' She edged closer to him and whispered, 'They're twelve and six, Joe,' she paused. 'I've only got ten shillin'.' Looking into his face, she asked, 'Can you make up the difference for me? It's only half a crown.'

'No lass. Don't even think about it. I've nothing to spare, no job and no money coming in. No, Doris. Choose something else,' George said firmly as he moved away from her.

'But, I like these best. I've tried on hundreds and these fit perfectly and they suit me legs so well.'

George beckoned the assistant over, 'The lass has changed her mind thank you.' Turning to Doris, he said, 'Come on, let's away now.' Reluctantly, and sulking, she followed him out of the shop.

Three shops further down the street she surprised him again. 'Look Joe. A pawnbroker's,' she began putting her hand inside her coat. 'Look, I could pawn me brooch. Should get two and six for it I reckon.'

Shrugging his shoulders he said, 'You go in then, I'll wait further down road.'

'Brokers have a reputation for dealing badly with women,' she said as she took his hand and twined her fingers in his. Pressing herself against him she pleaded, 'Please George. You go in with it. You're sure to get a better deal. Please?'

'Just this once.' he sighed. 'I hate the bloody place, so don't you go telling anyone I was in there.'

She handed him the brooch and thanked him. It didn't take long to negotiate, and when George handed her the three shillings he'd got, she threw her arms around him.

'Hey, steady on.' he said shocked and he admitted to himself pleasantly surprised, 'we're in the road, lass. Anyone can see us.' The shoes were purchased as planned, but George never saw them again.

It was Friday morning when his cousin, John, in full police uniform entered the kitchen.

'Will you have a cup of tea? Some breakfast lad?' asked Hannah.

'No thanks auntie.' he answered. As he took off his helmet, he ran his fingers through his hair and asked quietly, 'Is Joe about?'

'Our Joe?' queried Joseph from his chair.

'Is he in?' persisted John.

Hannah sat down abruptly, brushed the hair from her face before asking, 'What is it John? Why do you want to see our Joe? Is he in bother?' John shook his head as Hannah called out, 'Joe, get yourself down here. Our John wants a word.'

As George entered the room, pulling his braces over his shoulders, everyone was horrified to see John take out handcuffs and hear him say, 'George Carr, you're under arrest.'

George laughed. 'You daft bugger. Stop playing about. What's up with you?'

'Put your hands out please. I'm serious Joe.'

'You bloody well tell me first what's up, before I do owt of the sort,' he retorted.

'There is a charge against you of theft.'

'Oh, Joe. What does he mean?' Hannah gasped.

'I've never stole in my life,' George bawled out, 'Never.'

'And I believe you,' said John cautiously, 'But Mrs Jarvis in Darlington, says you took a valuable brooch from her house.'

'Do you mean my friend's aunt?' George spluttered, 'Well, I never did.'

'But you did go there?'

'Aye I did, that's a fact, but I never touched a thing, I tell you.'

John took out his notebook and read, 'She says that nothing has ever gone missing before and you are the only stranger she's had in the house.'

George went across to Hannah, 'Mam, I swear on the Bible, I've nothing to do with this.' For a moment she held his hand and he sat down beside her, but turned back to John when he added, 'There's worse. More proof if you like.'

'Go on,' George sighed, and referring to his book again, John said,

'You were seen going into the pawnbrokers, Joe. And the fella in there said it was a brooch you bartered with.'

George sprung up from his chair and paced frantically about the room then began shouting, 'The little bitch! Set me up for a right patsy. I'll kill her if I get my hands on her.'

'Who, Joe? Who we talking about?'

George reddened as he remembered Mrs Robinson's words. 'She'll have your money and your good name.' The old girl was right, a tramp, a gold digger. He was that angry. Hannah will be angry with him, but that greedy bitch, wasn't going to get away with it. Taking a deep breath he said, 'You should go and talk to Doris.'

Slowly, John folded his pocket book and put the handcuffs away. 'I thought it might be something to do with her. Tell me about it, Joe.' Then turning to Hannah he said, 'I'll take a brew now auntie, if you've a mind.'

When George had finished telling his side of the story, John stood up, put on his helmet, and shook George's hand. 'You'll hear no more about it Joe. Don't do or say anything rash though, I'm warning you. Let the matter be. The law will deal with that lassie.'

As Hannah began to pour out his tea, she said, 'You're a good boy, John. How about a hot buttered teacake?' and as he smiled and nodded she turned sharply on George and pointed her finger at him. 'And as for you, I've a good mind to tan your bottom.' She paused, then muttered, 'if you weren't so big,' and everybody burst out laughing. George heard no more except for the teasing and jokes from his family and friends, but he knew that he had been close to losing his good name as well as finding empty pockets.

It was during the following week that the question of him staying on came up. 'If you've finished your jaunts to London, and thinking of settling back here Joe,' his father said one evening, 'there's a couple of things we need to think about.'

George was playing with baby Joe, and looked up in surprise. He turned to his little brother and said, 'I think our da wants a word with you. Are you off to London town?' but the child only repeated, 'My turn, my turn.'

'Aye so it is, but I've got to talk with da now. We'll finish tomorrow,' he replied. Hannah took the youngster off to bed. Getting up from the floor and reaching for a cigarette before sitting down, George asked, 'What do you mean da?'

Joseph tapped his pipe on the fender, cleared his throat and said, 'If you're staying on Joe, you need a bed of your own. Mother and I think it best if we give over the front parlour to you so's you got a place of your own. Give you a bit of privacy like, you being grown up now so to speak.' George said nothing and waited for his father to go on. Joseph sucked on his pipe until the tobacco glowed and George flicked the ash from his cigarette. Leaning back in his chair Joseph went on, 'Course you'll have to get a regular job. At the moment there's a place going for you at the pit.'

'Never,' exploded George, 'never, ever.'

'Don't take on so, son. Just listen for a bit.'

'Don't ask me to go down that hellhole, da. I just couldn't.'

'Now listen to me. Think on. Our Robert is leaving school next Easter, and down the mine he'll have to go. We thought it would be a good thing if his elder brother were there to keep an eye on him.'

George clenched his jaw. It went against his principles to argue with his father but the idea of hewing coal in semi darkness again was unbearable. 'You'd put the lad in the pit after all that's happened in this family?'

'It's how it is. You know well enough that it is the only work to be had around here, and, I might add, that's getting scarcer.'

'He could go away somewhere.'

'Where?'

George shrugged. 'I don't know. Be a page boy to the queen or work on a farm. He's bright enough to try for a civil service post.'

'That has to be paid for and there's exams wanting money too. Don't talk so daft.'

Hannah, who had been standing behind Joseph's chair said sharply, 'Keep your voices down. You'll wake the bairns.'

George, trying to keep his temper under control, at the same time trying to appeal to his father, said, 'Da, if you send Robert down the mine...' he thought for a moment then added, 'I won't ever forgive you or come home again.'

'That's enough. That's an end o' the matter. Stay or go as you please, but you'll not tell me what to do, or threaten me in me own home.'

Both men were angry now and Hannah, moving towards the kettle hanging over the red coals, intervened again. 'I think a cup of tea would be fine all round and then bed. Sleep on the problem and be sensible in the morning about this.'

'You don't want our Robert down the pit do you mam?' George pleaded. Hannah said nothing. 'Forget the tea, I'm, away to my bed,' he muttered.

Throughout the night he was disturbed by haunting dreams, and was awakened early by Robert, who whispered, 'You awake our Joe?'

'What's up? Whatya want?' George grunted from under the blanket. Robert nudged him, as George appeared to be settling down to sleep.

'Wake up. Come on. I want to know what the row was all about last night.' George gave a low moan, then leaned on his elbow and cupped his head in his hand. 'Come on Joe,' Robert whispered, 'tell me. It's about me isn't it?'

In the early morning light, George thought how young and vulnerable Robert looked, and the idea of his young brother trapped in the pit filled him with determination that it should never happen.

'How do you feel about becoming a miner?' he asked. Robert remained silent. 'Does that mean, you haven't thought about it yet, or did you not realise that is what da has in store for you?'

'What else is there our Joe? Mam doesn't want me to go away like you. Broke her heart she said.'

This surprised George. Had he broken his mother's heart he wondered. Surely not, she was tougher than that. Upset maybe, well yes, of course, but broken hearted? 'Take no notice of that lad. That's just women's talk. They all think their babies never grow up.' They chuckled softly together, one already a man and the other on the verge of manhood, and both thinking of themselves as babies.

'Now then Robbie boy, tell me honestly, is it pit work for you?'

Robert sighed. 'That's all there is around here. Coal, bloody coal.' George took a deep breath,

'Now listen, if it's not what you want, don't do it.'

'I can't go against da now can I? He'll beat the living daylights out of me.'

George thought for a moment, something he had thought carefully about during the long restless night. 'Listen our lad, I've been think-

ing. I can't bear the idea of you trapped in the mine like me and da.'
He paused for a second, 'Aye, and our poor Tommy. It is a hell on
earth. I don't know why they think it's all there is for you.' He
scratched his chin, feeling the new growth of bristle needing a shave
then said, 'When the time comes lad, be firm, and say that you are not
going to dig out coal.'

'But...'

'Oh aye, there'll be rows, but write to me and I'll send you the fare
to London. I'll find something for you, a trade like mine if you like,
but something so's you can make your own way in a few years.'

'You mean it don't you? You'd do that for me? We'd both be in real
trouble with mam and da.'

'I think after a time, especially if you prove yourself, that they'll be
proud of you. Any road, it will be better than slogging down yonder
hell hole.' Robert wriggled closer to George who promptly began to
wrestle with him. Giving as good as he got, Robert tickled George
until he gave in, but then George suddenly turned on his younger
brother, and squeezed him in a bear hug, until the boy begged for
mercy, and said, 'That's for swearing and you not even working yet.'

'Breakfast for them that's awake,' It was the first call of the morning,
and Nancy would have to call twice more before everyone was fed.
Robert, always hungry, quickly dressed and as he passed close to the
shared bed, George grabbed him and pulled him close, 'Mind you say
nowt about what we been talking about our Robbie.' Robert nodded,
'we'll talk some more nearer Easter. Right? Now, go on, scamper
away for your bait.'

Later that morning when Hannah was kneading bread dough, and
Joseph was reading the paper, George spoke quietly to them, 'I've
made up me mind. I'm away back to London for a spell. There's more
work to be had there. I'll write to my gaffer today and ask him what's
going.'

Hannah wiped her hands down her apron, Joseph sighed. 'We were
hoping that you'd not go back son. Aye work is scarce, but you're our
lad and we want you close,' Joseph said.

'Our firstborn,' said Hannah softly as she sat down. 'Stay on Joe, for
a while longer. Something could turn up for you.'

'It's no good mam. Just looking out of the window and seeing the
pithead gear makes me shudder somehow. I've...I've got to get away,

but I promise you, I'll come back as often as possible.' George went across to her and put his arm around her shoulders. 'Honestly, I promise, perhaps twice a year, if I've the fare.'

Taking his time before he spoke, Joseph tamped down fresh tobacco into his pipe, lit it and inhaled its fragrant smoke. 'I've been thinking our Joe, you've a good head on you. You ought to be able to get better work than breaking roads. Didn't you once talk about becoming a reporter or something like that?'

Laughing, George answered, 'Yes da, but I was young and daft then. You get nowhere in this world if you don't know the right folks to start with. And then I'd have to improve me English for a start and…'

'Aye lad, and I was thinking you might find out about them night courses for…' frowning, he tapped his fingers on the arm of his chair, 'I think they's called Adult Classes or some such name. Ye could get yerself some qualifications, you're bright enough.'

George was surprised and pleased that his father had accepted he was adamant about refusing mine work, and had thought of his future. Not only that, da had come up with a reasonable idea. 'Aw da, that's a grand notion. I'll have a look round and see what's what.'

Hannah covered her dough with a clean cloth and placed it near to the fire to rise, and after smoothing her hair turned to her menfolk. 'I'm away next door, see how the bairns are with their chicken pox.'

After she'd gone, Joseph said, 'Now our lad, come down to the shed. I'm sure I've got a few tools you could be using.' George followed his limping father, who went on slyly. 'I bet anything you like son, you're a better carpenter than a, a…stonemason did you say?' He chuckled, 'more like a bricklayer's labourer by all accounts.'

'Why didn't you stick at being a carpenter da? Would have saved you from having that bloody awful accident.'

'Well, I suppose I can blame your mam for that.' And George heard the laughter in his father's reply.

Mam?' Women, he had always understood, did not interfere with men's work.

'Aye,' and seeing the look on his son's face, grinned. 'It were like this. As I told you before, I started work at twelve as a chitter picker, picking out the unwanted spoil. By God it were that noisy as the belt moved the coal along to the storage bays.' He bent down and rummaged in a large wooden box, picking out tools he no longer used, then straightening up continued, 'I did that until I was nigh on fourteen or thereabouts. Then my pa, apprenticed me to the trade of carpenter joiner, best years of me life.'

'Yes, but how does ma come into you leaving a skilled job?' George queried.

'Ah well tha knows, we wed in a bit of a hurry like, and you came along, then your sisters and the pay wasn't enough to keep us all together, so I went underground.'

'I can't see why you blamed ma,' said George indignantly.

'She were a bonny lass, so I'll say no more,' laughed Joseph. 'Any road, my time wasn't wasted was it? I taught you all I knew. Made some grand fiddles didn't we?'

George nodded remembering how he loved the feel of wood in his hands and how he used to sandpaper it until it felt like warm silk. 'I remember,' he said, 'and I remember the smell of animal glue as it warmed in the pot over the fire, and didn't mam go on about it!' They grinned at each other, as they recalled Hannah's sharp reproaches. 'But the best part was seeing the instruments finished. French polished. Coat after coat we gave them until they looked as if they were covered in glass.'

Joseph sighed, 'We had a grand time then, son. Working together at home and down the pit I reckon.'

'I would have loved to keep me own, but needs must when the devil drives so to speak and I needed the money to get away.'

Joseph looked at his eldest then said quietly, 'I too, had to sell mine lad, when the accident happened. The shillings kept us going until your postal orders started coming.' He clasped then shook George's hand, 'Thanks son,' was all he said, and George felt a lump in his throat and knew that he was loved.

After writing to Charlie, George set out to post the letter and meet Mary from school. The bell rang, and George was amazed to see Mary rush out, arms and legs flailing, and beaming with happiness. Something wonderful had happened for his little sister he guessed and was pleased to see her so happy. Dancing around him she screamed, 'I can read! I can read!'

George sat her on the school wall. 'Why, you clever lass. Let's hear you then.' Mary took the book out of her pocket, and slowly mastered each word, words that were repeated over and over again, probably no more than ten George thought. When she had finished he gave her a big hug. 'My word, da will have to hide his newspaper I'm thinking if you carry on like that. Thou's a canny lass our Mary.' He lifted her down and she slipped her hand into his.

'It's true isn't it Joe? I can read now can't I?'

'Course you can,' he replied as he began running towards the sweetshop, and dragging her along. 'Let's get some sweeties to celebrate, shall we?'

Later that evening, George said to his father, 'You know da, I was thinking maybe I could be a teacher.'

Joseph eyed his son and shook his head, 'Eh, lad. First you want to be a reporter, then a musician, then a singer, then a stonemason, then a carpenter and now, God help us, a teacher.' He pulled on his jacket ready to leave for the night shift and chuckled as he added, 'Well why not go for the whole hog and become prime minister?' As he went through the door he called back over his shoulder, 'Your grandda began teacher training, but it was hard for him.'

'In what way,' asked George walking beside his father to the gate.

'Well like, you could say moral wise.'

'Morals? What do you mean?' Joseph stopped and looked at George.

'You like girls and dancing, a drink, a little bet sometimes lad? Well your grandda was playing shove-h'penny in the inn one night, and didn't someone report it to the authorities? They threw him out smart, like. A danger to the children they said. Could've made it he used to say, but he ended up a publican in the end. Wonder where you'll end up?'

CHAPTER TEN

Charlie's letter came by return post. Yes, he wrote, there was at least four week's work he could offer starting next Monday. After that being October, and the beginning of poor weather, work would be scarcer, but come anyway. Digs would be no immediate problem as Bert's sister had moved into a new council house, and could put him up for a few days until he found something suitable. George decided to leave immediately, and as he embraced his family in turn, his father shook his hand, patted him on the back, and said, 'Good luck, son.'

Hannah stood upright, stoic, but her voice cracked a little as she too said, 'Good luck, Joe.'

Ethel, Bert's sister rented a newly built council house with a generous size kitchen come diner. There were tiled walls, and water laid on, in the working area, and her pride and joy, electric lighting. There was also a front room parlour and, in keeping with tradition, a new three suite piece kept for visitors, who alone, would sit on it. George knew that his stay there would be short. So that he could have a bed to himself, the youngest child slept with his parents, an arrangement that made George feel a little guilty. It was when Ethel asked him to say he was her cousin if he should be asked, he realised that she was breaking the council conditions of 'no lodgers'. Within days, Ethel found him lodgings with her friend, and within a week he had moved into Emma's terraced house.

On the whole he was happy there, and although a number of small things irked him it was far better than, 'Clara's Joint', as Harry had nicknamed it when George had told him about the goings on of the girls.

Always, without fail every cup of tea George had in Emma's house was stronger than that drunk on site, and sweetened with lashings of condensed milk which he hated. Try as he might to change this, by buying his own fresh milk or drinking it black with sugar only, his efforts were quietly ignored, and quickly replaced with the offending white, cloying syrup. Newspapers served as tablecloths, a fresh one daily laid on top of yesterday's, so that by the end of the week there was a thick, and sometimes unwholesome, pile. On Sundays the whole lot was thrown away. George had no objection to newspaper tablecloths, but truth to tell he preferred his mother's well scrubbed table.

As George entered the house, his downstairs bedroom was immediately on the left of a long tiled passage. The room opposite his had been turned into a shop. The parlour shop, as Emma called it, was an

Aladdin's cave – everything from candles, string, sewing thread, bread, eggs, paraffin, sugar, sweets and condensed milk, could be purchased. Open from early morning, before George set off for work, and late at night and sometimes after he had gone to bed, there would be a customer. Often, George noted, Emma was quite happy to serve in her dressing gown, but if her hair was in rag curlers she exclaimed, 'I wouldn't been seen dead in them,' and she was quite happy to yell out for him to serve, '…if you don't mind darling. You can pay yerself with a sweetie or two.' Naturally, George obliged.

The four weeks' work Charlie promised stretched into nearly six for them both, along with Bert and a few others. In the middle of October, it persistently rained and most, including Bert, were laid off until the weather improved. As luck would have it, George, being the youngest and paid the least, was best suited to a labourer's role and was kept on by the Company. No promises were made as to how long, but he knew he owed this chance to Charlie, who had been kept on as carpenter. It was the third day of rainfall, George had exhausted all the work found for him, mostly tidying the site in the rain, when Charlie asked him to sweep the workshop he was working in. At the doorway George stopped, and breathed in deeply the smell of freshly shaved wood. As he was gathering up after Charlie, the Company manager entered with a new batch of drawings. He spoke earnestly with Charlie for a few moments saying as he left, 'By Thursday Drew. Understand? They're for Mr Foster's new house and he wants them in place by Saturday.'

Officiously he left the building as Charlie began to protest about the short notice, yelling after him, 'Bloody impossible with me on me own. What do you think I am?'

'Get on with it man or you'll be looking for a job come Monday,' was the sharp reply.

Charlie threw down his hammer and picked up the drawings. George watched as Charlie ran his hand over his head and frowned in bewilderment as he squinted at the documents.

'Sod it,' he said, 'this is specialist work. Doesn't mean I can't do it, but it all needs time and care.' He sighed, 'Why has that idiot manager made such promises to Mr Foster?'

'Come on Charlie,' said George. 'You know as well as I do. He wants to show he's needed around here. Making sure of his own job I reckon.'

'Well can't be done. Site's waiting for these skirtings, the whole job will be held up if they aint finished by the weekend. He can go boil his bloody head. I owe it to the lads on site first.' George watched as he threw the papers on the bench, picked up his saw and began work again.

'Shall I get you some char, Charlie? Give yourself a chance to think for a moment or two?' Charlie nodded his thanks. Whilst waiting for the battered enamel kettle to boil, George sauntered over to the bench, and began looking over the drawings, pondering, then nodding to himself. After he'd given the tea over, he picked up the papers, tapped them gently then hesitantly said, 'You know Charlie, I can cope with some of this if you'll let me have a go.'

'Getting a bit above yourself aint you lad? I couldn't make head nor tail of the buggers so how come you think you can?'

'I turned them upside down and then they made more sense to me.'

'Upside down?' Sheepishly, he put on his spectacles. Then the truth struck him. 'You cheeky blighter. You mean I was holding them the wrong way up don't you?' He turned the papers himself, and saw there was a lot of work, but it all looked a bit more reasonable.

'Give me a chance Charlie. Something simple to prove meself. You won't be sorry.' George said as he picked up one of Charlie's planes.

'What about tools? I need mine nearby all the time,' he replied taking the plane off George. With a flourish George opened his tool bag and displayed the array of tools inside.

'Blimey. Where'd get that lot?'

'Told you ages ago I was a carpenter like me dad. He set me up with this lot. Told me to better meself.'

Charlie hesitated for a moment, took a large swallow of his tea and making up his mind, said, 'Better get cracking then. See what you can do with this,' and he shoved the measurements of a door frame into George's hands. Delighted, George began work. He placed his feet apart to give maximum balance and then his body took on a steady rhythm as he sawed and planed the wood, until it was smooth and white. Charlie quietly noticed how he referred time and time again to the drawing, measured the wood and handled his tools like a man born to the business. When he was satisfied himself with the finished job George nodded to Charlie. Charlie ran his hand over the wood, made checks on the door frame, made sure it was square and the joints fitted together, were true. Charlie looked across to George, and noticed he had a pencil tucked behind his ear, like someone with years of knowledge behind him. He grinned.

'I suppose you think yourself master of the trade with that pencil, lad.' He inspected the frame again, George was on tenterhooks, waiting for the verdict of his afternoon's labour. Charlie stretched himself, and lit a cigarette before adding, 'I'm not one for giving out praise lad, all in a day's work. Always expect the best from my crew. But to be honest, you've bettered my expectations. Well done lad.' George glowed.

'And...?' The question was soon answered.

'I'll speak to the manager in the morning. Show him your work. He'll be more than surprised I can tell you. He's got no time for youngsters as a rule that one. Anyway, he leaves it to me to pick me men so yes, my young fella, more carpentry jobs for you from now on.' Lying in bed that night, he thought about how his life was going forward.

As his father had suggested, he'd enrolled at the local College for Adult Evening Education and was learning shorthand typing towards his dreamed of career as a journalist. So, he told himself, the little squiggles of shorthand were a devil to master, and at the moment his fingers seemed to be all thumbs on the typewriter, but by God I'll get there he promised himself. In the meantime, he'd had good training from Bert, and could lay bricks with the best of them. Even better, today Charlie had promised him more carpentry work.

Sighing, he thought about the folk mainly in Newcastle, not too far from home, who were steadily losing their jobs, especially in the shipbuilding industry. It would be lovely, he thought, to tell someone of his satisfying day, but he rarely saw Jessie, never Emily or his other sisters although he had letters from all, except Emily. It seemed that they all had restrictions regarding time off from their employers. His thoughts were divided on this, he resented the tardiness of those issuing them but, at the same time, realised that the girls were lucky to be employed at all.

In no time at all it was Christmas. Through fair and foul weather George had been kept in work. Steady progress was being made with his shorthand and typewriting, and he had danced and sang through the weekends. A number of girls had caught his eye, but nothing lasting. Not that it mattered, there were very few dates with anything more than a kiss and cuddle and, he admitted to himself, that the arrangement he had with Pat could never be repeated with anyone else.

Work had been found for Bert and during the lunch break and relaxing with a cigarette, George was surprised when Bert asked suddenly,

'What you doing tomorrow, Christmas Day Geordie?'

George shrugged, stubbed out the cigarette and answered, 'Probably sleeping.' Seeing Bert raise his eyebrow in surprise he added, 'Write a few letters, and practise my homework I expect. Emma's going to her sister's so I'll have the place to myself. Might rob the shop for something I can cook easily.'

Bert was quiet for a few moments, then having made up his mind said, 'Well I was thinking like. Maybe you could come over to us for the day. We got plenty, and one more won't make any difference to my Sarah. Whatcha say?'

To be honest with himself George had been dreading being on his own. There were so many Christmases at home when the house had been crowded with neighbours and relatives and there was enough food for all. Where his mother got it all from he never knew. George was glad of Bert's offer, but couldn't be sure if he was kidding or not. Pulling on his ear he asked hopefully, 'Really?'

Bert nodded, 'Yer, why not? No point being on yer own.'

Giving a wide grin, George answered, 'Thanks Bert. I'd appreciate that,' and turned away quickly to wipe a sudden wetness in his eye.

It seemed Bert noticed, and came across to him, slapped him on the back and said, 'You daft bugger, give over. 'Course you're more than welcome. Be there by twelve sharp then we can have a beer or two before dinner.'

George approached Charlie later in the day and asked about Bert's family. 'He's got four kids, three boys and a girl and another on the way. Let me think now...' George watched as he quietly counted on his fingers, 'Yes, the boys are nine, seven and six 'cos their birthdays are close to my own kids and the girl is about three I think. Is that what you want to know?' George nodded.

As it was Christmas Eve and getting dark they finished work around four o'clock. Straight away, George made for the shops. No way, he thought was he going to go to Bert's empty handed. Toys were bought for the children, a fresh pineapple for Sarah – to hell with the expense he thought. A present for Bert was a bit more difficult, but as George wandered about the town he suddenly saw the very thing, a blue cotton kerchief with white spots, Bert always wore one around his throat, almost like a cockney badge, and George was sure it would be a hit. He added some penny bars of chocolate and a couple of paper screws of jelly babies to his purchases, just in case. He wouldn't like to miss anyone out.

On Christmas morning, mild for the time of year and not raining, he put on his suit and striped tie both of which he had sponged down the previous evening. He also wore the presents from his mother, a thick hand knitted wool jumper and socks. In a stout brown paper carrier bag were the presents he'd carefully wrapped in colourful magazine paper and tied up with string. There were a couple of bus changes to be made before he reached Bert's house, but he arrived in good time. When the door was opened by the eldest boy to his knock a wonderful smell of cooking filled the air – spices and fruit mainly, mixed in with the smell of roasting meat.

'You Geordie?' enquired the lad. 'I'm Ted. Dad said you wos a big bloke so you must be 'im.' George laughed at this introduction and nodded. 'Better come this way then, into the parlour dad said I wos to take you,' and he led the way. Inside the room it seemed as if children outnumbered the adults. There were a few garlands stretched between the picture rails around the room. There was paper strewn about the floor along with toys and books. George was relieved, just like Christmas morning at home he thought.

Bert rushed over to him his hand outstretched, 'You made it then. Good lad. Merry Christmas. Meet the gang.' Everyone seemed to be nodding and smiling at him, and the children, suddenly hushed by his arrival, stared. The two men were Bert's brothers and they stood up, shook his hand and wished him a 'Merry Christmas' as they were introduced. The only woman, somewhere in her sixties, was cousin to them all, but she smiled and murmured a shy welcome. 'Come into the kitchen Geordie and meet my Sarah.' George followed him into the steamy room where Sarah stood hot and red in the face, with her hands on her hips directing another two women to various tasks. 'Both our sisters-in-law,' whispered Bert. Sarah, my love,' he called, 'come and meet Geordie.'

Wiping her hands down her apron, she smoothed her hair, and smiled, 'So you're the Rob Roy wonder keeping my Bert on the straight and narra. 'Ow d' you do?'

'That's me, George Carr. I don't know about the Rob Roy bit. If it wasn't for Bert I'd still be a labourer.' As he took her hand to shake he said, 'But I think Bert's forgotten my real name.'

'Blimey, so I had,' exclaimed Bert. As George put his carrier bag on the table, "Ere let me take yer jacket,' and he carried it off to a peg on the door.

George said his thanks, and looked around the kitchen. Every surface had a full dish, but what caught his eye was a large roll of hot roasted beef, the largest he had seen for a long time. Hoping no one had heard his stomach rumbling, he turned to Sarah. 'Something smells absolutely wonderful. I think it must be that roast over there. You cook everything yourself?'

He saw her preen a little and then with honesty, she said, 'Nah, we all muck in togever. We all puts a penny or two every week or so into a club at the co-op.' The other young women nodded in agreement. 'Mind I start somewhere in August, making puddings, then a cake in November 'cos they keep.'

'That's just how my mam does it. Every year the same.'

Sarah turned to the oven and basted the two chickens just turning golden, then turned to one of her helpers and asked her to, 'Put the spuds on love, everything's just about ready.' Turning to the other woman she asked, 'Are the places set and the plates warm enough yet?'

'Stop worrying, everything's in hand gel,' was the quick reply.

'You can see who's boss in this 'ouse, can't you?' Bert said turning to George who was rummaging about in the carrier.

'Bit like her old man then,' answered George.

'Gotcha there Bert,' Sarah laughed. She looked around for an empty chair and thankfully sat down for a moment.

'A bit tired I'll bet?' queried George, as he handed her his gift. 'I er…I didn't know what to get you Sarah, I hope you like it. My mam always liked some fresh fruit, the more exotic the better when she was er…' All the women pealed with laughter as he struggled to find the right word.

'You mean up the duff.'

'In the club.'

'Expecting.'

'Pregnant.' Everyone had their own name for Sarah's condition. George felt himself going red, but by now Sarah had unwrapped her gift. George watched as she carefully felt all over the knobbly thick skin, then raised it to her nose and took a long sniff of its distinctive smell. Awed, she whispered, 'Why George, it's perfect. I've never had a fresh pineapple before but I've often fancied one. Thank you ducks,' and she stood up on her tiptoes to kiss his cheek as the others handled the fruit in turns, and Bert beamed his approval.

'I haven't forgotten you Bert. Here, catch,' George said as he threw the parcel to him.

Bert fingered the scarf. 'Look at that Sarah love, aint that smart.' He fastened it about his neck, then went across to the mirror to admire the effect.

'Blimey, watch out Bert, you'll have all the girls after you now you've got something new,' said one of the women. Sarah laughed,

'They're bloody welcome to 'im especially today wif all this crowd.' As a fleeting stricken look crossed George's face, she quickly added, 'Only kidding Geordie, only kidding. We loves to do this every year don't we Bert, girls?' Three heads nodded vigorously then Sarah said, 'After lunch George, those in the parlour have to clear up.' She chuckled as she continued, 'they can't cook. Well, I dare say Em can, but as we don't like washing up we leaves it to them, so's we can put our feet up before the evening lot arrive.'

Dinner was beyond George's expectations. He realised it was not just that the food was perfect, but those sat at the table with him had made him welcome. Joking and teasing each other and him, added greatly to the occasion. The children sat at a table set aside for them and had crackers which they pulled without warning so that, Sarah, when startled, threatened to have her baby there and then.

'You'd better not,' threatened Bert, 'I aint had me pudding yet and it's my turn for the joey*.' When the meal was over, the three brothers stood up, pulling George to stand up with them, and announced their intention of going down the pub for a beer or two.

---

* Old money

'What! Leave poor Em on her own with all this lot? No you don't, me lad,' said Sarah grabbing hold of Bert. Each woman held on to their husband and Em quickly clutched George's sleeve.

'One of these days Bert, we'll just sneak away, won't announce to the girls where we're going,' laughed someone.

With a big mocking sigh, Bert began collecting up the dishes, 'Right,' he said, 'whose turn to wear the pinny?'

'I'll give a hand if you like,' volunteered George, and then added quickly, 'without the pinny.'

'Nah, it's alright lad, we'll manage. Got a system. I sits in Sarah's chair wif a fag, and tell the others where everything goes!' Both his brothers thumped him, and the pile of dishes wobbled in his hands. 'Tell you what, Sarah's going to have a lie down upstairs. Yes you are,' he said as she began to protest, 'and you George, can you sit in the parlour for a bit to keep an eye on the kids?'

'Fine, anything to help. Yes, I've got something for them. Should have given it before but dinner came and well, I wasn't going to miss that for anything.'

Sitting on the settee, the children, Bert's four and their two cousins eyed him curiously and seemed overcome with shyness. He called Ted over, 'Better tell me their names,' he whispered, 'they all look frightened to death of me.'

'Get over 'ere you lot,' summoned Ted. 'Now then, this is me bruvver Walter, wot we calls Wally.' George solemnly shook hands with him. 'Come 'ere Tinker.' Ted pulled another boy over, 'and this is me other brother, we calls Tinker but 'is real name is Terry.' Again George shook hands. He was surprised to see how gently Ted led the smallest of the girls over to him. 'And this is Pearl, me little sister,' he said proudly as he tried to push her forward but she insisted on hiding behind him.

'Well, no wonder Bert, er your da is proud of you all Ted. Such good manners. He turned to the two remaining children, a boy and a girl, 'and who are these two young people I wonder?'

Bold as brass the girl said, 'We're their cousins. I'm Daisy and this is Paul me brother. Uncle Bert is me uncle.'

'Don't take no notice of 'er,' said Ted, 'always says that, as if we didn't know.'

'Well now, I'm George, though I expect you know me better as Geordie from your da.'

'We don't say da, we say dad in our house,' said Tinker, and Ted promptly cuffed him about the ear.

'No need for that Ted,' George rebuked, 'I shall remember to say dad from now on. It's only fair in your house, but in my house we say da. Now, Tinker you go and find my carrier bag. I think I left it in the kitchen.' The lad soon hurried back with the bag, and George, slowly pulled out a parcel.

'Now, I wonder who would like this?'

The children's faces lit up, their eyes danced, then altogether they cried, 'Me, me.'

George handed it to Ted and then in turn he gave each of Bert's boys the same. All had a model wind-up tin car but each was a different colour so there would be no arguments. He had brothers and sisters of his own so there were some things he'd learned. Putting his hand into the bag he said,

'I wonder what this is? I wonder who it is for?' Pearl crept a little closer, 'I think this must be for a little girl called, let me see,' he turned the parcel over in his hand, and announced, 'Why I do believe it's for Pearl.' Wally helped her pull the string off and George watched her little face light up when she finally reached the white fluffy toy rabbit with long ears. How George wished he'd got a present for the two cousins, but they were happy with their chocolate bars and sweets.

The room was warm, the boys raced their new cars and George had a job keeping his eyes open after his big meal. Pearl climbed up onto the settee beside him and asked, 'Did you have any dollies when you was little?'

'No pet. I'm a boy and boys don't play with dolls now do they?' A frown crossed her face. 'But I tell you what, you know that tar on the roads you see.' Pearl looked solemnly at him not quite sure. 'You know, it smells a bit when it's hot.' She nodded. 'Well, they make tar where I come from, and...' George waited while she settled herself more comfortably on the settee, 'my little sisters, just like you, used to make dolls out of it. They called them tar babies.' Pearl's eyes widened at this. George laughed as he said, 'My word, they used to get their clean pinnies in such a mess, all black and sticky, and when they got home they got a slap around their legs. You wouldn't like that would you?' Pearl smiled sleepily and shook her head, then put her head on his lap, curled herself up and quickly fell asleep.

Almost asleep himself he vaguely heard one of the boys who had been busy lining up his new lead soldiers say, 'Look he's nearly asleep,' and wondered if mischief was about to be planned, but Ted ever protective of his little sister, said, 'So's Pearl so keep yer racket down.' George half smiled and thought, Ted's just like me where youngsters are concerned, then allowed himself the luxury of forty winks.

Throughout the rest of the day, Bert's neighbours drifted in and out of the house all sharing their beer and food. The tired out children were put to bed, and the adults began singing popular songs accompanied by someone playing the mouth organ. Bert knew George sang at the dance halls and asked him give a song. As soon as he began the first line the organist was able to pick up the refrain. George knew he was showing off as he sang 'Aint she sweet', 'Only Make Believe' to start with. Then he quickly pulled off his jumper, locked his thumbs into his braces, adopted the east enders strut, and to the delight of everyone, sang their favourite – 'My Old Man said Follow the Band'. Everyone, in loud voice, joined in the second time round.

'Cor enough racket to wake the dead leave alone the kids,' said Sarah.

'It's the same every year, and you always say the same fing,' teased Bert.

'How d'you like London town mate?' one of the men asked as he filled up George's glass.

'I like it well enough,' he replied.

Before he could say anything further Bert slyly interrupted, 'Except for landladies.' George knew at once what he was referring too. 'Go on Geordie, tell them about some of them.'

As he was telling everyone about the house of wretched women in 'Clara's Joint' there was a mixed reaction, mainly from the women who tutted and gave out little gasps of horror. Bert though wasn't satisfied with George stopping there.

'Go on Geordie, tell 'em how you got your own back.'

Sheepishly, George related the baby's potty incident, which caused them to cheer him enthusiastically. When he had finished, Sarah said,

'I wouldn't like that lot living next door. Sounds more like a brothel if you ask me.'

Bert cocked his head slightly, gave an exaggerated wink to all then giving out a long deep sigh said, 'Ah, but Sarah gel, be bloody 'andy wouldn't it?' and everybody roared out laughing as Sarah boxed him soundly round the ears. Yes, thought George, just like being at home.

CHAPTER ELEVEN

Early in March there was a letter waiting for him. He was surprised to see it was from his mother. Surprised because he always wrote to her on a Friday and she wrote back without fail so that he got a reply on Tuesday and today was Thursday. There must be some trouble at home, he thought, and grew uneasy wondering what it could be. Surely not his father, he was well over his accident now and back at work. Perhaps they needed a few shillings for something urgent or someone was ill. Nodding a 'Good evening,' to Emma he quickly closed the door of his room, unfolded the letter and saw that the writing, so unlike his mother's careful hand, was scrawled as if in haste. George read the letter twice. There was no mistake. Robert had run away. Hannah, he could tell, was frantic and had written,

Is he with you Joe? Just let us know he is safe as soon as you can. We do not know why he left, there has been no argument or trouble at school. No one saw him leaving the village, and he has been gone these last two days. A few of his clothes are missing and we don't know if he has any money. Did you give him any? I am so worried that he might be lost or hungry. If he is with you Joe, tell him we are not angry with him, but want to know he is safe and that he can come home whenever he is ready. Da is keeping his job open at the pit. Please reply as soon as you can.
Mam.

Well, thought George, there's your answer mam. No way was Robert intending to go down the mine. Silly little beggar, thought George, I told him to let me know if he was coming to London.

Wonder where he is? How did he get money, if he has any? Hastily he wrote back to his mother telling her that Robert was not with him, and that he had not given over any money. He assured her that Robert was very bright and quite able to look after himself, and no doubt will get in touch with her soon. In the meantime she should try not to worry. He promised her that for the next few days he would go to Kings Cross station to see if Robert might be hanging around there and enquire if anyone had seen him.

If he turns up, I'll tan his hide myself and put him on the first train home. He also added, *If he hasn't already told you himself, he does not want to be a miner, but what he wants to do I don't know.*

As promised, George spent all his spare time during the next few days at the station, pestering whoever was on duty, but no one remembered seeing a lone, young blond boy with a northern accent. After a week, George gave up looking, and convinced himself that the boy would turn up before long.

Jobs had been sporadic through the winter months, and the current contract the gang were working on, was almost complete. One morning in late April, Charlie came over to Bert and George. They could tell he was excited about something. George was hoping it was news of his brother on another site perhaps, but the news Charlie had was almost as good.

'Listen lads. A Clerk of Works has been nosing around these last few days, had you noticed?' Both shook their heads. 'Seems he likes what he's seen. Likes the way we work as a team, likes the standard we got,' he looked at them smugly. 'That's my doing of course, making all of you toe the line.'

Bert and George grinned at each other as Bert said, 'Let 'im think that Geordie. Keep 'im sweet.'

'Oi, you! We may have been mates for a long time, but I don't want any of your lip.'

'Give over, you silly beggar.'

Charlie laughed and replied, 'Only kidding. 'Cos if it's all right with you two, we got work for about nine months.' Bert's mouth fell open, and George threw his cap in the air. Charlie sat himself down on an upturned bucket. 'Thought you'd be pleased.'

Bert took off his cap and scratched his scalp. 'Well,' he said, 'I must say I woz getting a bit worried. When you hear all that stuff coming out of America, I mean, the people there can't make ends meet, and wot 'appens there usually follows over here don't it.'

Charlie broke in, 'Ah, you mean the crash, I think it was called the Wall Street something or other that happened a couple of years back.'

George nodded and said, 'You're right. Since then my cousin who works, no worked in the shipyard in Sunderland says that no new orders for shipping came in after that, so they're mostly all laid off. Ruining other trades in the north too it seems.'

All were silent for the moment, until Charlie spoke, 'Could be worse to come I reckon, so lads what do you say? Seven months guaranteed, the bloke said.'

Jubilantly, Bert burst out, 'Blimey! Seven months! So where is this to be?'

'What's he offering?' asked George.

'It's a big new housing estate in Purley, not too far away from here. Houses, four and five bedrooms with all modern stuff in 'em. There'll be roads and sewers and the like and plenty of carpentry.' He looked at their faces, they looked at each other then nodded in unison.

'Wages the same as we get now, but there'll be extra for working weekends, if we want.' The two nodded again and then all three shook hands.

'Go tell the bloody pitch and toss he's lucky to get us,' said Bert. George raised his eyebrows. 'Work it out son,' smiled Bert. Seeing he was still puzzled Bert said, 'Will you never learn Geordie? Pitch and toss — boss. Get it?' George grinned then offered the other two a cigarette each to celebrate.

Two weeks later George reluctantly said goodbye to Emma, and found new lodgings, more like a small hotel where he seldom met other boarders. Arriving at the new site, a couple of fields with a large barn in one on a chalky hillside, they could see that already markers had laid out the plans for the new estate. There were a few older houses close by on a wide road and George knew one of the first jobs would be to dig this road up for pipe work. Charlie strode across the field to the temporary office to find the Clerk of Works, and brought him back to the others.

'This is Mr Mathews, lads. What he says goes. Understand?' They nodded then both put their hands forward as Charlie introduced them.

'This is Bert Smith and this is George Carr. Both stonemasons, brickies, labourers and Geordie, Carr, can turn his hand to a bit of carpentry.' George was quietly pleased with his introduction, and as he shook Mr Mathew's hand was surprised to see how young he was, only ten years or so older than himself. Bit of a fool wearing a suit on a building site he thought, but then noticed the boots, which by their appearance, had seen duty in plenty of mud.

'Well lads, pleased to meet you. Seen you working, like what I saw, so all I ask is a good day's work from you and I'll see you alright. Fair enough?'

'Fair enough sir,' answered Charlie. It was obvious to George that Mr Matthews had a university education. He was briefly envious, as he remembered he'd passed the eleven plus examination, and had dreamed for weeks of going to university himself – until his mother, fed up with his unrealistic daydreams, had told him firmly there was no money for grammar school let alone university. The three men stood, and watched Mr Mathews stride away, not a talkative man but it was clear to all that he was confident and fully in charge.

Less than a week into the job as George was digging out the road, a young woman, carrying letters, came through the gate of one of the houses. It was not until someone nudged him that he saw her walk by. Admiring calls and whistles, including his shrill one filled the air. The girl, about nineteen, kept on walking steadily looking neither left nor right. After she had passed by for a few moments there was speculation and bantering amongst the men, including George. There had not been a chance to look at her face, but he'd noticed that her dress was calf length and clung to her slender body, the hem swinging a little as she walked, and her shoes were black with a strap buttoned across the instep. The slight heel added a little to her height, somewhere around five foot eight he reckoned, up to his shoulder, which he patted as if to confirm this. It seemed that it was a routine of the girl to post letters at the same time every day and, for a short time, she was the subject of the men's interest, but most soon stopped as the girl took no notice. As the days passed, George noticed more and more about her. He saw that her incredibly black hair, parted at the side, was finger waved and fastened in a bun at the nape, other times there was a plait. Her breasts were high and well rounded above a pronounced waistline and her bare, smooth arms swung gently as she walked. George began to look out for her every day, and every day she appeared at the same time.

As usual he went dancing on Saturday evening, and found himself looking out for the girl, even asking those with a likeness for a dance, though none truly bore any resemblance to her. Sometimes he imagined he was actually dancing with her. Much to his surprise, Mr Mathews was also at the dance. He made his way over to George, shook his hand and said call me Cyril, 'Outside of work of course,' he added. Although George didn't know it at the time, Cyril was to play an important part in his life.

On Sunday when George went out for a stroll he hoped he would see her. Constantly over the weekend he found himself thinking about her, he had never before given as much thinking time to a girl. There was something special about her, and he admitted to himself, that Monday couldn't come quick enough.

Sure enough, around eleven on Monday he heard the click of the gate and saw her approaching. Bert said, as he winked at the others working with them.

'Here's that gal Geordie. I reckon you're a bit smitten on her. Better get yourself wed to her quick before she disappears.'

Without a second thought, George leapt out of the ditch and dropped on his knees before her adopting an exaggerated pose of Al Jolson. He snatched his cap from his head and clasped it in front of his heart, 'Marry me,' he pleaded. The men close by rested on their shovels and cheered, then laughed as the girl pulled her skirt closer, as if afraid of contamination then calmly edged around him. Feeling a little foolish and dusting down his knees, he rejoined his mates and grinned at his own audacity. He made up his mind to say sorry for the embarrassment he'd caused her on her way back, but she did not return.

It was raining when George and Bert arrived at work the next day, and there was little that could be done. They spent their time sitting around playing cards and smoking under lean-to tarpaulins. 'Well, if it's like this tomorrow, we'll be sent packing, you can bet on that,' moaned Bert. Sure enough it was raining the next day and the site was a greyish slurry, impossible for anyone to dig or lay bricks. Bert was right in his prediction, and along with others he and George were sent away. Bert was worried. Worried about one of his kids with a nasty cough who needed the doctor, and that cost money and worried about money in general.

'Just turn up as usual tomorrow, Bert. Something will turn up. Charlie will sort something out for you. Not too worried meself at the moment.' He hesitated then said, 'I could help you out a bit, got a few bob handy if you like.' Putting his hand in his pocket he drew out five shillings. 'Here take it for the bairns.' Bert lost his temper.

With closed fists and a fierce look in his eye, he turned on George. 'You bloody trying to insult me,' he yelled. 'I'll look after me own bleeding kids, ta very much. Shove yer money,' and he stalked away from George who called after him.

'Be here tomorrow usual time, you daft bugger.'

Both arrived in good time on Thursday, and it was still raining. Bert quietly stepped beside George, 'All right mate?' he asked and then sheepishly mumbled something about his quick temper.

George gave him a nudge with his elbow, and they both joined the queue of waiting men. One or two were allowed to enter and George began to hope they had a chance. Leaning closer to Bert, he said, 'I've got a plan. I think it will work.'

'Wot you on abart Geordie?'

'Want to work don't you?' Bert nodded.

'Well, do as I say. Don't make a fuss. All right?'

Bert grinned. 'Wot you up to lad?'

George looked about to make sure that they could not be overheard. 'This is what we'll do. When we get to the gate all you got to say is you're a carpenter and I'm your apprentice.'

'You what?' exploded Bert.

'Near the end of my time you can explain if they ask.'

'Blimey, I couldn't handle a plane let alone a saw. You sure abart this?'

'Yep. I'm the carpenter and you're going to be my apprentice for today. I reckon we can get away with it.' Bert was astounded at the plan.

'You think it might work?'

George nodded and pointed to the barn. 'That's the temporary workshop. Plenty of work going on in there. What do you think?'

'I reckon it's werf a try Geordie. Does that mean I'll be at your beck and call all day?'

George laughed, 'You bet you lazy blighter. I'll make your life a misery. Sweat, you'll know the meaning of the word at the end of this day!' Together they approached a man checking on the gate. George could feel his palms were clammy, and Bert kept taking his cap off to wipe his forehead. At last their turn came.

'Trade?' the man on the entrance demanded, without looking up from his sheaf of papers.

'Er…' Bert swallowed nervously.

'Well, what's your trade? Come on, buck up, aint got all day.'

George answered for him. 'He's a carpenter, can't you see his toolbag?' There was a sigh from the man. 'Name? Got a name I suppose?'

'Bert Smith and er George Carr.' The man looked up sharply. We're done for, thought George, he's caught us out, but the man smiled at them.

'So you're Bert Smith. Mr Mathews said to look out for you. This your mate?'

Bert nodded. 'One of you a stonemason and the other a carpenter right?' They both nodded again, and held their breath. 'Right then lads. Straight on through to the barn. Use the duck boards mate. Carpenters needed today. Mr Mathews don't like wasting time. He thinks we should get ahead with the internal stuff, doors, window frames, anyfing made of wood if you ask me. You know what I mean. See you tomorrow then lads. Good luck.'

Delighted with the outcome they made their way to the barn, where they found Charlie. Bert, relieved that a day's work, possibly two was available, was the cheerful 'goffa' for both carpenters all day. He called himself that. 'I'm the 'goffa'. Go for this and go for that, but you carry on lads. I'm enjoying meself and maybe I'll be a carpenter meself one day,' he joked.

'Gawd help us,' was Charlie's horrified reply.

It finally stopped raining Friday evening and by the following Tuesday the site had dried enough for the men to work outside again. It was Wednesday before the girl re-appeared. When she reached the site, egged on by Bert who moved his head and eyes sideways to indicate her, George jumped out in front of her and barred the way with his arms outstretched and his legs wide apart.

'Hello, I'm George Carr,' he bragged. The men stopped work to see her reaction. For a moment she looked into George's face, and besides her disdainful look, he saw that her eyes were the greenest he had ever seen, that her face was oval and her flawless, creamy skin was lightly flushed. To him, she seemed fragile and he felt compelled that he had to take care of her. From that moment on he was certain he was in love. Then, without warning, she kicked him on the shin, not too hard or too gentle. As he hopped from foot to foot, pretending to be in pain, she ignored him and walked on. In love, so that was the special something Pat had tried to explain. With mixed feelings, he got on with his work. One or two of the men were still making almost crude remarks, and George longed to punch them into respect for her. To do so would show them his interest, and then there would be endless teasing or even worse, he could be sacked. This last bit of silly behaviour was out of character. He knew he had been showing off, and he was not proud of himself, indeed he was deeply ashamed. Worst of all, he realised that, any chance he might have had of seeing more of her was unlikely now. When she passed the following days he kept quiet, and didn't look her way at all.

As promised, there was plenty of overtime to be had on Saturday afternoons which George took advantage of. It was wonderful for him to have a few shillings, to be able to send postal orders home once in a while with a little extra and, best of all, to have a new set of clothes, especially shirts.

Finishing work one warm June Saturday afternoon, a bit later than usual, he was surprised to see the girl leave the house and turn in the opposite direction from her usual route. George felt his heart race, he slicked back his hair. This was a God given opportunity, for a second he hesitated, but even if she rebuffed him again, it was worth a try. Quickly, afraid of losing his chance, he sprinted along the road to catch up with her. When he reached her side, he quietly said, 'May I walk a little way with you?' Expecting a refusal, he was delighted when she nodded. He matched his step to hers then said, 'I'm George Carr.'

Without missing a step, she answered, 'I know.'

George stopped dead in his tracks and then ran to catch up with her. 'But, you're not English!' he exclaimed.

'Ugh, nor are you,' was her tart reply. Then she smiled, the first smile ever she gave him, and he thought she was beautiful. 'I'm from south Wales, from a mining village now dead because the pits are closing down.'

'And I'm from Durham because I hate being down the pit,' he answered. Feeling around in his jacket pocket for his cigarettes he offered her the open packet, 'Would you like a cigarette?'

Frowning slightly and then relaxing a little, she replied, 'No thank you. I believe they are not good for your health.'

Sighing, George lit one up for himself, 'That may as be, but they are a great comfort to a working chap.' Flicking off the ash, he went on, 'Now tell me, how come you find yourself in Purley?'

'Simple really. I have four brothers, all miners except one, and when they were thrown out of work, a couple of years back, they all came to London.' For a moment they were both deep in their thoughts of their own mining village experiencing hardship. 'Then three of my sisters, I have five, found work here. I stayed home for a bit looking after my father, but the boys persuaded him to come up. Plenty of work they told him, and so…here I am.'

George nodded. 'And you, what do you do?'

'I suppose you could say I was in service but it isn't quite like that.'

Nipping out the end of his cigarette, George threw the butt away and asked, 'What do you mean by that?'

She turned her head slightly and smiled, 'Well, besides some household chores, I am a sort of companion to a Doctor's wife who is expecting a baby in December and is not at all well at the moment.'

'So you run all her errands like posting her letters.'

'Mostly his. He is very famous, has a practice in Harley Street.' By now they had strolled into the high street, and ahead of them George saw a couple waving. The girl waved back, 'My sister Vi and her husband Bryn. Every Saturday afternoon we go to the Music Hall matinee. I meet them here after I've finished. I stay with them every weekend.' As she began to move away from him she said briskly over her shoulder, 'Goodbye.'

This was it then, the end. She had got the better of him again. He felt his heart sinking then making up his mind quickly called after her, 'See you next Saturday.' There was no answer and he watched as she embraced her sister, then they both looked round at him. His heart and hopes lifted as, his girl as he now thought of her, gave a half hearted wave. Feeling on top of the world, and with a silly grin on his face, which he tried but failed to control, he made his way to the tram stop.

Arriving at his lodgings that evening, he found a letter from his mother waiting for him. After reading it he almost whooped with joy. Robert had been found safe and well. Hannah had written that the lad had run away to Newcastle and had been taken on as cabin boy on a boat plying coal to London. The skipper had written to her asking if Robert Carr was her son, and if he was, that he had truthfully given his name and address. Skipper also wrote that Robert was an honest and hardworking lad about the boat, and that he would keep an eye on the youngster. The skipper added that he would instruct Robert to visit his parents next time they were ashore in Newcastle, and that she had no need to worry. Hannah ended her letter saying she couldn't be happier. Bloody hell, thought George, seafaring was as dangerous as mining, or so he'd heard, and yet, he supposed, it was marginally better, as the boy was not underground. Writing back to his mother he said he too was pleased to have the news and if she could find out the name of the boat Robert was on, and when it might be next in London, he would try to get to the docks and see his brother. What a day, George thought, Robert safe, and I've met my own special girl, my world is perfect.

It didn't occur to him until later when he was in bed that he didn't know her name.

CHAPTER TWELVE

To George it seemed an incredibly long week. Every day around eleven he made sure he was busy, just glancing up quickly to look at her as she went about her errand, then away again. Daily she calmly walked by, not even glancing his way, or if she did he didn't notice. Each evening he kept himself busy with his shorthand and English writing tasks, and was pleased with his steady progress. He went dancing and took evening walks, but the hours dragged somehow until Saturday. He did, however, buy himself some hardwearing dungarees to cover his clothes from the dusty chalk that seemed to coat everything in a dirty white film so that on Saturday he would not look too dishevelled to meet his girl.

One thing he did notice, every day without fail, there was a thin faced man who slouched at the site gate, with a cigarette hanging from his mouth. A number of men seemed to know him, they nodded to him then looked around furtively, and George recognised at once what was happening. One of his father's pastimes was betting. Until he started work, it was his job to hurry as fast as he could to the bookie's runner, a similar nervy man he was looking at now, with his father's stake money. George always knew when he had to make the two mile trip to the village pub. Joe would sit in his fireside chair, chewing a pencil and making marks in the paper. Hannah had made it clear she did not approve, but George knew his father still secretly laid on a bet. Whether he ever had any success, George never knew. Ah well, thought George, see no evil, speak no evil, let be and let live.

The weather continued to stay dry and hot. Quite often the men would help themselves to a refreshing drink from the hosepipe, and sometimes, catching their mates off guard, sprayed them unexpected-ly. This often led to a short water fight among the young lads, but the older men were wiser knowing that the white chalk would cling to their clothes like clay when it was wet.

Mr Mathews came almost daily to each gang of workmen, but always stopped and offered cigarettes to Charlie, Bert and George and after lighting up one for himself, stayed chatting to the three for five to ten minutes.

'A real gent,' Bert always remarked after he'd left. 'Wouldn't mind working wif him again.'

After a week, this remark was anticipated by George and Charlie, and in unison one day, they surprised Bert by beating him to it. 'A real gent. I wouldn't mind working wif him again,' they mimicked. Bert threw a handful of sand over the two laughing men.

At last Saturday came. George worked until three o'clock then washed himself as best he could in the temporary hut erected for toilet purposes, rubbed the toe caps of his boots down the back of his trousers then brushed his hands down his clothes, swilled his mouth in the hopes of disguising his smoke laden breath, and made his way to the gate, between a well maintained privet hedge, where he knew she worked. The gate had a highly polished brass plate stating: Mr Ralph Woodmarsh, G.P., F.R.C.S.I. of Harley Street. Impressed, George knew what the first qualification was and wondered about the second.

As she stepped through the gate, George fell into step beside her. She didn't seem at all surprised. 'Good afternoon,' he said. 'May I escort you to the High Street?'

Half turning towards him, she gave a faint smiled and answered, 'You may.' For a short way they walked steadily together neither speaking but George was content to be with her.

Then he remembered, he put out his hand to stop her. 'Hang on a moment Miss...? I nearly forgot.'

She stopped and put her head to one side. Puzzled she said, 'What? I'm not turning back. You can go alone. I don't want to be late for Vi and Bryn.' George grinned. 'No, I don't mean I've forgotten something, I mean, I nearly forgot to ask you your name.'

'I'm not sure I should tell you that,' she answered as they began walking on.

How he hoped he hadn't overstepped the mark, then thought maybe she was teasing him, her tone hadn't been sharp. Then he thought well two can play that game, I'll do a little teasing of my own. 'Ah, so you're on the run from the law are you? Now let me see what ever could a lovely girl like you be guilty of?' He pondered for a few moments, and with one finger, tapped his chin then triumphantly, 'I know, that's it.'

'Oh, and what is it that you think I've done?'

Putting on his most serious expression and in a low sad voice said, 'Breaking boys' hearts.' His heart leapt as he heard her giggle, 'Come on. Tell me please,' he wheedled and cheekily winked at her.

'George Carr! Don't you try your charms on me.'

'Why not? You like me don't you?' He could see her smiling to herself, 'Don't you?'

'My name is Evelyn Jones, and that's all you're getting.'

'Evelyn Jones.' George said it aloud, savoured it. 'Evelyn Jones.' he repeated. All too soon they reached the High Street and could see the waiting couple.

'Goodbye George Carr,' she said.

'Same time next week?' he asked hopefully.

'I suppose so,' she answered with another of her warm smiles.

Every day Evelyn passed by the site, and not once during the whole week did she look at George. Desperate to see her again on Saturday, he found time dragged by, and tried to keep himself busy, but quite often he was caught daydreaming.

'What's up wif you?' Charlie demanded. 'Not dreaming of going home again are yer? Got it made 'ere lad for while. Play yer cards right and you'll be in clover.'

George sighed, looked straight at Charlie then Bert, should he tell them? No, he decided. He wasn't sure what their reaction might be and he couldn't risk their questions or bantering as he couldn't bear the idea of any sly remarks or jokes about his girl.

At three o'clock on Saturday, George was surprised and pleased to see her waiting for him. Smiling at her, he offered her his arm, on which she laid her hand, and together they strolled towards Purley. 'So, what have you been doing with yourself all week er… May I call you Evelyn, or I'll call you Miss Jones if you prefer?' He looked expectantly at her, and as there was no immediate answer, 'Miss Jones then 'til we're better acquainted. Yes?' He smiled to himself when she answered him. Her soft, Welsh voice was one of the things he found fascinating about her.

'You may call me Evelyn if you like, but my family and friends all call me Eve.'

'If I call you Eve, does that mean we are friends?' She nodded and he was more than happy. 'Well now, Eve, what have you been up to this week?'

'You really don't want to hear all about my housework routine do you George Carr? Nothing could be more boring I promise you.'

They walked on in silence for a short while then he asked, 'Well what time do you get up?'

She turned her head to answer. 'Six o'clock.'

He waited, 'And?'

'What?'

'What do you do then? Have your breakfast?'

'I clean out the downstairs fire grates, relay the fire and get them going. Mrs Woodmarsh feels the cold.' Eve sighed, 'then I dust round. The ash seems to get everywhere, then I set the table, then…'

'All right, all right. Just the same routine as my sister Jessie. Certainly doesn't sound exciting, but it's a job after all.'

'And what did you do all week?'

Laughing he said, 'Would you believe, I thought non-stop about you.'

In amazement she let go of his arm and stopped walking. 'Me?'

He nodded then dared to put his arm around her shoulder. 'I've never met anyone like you before. I think of you as − special.' She let his arm stay as they began to walk on. 'Oh, I carried on as usual, working with the lads. They're a grand crew really.' She sniffed at the idea. 'Really they are, but you're right to take no notice of their fun.'

'You're going to say next that they put you up to all that nonsense a few weeks back. You could have hurt yourself you know, falling hard on your knees like that when you…'

He saw her blushing, pulled her closer and laughed as he said, 'Ha, you mean the proposal?'

Quickly she changed the subject. 'What else then have you been up to?'

'I go to night school twice a week. Hoping to be reporter one day, so need to get some qualifications like shorthand.'

He could tell she was impressed, but as she turned her head towards him, said, 'Getting above your station, as my mam would say,' then shrugging her shoulders, added, 'well, don't get your hopes up.'

He decided not to tell her he had an interview the following week with an editor of a London newspaper and thought, we shall see lady. 'Then a couple of nights a week I go dancing. It's the finest thing in the world. I just love the music and the dancing. Maybe we can go together one evening?' he asked hopefully.

'I don't think so,' she answered shortly.

George couldn't believe how hostile her answer had been. 'And why not pray?' He took his arm away, she brushed a hair off her face and they stood facing each other. 'You're going to tell me it's sinful aren't you? That your chapel folk are against it aren't they?' He thrust his hands into his pockets and took a step away from her, reached for his cigarettes and watched as her lips firmed into a thin line in anger.

Then, surprisingly she slightly lowered her head and muttered, 'I can't. I can't dance. Not one step. I've tried but my feet get tangled up.'

Can't dance! George's mind screamed, can't dance. He was appalled. For the last few weeks he had dreamed of nothing but holding this lovely girl in his arms, and dancing away countless hours. He couldn't believe it, then taking her hand he said confidently, 'When you dance with me, and you will after a bit, you will think yourself in heaven.' He could see she didn't believe him so he went on, 'You'll see, I'm a good teacher.'

All too soon they reached the town, and she withdrew her hand as they approached Vi and Bryn. 'I see your sister's waiting for you. Do you get Sundays off as well then?' he asked.

'Mrs Woodmarsh's sister comes every Saturday afternoon, and stays 'til Monday morning, so she does the looking after.' As she waved to Vi, she added, 'and it saves her paying me, doesn't it? But then, I'd rather have the time off, so I don't grumble.'

'You've got a good point there,' he agreed.

'Goodbye George.'

'Next week?' he asked hopefully.

'Next week George Carr. I'll be waiting,' she answered as she walked away from him.

The interview was on Tuesday. In order to get time off he told Bert he had toothache and was going to the dentist. Everything about him was as clean and fresh looking as he could make it, even his skin seemed to glow. Arriving at the imposing offices, he made his way to the receptionist.

'I'm here for the interview lass if you'll point me in the right direction.'

Looking down her nose at him, she said, 'You! For the interview!' then covered her mouth with her hand to hide a smirk. 'I think not.'

'Aye, I am. My name's George Carr, and I've a letter of invitation here.' He watched as she ran her finger down a list of names in front of her.

'Oh. Yes, I see. I'm not sure that Mr Webber will…'

Excited and a little anxious, George interrupted her, 'Where shall I wait? I don't mind waiting 'til he's free to see me.'

Pointing to a door she said, 'You'd better wait over there, with those other two…gentlemen.'

As he sat down both men looked at him, then at each other. Nothing was said, but George noticed that one winked at the other who raised an eyebrow before grinning back. George looked carefully at the competition. One had on a double breasted pin-striped suit, his shirt cuffs, fastened with bone links, protruded from the jacket sleeves. Matching tie and handkerchief completed the outfit. George noticed that he was nursing a bowler hat and cane. The other man wore a sports jacket, and long straight trousers with turn-ups, and had a trilby in his lap. Beginning to feel a little nervous, George twisted his cap round and round in his hands until a door opened and a voice boomed out, 'George Carr? Get in here. Haven't got all day.' George stood, pulled down his jacket, attempted to smooth his hair and made his way to the interview room.

'I'm Webber,' said the man sitting behind the desk, looking down at some papers which he marked with an indelible pencil.

George watched for a moment or two, then said, 'George Carr, sir. Come about the reporter's job.'

Webber sighed, put the pencil behind his ear, then looked up at George. He leaned back in his chair, gave a laugh of disbelief, tapped his teeth with an inky finger and sneered, 'You? A reporter? Not in a month of Sundays.' George was shocked by this response then indignant. 'What makes you think you're fit for the position?'

'I'm a good listener,' George answered, 'like to know what makes people tick and what makes the world go round.'

'It takes a darn sight more than that, my young bucko.'

'I'd appreciate it if you'd hear me out sir.'

'Hear you out, you say,' Mr Webber leant forward, 'that's it for a start, boy. Tell me how I can send you to interview Lady Carther's afternoon soiree with an accent like that? It would cut through ice that would.'

'There's nowt wrong with a northern accent.'

'No, there's nowt wrong with a northern accent in the right place,' mimicked Webber. 'And another thing, that suit's come out of the ark. Got to have a certain smartness about my lads especially if I have to send them to Parliament. Get my meaning?'

George was silent for a moment. Thoughts like I'd like to smash this man's face in were going round in his head, and for safety sake he put his hands in his pockets. 'My shorthand's good and my typing is up to speed,' he said then added, 'sir.'

'You've not the King's English, you're not wearing the right turn-out. Look at your hands, dry and calloused, who in hell would want to shake hands with you, and I don't care a damn about your qualifications.'

George looked at his hands, hands that gave him a good living. He had heard enough and stood up, lifted his foot onto the table and said, 'but, look, me shoes are clean. Not trod in any muck until I came in here.' Standing on his two feet again, he placed both hands on the table and leaned in towards Webber. 'Tell you what, sir. I've changed me mind about reporting. There is nothing in the world could make me as rude, arrogant or as insensitive as you. If reporting means bullying and harassing some folks who are suffering, if that's what it takes, I'm not for it,' and ramming his cap onto his head, made his way to the door.

Webber's voice bellowed behind him, 'You cheeky mongrel! Glad to see the back of you.'

George straightened his back and strode past the two waiting candidates noting their shocked faces, then finger-tipped his cap at the receptionist. Well, he told himself, I've already got a good job. What do I want to be like him for? Evelyn was right, I've no business stepping outside me class so I'll not say a word about it to her. Any roads, I'm happy as I am. Bugger it, I'll not bother again.

When Evelyn and George met up the following Saturday, George took her hand, and they swung their arms together as they walked. 'I've been thinking Eve,' he said. 'Do you get any time off during the week? I mean in the evenings. We could perhaps have an hour's walk and talk maybe?' He stopped for a second, 'I'd really like to see you more often.' He could tell by how her face lit up that she felt the same.

'I finish my chores around seven thirty most evenings and after that the time is my own. Although, I have to be in the house by ten as Mr Woodmarsh locks up then.'

'What day suits you most?' he asked. Anxiously, he waited, and watching her, he could see her thinking, and nodding off the days of the week.

'Wednesday, yes Wednesday would be best for me,' she said. George was more than delighted with this answer as it did not interfere with his own weekly commitments. Tuesday dancing, Thursday dancing, and Friday night letter writing. Saturday and Sunday he knew she was at her sister's. Wednesday evenings would suit him, although he admitted to himself he gladly would give up one evening of dancing if Eve had said a different day.

Over the next few weeks they met every Saturday afternoon and Wednesday evenings. Sometimes Eve was held up, and they had less than an hour. On Wednesdays they walked the leafy lanes around Purley strolling hand in hand, telling each other about their families. He remembered she had five sisters, and Eve said that besides Vi, Martha had come to London to look after their father. A younger sister, Iris, along with a nephew, whose mother, Esther, had died at his birth soon joined them. Ann and Sarah, both married had stayed in Wales, married to brothers who owned the village shop, so they were fairly comfortable.

'Although, now there is another baby on the way for Ann. Vi sends a few bits and pieces towards the layette,' Eve said.

George told her about his sisters and that he too had lost one to illness. 'But I have two brothers, one is at sea and the other is nearly four years old. There is close on eighteen years between us, he is called Joseph, and he thinks I'm his second da when I'm at home.'

'I have four brothers,' she told him. 'William is fifteen years older than myself. He has a large family and lives near Vi and Bryn. So does Paul, he married a London bar maid,' she was quiet for a moment. 'Well,' she said brightly, 'less said of her the better.'

George hazard a guess. 'A bit flighty do you think? Likes the men does she?'

'We're talking of Paul's wife here, so I'll say no more,' she snapped back. It wasn't the first time she had been sharp with him he recalled, well not sharp, a bit feisty he told himself. He listened as she told him that another brother, Daniel, had been a soldier in the war and that his lungs were ruined by the gas.

'He's constantly gasping for air and there's nothing we can do to help, except run his errands. He got married to a girl from the valleys. Bronwin, a good wife but she came with a son. Not our Danny's, though they have three girls now. Got herself in the family way with another soldier, who was later killed in France. She's devoted to Danny, and we're all very fond of her.'

'You said you had four brothers. So who is number four?'

'Frank. Now he is a little devil. Always teasing. He stayed behind because he's sweet on a couple of girls. He'll make his mind up one of these days. But I tell you what, he made living at home better, happier somehow.'

On another evening he asked about her father. 'Dadda? What can I tell you? He came from Devon, walked all the way to South Wales looking for work when he was seventeen. Got taken on in the pits straight away.'

'Don't mention the mines to me,' George muttered. 'I hate them. Even now I'm away from them they give me the willies. Do you know just getting on the London underground, just saying that word, makes me want to run a mile.'

'Oh dadda said he thought he was lucky. It was God's way of giving him a living.' As they walked on she added, 'He's quite a chapel man. He saved and saved until he could buy a little shop, then he married mam.'

'What about your mother. You've not mentioned her at all.'

Sighing, she answered forlornly, 'She died four years ago.' George wasn't sure what to say or do, but Eve went on, 'She could have had an operation but she was so scared. In the end the disease took her off.' She bit her lip, 'You know George, my dadda was beside himself. They met when he was seventeen and she was sixteen, he told me. He was pleading with her everyday as we all were, but she wouldn't budge. It nearly killed him seeing her suffer, but as mam said, 'she was going to meet her Maker.'

Silently they walked on, until she said, 'Do you believe in God, George?'

'Well, I was always at church like as a lad, being told this and that.'

'But do you believe? I tell you now, there can't possibly be. What sort of God is it that allows our good folk to suffer like mam and Danny?'

Gently he pulled her into his arms and said quietly, 'I was also taught not to question, but to accept.'

They walked on until they reached the gate, and as he opened it to let her enter, she said, 'A load of baloney. Goodnight.'

Something happened in the week before he met Eve again, that pleased George immensely. He was up and down the scaffolding like a monkey, carrying bricks or mortar, mixed by the labourer below, for Bert and himself when, early in the morning Mr Mathews approached Bert. 'Good morning Bert. Charlie not around?'

Bert touched his cap and answered, 'Sir,' then added, 'Charlie's checking a delivery at the moment. Can I help at all?'

Mathews nodded towards George, then said, 'I was wondering Bert if you could spare Geordie for the day.' Both looked at Mathews in surprise. Wonder what this is all about, thought George.

'Well, might slow me down a bit, but if you think it's important...'

'I thought maybe George could further his skills. It might be worthwhile him giving Alf a hand.'

'Alf? Ha, you mean the bloke what's doing the fancy stuff. Clever geezer that one.' He looked at George, 'What do think mate? Want to further yer ejucation?'

George didn't hesitate. 'Only if you're sure Bert. I don't want to let you down. You got your own reputation to keep up. Wouldn't like you to fall behind because of me.'

Mathews intervened. 'Tell you what. I'll send young David over to give you a hand. He's a willing lad. What do you say Bert?' George was hoping that Bert would agree to this, he was always ready to learn new skills.

'Alright guv, Geordie can 'ave the day orf.' Then as Mathews and George left he was heard to mutter, 'I wouldn't mind learning that craft meself.'

As they passed the nearly finished houses, Mathews pointed to the facades of some, 'See that George? See that lovely herringbone effect of the bricks? That's Alf's work. Reckon you'd like to have a go at it?' There was no doubt that the patterns gave the houses a distinctive, individual look. 'I've already spoken to him about you. He says it'll be good for a youngster to learn the trade. Here we are.' After the introductions, Mathews left them to get on with the work.

'Glad to have you around son,' Alf said. 'Need to pass on trade skills to young blokes like yerself. Who's to do it when I retire, I ask you? Nearing sixty-three meself, so not long to go, God willing.' He straightened his back, and adjusted the glasses that had slipped down his nose. 'Now then, climb up here and stand close by me for a bit lad. Nothing to it really. Everybody thinks I'm pretty good at it, but all it takes is a little patience.'

George watched as Alf slowly, treating each brick as if it were gold, carefully measured the amount of mortar then placed them into the diagonal herringbone pattern between the two upper windows. 'You go and practise a bit on the ground first lad. I've made up a wooden block the size we want for you. When you're satisfied I'll have a look, and if I thinks it alright, I might let you have ago up there,' he said pointing to the houses further along the new road. It took many hours for George to get it right. At first he struggled with the mortar, too thick, too thin, not enough applied then too much. In the end he was satisfied. It was just a question of fitting the bricks in a pattern into a given space.

The next day, after Bert agreed, he went back to Alf, who let him go ahead with his first effort. George was dismayed when Alf disassembled them hastily, and finished the job himself. 'One was protruding a bit, that's all. Soon 'ave it right son.'

Patiently George tried again and again, until at last, Alf was satisfied. 'There you are then. Told you so. Born to it you are. Well done.'

Next day, George explained it all to Bert and during their lunch break. Bert tried his hand, and was surprised how well George could quickly lay out the design.

On the following Saturday after Eve had joined her sister, and he had turned away to go to his lodgings, he suddenly heard her calling after him.

'George. George.' She was slightly out of breath and excited when she caught up with him. 'Can't stop, but Vi and Bryn said to ask you for tea tomorrow if you are free. You are free aren't you?' she asked hopefully, peering into his face.

He nodded, 'Aye lass, I'll be there. What time did you say and where?'

Quickly she answered, 'I'll meet you here at three o'clock.'

They both heard Bryn call for her to, 'Hurry up.'

'I've got to go. We'll miss the start. Yes, that'll be best. See you then.'

'See you tomorrow pet,' he answered. Things were looking promising, he thought. Maybe I'll officially be walking out with her, and we'll see where that leads.

Together, the next day, they caught a bus to Coulsdon, and walked along Chipstead Valley Road towards Vi and Bryn's terraced house. As they passed one house, a man's head appeared over the privet hedge, and pointing a gardening trowel at Eve, said in a strong Welsh accent, 'You watch your step my girl. Nineteen, and on a fellow's arm on a Sunday.' George was both shocked and prepared to defend her, until he saw that the man was grinning at him.

'Oh, shut up Billy. George, this is my brother William. Take no notice of him. Cheeky blighter.' As the two men shook hands, George could see William was in his early forties at least. From a big family over twenty odd years between the eldest and youngest, just like my own folks, he thought to himself.

'Well, dadda would say that if he knew what you were up too my girl.'

'We're away to Vi's for our tea. Dadda wouldn't mind that, her being my chaperone.'

George was beginning to wonder what 'dadda' was like. It sounds as if her dadda still liked to rule his family's lives. Then he remembered Jessie and Ron who had asked him to keep their courtship a secret from his own parents for the time being. The same sort of attitude, he surmised then in most families.

It was almost four o'clock when they reached Vi's, and immediately she sat them down at the table. George felt clumsy as he tried to handle the fragile china cup of tea. A plate of dainty cucumber sandwiches was offered to him, he daren't take two, and thought I'll be going home hungry. After the sandwiches came tinned peaches with evaporated milk poured over them, and he noticed that the others ate theirs with bread and butter, so he followed suit. More tea followed, then a large slice of Victoria Sponge.

'Eve and I will clear up while you two go for a smoke,' said Vi.

George followed Bryn into the garden and was surprised at how tall he was for a Welshman, he always thought they were shorter than the English somehow, how wrong could you be, he asked himself?

Once their cigarettes were lit, Bryn in a soft, strongly accented voice said, 'We look after Eve you know. She's a good bit younger than Vi who treats her more like a daughter than a sister.' He looked sideways at George, 'So boyo, how do you feel about our Eve?'

George drew on his cigarette and flicked off the ash before answering. He didn't feel ready yet to admit to anyone of his love for her, he was after all only coming to terms with idea himself. 'She's a grand girl no denying that. In fact I'd go so far as to say she is very special to me.'

Bryn growled softly in his throat. 'Well that's the point. How special? I mean you've been meeting up now for nearly two months and all we get every weekend, is George this and George that.'

'Well I hope it's all good that she tells you.'

'Do you mean there's something we ought to know about?'

George was beginning to get a bit flustered, and felt that somehow he was being warned, but not sure of what. Almost angry but remembering he was a guest, he demanded, 'Just what do you mean? Do you think I'm a criminal? That I go around picking up girls? I have a great deal of respect for Evelyn, and to be honest my friend, I think that what goes on between us is none of your damned business.' He could see by Bryn's face that the man was startled by his almost fierce reply.

'No need for you to get yourself into a state boyo,' he replied. 'It's just that we know when your present job is finished you will likely be moving on. We don't want to see Eve hurt, but we can't make her understand that she shouldn't think that this...' he paused for a moment looking for the right word then went on, 'this friendship between you is nothing more than that, a friendship with an itinerant worker.' Both stubbed out their cigarette butts. George put his hands in his pockets as he was taught to do at school when as a young lad his temper flared. Bryn bent down to pull up a weed between the flagstones. 'You see what I'm getting at George? We don't want to see her hurt.'

For a moment or two George thought about what Bryn had said. 'I don't wish to hurt her either. All I can say is that I intend going on seeing her if she is agreeable, and that neither you nor I can possibly know what lies in the future.'

Bryn patted him on the shoulder as he said, 'Fair enough George. Let's join our womenfolk.' Then grinning asked, 'Is it true that some of the men call you Geordie?'

'Aye, they do, but they're wrong,' laughed George.

As they sat in the lounge, complete with a three piece suite, Bryn, turning a handle on his new gramophone was able to play some popular music. George surprised them all when he sang, without any embarrassment, one of the latest songs.

Vi and Eve left the men after a while, and Bryn poured himself and George a beer. It was eight o'clock when Vi called out for them to come for supper. Supper! George, who had thought he was there for tea and had found it a bit mean, was astounded. More so, when he saw the table laden with platters of cold meats, pasties, hot potatoes and green peas. 'Tuck in boys,' said Vi cheerfully, 'I don't want anything left after I've gone to all this trouble.' George didn't need a second bidding, and gladly set to.

George was to escort Eve back to the Woodmarsh's and as he thanked Vi and Bryn for their hospitality, Vi invited him to come again soon. On the corner of the road where Eve worked, was a pillar box. They stopped beside it for a moment, 'How come you don't post Woodmarsh's letters in here instead of going into the town?' he asked.

'Without stamps? Besides the walk does me good and...' she laughed, 'I get to see some good looking fellows on the building site.' It was then, as she gave another small laugh, that he kissed her. Kissed her, for the first time, on the lips, and what's more he realised, she hadn't stopped him. So began their courtship, every Wednesday and Sunday evenings once they reached the pillar box, they kissed.

CHAPTER THIRTEEN

One October Saturday evening, George asked Eve if she would go to the dance with him. They had been practising the waltz, the easiest of dances, in Vi's parlour a few times. George admitted to himself that it was rather like pushing a cart horse around the room. Placing his hands on her shoulders and hers on his, he told her to watch his feet and follow, but somehow she got her feet muddled, and her long, thin legs splaying out like an untrained colt. At one point she complained, 'I can't go backwards, I can't see where I'm going.'

Hiding his impatience, had answered, 'You're supposed to trust me, let me guide you. That's how it's done.' One thing he did notice was that she kept a good distance between their bodies, so that when she had progressed enough for him to hold her in his arms and she could no longer see their feet, it was as if they were back at square one. Often Bryn was in the doorway, grinning at her efforts and shaking his head in sympathy with him. Neither dared tease her, both aware of her quick, short temper, and George, convinced if she were to get upset, he would never get her inside the ballroom. Instead, they encouraged her telling her she was improving, which she was, but very slowly. Sometimes, when they reached their letter box and if no one was around they'd dance a few steps on the pavement, she, occasionally faultless. George put this down to the fact that there was no one about, and they would laugh happily together, then kiss before parting. They were enjoying each other's company and at ease, sharing their news, in the main about Mrs Woodmarsh's expected baby and the variety of work he was experiencing on the site.

When George met her on the evening of the dance, he was delighted to see, under a shapeless cardigan, she had on a new dress. Made of some smooth material, with a leaf green background and covered with a dainty floral pattern. It had short puff sleeves with contrasting cuffs, a rounded collar matching the cuffs, a v-neckline and nipped in at the waist which showed off her neat figure perfectly.

'You look absolutely beautiful. Green suits you, shows off your hair to perfection,' he whispered as he took her hand. 'I'll be so proud to waltz you around the ballroom.' Then squeezing her hand firmly, said, 'I'll have to watch out. Every fellow in the place will be after you.' By the panicky look on her face he realised she was nervous. As they neared the dance hall they could hear the music and he sensed her misgivings as she hung back, 'Don't worry pet, I'll be there. You don't have to do anything you don't want. Trust me.' He began to hurry her along, dancing a few steps in front of her, 'See, remember?

You can do it.'

'Promise you'll not leave me alone.'

He stood still for a moment, then took her in his arms and said, 'Are you saying I can't dance any other dance other than the waltz tonight?'

'No.' Surprised at his idea, she went on, 'No, I didn't mean that. Just that if someone, a man should ask me, then...then I want you nearby. Not too much to ask is it?'

Trying to make light of her apprehension, he said, 'Wait 'til you get inside. You'll love it. I bet you'll want to come again.' He could see by the sceptical look on her face that tonight was going to be difficult and his spirits sank a little.

The first waltz was a complete disaster, as was the second. Tripping over his feet and her own, treading on his feet, and he on her, and bumping into other whirling couples, and he having to apologise, he finally led her off the floor. Eve's nerve had gone, and there was little he could do about it. They sat together miserable, Eve because she couldn't dance, and he because the music was enticing him to find a partner and enjoy himself. In the interval, the leader of the three piece band beckoned him over and invited him to sing while his group had a break. George had been doing this for the last few weeks. A girl from the crowd volunteered to play the piano and he began to sing the popular tunes of the day among them, 'Aint she Sweet,' and 'Stardust' the dancers showing their appreciation with clapping and whistles. When he began his final song he pointed towards where Eve was sitting, and told the audience that this song was for a special girl, and began to sing, 'Only Make Believe I love You', the last line declaring, 'To tell the truth, I do.' After the applause, the band returned and began the second half of the evening by playing a quickstep. As he made his way back to Eve, and before he reached her, he was asked to dance by one of the girls he sometimes met up with. When it finished, he made his way, breathless, to Eve.

Tight lipped and eyes narrowed, she demanded, 'Take me home,' but before he could answer, another girl grabbed him for a tango.

When he returned to Eve the next time, she again insisted on being taken home.

'Look,' he said, 'we'll have another go when a waltz comes up. Now you know what it's all about you'll probably do better.' She shrugged and turned away from him. Standing up and looking down on her,

'You're in a temper aren't you? You're determined not to enjoy yourself aren't you? Well you're not going to spoil my evening. Sit there till I'm ready to go, or make your own way. It makes no odds to me,' and with that he marched across the dance floor seeking out a partner.

Eve waited for him, as he knew she would, until the dance was over. There was no escaping the fact – he could tell by her tightly compressed lips that she was sulking. It was dark now, and without speaking they caught the last bus to Couldsdon and during the walk to Vi's neither spoke nor touched each other. Finally they reached the front gate and stopped. Eve turned her back to him, her loose hair swinging around her shoulders, which he was tempted to stroke.

Sighing, he lit up a cigarette and after a long inhalation he said gruffly, 'Well are you going to kiss me goodnight or what?' There was no answer. 'Does this mean then, that it is all over between us? You wish me gone out of your life?'

She whirled round to him, he saw her trembling, her face white with anger. 'Yes,' she hissed, 'Get yourself away from me.'

He took a few steps away from her, then turned and asked, 'So, what's upset you most? God knows I tried to teach you to dance. Just one dance, that's all I asked of you when there are hundreds.'

'I can't help having two left feet can I?' she stormed at him, 'but I'll tell you what I really hated shall I?'

He ground the cigarette butt beneath his heel, feeling partly guilty of some demeanour he wasn't sure of, and beginning to lose patience, snapped back, 'Whatever it is believe me it won't happen again. You and your blasted moods. I tell you Eve, I'm just about sick of them. You fly off the handle as soon as look at me.'

As she began to answer he stepped towards her, and was preparing himself for what was to come. He could see by how her shoulders were held back, and her arms akimbo, that she was determined to fight him. 'If you must know Mister Carr,' she hesitated, 'it was awful, embarrassing, I didn't know where to hide my face when you sang that…that silly song to me.' By now tears of frustration were spilling down her face. George put out his arms to comfort her, but she pushed him away. 'Oh go way! Leave me alone,' she said as she buried her face in her hands.

George dropped his hands to his sides, then turned his palms upwards as if pleading, 'Look at me will you, or at least listen to what I've got to say for once.' Eve didn't move and kept her face covered. Giving an exasperated sigh, he went on, 'When I sang that song, yes it was meant for you, but I only pointed in your direction. It could have been for any number of girls standing near you for all anyone knew.' He stopped hoping for some reaction from her, 'Just for you, I hoped you'd listen to the words and guess how I'm feeling about you.'

There was no response, but she hadn't finished, she screamed at him, 'And another thing...'

'Oh God, what now woman? I tell you lass you're going the right way to see the back of me for sure. What is it this time?'

'That dancing you're so mad about. I know why now. It's downright...' she struggled for the right word, 'downright immoral that's what it is.'

George spluttered, 'Immoral? What are you talking about. Immoral my eye.'

Stamping her foot, she shouted at him, 'Immoral, I said and immoral I mean Mister Carr.'

Quickly George put his hand over her mouth as he glanced around to see if anyone was about. Fortunately they were alone and as she tried to free herself he said between gritted teeth. 'Shut up you silly 'aporth. People will think something's up, and stop struggling.' Both stepped way from each other, both of them out of breath with their quarrelling.

A short, cold time elapsed before George regained some composure before he asked her to explain what she meant.

Eve too, had quietened down and said in a level voice, 'I mean George, dancing. It was really quite shocking to see how close you held those girls.' She stopped for a moment, 'I mean, I'm sure you must have felt every part of their...their bodies, and some of the movements you made were more than suggestive, and you, you just encouraged them, playing up to them.'

'I'm not sure I'm hearing this. It was only dancing like everyone is taught to do. There's nowt else. I think you have a bad case of jealousy my girl.'

Suddenly she stepped forward, and pressed herself against him, 'Like this George,' she said fiercely. 'Like this, that's how they were.'

He could feel her breasts and thighs against his own and his heart thumping wildly. Quickly he folded his arms around her, held her tight, and then instead of the tender goodnight kisses she was used to, he kissed her passionately on the lips. To his joy she responded with equal fervour. George held her away from him, crooked his finger under her chin to tilt her tearstained face and said, 'I love you Eve.' Her response was more urgent kissing. Half dragging her he took her into the garden where they could have some privacy, 'I'll be careful,' he murmured hoarsely as he felt her body soften at his touch.

'That was madness,' he exclaimed afterwards and covering his face said, 'I never intended anything like that to happen Eve. Honestly. I care too much about you.'

'Shh,' she said, taking his hands away from his face, and looking into his eyes, 'I don't remember stopping you. Do you?'

There was a chill now in the autumn air, and he noticed her thin coat. Opening his he pulled her close and wrapped it around them both, 'You're a grand lass,' he whispered, 'the best in the world.' They clung together both a little awed by what had happened.

With her face muffled against his chest she asked, 'Have you ever had a girlfriend before George?'

He thought fast, he was sure she would never understand the truth about Pat, at the same time he didn't want to mar this new stage of their relationship by lying. Cautiously he answered, 'Well there was a girl once I was partial to, up north like, but she found another so that just fizzled out.'

'What was she called? Was she pretty?'

Careful, careful he told himself. 'I called her Pat but her name was Patricia and aye, she was bonnie enough, but not anywhere as wonderful as my girl Evelyn.'

He heard her sigh happily before she said, 'I suppose I'd better go in. It's got rather late hasn't it. I've forgotten most of my Welsh but Goodnight cariadon.'

'Which means?' he asked.

'Goodnight darling,' and he kissed her again, their own tender goodnight kiss.

CHAPTER FOURTEEN

Mid November, and the contract was almost complete. Bert and Charlie were already fretting about finding a job before Christmas, as they both knew that work in the winter months was hard to come by, and there was a money crisis in the country which was beginning to effect most businesses. Finishing work one evening, Mr Mathews found George on his own, and after lighting up a cigarette asked him what his plans were. George knew he meant work wise. There was no way he was going to tell him that he intended to propose to Evelyn at Christmas. There was a tidy sum in his post office book now, and they could find lodgings once he had a new job. Vi had asked him to join them for Christmas day, and although he had thought of going home, he decided to go as soon as this job was finished instead, so that he could be with Eve for the holiday.

'I've no idea yet,' he answered. 'I'm going to see my folks for a week when we're finished up here and then I'll have to see what's what.'

Mr Mathews replied, 'I figured something like that.' Sitting himself down on a pile of bricks, he watched as George collected up his tools. Thoughtfully he said, 'I have something in mind you might be interested in lad.'

George turned to look at him hardly daring to hope there was a job in the offing. He chuckled, 'And what's that, sir?'

'Come into the Office where we can have a chat when you're done here. Alright?'

As George entered the office, he hoped that he wouldn't be kept there too long as he intended to go dancing. Eve knew, and didn't raise any objections when he promised he would be true to her.

'Take a seat,' ordered Mr Mathews when he arrived. George offered him a Woodbine cigarette, but Mr Mathews refused saying, 'I prefer these,' and so do I thought George as he accepted a Players Navy Cut, much more satisfactory. Leaning back in his chair Mr Mathews blew smoke towards the ceiling and both looked towards the window as rain had begun to splatter loudly on the panes. 'Going to get wet going home, I reckon. Well George, there is something I'd like to put to you.' He paused for a moment.

What now I wonder George asked himself? 'Yes, sir?'

'Oh please, call me Cyril. Respect is all right, don't get me wrong, and it can be useful when I'm trying to get some work done from some of the lazy blighters.' as he said this he extended his hand to George who shook it, 'I get plenty of 'sirs' when I threaten them with dismissal, believe me.'

'Right, then Cyril it is.'

'At present, what I am going to say is between us.' Leaning forward, he went on, 'The money situation in the country is pretty grim at present, although the building trades in the south here are keeping their heads above water I'd say.'

'Yes, I've read something about that. Seems there's more new factories being built this end along with housing for the workers. Right?'

'You're right. It also means that a lot of small businesses are finding it difficult to compete. So...' He stood up, stretched and stubbed out the cigarette. 'My brother and I have found a small building yard, come stonemason's, up for sale in Willesden.'

George swivelled in his chair to watch as Cyril went across to the window and continued, 'and it is our intention to buy it.' George waited, wondering what was coming next. Cyril came back to his desk and sat down. 'I believe George that I can offer you a permanent job, working for us in the New Year.'

George's head whirled and was quietly pleased with the news then felt he had a thousand questions. 'As what exactly?' he enquired.

'Alf has agreed to join us probably until he retires in a couple of years. Thought you might like to learn all he's willing to teach. He was mighty impressed with you, you know.'

George was excited, but hoped it didn't show, 'And I admire him and his skills, nothing would please me more than to be with him.' He hesitated for a moment before going on then blurted out, 'Mr Mathews, Cyril, I'm planning to get married next year sometime, so, I'm sorry but there's no way I can provide a home on me present wages.'

Cyril's laugh echoed around the office, 'Well, first congratulations and secondly we, my brother Keith and I, thought bricklayer's wages to start with.' More seriously he added, 'What we'd really like is for you, in say two three year's time, to take over, run the whole affair for us.'

George's mouth dropped with surprise, 'Me?'

'Why not? Everyone says you're a quick learner, thorough and honest. Best qualifications I can think of myself.'

'What about Bert and Charlie? I've been with them nearly two years now. I wouldn't like them to think I was ungrateful or anything like that.'

Cyril picked up a pencil and twirled it in his hand for a moment before answering, 'It's like this. Firstly, we can only employ a few to begin with, the place is north of the river and those two fellows live this side. As skilled men they should easily be able to find a job. In fact, I'll go as far as to say I'll see if I've got some contacts that might help, and lastly even if I could take one on, they've been together for so long now, that they'd turn me down.'

In his heart George knew that what he was saying made sense. Well, well he thought, a right turn up for me, a real glad and sorry day as mam would say. It would be madness to turn down such an offer.

'Tell you what,' said Cyril, standing up and putting on his coat, 'you have your holiday and let me know what you think when you get back.' He fished about in one of the desk drawers, 'here's my card with my address on it. Get in touch when you're ready, and mind you don't leave it too long.' Wrapping his scarf around his neck, he shook George's hand again and said, 'Goodnight Geordie.'

George watched Cyril lope across the new road to his Morris car and told himself, as he watched him crank the motor into life, the way things are going, I'll have one of those meself one day. That evening he wrote telling his mother that he was coming home on Monday for a week's holiday and that he had the promise of a job in the New Year. Although in an earlier letter he had mentioned that he'd met a girl from Wales, he didn't tell her of his future wedding plans.

Waiting for Eve the next evening to tell her his good news, he was shocked when she finally appeared. Although the light was dim beneath the street lamp, he could see her drooped shoulders, her untidy hair, her coat unbuttoned and pulled tightly around her thin body, and most disturbing of all her white, tear stained face.

His heart constricted with a longing to care of her, take on her troubles and concerned he reached for her, but she pushed him away. His own news forgotten for the moment, he asked, 'What is it lass? What has happened to upset you so?' His gentle kind words set her off weeping again. 'Tell me. It can't be that bad,' he took out his handkerchief, mentally wished it was cleaner, wiped her tears and put his arms around her. For a moment, he felt her relax against him, then wriggle away. 'Have I done something to upset you? Tell me,' he pleaded as he searched his mind for a possible misdemeanour.

Turning her back on him she sniffed then with sobs in between, said, 'Mrs Woodmarsh has lost her baby,' she paused for a moment, 'Born and died today. They are both so upset, she hasn't stopped crying and he, well he is so miserable, doesn't know what to say or do for the best.'

'Aw, that's dreadful. After waiting all that time and her so poorly too.'

They stood together for a moment, before Eve said, 'I must go back to her until her sister arrives. I just don't know what to do or say to help.'

George knew he had to tell her he was going away for a few days. 'Well, I'll see you Saturday shall I? Before you go in Eve, I'm going home for a week to see my family on Monday. Just for a few days,' he said quickly as he heard her give a little gasp.

'Once you get there, you'll never come back George. Bryn warned me ages ago you'd be off one of these days.'

"Course I'll come back. What makes you think otherwise?' he answered taking her back into his arms. He was surprised and alarmed when she again shoved him away forcefully.

'Get off me! Always pulling me about. Leave me alone.'

But, I thought…'

'You thought wrong. I'm sick of everything we do. We should never have…'

Quickly he broke in, 'That's not what you said on the night or since.' George could feel himself getting angry, as far as he was concerned their lovemaking had always been a joy to both of them.

Sharply she said as she turned her back on him. 'No more George,

I've had enough.'

By now exasperated, he replied, 'I was only trying to comfort you. Give you a shoulder to cry on, show you that I'm here if you need me, but as usual you have to jump in and spoil things.'

'I just want to be left alone. Can't you understand that? I've got too much on my mind to bother with you.'

'You'll feel better when all this baby business is over. By the time I get back from Durham, you'll see, you'll be looking out for me.'

'Oh clear off George. Go back to Durham. See if I care,' then spitefully she added, 'I dare say Pat will be free with her charms for you.'

My God, he thought, I said nowt, has the witch guessed? It must just be a shot in the dark to try to find out more. Angrily he replied, 'By, lass. You're downright evil sometimes. Where do you get your ideas from I wonder?' There was no answer. 'Yes, I'm away to my own folks and seeing as you feel that way about me, I might stay on longer now. When I return to London, which I shall, it won't be anywhere near you my girl, you can bet on that.' He noticed his hands trembling as he lit up a cigarette before striding angrily away. He felt as if his heart had been battered so ignored a small voice behind him saying just once,

'George. Wait.'

George had some misgivings as he said 'goodbye' to his mentors, but Bert and Charlie made it as easy as they could. They reminded him that in their trades people came and went almost daily, and that they had been lucky to have had him for so long.

'When Alf's finished wif yer, yer can call yerself stonemason proper, lad,' said Bert as he shook his hand.

Charlie was having none of that. 'A couple of more years and you can call yourself a master carpenter,' he forecast. 'Good luck son. Our paths are sure to cross sometime. I'll keep a look out for you.'

CHAPTER FIFTEEN

George had been home two days, but he was moody, snapping at baby Joseph, and rarely leaving the house. A letter to Cyril was already in the post, accepting the work offer and thanking him for the opportunity. It was at dinner time that in exasperation, his mother, when she had put a full plate in front of him, exclaimed, 'For heaven's sake, lad. Whatever is the matter with you?'

Poking uninterested at his food, he answered sullenly, 'Nothing.' He gave a sigh, 'nothing at all mam. Don't keep on.'

'I haven't started yet. Pull yourself together child. You're supposed to be on your Christmas holidays. You should be on top of the world. Home with your family, and a good job in the offing.' George pushed his plate away. Aghast she said, 'You're not leaving all that are you? Good money bought that lot for you my lad. Your da's money.'

'If it's money you want, I'll pay me way. Just give us some time will you,' he growled back.

Baby Joseph climbed onto his knee, 'Joe, shall we go Christmas shopping?' he asked. 'I want to buy some presents and for da…'

A brief smile crossed George's face when Joseph whispered in his ear. Earnestly the boy asked, 'Do you think he'll like that?'

George answered, 'The best a da could ever have. Have you enough pennies though?'

The child nodded, 'I think so.'

'Right, first thing in the morning, we're off to Darlington. See what they've got shall we?' By the look on his parents' faces, he could see that they were relieved he had made an effort for the child. If they only knew how my heart is aching he thought.

Returning home after the shopping expedition with Joseph, George was surprised when his mother handed him a letter. 'Came by the second post. From London,' she told him. At once his face lit up. Evelyn, he thought, she's come round, she wants me back. Smiling happily at everyone, he tore open the envelope and pulled out a sheet of white notepaper. Everyone looked at each other in amazement when suddenly George screwed up the letter and threw it angrily on the floor.

'You know, Joe,' said his father mildly, 'there's no need for you to show your temper like that when you get bad news.'

George sat himself down and held his head in his hands for a moment before replying, 'It aint bad news da. It's just…Well, not the news I was hoping for.'

'Good news then, lad. You should be celebrating. Going to share it?'

George looked at his family, all busy, mam at the range, Joseph secretly looking at the gifts he had bought and Mary struggling with a piece of grubby knitting with more than one dropped stitch. 'A pot holder for mam,' she'd confided in George. Standing up and retrieving the letter, he said, 'Sorry everyone. Very naughty of me eh Joseph? The letter is from Cyril Mathews, just wishing me and my family a happy Christmas and telling me to be ready to start work on the second of January. Good news after all.' He stopped for a moment, 'It's like this. I'm hoping for a letter from someone special.'

'That girlfriend you wrote about, I should have guessed,' said his mother.

George glared at her and nodded miserably, 'Something like that,' he muttered, reluctant to say more and wisely his mother kept her questions to herself.

Early next morning everyone was delighted when Robert walked into the room with a full kit bag over his shoulder. As he embraced his mother he looked over her head and winked at George, who crossed the room and thumped him heartily on the back laughing as he did so. 'That's for running away and scaring the daylights out of us all,' he declared.

Hannah was beside herself with joy. 'Oh! It's going to be a glorious Christmas with the boys home Joe, isn't it?'

'Aye, I dare say. Won't be long before they'll all be scrapping just like old times.'

Robert pointed to his bag, 'There's some washing in there mam,' he told her and everyone laughed then he added, 'there's some fish too.'

'Fish?' queried his father. 'I thought you were on a collier, loading coal and the likes.'

Robert nodded, 'You're right, but when we docked last weekend, skipper said that was it 'til after Christmas, and as there was a fishing boat putting out for three days looking for a cabin boy,' he gave a chuckle. 'And that's a laugh. More like dog's body. Anyway, I thought why not?'

George looked at his younger brother and couldn't believe how much taller he was, how muscular and how mature. Only thirteen when he'd last seen him and now nearing fifteen and almost a man. Although at first he had misgivings about Robert being at sea, it was obvious the boy was enjoying the life. 'Hard work is it, being at sea?'

'Well, at first,' confessed Robert, 'I was both homesick and seasick, but the skipper is a good fellow and he looked after me like his own son, who is my best mate by the way. You'd like him mam. Always sunny, cheering everyone up. Anyway...' he said, opening up the bag 'that's how I got you some fish for supper. Plenty there I think.'

'I suppose being on a fishing vessel is very different from the collier then?' da asked.

Robert sat and gulped down a mug of tea his mother had put before him. Then seriously he said, 'Yes da, the bloody thing caught fire!' Everyone looked at him, eyes wide and open-mouthed.

'Fire? You'd better tell us about it,' da said.

Pulling out a packet of cigarettes Robert lit one and said, 'It was like this. Cabin boy my eye. More like cook! I soon settled into a routine of cooking hearty meals, mainly with the frying pan.'

'Seems two of my sons can cook,' murmured da.

Robert and George grinned at each other. 'Sometimes the crew thanked me, but sometimes they were so surly. I soon realised their moods depended on the day's catch. A good haul and they were happy, but if the nets were not full, well, that was their main topic of conversation.' Hannah put before him two thick slices of fried bread topped with fried eggs. With his mouth full, he went on, 'There were five in the crew, the skipper, always fussing about the safety of the boat and his men. There were four of them, tough weather-beaten beggars, all around the fifty mark.' He forked another piece of bread chewed it then wiped his mouth with the back of his hand. 'They never stopped calling out instructions, laughing, cursing and hard working all day, and sometimes well into the night. When they wanted me they called out, 'Boy.' He mopped up the rest of the egg yolk with the last of the bread, and went on, 'I was constantly washing the decks free of fish waste. You wouldn't believe the stink.'

'If it's anything like you smell now, yes we can,' teased George.

'Who me? Good honest sweat that. I had to answer quick to whoever called out so no wonder I might need a wash.' He looked at his mother, 'A bath would be grand mam, if there's enough water.' She nodded and began setting out the tin bath.

'Mainly I was to cook.' He lifted his mug and saw it was empty. George lifted the teapot and filled it. After washing down the last of his meal, he said, 'Towards evening of the third day, our last at sea and now on our way home, we were just about half a mile from the harbour when the wind increased, and the sea started heaving. I mean really big waves and each time a wave slid over the bows I was scared to death. Nothing to worry about the rest of the crew kidded me, at the same time grinning as I was beginning to feel sick, and that hadn't happened for a long time I can tell you.'

Hannah sat down and twisted her hands in her apron. 'I'm not sure it's any better than being down the mine from what you're saying lad.'

Robert smiled at her. 'It's not so bad mam, honestly. I love being at sea as a rule. In fact...' George could see he was excited about something, 'in fact, I'm applying for a place in the Merchant Navy.'

'Sounds like a good idea son. Better pay, cleaner conditions and maybe you'll see a bit of the world. Go on lad,' da said, as he tapped out his pipe on the fender. 'Go on, what happened next?'

'Anyways, like I said, I went to the galley to cook the usual fry-up and suddenly the boat lurched again. The pan slid, the fat spilled and flared up as it splashed onto the flame. You wouldn't believe how quick it all happened. Cloths drying over the stove slipped then fell into the hot pan. Well, being so wet it caused the fat to splutter and flare. Then the flames just seemed to leap up and caught the rest of the towels. It was all so fierce and quick. Before I knew what was happening, the fire had spread through the galley and I was bawling out Fire! Fire!'

He looked at the faces of this family around him. Everyone was quiet and shocked at his story. 'Cheer up you lot. I'm here, safe and sound. Anyway, you should have seen the men. I never saw anyone move so fast. Two rushed to man the pump which wasn't much good, it was so ancient and the rest of us beat at the flames with anything we could lay our hands on. I had a moth eaten fire blanket, someone had a tattered piece of tarpaulin and the skipper used his oilskin jacket. As fast as we thought we had one fire under control another, fanned by the wind mostly, broke out somewhere new.' He paused for a moment. 'Well, any road, we won in the end. Nearly everything burned or scorched in the galley, though we saved the deck, just a little burned in places. Then another trawler came alongside and followed us into the harbour to make sure we were safe.' Swallowing down the rest of his tea, he chuckled as he turned to his mother and said, 'Eh, mother you should have heard the skipper swearing. Not only had his boat been damaged, but his hands were that badly burned.'

She smiled, then laughed as George said, 'I reckon then, you could have brought the fish home ready fried for us if you'd tried.'

It was later after supper when pa spoke. 'Did your mother write and tell you Joe, that the men who robbed and burned down the Manor House have been caught? In Newcastle I think.'

Surprised, George answered, 'No. She said nowt about that. Over a year now isn't it. Is there to be a trial?

'Aye, in the New Year.'

George sighed, 'I wonder what they'll get.' He thought for a moment, before adding, 'They'll hang if the charge is murder.'

'Well now, they wasn't to know the old lady was still in the house was they? If they're lucky it'll be a manslaughter charge.'

'Life. That's what they'll get then. I couldn't bear life in a prison meself, think I'd rather get the rope.'

'Don't talk daft lad. Things change, mark my words. If there's a war, and there's signs of one looming I can tell you, they could be enlisted or certainly set to work somewhere useful.'

'Aye, the bloody mines!' said George.

His mother tutted as she reprimanded him, 'Our Joe.'

'Sorry mam.' Thinking about the men he once worked with, he remembered Thomas's friend Andrew. 'Is Andrew one of them?' he asked.

'No,' replied Hannah. 'I met his mother only last week. She said that after the roof cave in, Thomas had told Andrew that he couldn't face going down the mine anymore. The next thing we knew he was dead.' George thought of the dreadful events that had happened.

'Are you saying...?

Putting her hand out she patted George gently on the knee, and not given to showing emotions, he knew it was to comfort him as she added, 'Seems that way son. Andrew was beside himself, his mother told me. Blamed himself, said he should have understood what Tommy was saying.'

George was dismayed. His cousin, suicide? Never.

'That's why they packed him off to Kent. Nearly out of his mind, she said. Got himself a little job in the village shop and he's feeling a lot better now.'

Bloody Harry, thought George, I'll murder the sod meself. Leading everyone to think the two lads were involved in murder like that.

'She's that disappointed. Says he won't be coming home ever. Can't bear the place she says.' George sighed, how well he understood that.

It was Friday, Christmas Day was on Sunday and the house was a hive of activity. George was helping Joe and Mary make paper chains and hang the finished garlands around both downstairs rooms. Robert had been along the hedgerows and had cut some large branches, and was now hanging the few baubles the family possessed onto them, along with some cotton wool. Hannah was baking mince pies but was losing the battle to keep them, for as soon as a batch came out of the oven the three boys just had to sample them. 'You're not too big for a slapping,' she warned them as she found targets with her dishcloth, but they cajoled and teased her and really, George could see, she was enjoying having her family around her.

It was Robert who brought up the question about Aunt Lizzie.

'I hope, mam, you haven't asked Aunt Lizzie to spend Christmas Day with us have you?'

Hannah's answer confirmed their worst nightmare. Lizzie was Hannah's widowed cousin, a lonely soul who came to tea every Sunday. Somehow she knew all the virtues and shortcomings of most of the members of the rest of the family and somehow, she conveyed their news waspishly. 'Of course she's coming. Can't leave the poor woman alone over Christmas, can we?'

The boys groaned, 'Well she's mighty fond of your apple tart mam. If you tell her that there's only pudding perhaps she'll change her mind,' George suggested.

Robert butted in, 'Have you forgotten how downright greedy she is when it comes to cheese, our Joe? I just watch amazed as she cuts off a piece and nibbles it, and before it's down her throat, she's cutting more! Got a wooden leg I reckon.'

'Behave you two,' Hannah scolded, 'and anyway if I remember rightly, you all seem to clear off when she's here. She asked me once where you'd all gone, and I had to tell her you'd gone for a walk to get up an appetite. Mind, the day any of you are without an appetite will be a wonder to me.'

It was Nancy who mimicking Aunt Lizzie, who had an unfortunate habit of sniffing, had them all, including Hannah, in stitches. 'I tell you Hannah,' Nancy gave an exaggerated sniff, 'that boy will be in prison afore he's twelve.' Sniff, sniff. 'And who his mother thinks she is, sending him off to piano lessons,' a sigh, a shake of the head followed by another sniff, 'airs and graces that one.' Everyone began to laugh, as Nancy pretended to search in her sleeve for a handkerchief and sniffed again. 'Mark my words,' sniff, 'he'll be down the pit and pub with the rest of them lads.' The little repertoire was finished by Nancy dramatically dragging her sleeve across the bottom of her nose before a final sniff.

'Bye, I ought to send you to bed you cheeky madam,' laughed mam.

Artfully, Robert said, 'Are those mince pies burning mam?' which prompted her to rush to the oven.

Around six o'clock, the last post of the day arrived. There were two for George. Although he had lost hope by now of hearing from Evelyn, nevertheless his heart fluttered a little when he saw London postmarks. Telling himself that it was probably more instructions from Cyril, he opened the first. There was a smile on his face when he saw it was a card from Bert and his family wishing him the best for Christmas. The second letter he thought must be from Cyril.

It was not. He read the first sentence and whooped with joy then read it a second time.

'George, I am writing to tell you that Evelyn is expecting a baby in early summer. She does not wish you to know or to have any further contact with you.'

George couldn't help it, his heart filled with joy, he was going to be a father. The second paragraph caused him to growl and say out loud,

'Over my dead body.'

'Joe?' his mother queried, 'what's up with you lad?'

'Give us a minute mam,' he answered as he read the shocking news again.

'Vi cannot have children, and so we have decided to bring up the child as ours. Evelyn will go to friends nearer the time with Vi, who will, to all intents and purposes, be the child's mother. Evelyn has agreed to this arrangement. I thought you should know, and agree that this is the best solution all round. We do not wish you to be involved. Bryn.'

George jumped up, elated, then angry then elated again. Striding about the room, he began to make his plans. The Woodmarsh's had said Evelyn could leave at seven o'clock on Christmas Eve, and need not return until the twenty-seventh of December. Well, he knew where she would be all that time. 'I'm away back to London tomorrow mam,' he said quickly.

'Joe, whatever has happened? Can't it wait until after Christmas?'

'No mam. No indeed. I've something to sort out pretty smartly.' Seeing her bewildered face but not sure what her reaction would be, he thrust the letter at her. 'Read it mam, and tell me I'm right in going down to sort things out.'

Hannah read the letter carefully, then handing it back to him and sighing softly, said, 'Poor girl,' then turning to her eldest son said, 'Think about this son. Whatever you decide is for the rest of your life.'

He nodded and was glad she was not reproaching him.

'Are you thinking of marrying the girl?'

'Aye, I am that mam. She's a grand lass.'

'You know lad, you could bring the bairn home here. I'll look after the child for you.'

'No mam, but thanks. I'll marry Evelyn as soon as I can.'

'But the letter says she no longer wants anything to do with you.'

George sat down, it was true he thought. What if she really meant it? Putting his head in his hands he sat down abruptly, then brightened as he remembered. 'She said she loved me mam. Else how...?'

Hannah stood over her son, and in an unfamiliar gesture stroked his hair. 'Love eh?' Taking her hand away she added, 'You realise Joe, if you wed this girl, any girl in fact, that it is for life, forever and that you will probably never have another penny to your name?'

Smiling at her, George said, 'Aye mam, but I've loved her from the first day I clapped eyes on her.'

'You think I don't know about love son? Some folk feel trapped, some find their soul mate, but it isn't easy believe me.' She sighed, 'and you still a boy in my eyes. Well now, I can't stop you. I'd best make up some bait for you, in case you're stranded over Christmas.' She turned away then added, 'Come home won't you Joe, if it doesn't work out lad.'

CHAPTER SIXTEEN

There was a chill in the air when, just after nine o'clock, George finally arrived at Bryn's house on Christmas Eve. Thankfully he put his case and tool bag down on the step, blew his warm breath on his hands then knocked at the door. While he waited for an answer, he gazed up at the clear sky filled with stars. They do say everyone's destiny is written in the stars he told himself, well if tonight's are anything to go by, I've got a bright future. Bryn opened the door.

'Where is she?' demanded George at once.

Bryn put up a flat hand to hold him back. 'Now steady on boyo. Evelyn doesn't want to see you. I made that clear in my letter.'

George tried to elbow his way past him, 'Don't give me any trouble Bryn, or you might find yourself on the end of my fist.'

Bryn stood his ground, before quietly saying, 'George, she doesn't want to see you.' He hesitated for a moment. 'Look, Vi has her heart set on this baby. She…'

'Over my dead body,' was the angry interruption. 'My child and my family when Evelyn comes round to my way of thinking. Man, you were quick to take bloody advantage of a girl on her own with her fellow away and he not even asked just told.' He glared at Bryn. 'Now where is she?'

'Can't you wait 'til tomorrow? I mean George, you come here this time of night, chucking your weight around...'

'Bryn, it's bloody cold on this doorstep. Let me at least see her. Now I ask you again. Where is she?'

Bryn nodded towards the back room, and resignedly moved to allow George to pass, 'In there. Asleep. She's been real poorly. Needs to rest a lot. Vi's been taking care of her.' As he picked up George's case and tools, he added, 'She's been working still. Says she needs the money, but we told her no need. We would look after...'

George turned round to face him, 'Our baby Bryn. Get it? Mine and Evelyn's. If she's still in the same mind, and really doesn't want me, then I'll take the bairn home to my mother.' Bryn reddened and was about to protest, but George had already reached the back room.

The room was almost in darkness, just one small table lamp and the glow of the fire. In an armchair, in front of the fire, he saw Evelyn, asleep. Looking at her he could see at once she was unwell. Her face was white and pinched although there seemed to be a healthy colour on her high cheekbones, a reflection of the fire he thought. On her brow was a fine film of sweat. A blanket was draped over her, and he noticed that her hands and wrists resting outside the cover, were stick thin. That feeling of loving and the need to care for her over-whelmed him again. Gently he lifted her hand, 'Eve, pet. It's me George.' She stirred, half opened her eyes and resettled herself. Carefully he squeezed her limp hand, 'Wake up my love. I need you.' More awake this time, he could see she was startled.

She sat up suddenly, looked about her and whimpered, 'Vi?' As she gathered her wits and saw George she thrust the blanket aside hastily then stood up. 'George,' she exclaimed. He wasn't sure if she was pleased to see him or not, as he stepped forward to catch her, and sit her down again when she swayed a little.

'Aye, it's me lass.'

Leaning against the back of the chair with her eyes closed, wearily she asked, 'What are you doing here George? What do you want? I told Vi and Bryn not to get in touch with you ever.'

Holding her hand and then kissing it lightly, he replied, 'What do you think my girl? You about to be a mother and robbing me of the chance to be a father of our own child. How could you even think about leaving me out of such a wonderful event?'

Giving a sigh, she said, 'I've been so sick George, believe me, it's not something I ever want to go through again.'

'I can see that and I'm here to look after you meself, and the baby, our baby.'

Slowly she withdrew her hand. 'Go away George, please. Leave us alone. Vi will be a good mother and Bryn a good father. We arranged it so that both you and I can be free to get on with whatever we want from life.'

George could feel himself getting angry, but knew a wrong action or word now would spoil his chances. 'How could you even think of giving away our baby?' he asked quietly. There was no answer. 'And yes, I do believe Vi would be as excellent a mother as would be my own mam. Anyways, I do believe it's against the law, giving away a child.'

'We are going to do it properly. Vi and Bryn will officially adopt it. So your mother wouldn't stand a chance.'

'She wouldn't need to adopt. I shall be there for our baby always, so no need for any rigmarole. I wouldn't let that happen you know. I'd have to put me oar in, so to speak, to keep the child with me.'

'It would mean you'd have to find work in the mines again, and I know you'd hate that.'

A flicker of dread moved through his body knowing it was probably true, but he answered firmly, 'So be it.' Evelyn looked at him intently, she could see he meant it. Taking her hand again, and hanging on to it so that she couldn't pull away, he said, 'There's no life for me without you Evelyn. You know that. I dreamed of a future with you and told myself that no matter what happened we would always be together. All this time apart I've thought only of you. I love you pet, from the bottom of my heart and always will, even if you send me away.' He saw the tears begin to trickle down her face.

'I don't know what to do?' she wept. 'Vi on at me, Bryn pestering for an answer, and now you.' She stopped for a moment and then softly whispered, 'This baby is mine, even though I feel rotten, I do care about it. I ought to be able to decide, but I just can't. Everything is too much to bear.'

George knelt down beside her chair, and holding both her hands he said, 'I've asked you before and now I'm asking you again, Evelyn, will you marry me?'

For a brief moment she flared up at him, 'You don't have to marry me, so that the child is not…' she hesitated before uttering the word, 'illegitimate. Yes, Vi keeps reminding me of that. Nor do I want you to think that you have to… to stand by me. No, George, I will not marry you. I should never allowed this to happen. Please just leave me alone. Vi says it's my own fault.'

George was stunned by the last remark and he couldn't help raising his voice a little, 'Are they making you feel guilty about all this? It takes two, or have they forgotten that? If it's guilt then believe me, I'm having my share of it too. It wasn't you alone that caused this.'

Bryn appeared at the door, 'Everything all right?' he asked.

George sensed the anxiety in Bryn's voice. He stood up and went across to him, 'Let me say it again Bryn. There is no way you and Vi are having my son or daughter. No way.'

Bryn, unnerved by George's threatening stance backed down and as he glanced at Evelyn and seeing her tears called, 'Evelyn, is he bullying you? Tell me and I'll give him a bloody good hiding.'

She shook her head, 'It's okay Bryn. Leave it be. I have to think and I'm so weary.'

As he left the pair he said to her, 'Call if there's any trouble, Eve. I'm just in the kitchen.'

The only sound in the room for a few minutes after he'd gone was the odd snap of the fire as its embers shifted. Then quietly George, said, 'I love you with my whole being Evelyn, please say you will marry me.'

She bent forwards and stroked his face. 'And I love you George Carr, and if you're sure…' she stopped for a moment, 'then yes. I'll marry you.'

Lifting her up he folded his arms about her. 'You'll never be sorry. I'll always be there for you.' Then as if testing it for sound he said proudly, 'Mrs George Carr. Mrs Carr wife of George Carr,' and she repeated it after him, 'Mrs George Carr.'

After two or three kisses, he chuckled as he said, 'Third time lucky, Eve. I had to ask you three times to marry me.'

Evelyn gave a little giggle, 'And I remember the first time. As I walked past you I thought to myself, if only. I felt somehow happy inside, and when I got round the corner I said, yes out loud.' She sighed. 'You were so sure of yourself and so good looking.'

George pretended to be half cross, 'You little minx,' he scolded.

There was a smell of steaming cocoa as Vi bustled in. 'So, made up your minds have you?' She put a tray holding two full cups and some biscuits down between them and smiling added, 'Sort that lot out between you,' then as an afterthought turned to George and said, 'you'll be staying the night then? I'll find a couple of blankets and you can sleep on the floor in here in front of the fire. Put the cushions on the floor. You should be cosy enough.' Turning to Evelyn she ordered, 'and you madam, bed as soon as you've finished. Got to be bright for tomorrow. Goodnight to the pair of you.'

'You're not too upset are you Vi?' asked Evelyn. 'We've talked it over, me and George. We want to be together, we're getting married and we want our baby.'

Sighing, Vi answered as she left the room. 'Well, you don't have to be a clairvoyant to know that. I think it's best really, though I insist on my fair share of cuddles when baby arrives.'

In the New Year, George began working with Alf at the yard as arranged, and was enjoying learning new skills. Rooms were found a short bus ride away, a large sunny first floor room in the front of a house overlooking the Welsh Harp Lake and park.

The wedding day was arranged for the twenty-sixth January. Snow had fallen, melted then frozen into small icy pyramids which sparkled in the winter sunlight, and crunched underfoot as they made their way to the Registrar Office. Evelyn wore a new wool winter coat. 'Will see you through a good few winters,' Vi remarked. A wide brimmed velour hat given to her by Mrs Woodmarsh trimmed with what looked like large silk pink peonies completed the outfit.

George had his suit pressed professionally and had treated himself to a new pair of shoes and a grey trilby hat which he tipped slightly to one side on his head and Evelyn remarked, ' You look just like a film star.' To complete his outfit he wound a wide white scarf with blue borders around his neck. Not quite the outfit he'd have liked, but as Evelyn had spent countless hours knitting it for him, he didn't want to hurt her feelings.

Mrs Woodmarsh had proved to be a wonderful benefactress. Not had she only been very understanding when Evelyn gave notice, but on the day she left, added an extra five pounds to Evelyn's wages, saying that she deserved every happiness, as she had been such a comfort to her during her own pregnancy, and to put the money aside for a rainy day.

George and Evelyn spent the money on setting up their home, 'There'll be no rainy days for us,' George said to Evelyn, 'just sunshine all the way now we're together.'

Mrs Woodmarsh also donated the entire layette she'd gathered for her own baby saying that next time she would want everything new, not a reminder of the one she had lost. Besides the palest primrose coloured clothes for the baby, there were terry towelling nappies as well as muslin ones, vests, bootees and even binders for the baby's cord, everything a baby could possibly need.

George and Evelyn had settled cosily into a couple of upstairs rooms in the large house, given over to varying sizes of accommodation. They loved finding out each other's faults and generous ways. George learned that she seemed unable to budget the housekeeping money he gave her, often towards the end of the week she would ask for a few coppers more to see them through to next pay day. Quietly, he laughed to himself when he found out she had a weakness for hats. Often in the evening when he asked what she had been up to during the day, frequently she would answer, 'I went to town and tried on a few hats.' Quickly she found out that he didn't care at all for vegetables with his dinner, so that always it had to be a meat dish, never fish which was cheaper. Something that really pleased her was that he always stripped down for a wash before going to bed. It was her job, he told her, to wash down his back, but to be careful not to wet the dry spot in the middle for fear of weakening him, a collier's, superstition.

'Same as I used to do for my brothers,' she told him, 'for the same reason, but I don't mind doing it for you.'

Below them lived a family of eight from Ireland, Mr and Mrs O'Reagan and their six children. George and Evelyn giggled every evening when Mrs O'Reagan, 'Call me Peggy,' yelled from the front door for her brood, starting from the eldest downwards. The elongated cry of each name would echo around the street, 'Ma…ry, Brid…jet, Li…am, Mide…ey, Sean, Patrick.'

'Who the hell is Mide…y, I wonder?' George mimicked one evening.

'That'll be Michael, Peggy's favourite.' Peggy had befriended Evelyn, asking her down for a cup of tea some afternoons, and asking after her 'condition'. 'How she keeps the place so spotless I don't know,' Evelyn remarked to George.

George, returning from work one evening, saw the O'Reagan's door was open and just as he was about to go up the stairs, Peggy poked her head out. 'My, that's a wonderful smell you're cooking, Mrs O'Reagan,' George said.

''Tis me famous Irish stew.' She beamed at him, 'Wait there, I'll fetch you a dish.' She returned with a small enamel bowl filled to the top on which floated an enormous dumpling. 'There now, me darling, just you try that for your supper.'

Waiting for his own dinner, he sampled it, and offered Evelyn a taste. 'It's great Eve. You should've tried some. The dumpling was as light as a feather.'

'That's good, but I hope you've left room for your dinner.'

'Oh, I'd never pass up anything you've cooked, pet. You're the best ever.' Once a week, George was treated to a bowl of Peggy's stew complete with a dumpling.

One afternoon, Evelyn called on Peggy with a few biscuits she had made for the children. When Peggy answered the door her hands were covered in flour, as was her none too clean apron. 'Come in. Come in. Just making up a few dumplings for the children's supper. Your Mister likes them so I'll set aside one for him as usual shall I?' Evelyn sat down, hypnotised as she watched the plump hands rub the fat through the flour in a white china bowl. She watched as Peggy added the water, formed the balls then scrape round the bowl so that nothing was wasted. She had to hide her face, so that firstly, the shock and consternation didn't show, then to hide her laughter.

When George came up the stairs that evening, she was waiting at the door for him and as he entered the room, she quickly snatched the steaming dumpling from him.

Bewildered, he asked, 'What? What's going on?' Evelyn began to giggle.

'Come on kid, what's going on?' he asked again.

'Oh, George. You won't believe it,' and almost choking on her laughter she said, 'Those dumplings you're so fond of...' she could hardly speak for laughing now, 'She, Peggy O'Reagan. I saw her making them today and you won't believe this.'

'Stop laughing and get on with it, will you?'

'She mixes them up in...' Doubling up with laughter again, told him, 'She mixes them in a goesunder.'

'A goesunder? What in God's name is that woman?'

'A jerry, po to you, George. A po. The pot that goes under the bed.' George was aghast, and sat down abruptly. Wiping her eyes she looked at his face, and began giggling all over again. 'Oh don't look so tragic, George. I expect she cleaned it out well before using it.'

'Oh my sainted aunt,' he exclaimed. Then gradually he began to see the funny side of it, and for the rest of their married lives every time they had dumplings and stew they would smile knowingly at each other.

One evening after finishing their meal, Evelyn, from a family of nine, surprised George by timidly asking, 'George, how is this baby going to come out?'

Anxious not to alarm her, he lit up a cigarette smiled and answered, 'The same way it went in pet. The same way.'

She was silent for a moment, then said, 'We know the date but how can I be sure? I mean, will I get any warning?'

'Aye, lass there'll be plenty of warning. Anyways, I'll be close by, I'll know when.'

As he helped her by wiping up the supper dishes, he casually asked, 'Why was Vi and Bryn so keen to have the baby, Eve? I mean can't they have one of their own or what?'

Emptying the soda water down the sink she answered, 'No, George it seems they can't. They keep trying but nothing so far as you know.'

'But, all that to-do, that carry-on about adopting ours, whose idea was that?'

'Oh that was Vi's. Thought it would please Bryn until one of their own came along.'

'What do you mean, please Bryn? Didn't she want it as well?'

'Of course she did, but...'

George stacking up the plates interrupted sharply, 'But what?'

'Best not say anything George, but each month, you know, nothing happened. Vi would cry and Bryn shout, call her names and a couple of times...' she looked at George, 'You'll not say or do anything daft now will you?'

'What did he do a couple of times?'

'He landed one on her or as you'd say, showed her the end of his fist.'

As Evelyn's eyes filled with tears for her sister, George put his arms around, 'Give over lass. Nothing you can do about it, but if I see or hear him playing your sister up, you're right, he will see the end of my fist. Now then woman go and put your feet up.' Over the last few months he had seen Evelyn blossom, smiling and happy to be his wife, just perfect to be the mother of my children, he told himself.

CHAPTER SEVENTEEN

It was Wednesday the fifteenth of June nineteen thirty-three, when Evelyn began her labour pains. They started quite early, before George went to work, but she said nothing not being sure what they were. Feeling uncomfortable around ten o'clock she wrote a note to George telling him she was at Park Royal Hospital if she wasn't back when he arrived home. It wasn't far to the hospital by bus, and by two thirty in the afternoon she was the mother of a daughter.

As soon as he found the note, George quickly washed and changed into his suit, I am after all going to meet my new son or daughter, he thought. He rather hoped for a son, they'd discussed names and had easily decided on Frederick Joseph, named after their fathers, for a boy. They briefly thought about names for a girl but had been undecided. Swallowing down a cup of tea and a slice of bread and dripping, he promised himself a fish and chip supper on the way home.

Visiting time began at seven o'clock, and George was first on the ward. Rushing to Evelyn he kissed her again and again, then noticed other new fathers had bought flowers and gifts. 'Tomorrow, my love, I'll bring you the largest bunch of flowers you ever saw in your life. How are you feeling?' Again he couldn't believe how frail she looked, but this time he could see although tired, she was radiant and happy.

'I'm fine,' she answered, 'just fine. A bit tired, it was hard work I can tell you, bringing that baby into the world.'

George looked around him. 'And where is that baby? You haven't said yet. Boy or girl?'

Half teasing him she answered, 'Well what would you like?'

'As long as you're both alright, I don't mind. Now come on lass don't keep me waiting any longer,' he pleaded.

Evelyn put her arms around his neck and whispered, 'We have a seven pounds five ounces –' she looked into his face, 'daughter.'

George's heart leapt and he knew a silly grin was fixed on his face but was surprised when he felt Evelyn relax. Had she been so nervous of disappointing him he wondered. 'So where is she? Can I see her?'

Evelyn nodded. 'Just ask the nurse over there, she'll take you to her.'

The nurse led him to the nursery. 'Here you are Mr Carr,' she said, 'your daughter.'

George gazed at the tightly wrapped bundle in the cot, although he could see one tiny hand had escaped, a hand that seemed not much larger that a penny. Tentatively, he touched the tiny fingers, and was surprised and delighted when those same fingers curled naturally around his. The feelings in his heart were none that he had ever experienced before, and he knew that this first born would always have a special place in his life. 'Hello pet,' he said, 'welcome. I'm your daddy.'

The next evening he arrived on time with flowers and a couple of penny bars of chocolate and after greeting Evelyn with a kiss, he made his way to the nursery to see his daughter.

'So Mr Carr, what is the baby's name? She's a good baby, sleeps and feeds, not much wailing from that little one,' said the nurse as she smiled at him gazing at the baby.

'We haven't decided yet. Had plenty of ideas for a little lad, but, well you see we was kinda hoping for a lad,' then he added hastily, 'but now she's here, well that makes all the difference doesn't it? I mean who couldn't love a bonnie bairn like this one?'

Returning to Evelyn, he told her the nurse had asked about a name for the baby. Leaning over to her bedside locker, she searched among her things and brought out a list, 'Yes, George, I've been thinking about that myself,' and handed him the paper.

George glanced at it, the names he had in mind were not on it. 'I was thinking Hannah would be good,' he suggested.

Evelyn looked at him aghast, 'You mean Hannah after your mother? What about my mother, Bertha? What's wrong with that? Hannah, indeed.'

George winced, as he could see the telltale signs of the start of a tantrum. 'Bertha?' he pondered for a few moments. 'I don't know. It sounds a bit old fashion to me. Wasn't there a gun named Bertha? Wouldn't like to think about war every time I said her name.' He hesitated before he went on, 'How about Patricia? That's a very popular name at the moment.'

Abruptly she sat up straight in the bed and almost screaming at him, she spat out, 'Patricia! Patricia as in 'my friend in the north Patricia' no doubt, as you keep telling me.'

'Settle yourself will you. It was only a suggestion.' He urgently felt the need for a cigarette, but instead helped himself to a piece of chocolate.

Evelyn crossly slapped his hand away, 'I thought you bought that for me,'

George sighed, 'Well, we can't go on calling her it can we? Let's have another look at that list.' Out loud he put girls names to Carr, 'Jane Carr, Ethel Carr, Sybil Carr, Edna Carr, May Carr.' To him none seemed in tune. By now Evelyn had slid petulantly beneath the bed covers. George asked himself, will this woman ever grow up? He handed the paper back to Evelyn, and said, pointing at the list, 'Well there's none there I fancy.'

I'm over the bloody moon with me daughter, he thought, and here we are at loggerheads with each other over the child's blessed name. Idly he turned the pages of a magazine on the bed, and Evelyn closed her eyes wearily. Nothing was said between them for a while until George exclaimed, 'Got it!' Handing the magazine to her he said, 'Look, there. See. How about it? Sounds just about right to me.'

Taking the magazine from him she looked at the name he was pointing at, then tried it out. 'Belinda,' she breathed softly, 'Belinda. Belinda Carr.'

'Perfect I reckon, don't you?' said George, 'and think on a moment, Belle is French for beautiful, and no one can deny that she is a little beauty, and the Lin part can be after you. See what I mean Evelyn, part of your name? What do you think? I like it myself.'

As George waited for her decision, he saw her face brighten and putting her arms out towards him nodded as she said, 'Perfect. Yes, I think that's a perfect name. Trust you George to get it right.'

He sighed with relief, now that a row had been avoided, as he leaned forward and as he embraced her back. 'Aye, and the last bit is da, which is for me.' he added proudly.

Evelyn and Belinda had been home from the hospital for nearly six weeks, when George, after receiving a letter from his mother turned to Evelyn and said, 'Well love, I think it's about time you met my family in Chilton. Mam says she is longing to meet you and her first grandchild.' He saw her face cloud over, and decided to ignore the signs. 'After all pet, Vi and Bryn have met our Belle and your dad and sisters in law.'

Evelyn shrugged as she answered,' It's a long way to travel with a baby George. I mean there will be lots of her things to carry.'

'Aye, but I'll be there to help you.' Not waiting for her to agree he went on, 'We'll go up next Saturday morning, stay the night and be back Sunday evening. That way I can be at work on the Monday, and we will be able to keep the luggage down. What do you think?'

'I think they don't like me, that's what I think. I mean they never write to me do they?'

George was tempted to say that she had never written to his folks when she should have done once they were married but held his tongue. 'Right, we go on Saturday and once they meet you they'll love you as much as I do.' The only reason she hadn't argued with him he realised, was that she was tired. Why was she always so tired he asked himself?

The welcome was warm enough when they arrived at his parents late on Saturday afternoon. Hannah embraced them both, and his da stood up as Evelyn entered the room. Baby Joe rushed across to be lifted up, and Nancy, ever laughing, gave George a big kiss on his cheek. Hannah picked up the child straight away, even though Evelyn half heartedly protested, and made all the right sounds as far as George was concerned.

'Eh, our Joe, she's perfect, grand. Just look at her little fingers.' Examining the child's face she turned brightly to Evelyn, 'She's got

Joe's eyes don't you think and look at that little dimple beside her mouth, just like our Jessie's.'

Evelyn looked fiercely at George, then taking the baby sharply from Hannah said coldly, 'She looks exactly like my mother. All my family say so.'

George could see that his mam was bewildered by Evelyn's attitude although he could tell that when she answered she was doing her best to smooth over the uneasy atmosphere that seemed to have invaded the room.

'Of course, my dear. Silly of me. Just for a moment I thought I could see a likeness. But she is the bonniest bairn I've seen in a long time. Now I think it's time we had a bite to eat. I've some meat pasties in the oven. George loves them.' Then seeing Evelyn's unsmiling face added hastily, 'Well you know that of course. Now sit yourself down at the table. All of you.'

Nancy, George noticed, made sure she didn't sit next to Evelyn, and his baby brother sat on his knee, carefully watching the baby and Evelyn. Although George did his best, the twenty-four hours with his family were without doubt, strained. Evelyn seemed to guard Belinda ferociously, only allowing the baby to be viewed asleep and not letting anyone nurse her. When anyone spoke to her, she answered abruptly in as few words as possible. Nancy had whispered to George, 'What's up with her our Joe? As prickly as a hedgehog that one. Thinks we're not good enough for her or something?'

'That's not fair,' he answered defensively, 'she's just tired out after having the baby and the long journey. Take it out of anyone. And besides,' he added, 'she's quite shy you know. She's just overwhelmed by everyone. Remember you are all strangers to her. Try to be nice, there's a good girl.'

'I'll try Joe but she is so standoffish.'

'Now then, I…'

'Yes, yes I will go and talk to her now if you want,' she said as she walked away. George swore under his breath when, five minutes later, Nancy returned scowling and her face red said sharply, 'Well I tried, so there.'

All that was said, by Evelyn, on the journey home was, 'We shan't be going there too often I can tell you. In fact, don't even think of it for a hundred years.' George thought it best to keep quiet. The problem he knew by now, was that she was both jealous and possessive where he and the child were concerned. This was obvious when, Belle dressed in her best, and cradled in his arms was admired by the many people he met when he took her to the corner shop for his cigarettes each weekend. Evelyn tried to insist that Belle be left with her or put in the pram out of reach to admirers, but he loved to nurse his baby girl, to show her off.

Returning from work cheerfully one evening when Belle was about seven months old, he opened the door, threw his cap at the peg and missed as usual, then picked up Belle and said as she grinned at him, 'And how's my little princess?' Too late he saw, out of the corner of his eye, Evelyn turn to smile at him, then abruptly turn back to the stove where she was stirring a pot. Quickly he tucked the baby under his arm, and strode across the room to his wife. 'And you, my darling, are my queen.'

'Leave me alone, George. I'm warning you. I'm not in the mood for your carrying ons.' He was surprised by her retort. Usually she was so glad to see him. Every evening, she'd told him, just before he was due home, she would wash both herself and Belle and both had clean dresses. 'Just for you, George,' she'd said. Now he noticed that not only had she not changed out of her wrap around overall, but that she had not even tidied her hair. Something was up, he was sure.

'Had a bad day have you pet?' he asked. 'Belle been fretful with her teething again?'

'Yes George, I've had a bad day,' she snapped. 'And I'll tell you now, a few more bad months ahead too.'

'What's that supposed to mean?' Careful George, he told himself. Something has unsettled her.

Turning back to him and pointing at him with the ladle she said, 'Put Belle back in the cot, George and go and wash then I'll dish up your dinner.'

'Not 'til you tell me what's eating you. I mean, I come home happy as a sand boy, and wham, I find you in a mood.' At this she burst into tears. George was at a loss and after putting Belle safely back into the cot, he went across to her. Gently putting his arms around her, he asked softly, 'Tell me, my love. What's upset you so badly?'

Pushing him away, she muttered, 'If only you'd leave me alone. Always pulling at me.'

Alarm bells rang for George. He'd had a similar conversation like this before. In fact, he remembered, it was before they were married. Turning her round to face him, he kissed her softly on the lips then said, 'There's another bairn on the way. Is that it?' Sobbing in his arms, she nodded. 'But that's wonderful,' he said, 'How can you be so upset?' he could see she was pleased with his reaction.

Wiping her eyes she said, 'It's too soon George. How will we manage?' He put his fingers on her lips. 'We'll manage hinny. Plenty of others have done so with much larger families. 'Sides, it will be good company for Belle, they'll grow up together as friends.'

'What will people think? I mean, so soon after Belle?'

'Bugger what people think or say. None of their blinking business. Didn't I say I'd always look after you?' She nodded. 'So then missus where's my dinner?' Although he'd said all these things, his stomach was in a knot. How in God's name are we going to manage, he asked himself?

Alf was quick to notice that George was down in the dumps the next day. 'What's up lad? No smiles, no laughing, no mucking abart? Somefinks up I can tell.' George shrugged his shoulders then bent over the work he was doing. They worked together in uneasy silence for about ten minutes, when Alf hit his thumb with his hammer. 'Sod it,' he said, 'your bloody fault. Got a face like me gran's bum on you.' George couldn't help it, he burst out laughing. 'That's more like it lad. Make a brew then we can have a talk. Sometimes it helps to talk things over with a mate.'

Sitting together sipping out of their enamel mugs, Alf said, 'Ah, that's better. Just the right thing for a bruised thumb. Now tell me what's up with you?' After he'd listened to George who declared he loved children but not just yet, that the money he earned now was enough for three not four, that there was only one bedroom and that Evelyn was so tired, Alf held up his hand. 'Son,' he said, 'count your blessings. You've a job, a roof over yer head and the clinic will take care of your missus. Think of those poor devils who've lost their work and are on the dole and expecting another any day. I reckon you're one of the lucky ones.' He paused for a moment, 'My old lady had five before we got two bedrooms, and we managed alright.'

George lit a cigarette, 'Ah, well, I'd like to earn enough to put something by for an emergency like,' George said, 'and give my kids a good start in life.'

Stroking his chin and nodding to himself, Alf turned to George and said, 'I think I might be able to help you there.'

George was immediately alert. Anything to avoid poverty, the real poverty that he'd witnessed before leaving for London. 'I'm all ears, man. What're you thinking?'

Alf chewed on his lip before answering. 'Now it might not come off, but I often make a few bob working Saturday afternoons, sometimes Sundays for those that want me.'

'Doing what?' George was surprised by what Alf had told him. 'You're so close to retiring, surely you've saved enough for your pension?'

'Mind your own business, you cheeky blighter. Just keeping me hand in.' He patted his pockets until he found a piece of paper which he handed to George. 'Take a look at that.' George looked at a crude diagram.

'Can see a house, but can't make out the rest.'

'Aye, it's a bit rough and ready but it's for a bloke, a well off bloke, who wants his garden laid out proper for next summer. How about you coming along with me on Saturday afternoon to help out a bit. Lugging them stones is getting a bit much for me. If you feel up to it afterwards, I'll see what I can get you for the odd weekend in the way of some extra work. How about it?'

'But you can't lay out paving and such in winter can you? Even I know that.'

'No lad, you're right you can't. But you can get the stones dressed ready for when the weather improves can't you? What's more the fellow will pay by the hour. Nice old geezer 'e is.'

Helping Alf out some weekends meant that George had the means to afford new lodgings for his growing family. The basement rooms he found were close to his work and comprised of two rooms plus a kitchen. All the rooms seemed damp and airless. Evelyn was shocked at his choice. 'I trusted you George,' she wailed, 'How can I bring up babies in this dank and dirty place?' She ran her finger along the picture rail and was horrified at the dust she found. 'Look at this,' she burst out, 'we'll all be ill before Easter, mark my words.' Looking out of the grimy window she added, 'and the lavvy's outside.'

George looked about him sheepishly. When he viewed the rooms he thought they'd be fine, but as Evelyn pointed out one fault after another he realised he should have had her with him at the time. 'Well, lass we'll have to make do. I've signed up for the year.'

'You what?' Evelyn screamed back at him.

George nodded miserably. 'As soon as the new bairn arrives we'll move on. I promise. We should have a bit more cash by then if I get enough weekend work.' Belinda began to grizzle, and Evelyn began rummaging through the suitcases and sacks holding their belongings, searching for Belle's dummy.

'It's only for a little while and look there's a backyard for Belle to play safely when she begins walking. That'll be useful won't it?'

'Safe? You call cobblestones covered in that green moss safe? It might be alright where you come from, but not for my kids.' She sat down wearily on a kitchen chair.

George went to her side and kissing the top of her head said, 'I'm sorry pet.'

He heard her sigh as she said, 'I'll get started on cleaning up as soon as you've made me a cup of tea,' and glancing around the kitchen again she added savagely, 'and it could take some time.'

George was always pleased to have letters from his family. They, along with him had been schooled in handwriting so that it was difficult to know from the envelope who had written, and part of the pleasure of opening it was guessing who it was from. He was surprised, when glancing at the signature, to see that it was from Emily. Briefly he noticed that the usual love and kisses the others sent were missing. Wants something, he told himself but nothing prepared him for her request. Shocked he read,

Dear George,

I find myself in a somewhat difficult situation in that I am to have a baby in two month's time. The father is already married so there is no chance of legitimising this child. Would you and Evelyn consider adopting the child from birth? I will contribute to its welfare, but cannot keep it myself. You are my only hope. The parents and others do not know of this so I would like you to keep it a secret. Please help.

Yours, Emily.

'My God,' he breathed out quietly. 'My God.'

'What is it George? What's wrong?' said Evelyn looking up from her sewing.

'Nothing wrong,' he answered. 'Well, I suppose it is in some respects.' He held the letter out to her, 'Here, read it for yourself.'

After reading it, Evelyn laughed quietly, 'So, George, you're not the only black sheep in the family. Well, I must say, I do feel a bit sorry for her.'

'Aye me too. You haven't met her, but I can tell you she was the one who was always at church, coming home and preaching about sin to us all. Butter wouldn't melt in her mouth. Disapproved of laughing that one and as for dancing, well you should hear her carry on.' He tapped the letter, 'Even in this letter she is so matter of fact.' He sighed, 'I can't understand how she got into this.'

Evelyn snorted. 'Can't you George?' She got up and said, 'I'll put the kettle on. Fancy a cup?' He nodded. As she waited for the kettle to boil she turned to him. 'I expect he was very charming, persuasive and promising all sorts if my memory serves me well.'

George was indignant, 'Now hang on a minute lady. Are you saying that is what happened between us? As I recall, we loved each other, although it took a while for you to notice.'

'Water under the bridge George, water under the bridge.' She made and poured the tea and they sat for a few moments sipping their drink when George said, 'I'll have to write to her.'

'And tell her we can't have her bastard,' Evelyn said sharply. 'I mean it George. If you think you can go out all day and leave me with three babies all under two, think on.' Then, to his surprise she gave a small laugh. 'In any case George, according to a gypsy this afternoon, she told me I would have five children, and all of them will be taken away from me.'

'Well she's wrong there,' he snapped, 'these two will do for us.' He lit up a cigarette, he always felt he could think better whilst smoking. 'Going back to our Em. What about Vi and Bryn? Do you think they might…'

'Don't be so daft. It's not one of the family is it?'

'Yes it is. One of my family.' Evelyn didn't reply and neither spoke until bedtime when George said, 'I'll write to her and tell her you're expecting again and we can't help and her best plan is to speak to mam.'

Sleepily she answered, 'That's the best I think. As long as it doesn't land on our doorstep. Goodnight.'

George lay down beside her, aye he thought, mam will love having a bairn about the place. Look how she loves my Belle, but as his eyes closed he was saddened as he remembered Evelyn's uncaring response to his sister's dilemma. Emily had not replied. It was almost ten weeks later when a letter from his mother told him of the abandoned child. Hannah's letter, although sad, expressed her joy at having a baby to care for. *A lovely little lass, blonde and blue-eyed, plump, feeding well and seems content.* This good news was offset by Hannah writing in the same letter that,

> *Emily doesn't want to know the child at all, even going so far as to say that she wouldn't ever come home while the girl was there. She wants me to arrange the adoption of Alice. I can't do that George, not one of my own flesh and blood.*

George sighed when he'd finished reading the letter. Poor Em. he thought, and poor Alice, mother and fatherless, but he was content to know that the baby would be cared for within the family.

The extra money for the weekends he was able to work was useful. Cyril ensured that George, as promised, had begun to learn the office side of the business. It seemed to come easily to him, keeping the books, answering the telephone, meeting clients, dealing with deliveries and customers. He was happy enough to run the office when Cyril was away, but to himself, he admitted that he would rather be working with Alf and learning as much as possible when time was slack in the yard, Alf, who in the past had carved headstones, began to show him how to carve stone.

One day an irate customer stormed into the Office complaining that the workmanship of his newly laid landscape garden, was not of a professional standard. George knew the account had not been paid, and he also knew that his and Alf's work was as near to perfect as damn it. Neither would ever be satisfied with less. In fact, Cyril had inspected the work and told them that a passer-by had praised the finished garden, and expressed enough interest to ask for a quote for his own large garden. George listened to the man quietly, then said, 'So what is it you want exactly?'

The man, satisfied that he was being listened to, answered, 'As it is now, the stones are the wrong colour and there are some that are not level, so that I'm afraid my wife will fall.' George watched as the customer's face puffed up as he blustered, 'I'll not part with a penny. It will have to do as it is, but there is no way I'll pay or recommend you.' With that he swung his walking stick and made for the door.

George was fuming knowing that the stone, design and work was of the best. He also knew that there was a financial crisis looming over the country. Probably this man might be a victim, but George had seen the opulence of the man's home and his wife. Both showed no signs of being without the best. Convinced the man was looking for an excuse not to pay, George held open the door, 'Good day to you, sir,' was all he said tightly, as the man left the office.

'You can't do that,' laughed Cyril when George told him later that day of the man's visit, and had suggested a ploy to get their money.

'With your permission, I can. Try me,' George pleaded. 'It will show others that we won't be victims of this slump. In fact I'd go so far as to say, that it will be good for business, as our suppliers will be happy to see we keep in credit.' He watched Cyril, his hands clasped together and his two index fingers tapping his lips thinking over what he had just said.

'You've got a point there George, I can see,' he paused and looked at him, 'You think it will work?'

I'm bloody sure it will.'

'Right, go ahead, but there's to be no roughness, no fists, or the law brought in. Understand?'

George was pleased and nodded. 'You wait. You'll see I'm right. I doubt there'll be any trouble.' In the yard, George told Alf to be ready at six the next morning.

'What you up to lad?' Alf asked. George explained his plan, and Alf slapped his thighs and chuckled for the rest of the day.

Early next morning George and Alf, armed with their tools, made their way to the customer's house. It was not yet seven o'clock when they started work. Crouching down they began to gently loosen each stone slab and were neither noisy nor quiet. They had lifted around ten pieces and stacked them neatly, when out of the corner of his eye, George saw the customer rushing down the path towards them, his arms flailing in a loose dressing gown and tripping over his slippers. 'What the hell do you think you're doing?' he yelled at them. George and Alf went on working, ignoring him, until he used his foot to nudge Alf off balance, who went sprawling backwards.

George sucked in his breath and immediately stood up and using his height to advantage, put his hands in his pockets and took a step towards the plump, angry man. 'Was that an accident sir, or was it intentional?' he asked, far too politely.

The man seemed to recognise the threat in George's tone, and backing away a little shouted, 'You are trespassing, both of you. If you don't leave at once, I'll call the police.'

George smiled but took a risk as he remembered Cyril's warning, no trouble, no police. 'We'd be happy for you to do that, sir. I'm sure they'll be more interested in these stolen slabs neatly laid in front of your house.' He paused for a moment as he pulled Alf to his feet, then added, 'and of course, there could be a charge of assault on my friend here.' George looking over their hard work added, 'I would go so far as to say that Alf here and myself think this is one of our finest jobs.' He saw Alf nod his head in agreement.

The man hesitated before answering. 'How do you mean? Stolen? You mean your company stoops to stealing their material.' Both Alf and George laughed.

'No, not us, you sir. You haven't paid for the materials used, so technically that makes you the thief.'

The man stepped forward. George could see he had been shocked by the answer, but was surprised when the man made a fist and aimed at him. 'Why you, you scoundrels!' he bellowed as he missed George's grinning face.

'Call the police, please sir,' he begged as he danced away from the fist, 'then I can add another assault to our claim.' Alf had begun working again and George joined him. The man stood for a moment bewildered by what was happening, but the arrival of his wife calmed him a little, and after a few quiet words with her, George overheard the words 'neighbours think.'

He turned to George and asked, 'What is it you want?'

George jumped up quickly, smoothed down his clothes and took out a cigarette before answering. 'The Governor, Mr Matthews, would like full payment by lunchtime for the materials and work carried out on these premises, according to the contract you signed. If not, then he has no other alternative but to claim back at least the materials used.' The man looked with dismay at the bare sandy unkempt area where the landscaping had already been removed. George went on, 'Our lunch break ends around half past one and we shall be back then, when we shall either relay the stones or remove the rest. It's up to you, sir.'

Tutting and defeated the irate client turned to his wife and said, 'I have little choice my dear,' and she nodded in agreement, the relief apparent on her face. 'I'll be there by twelve,' he snarled at the men, 'but believe me, my friends and acquaintances will never do business with you.' George was tempted to say that we don't need their business if any of them are like yourself, but times being what they were, he said nothing.

CHAPTER EIGHTEEN

In the months before Lydia Ann's birth in September, as George had suspected, jobs got scarcer and scarcer. Cyril often sent him a good distance from the yard to seek out and close deals on work. This meant that George was often late home and if he hadn't collected his pay on Thursdays, Cyril took it upon himself to take it to Evelyn. Arriving home one evening, George was surprised to see that Evelyn had opened the wage packet. He was also surprised at how angry this made him feel. Before he had removed his coat or picked up his princess, he strode across the room to Evelyn and roughly grabbed her upper arms and shook her as he said, 'Don't ever do that again. You hear me? Leave my wage packet alone.'

Bewildered at first, Evelyn pulled herself free. 'What do you mean? Don't you trust me?'

It's not that. It's mine, addressed to me.'

'But, but...' stammered Evelyn, 'surely it's ours?' She hesitated before going on, 'and what's more George, having seen what you get, it's time you gave me a bit more housekeeping. How you expect me to manage on what you give me a week I don't know. There's another mouth to feed shortly and Belinda is growing fast out of her things. I...'

George was furious. 'It's none of your business what I earn. Earned my girl by grafting damn hard. In future, leave it alone. Understood.' He strode away from her and took off his coat, washed his hands ready for supper and pulled up his chair to the table. Without warning his dinner was slapped heavily down in front of him slopping the gravy over the side of the plate. He looked up and saw Evelyn's angry, white face.

'And how do you think this got cooked?' she asked indignantly. 'Oh, yes. I remember now. After I'd pushed that heavy pram up the hill, brought all of it home, to a clean home I might add and then cook it on just two gas rings. And...' she thrust out her bulging stomach, 'and carrying this lot as well.' She sat down heavily and burst into tears, then sniffed, 'Think you could do a day's work with this inside you George Carr? Think that isn't as hard as grafting?'

Picking up his knife and fork George took a mouthful of mashed potatoes before answering slowly, 'Aye, I see you've got a point,' then almost sheepishly he added, 'Just leave me packet alone in future and we'll say no more.'

'Yes we bloody well will,' she exclaimed. 'You've got to give me some extra money George. Besides the food, you expect me to find money for the rent and the gas, and,' he heard her take a deep breath, 'and I have to buy you twenty fags a day.' George went on stoically eating. 'And another thing, if you'd only eat some vegetables with your meal sometimes, that would help. Buying lamb chops or steak nearly every day runs away with the money.'

With his mouth full, he muttered, 'You're nagging woman. Shut up for a while will you so I can eat me dinner in peace.'

Evelyn brought Belinda to the table and sat her on her knee and began to spoon sieved vegetables moistened with gravy into the eager mouth. George watched and then mashing his potato with the meat juices he leaned across with a loaded fork and gently put it into the child's mouth. Smiling, he looked across to Evelyn who smiled back. Their love for the child had, for the moment, created an uneasy truce, but George knew it couldn't last.

Leaning back in his chair, he lit up a cigarette and sighing, he said, 'You know Eve, if you didn't spend it all as soon as you get the money, you could make it go through the week. But no, not you, straight out and it's all gone by Monday.' Wagging his cigarette in her direction, 'then you come on my earhole for more.'

'And what a performance that is! A great show of patting your pockets and going through your coats for a few shillings.' She took a breath, 'and as for spending it at the weekends, that's the time the rent has to be paid, that we need the gas fire on because you're home and moaning about the cold, a shilling at least there, George. Oh, and then there's your dinner, the works, as you put it, like your mam puts up. Well, I tell you now George, it can't be done, not any longer.'

They glared at each other for a few moments and then as she began to clear the table, he said, 'Tell you what we'll do then. I'll give you some more,' he hesitated, 'how about another half crown, that should do it.'

He was taken aback when she threw her arms around him saying, 'Oh, George. That would really make a difference and I'll really try to go the whole week.'

Settling her on his knee he said, 'Well, I've had an idea about that too. How about I give you half your money on Thursday evening and the other half say Monday mornings? What do you think? That way you won't be tempted to spend out on something special for me Saturday tea.'

There was no immediate answer, then looking into his face, 'You do trust me with money, don't you George. I mean I never go to your tin box under the bed and take some out, you know.'

He laughed, 'It would be a bit of a job woman! I keep the key with me in my pocket.' Immediately he could see she had begun to flare up again.

'There's more than one way of skinning a cat George, as my mother used to say. Believe me, if I got that desperate I'd get to that money.'

'Aye, aye, I dare say. So are we agreed with the new arrangements?'

'Yes, that ought to work out. We'll give it a try.'

After sorting out the first half of her money he reached into his pay packet and drew out a ten shilling note. As he folded it into her hand, he said, 'Tomorrow, see if you can buy whatever Belle needs, and if there's any left over, treat yourself.' He was rewarded with more hugs and kisses.

Thinking about it later, George realised that it was only the pleasure of opening the envelope that had made him react as he did and, he admitted, the pride he felt handing over the housekeeping. However, things should work out better now he reasoned.

Although George was never out of work, early in nineteen thirty-seven they still lived in the same rooms. George felt reluctant to move in case he lost his job and couldn't afford the higher rent of a bigger place. In any case, there were not many places to rent available. Also the new business of Cyril's had not yet picked up enough work to justify an increase in his wages. Cyril's brother had left for South Africa to start up on his own, but the savings made by this departure were quickly ploughed back into keeping the yard open. Last year Jessie had got married. There was no way they could attend the ceremony, but George did manage to send a ten shilling postal order to her, and told her to buy a gift of her own choosing.

There had been another addition to the family. A boy this time. They called him William, although from the day he was born, he was known as Billy. Neither George nor Evelyn were practising Christians, but they did have their children dedicated in church, a ceremony similar to a christening, but not so elaborate. George's view was that if there was a Heaven, then his kids should be allowed in, he wasn't going to spoil their chances.

Evelyn seemed to take a long time to get well after Billy's birth. Often when George got home, he found her too tired to lift and empty the zinc bath in which the children had been bathed before bed, or the meal only half started. Since the day they had married, she had been tired, but this was something different. Often he found her crying, not loud sobs, just silently weeping as she went almost mechanically about her work. There was no doubt in his mind that she was a good mother, his family were always clean with fresh clothes daily and were fed adequately. He did his best to help when he could, but what was beginning to cause him some disquiet, was that four-year old

Belle was fetching and carrying for her mother. The child didn't complain and he could see that Evelyn was struggling to manage, but he was concerned. Billy's birth had sapped her meagre energy and taken a toll on her health. Dismayed, he learned that she had severe gingivitis and they were told that her health would probably improve if all her teeth were removed.

On the morning of the day the visit to the dentist had been arranged, he kissed her goodbye, and went off to work as usual. When he returned that evening the rooms were in darkness and wondering where they were he went to the door to see if they were in the street. It was ten minutes later when he saw her, almost collapsing, as she struggled uphill with the basinet pram holding his three sleepy children. My God, he thought as he rushed towards her. When he reached her he supported her with his arm around her waist, and pushed the heavy pram with the other. Once inside, he left the children in the pram, undressed Evelyn, and put her to bed. She could hardly speak, and he was appalled to see her mouth swollen and caked with blood, when she whispered the children needed to be fed. What on earth can I give them that is quick he thought, and thankfully remembered his mother's solution for poorly children. Quickly he put on a pan of milk to warm then poured it over some bread and sprinkled it with sugar. The two girls ate it in a flash, and he carefully spooned some into Billy's mouth. Wiping their mouths he said, 'That will have to do for tonight,' undressed them and got them into bed. Gently he fed Evelyn with the milky slop blowing on it so that it was not too hot. Wiping her face with a cold flannel, he told her to go to sleep then added, 'I'm sorry pet. Love you,' and kissed her forehead as she closed her eyes. He resolved to help her more and, more than anything, be careful in their lovemaking.

It was just six weeks later that he learned that his children were showing the signs of rickets. Evelyn had taken Billy to the clinic for a check-up and the health visitor had told her that the children could be helped to avoid serious damage to their bones, and suggested that they should attend the clinic three times a week for ultraviolet treatment, a fairly new idea, to help strengthen their bones. Evelyn told George that the lamp had the same effect as the sun, and he felt both guilty and ashamed. Guilty because the sun never reached the gloomy back yard where the children played, and ashamed that he couldn't or hadn't done more for them. Both Evelyn and George were sick with worry but cheered up when Belle told him that they all wore goggles, had been undressed and allowed to play with some lovely toys on the mat. 'And mummy was smiling at us the whole time,' she told him.

It was mid summer when the business began to improve. Alf had retired, but had told George he could always ask him for advice, 'Although I don't think you will be over very often. You've done well these last couple of years.'

There was a large increase in house building all around London, and Cyril was determined to make a name for the Company. George listened as Cyril explained, 'The new houses are small and cheap George, to appeal to workers with low but regular incomes. These workers need a home as they're beginning to find work in the new factories and are prepared to make monthly repayments for at least twenty years, so you see man, we must get in on the act now.' George agreed to supervise the bricklayers and carpenter joiners on one lucrative site being developed some good distance away in the new suburbs.

'You're a fussy bloke George, so I know you'll not stand for any shoddy work, and you have my permission to sack anyone not up to scratch.'

George looked at the plans, about twenty semi-detached houses, set each side of one road. The surrounding area was given over to parks and other new building concerns which might come their way in the future. He nodded confidently. 'A bit of a way out and, yes, it'll be a challenge but right up my street.' They both laughed at the unintended pun.

'Means you'll be home later than usual, so if you like I'll take your wages round to your Mrs, save you coming back here for them,' Cyril offered.

'That'll help. Like Evelyn to have her housekeeping for the weekend.' George replied.

'Not bad, eh Eve?' George said, on the evening of his promotion, 'me just gone twenty-seven and in charge.' He didn't tell her that he had been given a rise, enough for the train fare and to put a little away for a rainy day.

There was little improvement in Evelyn's, health and the warmer weather seemed to drain her. With the extra shillings in his pocket, George decided to buy her a bottle of tonic wine to see if that would perk her up. If it did, then he could afford to buy her another bottle. That should do the trick he told himself. He placed the bottle before her.

'What's this George? You're not taking to the drink now? Full of yourself with your work aren't you?'

Winking at her he fetched a mug and poured a generous measure into it. 'No my love. This is a tonic wine. I bought it for you. Should make you feel a heap better if you take it every day for a few weeks.'

She eyed him suspiciously, lifted the mug and sniffed at it. 'It smells like strong drink to me. You trying to get me tipsy or something?'

'Just try it will you?' She looked at him again. 'Trust me will you? It will do you good.' Carefully she raised the mug to her mouth, sniffed it again, then took a small swallow. She sprayed George as she spat it out instantly.

George was amazed by her reaction and couldn't stop laughing. 'Your face,' he laughed, 'you should have seen your face. A picture if ever there was one.'

Rushing to the tap for some water then rinsing her mouth, she gasped, 'That was disgusting George. Worse than any medicine I've ever had.' She wiped her mouth then asked, 'Whatever made you get the stuff?'

He picked up the bottle, 'It says here that it will pick you up if you are suffering from tiredness or feeling generally unwell.' He read a little more. 'And it says it contains iron. That will give you muscles my girl, improve the spuggy kneecaps you've got at the moment.' He laughed at his own joke.

'What the devil are spuggies' kneecaps for Heaven's sake?'

'Up north anyone with flabby little muscles, is said to have spuggy kneecaps and spuggies are sparrows. Get it? You can't get smaller muscles than that.' While he was talking, he got a mug and poured a generous helping for himself. He sipped it first to test it, then took a good swallow. 'It's not so bad, Evelyn. I quite like it. A bit on the sweet side, but not unlike me auntie's Christmas sherry. Always brought her own bottle of sherry when she came for Christmas.' He took another mouthful before adding, 'Yes, just like that sherry. Me and Robert used to wait until she nodded off after dinner, then take a swig from the bottle.' He smiled to himself then went on, 'We got caught by our da one year, and he laughed and said serve you right, when we started giggling and feeling a bit sick. Had a bit too much that time I reckon.'

Evelyn lifted the bottle and exclaimed, 'It says the alcohol content is at least six percent George.'

He nodded as he took another mouthful, 'And no one will ever get drunk on that, I can guarantee.' He looked into his mug, 'Well I'm blessed. It's all gone,' and lifting the bottle, 'Sure you won't try to take some lass, it'll do you good you know.' Evelyn shook her head, he shrugged his shoulders and said, 'In that case, I'll have to drink it meself. Can't waste it.'

It was about half an later, Evelyn was mending and George leaned towards her, 'You know what girl, thish, this tonic ish very, very good.'

He saw her lift her head sharply, 'I do believe George that you are, well, how did my father say, yes, a bit tipsy.'

'Not, so there,' he said a little petulantly.

She laughed out loud, 'Yes you are. You are slurring your words. Jush like thish!' and laughed again.

'No, I'm not.' He paused then said, 'Tell you what though it makesh me...' he put his arms around her and kissed her softly on the lips. 'It makesh me...Can't think of the word for the moment.'

Still laughing she said, 'I think you're trying to say it makes you frisky.'

'Aye, that's it lass. Frishky. Sounds like fun to me.'

'So I'm expected to sleep with someone who's tipsy and frisky, right?' She smiled at him as she laid down her work, and loosened her hair. She tilted her head as she gazed into his eyes, then slowly lowered hers. George thought to himself that he wasn't too drunk to know she was flirting with him, and nodded when she moved closer to him and whispered, 'Time for bed?'

Early in nineteen thirty-nine George was working later and later, and further out in the countryside fast turning into suburbia, and was relieved that Cyril was able to get his wages to Evelyn. Calling at the Office one February Monday morning, George was surprised when

Cyril, after talking through the week's work schedule, turned to him and said, 'You know George, your Evelyn is unwell.'

'Aye, not as bonny as she could be but she'll be better when spring arrives.'

Cyril put out his hand and restrained George who was making for the door. 'No George, I mean seriously ill.' George felt himself getting angry and put his hands in his pockets, just in case. 'I know you'd like to tell me to mind my own business, but those children will be motherless by Christmas if you don't do something.'

'Like what?' George growled.

Cyril recognised the tone, and quietly said, 'Sit down will you and listen to what I have to say?'

George sat, leaned forward with his hands clasped between his knees. 'You think I'm not looking after her, that's it isn't it? Well, I tell you...'

'Now hang on a minute George, I never even thought that.' Pushing a packet of cigarettes towards him and taking one himself, Cyril went on, 'You're building all these houses George, and they are well constructed, but have you ever thought of buying one yourself?'

George spluttered. 'What makes you think I have that sort of money?' he asked. 'I've three kids remember?'

Married and childless Cyril smiled. 'And damned lucky you are.'

George recognising Cyril's disappointment, muttered, 'Sorry.'

'Well now,' Cyril said briskly, 'here's something for you to think about.' He stubbed out his cigarette, and continued. 'Go for one of those houses George. Somewhere out in the countryside. I've made a few enquiries and it seems you can have a good loan at two percent for twenty years, pay a few shillings a week. I bet it won't be much more than you already pay out for your lodgings now.'

'Aye, but there's the deposit to think of. I've a few pound saved up but they're asking ten percent.'

'No George, builders are so keen to sell that they'll take five percent.' George took a few minutes to think things over and he saw Cyril watching him.

'I could help you out there. What if I give you a loan and you can pay me back out of your wages? It'll be easy if I give you a rise. Go away and think about it. Talk it over with Evelyn. Let me know by the end of the week and if your answer's yes, we'll set the wheels in motion.'

The journey home that evening had been difficult. A cloudburst had all the streets awash with storm water, and like most of the people around him, he took off his shoes and rolled up his trouser legs. Turning into his road, he saw his two daughters on the raised doorstep looking out for him. He waved, and began deliberately kicking the water to make splashes over the laughing girls. This wasn't the first time they had nearly been flooded out, another good reason to think about moving, he thought. On entering the kitchen he could tell that again Evelyn had been crying.

Sighing deeply he said, 'What is it pet? What's made you cry today? Can I put it right for you?'

'I sorted it out myself, George. Something happened at school today.' Belle had started school last summer. Both of them had been wary of her going there as the children were from all sorts of backgrounds, and some, although only four or five, were uncared for, aggressive, and in their eyes, common. 'It seems,' Evelyn went on, 'that the teachers had a meeting today, all sitting on the stage and the children sitting on the hall floor and told to keep quiet. Belle told me this. Anyway, it seems one of the teachers heard a dirty word from a child and she thought it was our Belle.'

'Our Belle you say? If I thought that for one moment, I'd smack her meself. Never, not our Belle.'

'That's what I told the teacher. When Belle came out she was so upset. I didn't know what was wrong until she said that Miss Fletcher had taken her to the cloakroom and told her she was a wicked little girl, and she was going to wash her mouth out. Belle said she had the soap in her hand and told her to open her mouth.'

George was aghast, 'I'll be there tomorrow just you watch my girl. I'll give her bloody soap.'

'No need George, I've spoken to her. Anyway, seems our Belle answered back and refused to open her mouth. What she was most upset about, was that Miss didn't believe her. By that time it was home time, and Miss Fletcher brought Belle to me, complaining about bad language.'

'And?'

'Bad language, I said, I'll give you bad language. No one in my house uses bad or dirty words, we have no need for them.' Evelyn sighed, 'I said a lot more and in the end she believed me and Belle and apologised. So end of story, but I'm afraid Belle might get picked on now.'

'We can sort that out if it happens and in any case it won't be for long because now I have something to tell you.'

When he had finished telling her what Cyril and he had in mind, he could see she was excited by the plan, her face lit up as she said over and over again, 'Oh George, oh George. We'll make it work. I'll manage on less if you like.'

'No need. Going to get a rise, aren't I?'

On the tenth of May, Mr and Mrs George Carr and their three children moved into a newly built home in Ruislip. It was in a crescent with a large garden and far from any pubs or theatres, although there was a new picture house a mile or so away, and Northolt race course, which, George promised himself, he would go to one Saturday afternoon.

Their neighbours were tradesmen from all parts of the country who had left their family ties to become house owners. George and Evelyn were proud of their new home. Evelyn made curtains and bought new linen, George laid linoleum in the two downstairs rooms, the two bedrooms and down the staircase. A Working Man's dwelling it declared on the house deeds. There was a tiled grate with a back boiler for hot water, hot water alone was worth every penny of the mortgage Evelyn declared. The beds, large kitchen table and chairs were second-hand and well scrubbed before Evelyn was satisfied. George had a new interest, gardening. It took some months before he was satisfied with the end result of his labours. Using stone purchased cheaply from one of the company's suppliers, a kidney shaped rose garden was built close to the back windows where Evelyn was able to see it. There was a lawn, complete with a swing, for the children to play, and at the top end of the garden he grew vegetables and soft fruit. Beyond was a field and a gate was installed so that the children could run freely into the field which was rich with wild flowers. Later, he added a shed where he built a treadle lathe, and most Sundays he would turn wood to make standard and table lamps to sell.

Evelyn did not make friends easily and was often a little envious of the neighbours. She was convinced they did not like her. It dismayed her to see their habit of allowing their children to scrape out the porridge saucepan in the garden, as if they had no plates. When Belle, Lydia and Billy had new clothes, she would wait until Sunday, dress them up and send them down the garden to the shed for their father to admire them. 'Go on,' she said to the children, 'just show that Ethel Franklin next door.' George understood her ploy, this way he realised, Evelyn was showing the neighbours that the Carrs were not so poor.

Evelyn and George were more than happy. Early every morning on his way to work across the field, George would give a long whistle to Evelyn when he reached the other side and she would whistle back. It was like a code to each other, saying I love you.

One morning George's whistle was repeated and repeated, but not in the evening. This happened every morning and as Evelyn was clearing the table one evening after their meal, she said, 'George, why don't you go straight to the station instead of whistling again and again to see if I answer?'

'I don't. If I don't get that workman's ticket before seven, I have to pay almost double. I'm straight off I can tell you.'

'In that case, someone is whistling just like you.'

'Aye, someone fooling about maybe. Hiding I should think to see how we react. Well take no notice. I'll just whistle once and you whistle back. They'll soon get fed up if we take no notice.' It was roughly four weeks later that Evelyn saw a cheeky blackbird on the back gate, and as George whistled, the bird mimicked him. George couldn't believe it and on the Saturday, not a working day, he was able to see and hear the bird for himself.

'You cheeky little blighter,' George said, 'trying to steal my missus. Go find your own,' but truth to tell they both grew a little fond of the bird.

News from Hannah always added to George's contentment. Every two or three weeks he had a letter from his mother full of family gossip, mostly of his brothers and sisters. This particular letter pleased him greatly. She had written that the gang da was working with, were allowing him to take his own time to get to the coalface.

It usually took him about ten minutes longer than the rest, and then, just before the shift ended they sent him off ten minutes early, so that when the rest of the gang caught up with him, they could all ascend together, fooling the management that da had worked a full shift. George was relieved that his father was able to go on working, and chuckled as he read the letter, he was all for pulling the wool over management eyes.

Eventually George was able to buy a second-hand wireless for himself. It was a large wooden box, the type that held an accumulator battery. This was placed high on top of a cupboard so that the children couldn't reach it. Every other Saturday after work, he would go to the local garage to have the heavy accumulator recharged. There was no doubting his love of music and he danced Evelyn around the kitchen to the modern tunes until, at last, she mastered some of the simple steps of the foxtrot and waltz. Everything was just fantastic in their lives until…

One Sunday morning, George wanted to work in his shed, and hear the music at the same time. Without thinking he turned the wireless volume up to its loudest. Twenty minutes later, lost in his work while he listened, he couldn't understand when suddenly the music stopped. Thinking Evelyn might have turned it off, he strode crossly back to the house. As he stood in the doorway he couldn't believe his eyes. Evelyn was in tears, standing on a chair with a poker in her hand and his precious wireless smashed to pieces. At once he could tell she was really scared of his reaction, but keeping his eyes still on the shattered bits and pieces, he said, 'Get down before you fall down.'

'George,' she whispered, 'George the noise was unbearable. I couldn't stand it a minute longer. I called to you but you didn't answer so…so.'

Helping her down he said softly, 'Sorry lass. I didn't think.' The wide eyed children stood silent and he turned to them and said, 'Well that's the end of dancing for a while eh? You'll just have to sing so's your mammy and daddy can have a dance.' They nodded then smiled. George really didn't know how he kept his temper, but knew he never wanted to see fear of him on Evelyn's face again.

The girls had been enrolled at the local school, and every evening George would stand them in turn on a kitchen chair and ask them what they had learnt in school 'today'. Both would quote times tables, or a story read, or rules of writing. Belle was always first and one evening when she had finished, Lydia stood solemnly on the chair.

'Did you learn anything special today pet?' George asked her.

'Yes daddy.' She stood there for a while fidgeting from foot to foot.

'Well are you going to tell us or not,' Evelyn said sharply.

George frowned at her, then Lydia her blue eyes saucer wide, said, 'Promise you won't smack me if I tell you?'

'Eh lass, is it that bad?' There was a slow nod from the child.

'I don't think it could be too bad. Just tell us what happened and I promise I...' he looked at Evelyn, who nodded back to him, 'and mammy won't smack you. Alright?'

Swinging her little body from side to side, Lydia gave a sigh before she began. 'I learned a new word today. Paul said it first,' she said hurriedly.

'And what was that?'

'Paul said...' she hesitated, 'you promised.' The parents smiled at each other both wondering what was to come.

'We promise,' said Evelyn.

'Well, Paul said, he said...BUM.'

George tried hard not to laugh and half choking lifted Lydia down and gave her a cuddle. 'And what did Mrs Thomas say to that, pet?'

Lydia, looked from one to the other. 'Mrs Thomas smacked him, very hard, on the legs and said it was a naughty word.'

George put on a serious face, 'It is a bit rude I suppose but there are lots more ruder words in the world. Anyways, off to bed now lass.'

When finally the children were in bed, Evelyn and George, bandied the word between them, popping the word into any conversation they were having and laughing themselves silly. 'I'll have to write to mam and tell her that tale,' George said. 'You did read her last letter didn't you? Great news for Robert, don't you think? A steward on the Mauritania the newest liner to New York'

'I did that and I thought he could make some good tips as it's only the nobs that can afford to cruise on luxury liners like that.'

'Aye maybe you're right. A few extra bob is always useful to a young lad. Good luck to him I say.'

'I do feel a bit sorry for your mother though.'

With mock surprise, George said, 'What, you going soft on me mam? What's the world coming too?'

Evelyn gave him a gentle push, 'Oh, you George. You know what I mean. Your sister Emily. How would we feel if Belle or Lydia never, ever wrote or came to see us? I couldn't bear that. I just couldn't.'

George sniffed full of despise for his sister, 'I reckon she's a selfish cow, hurting mam and da like that and never a word of thanks for taking on the wee bairn. Not that they mind like, love the little lass to bits according to the letters.'

One Thursday evening returning from work, George, tired and cold noticed as he kissed Evelyn his wages packet, unopened as usual, on the table. As he looked, a dreadful feeling came over him. Cyril had called. It was a standing arrangement, he knew that, he had agreed to the arrangement, but tonight there was a feeling of uncertainty and sadness, as if he'd lost something. While he was eating his dinner he brooded over his feelings, He began to feel cheated, betrayed although he knew it could not be so. Evelyn and Cyril! He imagined them laughing together, her sitting on his knee like she did some evenings with him. Did she stroke his hair, kiss him? Oh God, he thought, does she kiss him like she kisses me? As if mocking him a voice in his head reminded him that Cyril was over concerned about her health last year. Roughly he pushed his half eaten dinner away, and hoping his voice didn't betray him asked, 'How long was Cyril here today?'

'What do you mean? How long? Long enough to leave your wages, and have a drink.'

'A drink? What sort of drink?'

'Just a cup of tea.'

'You mean he came into the house?'

'Well, of course he came into the house. Couldn't leave him on the doorstep while the kettle boiled could I?'

A fear came over him. Cyril in the house. No one could see them together. What did they get up to? 'And?' he asked.

'And what George? What are you going on about?'

'When he came in, what did he do?'

'Do? Do? He sat on a chair and waited. Told me about some gypsy coming to the yard, and trying to sell ex-lax to one of the apprentices, told him it was chocolate.'

George saw her smile as she remembered. 'He's quite nice when he laughs. Always so much of a gentleman, raises his hat and says Good afternoon or evening or...' she stopped when she saw George's white face.

'When, if he comes again, you leave him on the doorstep, do you hear me woman?'

Billy started crying and as she picked him up she said wearily, 'What are you on about George? He's your good friend. We, I won't be that rude to him.'

Reaching for the comfort of a cigarette, he said, 'You heard me Eve. I don't want him near you. Oh he's charming enough, plenty of money. I'll never be able to match what he could give you, a labourer, that's all I am.' He was quiet for a moment, remembering his failed ambitions to be a journalist or bandleader, then said, 'But you're my wife. Let him try his luck somewhere else.' He looked at Billy in her arms, and he choked on his suspicions. Surely not, the child must be his. Got the Carr golden curls, and grey eyes. He did his best to convince himself he was the father, and yet? 'When did he first start coming into the house Eve. Tell me that.'

'For God's sake George, whatever is the matter with you?'

'When woman, I'm asking you? When?'

She shrugged. 'I can't remember. A good while ago.'

'Before or after Billy was born?'

'Well, only once or twice when we were in the rooms, but...George Carr! I do believe...No, I can't believe that, that you think...' She burst into tears and ran from the room.

Of course she would deny, it an angry voice taunted him in his head. That's why she couldn't face him – guilty of adultery. Betrayed by the two of them, one he loved more than life itself. In his anger he swiped the dishes off the table, grabbed his cap and slammed the door as he went out. For hours he walked the streets, turning over and over in his mind what might have been said between them. Gradually, he calmed down until at last he realised that he'd experienced a really bad fit of jealousy. As he turned towards his home he felt desolate, by his own suspicious mind, he may well have lost the love of his life, his Evelyn. Loneliness overwhelmed him and he gave way to tears as he wondered if she would ever forgive him. As he climbed into bed later beside her and said 'Sorry pet.' He knew, as she turned her back on him and her silence that it would be a long time before she would forgive him or before he could forgive himself.

Never wanting to experience such overwhelming doubts again, he decided to tell Cyril that in future there was no need for him to put himself out to deliver his wages.

Before he could say anything, Cyril called him into the office, 'Saw your wife yesterday George. My word the move has done her good. She's looking so bonnie now, don't you think?'

Not stopping to think, George's temper flared immediately. 'I'll thank you to not visit my wife again Cyril. I'll collect me wages meself no matter how late. I don't want you calling again. Not ever. Understand?'

'Good grief man. What's got into you?'

'You and…and my wife,' George hesitated. 'I don't like her being alone with you. In any case, neighbours will be talking, you visiting so regularly. Just stay away.'

Cyril stood up. 'If we weren't friends George Carr, I'd punch you. You've a good woman there. She's always talking of you. You do her an injustice.' They glared at each other. 'In fact George, if she was anybody else's wife I might…' George saw red and swung his fist into Cyril's face and although he dodged away the fist found his nose.

George made for the door, and called over his shoulder, 'I'll not be back.' Fortunately, the reputation of his working skills was well known in the local building trade and he was able to walk into a job before going home. Evelyn shrugged at his news, and not caring one jot, plonked his meal before him.

The cool atmosphere between them continued for several weeks. They spoke civilly to each other in front of the children, even made love, albeit unsatisfactory. Evelyn had never really got on with the neighbours, and it was on a Friday, the wedding day of the eldest daughter next door when everything came to a head. It was almost one in the morning, and George and Evelyn were unable to sleep. Like their own staircase, next doors was also covered in lino, and, as they lay in bed, they could hear the bride, running up and down the stairs, shrieking with laughter as she tried to dodge her new husband. Not once, but many times, George groaned at the noise, then finally punching his pillow said, 'Something has got to be done about that bloody woman,' but he did nothing. Eve got out of bed and put on her dressing gown. Thankfully, the noise stopped suddenly, and he fell asleep, unaware when Evelyn crept back into bed. Someone hammering on the front door the following morning just before six woke him with a start. Almost staggering down the stairs he shouted out, 'I'm coming, hold on will you?' He opened the door and was surprised to find two police officers.

'Mr Carr?' one enquired. 'Husband of Evelyn Carr?' Bewildered, George rubbed the stubble on his chin as he nodded. What the hell he thought?

'Is your wife inside?'

Only half awake, George hardly grasped what the officer said. 'My wife? What in God's name is going on?'

'She's to appear at Willesden court this morning on a charge of assault,' one of the officers replied.

George was astonished. 'Assault, what do you mean assault?'

'If you could both be at court by eleven this morning, sir.'

'But who? When?' he asked.

'Your neighbour reported an incident last night.'

Last night. All that racket. He began to explain, 'But...' then decided to hold his tongue, as one of the officers licked the end of his pencil ready to write down anything George might say. Resigned, he said, 'Eleven o'clock you say?'

'Yes sir. The magistrate is well known for his leniency, so with luck she'll avoid a spell in prison. We'll be off now sir.' Oh God, oh God, he thought. Evelyn shrugged her shoulders when he told her to get ready for court.

'What in God's name have you been up to woman?' he demanded.

And she muttered, 'Perhaps I'll get some peace now.'

'That's no answer. What's been going on?'

As she slipped her dress over her head, she snapped, 'You. You moaning and groaning all night about the noise next door. Tossing and turning.' Struggling with the buttons at the back of her dress she turned to him for help. 'So I thought, if I want any rest at all, I'd better put a stop to her shenanigans.'

'Well whatever you did, has landed you in court my girl,' he waited for her to go on. 'And?'

'I went round there. I asked very nicely if they could be a bit quieter, I told them you had to go to work in the morning and the three kids needed their sleep.' George watched her chew her lip for a moment before she went on, 'But they took no notice. She ran up the stairs again, so I followed her. All I wanted to do was to make her listen so I grabbed her and...'

'What? And what...?' George held his breath afraid of what was coming next.

'I think I must have poked her, gave a little nudge or something and,' she took a deep breath, 'and she took a tumble down the stairs.' Then as an afterthought, added sullenly, 'She deserved it.'

'By heck, you can be so spiteful. Just watch what you're saying woman. Say something like that to the magistrates and you'll find yourself inside Holloway.' George went across to Evelyn and put his arm around her, and for once she didn't push him away. 'Eh, our Eve, you're always getting into a spot of bother. I tell you what though, some bugger was mighty quick to get to the phone box to call up the police.' He sighed, 'If only they had waited, we might have been able to smooth things over this morning.'

George rushed round to a neighbour Evelyn sometimes talked to, and asked her to look after the children, not telling her why they had to be left at home.

It was as the police officer had said. The magistrate had indeed been lenient. After the initial proceedings, he had fixed his eyes on Evelyn and said, 'Mrs Carr the charge of assault is very serious. What you did to that young bride by pushing her down the stairs is assault. I have it in my power to send you to prison for fourteen days. As you are a mother of three young children this would make life very difficult for them and your husband, and...' he looked sternly at her, 'prison is not a place you would enjoy.' She stood still in front of him, saying nothing, and looking at her George knew she had acted on the spur of the moment. Again his temper had caused trouble.

The magistrate wrote on a sheet of paper before him, tapped the desk a few times with his pen. 'Therefore,' he went on, 'given that you were provoked and denied sleep, I intend to fine you in the sum of ten shillings.' George had mixed feelings, she'd been spared gaol, but ten shillings, then gasped as the magistrate added, 'and ten shillings costs. You have a week to pay.' Well, thought George, that'll make a hole in the savings, but better than my wife in prison. On the train home they held hands, the coolness between them over at last.

CHAPTER NINETEEN

The promised trip to the racecourse was made just before the Second World War broke out. With Belle on his shoulders, he walked the three miles as there was no public transport. At once, he was engulfed in the exciting atmosphere created by working men like himself, and the gentry. Somehow, it reminded him of the easy going camaraderie of Petticoat Lane he'd visited years ago. Most of the men were placing modest bets on the races, and George, fascinated by the waving antics of the tic tac men, gave into temptation and placed his own. Belle, still on his shoulders was treated to a lollipop and a colourful balloon, bounced up and down on his shoulders with excitement. He watched his chosen pony, its head pulled up, and with the regulation high stepping trot, pulled the sulky, its large wheels supporting the light frame. The jockey seated within the frame, was leaning forward, his cap askew and flourishing his long whip over the animal's back. Ruefully, George saw it finish fourth. All too soon, the afternoon ended, worth every penny he told himself, and smiled as he remembered his lost bet. Although he didn't know it at the time, it was the last meeting ever to be held there.

By the end of nineteen forty-one, George was seconded to a local factory designated to build spitfires. The place was within walking distance of home, and was also too close to Northolt Aerodrome a prime target for enemy planes. Besides working long hours during the day, George, along with his neighbours, was on fire watching duties during the nights there were air raids. Every evening the children were put to bed and, later every evening when the siren warned of an imminent raid, brought downstairs again. George rigged up bedding under the large, sturdy well scrubbed kitchen table, on top of which he placed a billiards table, payment for one of his earlier weekend jobs. Knowing he had done his best for his family, he joined the men and women in the field at the back of the house, where sometimes passing troops camped overnight and where his children played. The field was often lit up during raids by incendiary devices dropped by the enemy seeking out the air field. Although exhausted in the early years of the war by these almost nightly events, George found himself somehow exhilarated and felt he was doing his bit. What he enjoyed most, was when he was scheduled to be on fire watching duty at the factory. A great deal of the time was spent on the roof when the siren sounded, but until then, he along with others, loitered in the canteen. It was here that there was some fun to be had. Refreshments were served by lonesome women whose husbands were away in the army, and it wasn't long before someone brought in a wind-up gramophone. Others contributed records and the few men available were besieged by the women to dance with them. It was a long time since George had been dancing outside his family, but he was more than happy to realise that he hadn't lost his natural ability. For a while George kept quiet about his nights of dancing as he knew Evelyn would be jealous and imagining all sorts of carrying-ons. Not that there wasn't the opportunity, by heck, he thought, if I were single I'd think it was me birthday every day but he resisted the overt offers, he loved Evelyn and his kids too much to risk any hanky-panky.

George learned that Robert had joined the Royal Navy, and was once again concerned for his younger brother's safety. He'd heard the North Sea run was the most dangerous with ships and personnel being lost, and hoped Robert's ship was elsewhere, but he knew at sea no one was really safe.

One winter Saturday afternoon he took himself across the field to the local town just over a mile away in order to recharge the cumbersome wireless wet battery. Returning home across the field, the air raid siren sounded a warning. Evelyn was at the gate looking for him, when suddenly out of the clouds an enemy plane came low, all the while firing its machine guns. George threw himself on the ground. It was all over in a matter of seconds, now all he could hear was the receding engine of the plane, and Evelyn screaming his name over and over again. Gingerly he stood up, felt himself to be in good order, dusted himself down and looked towards Evelyn. Waving he began to run towards her to re-assure her he was alright, and watched astonished, as she fainted and slumped to the ground. That night in bed they clung fiercely to each other.

Walking with an Air Raid Warden towards the factory the next evening, George told him about being targeted by the crew of a German aircraft. The warden, laughed making George feel foolish and a little ashamed of his fear. 'I tell you, I was that bloody scared,' he said, 'it just came out of nowhere, aiming straight at me.'

The warden paused in his walk and pointed at a chink of light showing in one of the houses they were passing. With a hint of self importance he yelled, 'Put that light out!' and they waited until it was extinguished. 'Now then lad, a light like that invites trouble don't it?'

George nodded and checked his torch beam was directed onto the pavement. 'The bullets, there must have been fifty or so at least, all aimed at me. Thought my time was up for sure. But what I can't understand is why me for God's sake?'

The warden laughed again. 'You daft sod. What makes you think he was after you?'

George, bewildered by his off-hand reply said, 'Well, you'll know if it ever happens to you.'

'I dare say, but you know lad, when one of them gets lost, they have to come out of the clouds to see if there's anything to give 'em a clue to their whereabouts, and when they do that, they just keep firing in case, you know, just in case one of our blokes is waiting for them.'

George wasn't entirely convinced, 'I tell you, he was firing straight at me. My wife was yelling blue murder at the time, she'll tell you.'

'And I tell you, he probably didn't see you at all.'

'I'm a damn sight bigger than that chink of light we just passed so, if as you say he didn't see me, how come he could see that?'

The warden cleared his throat, 'Just doing what I'm told, what everyone's told mate.' They walked on in silence for a moment or two, then the warden added thoughtfully, 'you know what, that Jerry wasn't so lost was he? I mean so close to the airfield, that's what he was after, and by golly he must have just missed it. Anyway, you had a narrow escape lad. Thank your lucky stars for that.'

They parted at the gate of the factory, and as George made his way to the canteen, he remembered the passionate moments in bed the night before. The night that eventually led to the birth of their fourth child.

George knew he'd made a mistake, and thinking about it he realised he'd actually made two. God, that was a mistake of the highest order, but both he and Evelyn were resigned to adding to their family until Thursday that is. Sighing, he recalled his second mistake. It was his night for fire watching duties and he hoped that he would not be called on to help as a dance band had been hired for the factory workers. He hadn't told Evelyn about this, knowing full well she still held that dancing was likely to lead to trouble. Instead, he had washed his face and slicked his hair all the while Evelyn watching him.

'Well, you're making a fuss of yourself to go to work in the dark George,' she smiled as she spoke.

'Aye, I might meet the fairy Queen,' and the children laughed. It was as he was leaving that he made the fatal mistake. Casting his eye around the kitchen to make sure everything was as safe as he could make it, he kissed Belle, Lydia and Evelyn goodnight then, hoping Evelyn busy knitting for the new baby wouldn't notice, as casually he tucked his dancing shoes inside his coat. They were still supple and after a dusting were as good as new in his eyes.

'What on earth are you taking those old things with you for?' she said as she looked up from her work. 'I hope you're selling them. A few bob would come in handy right now.' George felt himself redden as guilt overwhelmed him as she looked at him. To himself he said, now for it, and he was not mistaken.

Putting her knitting down, she demanded, 'Something's on isn't it? Something you're not telling me, George. I'm right aren't I?' The girls stopped their play then they looked from one parent to the other. Like himself he thought, they knew when one of Evelyn's temper storms was about to erupt.

Turning back from the door, he said, 'Now Eve, pet. Don't get yourself all lathered up. It's nothing for you to worry about. Just that the managers have asked a few lads to play some music and I thought...' he hesitated, 'I thought that there might be a bit of dancing like.'

Her reaction was immediate. 'Dancing?' she exploded. 'Dancing. You dare to tell me you're fire watching, leaving me here with the kids, sick with worry if you'll be coming home, and and…' She burst into angry tears, 'and all the time you're off to have a good time,' she finished by screaming at him, 'dancing.'

Two childish voices wailed, 'Mummy. Daddy.'

'Get yourselves off to bed. Don't want you to hear about your father's philandering. Get out of my sight now,' she yelled at them. George watched as his two daughters holding hands and in tears started to leave the room.

At the door Belle turned to him, 'Daddy? Philan…?'

'Don't you worry pet. Everything will be better in the morning. Now you just take Lydia off to bed, there's a good girl.' He watched them go then turned to Evelyn, 'There's no need to take it out on the girls, like that.'

'No indeed,' she snapped back.

George was always surprised at how strong her Welsh accent came through when she was in a temper. Funny that, because he hadn't noticed it in their everyday talk. Lighting up a cigarette, 'You don't really mind do you, love? It's a bit of fun for all the workers once in a while.'

'So, there is a dance then. Not a maybe one but one definitely arranged.' She paused then said, 'And I suppose wives or husbands were invited?'

'Aye, you're right. They are, but I thought you wouldn't be fussed seeing as, well, you're expecting.'

Evelyn was dangerously quiet for a moment or two, then she jumped up, snatched the shoes from inside his jacket, threw them across the room and began pummelling him. 'You bastard,' she raged, 'you did it on purpose. Made bloody sure I had to stay home so you could go out and dance with every smitten tart you work with.' George tried to ward her off and wondered where she got the energy to keep up her attack. 'And I bet there's other fun and games afterwards.' Slowly the blows got lighter but with each one she shrilled, 'Isn't there? Isn't there?' Exhausted she reached for a chair and buried her face in her hands.

He drew on his cigarette and sighed before answering, 'Evelyn, you know that's not true. You are my only love, you should know that by now.'

'Clear off, George, just leave me.' Then as an afterthought, 'For good if you like. I've had enough.'

For a moment George stood watching her. Dance or no dance, he had to present himself for fire watching duties. 'I've got to go. You can believe what you like, but I am fire watching tonight. I'll see you in the morning, and I only hope to God that we all survive the night, and you'll be in a better mood.' He picked up the shoes and before opening the door quietly added, 'Just learn to trust me for once will you?'

As it happened, there was no dancing that night. It seemed that the German's were intent on attacking the airfield, and although the field received a few bombs, the majority fell in the surrounding area. Houses and roads were so badly damaged that George, and the others were busy all night long. Frantically, they clawed at the fallen debris, pulling out frightened children crying for their mothers, and old folk. Thankfully, all were alive but George could see there were some very serious injuries. People milling all around bewildered by the events. Some were calling for their loved ones and others swearing everlasting revenge on the destructive night visitors, in the best bad language George had ever heard. Half hearted cheers went up every time the gun stationed nearby and nicknamed Big Bertha fired, even though the noise was almost deafening. A smell of gas put everyone on their guard after someone called out, 'No smoking', as if we had time thought George. There were holes in the road to be filled and rubble to be cleared before the services, ambulance and fire engine crews could get near the devastated area. As he worked, there were more bombs being dropped. He listened to the eerie whistle of their descent, then the crump as they hit the ground, followed immediately by the petrifying explosion. He felt desperate, longing to know if his family was safe and every time he heard the bombs exploding nearby, he was filled with dread, but knew he couldn't leave.

At last the all clear sounded, the services had taken over the jobs, and George was free to go home. It was still dark, and his heart was full of dread as he turned the corner of his own street. He could have wept with joy to see that every house in the small crescent was standing, although on a closer look a house a few doors from his own seemed to have a gaping hole in the roof. Quietly, he let himself in and put the kettle on for a cup of tea.

All through the long night the women had been plying the rescuers with tea and sandwiches, but like everyone else, he'd put the drinks aside with thanks, and forgot about them. Pouring out a cup for Evelyn, he made his way to the bedroom to be greeted grumpily with, 'You decided to come back then?' as she sleepily sat up to take the cup from him. He heard her gasp before she said, 'George, your hands. What have you been doing?'

George looked down at his hands. He had not felt anything was wrong but now he could see that every knuckle was scraped, his palms were criss-crossed with surface and deeper cuts, and were caked white with a crust of dried cement dust. 'And your face George, covered in brick dust and black in places with soot.'

Astonished, he watched as she got out of bed, 'Get in,' she ordered as she went downstairs, and quickly returned with a bowl of warm water. 'Here we are,' she exclaimed cheerfully, 'put your hands in there. Yes, I know it stings a bit, but we need to get those cuts cleaned out. Good boy,' she said when he winced as he slowly put his hands in the water. Again she surprised him by getting a clean flannel and gently washing his face. 'There my love. A bit better?' Gently she patted his hands dry then slathered them in Vaseline. 'Go to sleep cariadon.' Then brushing his forehead with her lips she added softly, 'I love you George Carr.' George felt hot tears under his eyelids. They might fight like cats and dogs he thought, but by God we do love each other.

Wearily he went over the night's events in his mind. The only time he remembered sitting down, was when he sat on a piece of masonry to cuddle a wee girl, no older than his Lydia, crying for her mother, trying to reassure the child that she'd turn up soon. As he drifted off to sleep he recalled another picture of the night, a woman, no older than Evelyn, in her nightdress sitting on a garden wall, her head in her hands and silently weeping. It could have been my Evelyn, he thought, there but for the grace of God. With a bit of luck he knew he could have a couple of hours sleep before going to work, a seven o'clock start, but he told himself he'd rather lose an hour's pay and sleep on a bit.

It was nearly eight o'clock when he made his way to the kitchen. The children, bright as buttons, were enjoying their breakfast of porridge. 'My, that smells good,' he said.

'I'll get you a bowl right now,' said Evelyn, then added, as she poured a generous helping of syrup over it, 'Now you eat that while I fry you some bread and an egg.'

Tapping her bottom lightly, he asked, 'We back on track then, kid?'

Brushing his hand away, she whispered, 'Not in front of the girls, George, please,' and as she looked at his expectant face, smiled, 'yes, we're back on track.' They examined his hands and agreed that, in the main, the cuts were not as bad as expected now they had been cleaned. He was whistling as he left cheerfully for work.

On his way to the factory he noticed that despite the gaps where houses had fallen and the resulting piles of debris, nearly everything seemed normal and everyone getting on with their lives. Returning home that evening, there was a shock in store for him. Always, his dinner was put up on a plate ready for him. On entering his home this time, he was surprised to see Evelyn just beginning to peel potatoes and left handed Belle setting the table, and Lydia with her podgy arms swilling cabbage leaves. 'Something amiss, Evie?' he asked mildly as he gave her his customary kiss on the cheek.

Red in the face and flustered she said, 'Oh George. We...'

The girls interrupted excitedly,

'We went to the park,'

'We had a picnic.'

'There was a bomb.'

George looked at their flushed faces, both bursting to tell him about their day. As he heard the word bomb his heart turned over. 'Evelyn? What's been happening? Come and sit down a minute. That can wait.'

Sighing, she sat at the table and said, 'Oh George, what a day. I'm that tired.'

'I can see that. I'll give you a hand in a moment, but tell me what's been going on.'

Belle and Lydia both spoke at once, 'We...'

George put his finger to his lips to quieten them. 'Wait a minute girls. Let mummy tell me first then you can tell me about your day.

All right?' Together they nodded. 'Right now mother, what have you all been up to?'

'Well George, it couldn't have been more than ten minutes after you left this morning, when there was a knock at the door. I had the fright of my life, I can tell you.'

George leaned towards her, 'Who the hell was it? I mean it was only about twenty past eight. Was it the post?'

'No, no. Let me finish. It was a couple of army blokes all very serious and they said that I had to leave the house immediately.'

'Good God. Whatever for?'

'I told them straight. I couldn't. I had the girls to get off to school, and a baby still asleep, but they wouldn't listen. They insisted that I had just ten minutes to collect whatever I would need and leave.'

George frowned. 'Did they say why? It must have been something serious.'

'Oh it was serious alright.' She paused for a moment, 'You won't believe me George, but you know Mrs Putman, two doors down?' He nodded. 'It seems there was an unexploded bomb in her bath! Can you believe that?' A serious look exchanged between them that seemed to say, we've had another narrow escape but let's not frighten the children.

'Good God,' he exclaimed. 'So that's why there was a hole in her roof. Saw it when I came home last night. Thought a few tiles had slipped or something like that.'

'So we couldn't come home 'til half past five and that's why I'm rushing around now.'

'No need lass. As long as we're all together I can wait.' He turned to Belle, 'So, that's where you went, to the park instead of school.'

Nodding her head she told him, 'And we had chips for our lunch, and lots of people were there.'

George winked at Evelyn before seriously saying to the girl, 'I wonder what your teacher is going to say, missing school for the day.'

Lydia began to cry when Belle said, 'We'll probably get the slipper.'

'You what?' George couldn't believe his ears. 'The slipper? I'll be up that school meself on Monday. The slipper indeed. Don't you fret about it. I'll sort her out.'

Evelyn laughed quietly, 'The school was told George. There'll be no slipper.'

'Aye, not ever, not on my kids. Damn cheek of them.' He picked up Billy for a cuddle, and asked, 'Well then girls, let's get on with me dinner.'

Their second son, Francis, named after one of Evelyn's uncles, was born at home in October nineteen forty-two. Again the pregnancy and birth took its toll on Evelyn's health. Confined to bed for two weeks Mrs Morris, a council helper, had been brought in to run the home. After a few days, Evelyn suspected that the woman was not being honest when she asked for a little butter for her bread.

'I tell you George, that woman is not to be trusted,' she said. 'I'm sure she's helping herself.'

'She's gone by the time I get in. Everything's ready, the table laid, the dinner on, the kids washed and ready for bed. We're lucky to have her.'

Evelyn huffed, 'We'll see. Just you wait.'

Reaching home the next day, George was amazed to see Evelyn dressed and working at the stove. 'What the hell are you doing woman!' he exclaimed. 'Get back to bed. You need your rest. Why hasn't Mrs Morris done all this?'

'Gone. Rest indeed. Laying up there fretting over that woman, I told you I had my suspicions and I was right.'

Taking the spoon out of her hand he began to stir the gravy as he said, 'Sit down will you. I'll do that. Sit at the table and I'll bring the pans over and you can dish up.' When everyone sat down at the table and began eating, George asked, 'Now, tell me, what's been going on?'

Evelyn put down her knife and fork. 'I couldn't be sure until today, but everyday she used to bring me up some toast with margarine on. I hate that stuff George, rather have plain bread than that muck. I told her that I should be having butter. God knows, we don't get much of it, and well…' She stopped for a moment.

'Go on, what happened?'

'Well George, I crept downstairs and there she was, as bold as brass, eating toast and our butter ration. Like the cat with cream if ever there was one. So I sent her packing, told her I was going to report her for theft to the authorities. Oh, she swore it was only the once but if that's so where has it all gone, tell me that?'

Throughout the pregnancy, Evelyn had denied herself the meagre rations in order to feed the children, and keep George fit for work. It was what mining families did, ensured the man of the house was able to earn a wage so they always got the best of whatever was put on the table. Consequently she became extremely thin, undernourished and was often poorly with a cold or raised temperature. Belle was sent to the shops over a mile away on Saturdays, but during the week she often queued for an hour or two when it was rumoured something in short supply was available. To ensure George had cigarettes, she scoured the shops, sometimes having to go twice in one day if a supply was to be made in the afternoon.

February nineteen forty-three the coal cellar was empty, and being rationed, there was no telling when the next delivery was to be made. Workers in the factory were allowed one carrier bag of wood off-cuts that couldn't be used in any other way. George made a small wooden attaché case which held the same amount as the bag. When he got it home the children played with the bits, building or drawing on the smooth surfaces. Often Eve would turn on the gas oven for warmth, but this was expensive. One day, hoping to increase the supply he told the foreman, 'This little lot will just about get the fire going. Doesn't give out much heat but plenty of sparks. I suppose there's no hope of...' but he got the familiar answer,

'There's a war on.'

One afternoon in desperation to keep the family, especially her baby, warm, Evelyn unlocked George's shed, took his best saw and successfully cut down one of the smaller trees that separated the field from the garden. Although pleased with herself she was completely exhausted by her efforts. For weeks she had been suffering from a tickly cough, but her exertions on this day caused her cough to worsen during the night. George was horrified to see specks of blood on her hankie, and much alarmed, told her, 'Get yourself down to the surgery first thing tomorrow Evelyn,'

'Don't fuss. I'll be alright in a day or two,' she answered as she began coughing again.

'I'm putting my foot down over this hinny. You get yourself there first thing. I'll stay with the bairns 'til you get back.'

'But...'

'No buts, Eve. Doctor's first thing. You're going even if I have to drag you there meself.' Going to his locked tin box under the bed in which he kept their meagre savings, he gave her the three shillings for the consultation. 'We can afford it. I want you feeling better as soon as possible. That blood worries me.'

On her return from the surgery, George, who had taken time off work to mind the children, could see the relief on her face, and guessed her news couldn't be too bad. 'I've made some tea pet. Sit down and tell me what he said. Good news eh, by the look on your face?'

Evelyn sat down and reached for her cup, then sighing said, 'It depends on how you look at it George.' Taking a sip of tea she looked at him over the rim of her cup then quietly and seriously, 'George, he said that I must rest and to my mind that's good news.' Sighing, she went on, 'Well, you've got to know sometime, he said that he suspects a chest infection and that I need an x-ray.' George was dismayed. An x-ray? He told himself that only very sick people had x-rays. 'So, while I was getting dressed, he telephoned. Told me that he phoned his colleague at the hospital who would see me this afternoon, and I would have the x-ray there at the same time.'

George went across to her, put his arms around her, and shocked, whispered, 'Did he say what it might be? I mean he must have some idea if he's sending you to the hospital.'

'No, he just smiled. He's very kind you know. Said, go home now Mrs Carr, rest for a while and see that you're at the hospital at two thirty. Ask for Mr Graham. Say I sent you. He wants to see me again in a day or two.' Draining her cup and making her way to the armchair, she said, 'You will come with me won't you, George. In case...You know, if it's bad news.'

Nodding his agreement he said, 'As if I'd let you go alone you silly woman,' and kissed lightly on the cheek as she grabbed his hand. She's as frightened as I am, he thought, and immediately made plans for a neighbour to take care of the children.

The diagnosis was devastating. Together they had sat in the consulting room with Mr Graham, who had questioned them relentlessly. Finally he said to George who was holding Evelyn's hand, because she was shaking, anticipating the worst.

'Mr Carr, your wife is dreadfully undernourished,' then held up his hand quickly when George began to protest. 'No one's fault Mr Carr.

No one is blaming you.' Mr Graham smiled at Evelyn who had gasped, and whose pasty face seemed to emphasis her illness. 'It's alright my dear. Soon have you well.' Turning back to George he said, 'This tiredness should have been investigated earlier.' He stood up, went across to Evelyn and put his hand on her shoulder, 'There is no way I can soften this blow for you my dear,' he said. 'You have advanced tuberculosis. The tiredness you've suffered all this time is the very slow onset of the disease, coupled with the fact that you are very anaemic. I cannot stress enough that you must have treatment immediately.' As tears gathered and spilled over, he sighed, 'We'll do our best for you, but you need good food, fresh air and plenty of rest. The best way to achieve that, is for you to enter a sanatorium as early as possible.'

'I can't leave the children,' she gasped. 'What will happen to them if I go?'

Mr Graham immediately answered, 'Ah, the children, they must be seen at once. X-rays to see if any are infected, and after that there is a very good vaccination available.' Evelyn, wide eyed clung to George who had gone white, but sensed Mr Graham was sympathetic. 'Trust me,' he said. 'Mrs Carr, you will see such a difference in a year, feel so much better, I can assure you.' His confidence was relayed to George when he shook his hand although he quietly said to him, 'Your wife would have died within three months if she hadn't come here today.'

A coldness touched George's heart and his eyes filled with tears as he nodded and said, 'I'll take care of her. She'll have the best I can give her. Thank you doctor,' and decided to keep this awful news to himself.

Events happened swiftly during the next two weeks. Evelyn, defeated, had given in at last and organised her household and family from their only armchair. The two girls, Belle nine years old and Lydia seven and a few months were schooled in the more simple household duties. They prepared and cooked the evening meal, washed and wiped the dishes and got Billy dressed for nusery. A health visitor had called at the house the next day and Evelyn told George in the evening that the woman was almost cruel, 'She said that the children would have to be fostered. Somewhere in the country. I asked if they could all be together, and she answered, as if she didn't care, that it would be impossible.'

With a heavy heart George wrote to his mother of the illness, and the separating of the children. As he wrote he was suddenly aware that there was an argument going on between Evelyn and Belle. He heard Belle shout, 'I won't!'

'Yes you will,' countered Evelyn. 'If I say you have to wash the dishes I mean that you wash them, and Lydia will dry them.'

'I want to dry them, why must I always have to wash them?'

'Because, Lydia is to be a seamstress and must keep her hands nice.' George was outraged. 'Evelyn! What are you saying to the child? They're wee bairns. Nothing has been said about their future. That was downright wicked to say that to our Belle.' He glared at her, she might be ill he thought, but by God she's not getting away with that. He watched as she closed her eyes in weariness, then he said quietly, 'Belle, you wash up tonight, and tomorrow Lydia will do it, and from now on you take it in turns. All right pet?' Belle nodded, but he noticed Lydia's sulky face.

Every day they waited for letters to tell them what had been decided for the children, and the name of the sanatorium for Evelyn's recuperation. A doctor from the chest clinic came and gave the children their first and second injections.

'They all cried George,' Eve told him later. 'She said she would be back on Friday to give them the last one.' Friday came and George laughed out loud when he heard that the children had run away over the field. Evelyn was too ill to race after them and the doctor hadn't time.

'Although she waited over an hour, the little devils didn't come back for four hours. I was that pleased to see them.' She smiled then added, 'but I didn't tell them she was coming back tomorrow.' They both chuckled and George could see in his mind's eye, his two long legged children dragging little Billy to keep up, scampering away over the hill and fields.

He wasn't so pleased the next evening when Evelyn told him, 'That bloody doctor was more than vicious as she shoved the needle into their arms, George. Made all of them cry again and then had the cheek to tell them off for running away yesterday. I told her you'd already had a go at them, and to leave it to us to tell our own kids off.'

That night George decided to tackle the ever growing pile of washing and kept Belle from her bed to help. Evelyn supervised from the chair, white and exhausted. George kept looking over at her and in his heart he longed for her treatment to start, but at the same time dreaded her being away from him. The copper loaded with the whites was set to boil. People had often commented on Eve's sparkling white wash and she was determined no grey washing would grace her line. Soon he was rinsing, 'three times in cold water, George,' Evelyn directed. He was on his last rinse, when the back door was opened.

'Eh, our George. I never thought I'd see the day you at the washing.' George was delighted to see his sister Jessie. She took off her hat and coat, and said, 'Make us a brew, there's a good lad,' and promptly sent Belle to bed and began to fold and mangle.

When everything was cleared away, George asked, 'What are you doing here our lass?'

Jessie answered, 'You must be barmy. Do you think mam would let the family be split up? She sent me to collect your girls. We're all girls at home except for Joe and da, so we can manage.' George was overcome.

'Oh Jess, that's wonderful. He turned to Eve who was smiling, 'We've no need now to worry about the girls Eve, have we? I'll never be able to thank you and mam enough.'

With tears running down her face Evelyn was overcome with relief. Weakly she added her thanks then added, 'But what about our boys?'

George rubbed his chin thoughtfully, 'Perhaps…Er, perhaps…' He could see Eve looking at him expectantly. 'Well,' he went on, 'how about we ask your family. Vi and Bryn? They might help out for a few months. What do you think?'

Jessie said, 'Good idea, Evelyn. You'll be happier if you know your bairns are with family.'

'First thing, tomorrow then,' said George, 'I'll write to them see if they can help.' He helped Evelyn out of the chair so she could make her way up to bed, 'Should have a reply by Monday, eh girl?'

On Saturday morning Jessie spent the time ironing and packing the girls' clothes, shopping and cooking a good dinner, plus some pies ready for the next day. George was reluctant to go to work wanting to spend the last few hours with his children. It was mid afternoon when, the girls dressed in their best, left home for the six o'clock train from Kings Cross station. George could see they were bewildered by the speed of things, not really understanding why. He tried to reassure them that they were not evacuees, for some reason they seemed to think evacuees had a bad name.

Choking with his own emotions, he watched as tearfully they said their goodbyes. God knows what Evelyn must be feeling, he thought. Putting his arm around her, they stood at the door watching half their family cross the field. If things didn't move quickly now, she might never see them again. He hadn't told her just how really seriously ill she was.

By the end of the following week, he stood in his empty, silent house. He wandered about, touching coats hanging on the back of the door, cuddling a forgotten toy, thumbing through one of Belle's exercise books and lifting and lowering the lid of Evelyn's sewing box. There was an ache in his heart as he knew there were many empty days, weeks and months ahead.

Vi had written that they both were doing war work and couldn't have the boys, but Sarah had room and could he take them down to Wales. Wednesday saw another tearful farewell to Billy just six, socks around his ankles and his fair curly hair escaping from his school cap, and plump baby Francis. George was glad in a way, that Billy was excited at the thought of seeing a steam engine and listened as he tried to tell Francis about the 'monster' engine. Evelyn did her best to smile, but the pain of parting with her sons was plain to see, and George inwardly cursed and longed to wail out loud.

A letter arrived stating that a place had been located for Evelyn in the Grosvenor Sanatorium, in Ashford Kent and could she please make her own way there to begin treatment. They travelled together, holding hands all the way on Saturday. Both were appalled at the Spartan conditions. Evelyn was soon in bed and when the doctor said that the bed would be pushed outside day and night once she was settled, they looked at each in shocked surprise.

'Even in the rain?' George queried.

The doctor smiled and answered, 'In the rain, snow, mist and sunshine. Take a look outside.' George went to the windows and saw rows of beds, all occupied, under a glass roofed veranda. 'Fresh air is essential for recovery,' the doctor said. He smiled at them both before adding, 'Best of all, we now have a new drug, penicillin which will rapidly improve your health. You've probably seen it in the newspapers. They call it a miracle cure. A wonderful drug helping our wounded men no end. Good news, now everyone can have it.'

George said his goodbyes and as he left, the sister of the ward told him he could visit once a month. 'But should your wife begin to fail, we will send for you straight away,' she added.

'See you soon, love,' he whispered to Evelyn, not having the heart to tell her himself that it would be a long month.

CHAPTER TWENTY

When George explained his Saturday absence to the foreman, he knew it would not be long before the news was all round the factory. During lunch time he was plied with questions from the sympathetic women workers. It wasn't long before they offered more practical sympathy.

'A cake George. I expect you're missing your Eve's cooking,' that was from Beryl. Joyce offered to do his washing. Nelly was prepared to take on his mending, but he drew the line at Phyllis coming round to the house to tidy up. That would put the cat among the pigeons, he thought, as he remembered putting his foot down over Evelyn's visitors, particularly Cyril.

Picking up the post on entering the house one evening he noticed a buff envelope, and for a moment his heartbeat seemed to flutter. Emblazoned across the top of the envelope was 'On His Majesty's Service'. It was as he suspected his call up papers telling him to report to Acton Interview and Medical Centre. George had heard that the Government had planned to call up older men for service in the Forces, but hadn't realised he might be included. Coward he was not, he told himself he would do his bit but hoped he would be exempt, because he had been told he was in a reserved occupation. At worst, he could be sent back to the mines, he had after all, enough experience. By all accounts things had improved a little underground, and it may not be for long. Well so be it, he thought.

After passing the medical, George was pleased he passed A1, when explaining to the recruiting sergeant about his work, he was told sharply, 'Doesn't mean a thing, laddie. Now, which of the services will suit you best? The army, navy or air force?'

George didn't hesitate as he thought of Robert, there might even by a chance of being together, he thought. 'The navy would be fine.'

'The navy, sir?' was bellowed back at him.

George had the good sense to hold his temper as he told himself that he wasn't in the army yet by God, and repeated, 'The navy, sir.'

The sergeant snorted, made a few notes on the paper in front of him, muttering to himself, 'The navy he says.' Then in a loud bark, audible George thought that could be heard in Buckingham Palace, 'You'll go in the army me lad, and like it! You'll be hearing from us shortly.'

A week later the letter he had been dreading arrived. Turning it over slowly and reluctant to open it he sighed, then tore it open quickly. As he read a smile spread across his face. How he longed to share the good news. The letter informed him that, as his wife was in hospital for a long duration, that there was a real chance that he may not return home owing to the present hostilities, and that four children who could be orphaned should he and his wife not survive, he should remain in the vital occupation he was in at present. At once he wrote to Evelyn and his mother telling them the good news.

What surprised George was how quickly the month went by. In fact, he had little time for himself. The factory was now working overtime, there was his fire watching obligations and as he now had no immediate family at home, he was often called upon for extra duties. In his first letters to the girls, he wrote to them separately, he enclosed, as Evelyn had instructed, his and her sweet coupons. Oh, well, he told himself, I've still got my smokes. It wasn't long before Beryl found out and almost at once, there was a daily treat of a couple of boiled sweets or squares of chocolate. He never asked where she got them from, it wasn't the wisest thing to do and he had a horror of being involved in any black marketing he knew was happening around the factory floor.

Three times a week he wrote to Evelyn, there was little to tell her except of his love for her, and begging her to do everything she was told in order to come home as early as possible. Her few letters to him were in spidery writing, he knew just holding a pencil must be taxing her strength. Nevertheless, he was always happy to receive her returned declaration of love. George was looking at his garden full of vegetables and ripe soft fruit as he was writing to her. He felt, in all honesty, that he should tell her how the women were spoiling him, but was reluctant to do so. Any hint of his associating with them might upset and aggravate her fragile health, he thought. Seeing a blackbird helping itself to a raspberry, the solution suddenly came to him and he wrote,

I am so lucky, Eve, I thought all my hard work in the garden was going to be wasted what with you and the kids being so far away, but I take stuff down to the works and the girls are so pleased to have fresh veg and fruit that they bake me pies and cake as thanks. Isn't that kind of them, pet?

The following Monday, armed with bags of goodies from his garden, he put this idea into practice. Not only were pies and tarts offered in return by the grateful women but he was also able to sell some, enough to pay his fare to Ashford.

At the end of the four weeks, he made his way to the sanatorium, and was more than shocked to see how poorly Eve was. As he approached her bed, he saw her raise her stick thin hand to greet him and her dark hair spread across the pillow seemed to accentuate the whiteness of her face. After he had kissed her and held her gently in his arms for a few moments, he was convinced she was dying. Panicking at the thought, he searched round frantically for a doctor or anyone who might give him some answers. It was the matron who seeing his distress, took him into her office to calm him down.

'Now, Mr Carr,' she said as she handed him a cup of tea, 'let's get it straight. No my dear, your wife is not dying.'

'But she looks so shockingly ill. So thin and…and frail. I just can't lose her.'

'Yes, so she is, bless her. You probably didn't notice it yourself, but she must have been ill for quite sometime.' George reached for a cigarette but didn't light it as she said, 'This is a chest hospital Mr Carr. We discourage smoking. You can understand that, can't you?'

He nodded as he said, 'Aye, aye, makes sense.'

She smiled, took a sip from her dainty cup before going on, 'The good news Mr Carr, is that in fact your wife has just this week shown signs of progress.' George sat up straighter and leaned forward. 'Yes, indeed.' She rifled through some folders then opening one of them said, 'Yes, here we are. She has put on weight, just over half a pound this last week. That is good news for all of us.' She looked over the rim of her glasses. 'Pleasing news isn't it?'

'How is it that I didn't notice how thin she had got? I mean, we've not been apart since we married ten years ago.'

Matron answered, 'It is the same for nearly everyone Mr Carr. Being constantly with someone, people just don't notice the subtle changes taking place.' She paused for a moment, 'How many times have you heard someone say of your children, 'my how you've grown'. See what I mean? If you'd been away for a while you would have seen straight away any changes in your wife.'

'Aye, I can see that makes sense. Even so, I should have taken more notice. I mean she was always tired. I just thought it was having the bairns so quick like.'

'This illness, this T.B. as we call it quite often takes its time to develop, over many years. I suspect that is what has happened in your wife's case.'

'Her sister died of it. Did she tell you that?'

'Yes it's in the records. That's probably when Mrs Carr's own infection began.' She stood up and collected their empty cups and placed them on a tray. 'Good food, plenty of eggs and milk, she gets all that here, rest of course, the new penicillin drug and plenty of fresh air.' She laughed, 'I expect you've noticed that.'

George cleared his throat. 'So, you're sure she's going to make it?'

'No one can guarantee that Mr Carr. No one can say what the future holds, but there is a really good chance of a full recovery.' She held open the door for him and added, 'It is going to take a very long time, but at the moment, there is no indication of her dying. Now go back to her and tell her what you've been doing while she's away.' As he walked away, she called after him, 'and don't tell her you only wash up once a week!'

George laughed as he cheekily answered, 'Wash up. Wash up? What's that?'

At the factory the following Monday morning, he stood for a

moment looking along the rows of working women. All were in sensible dungarees which hid their feminine shapes. Some had their hair in net snoods, loose hair was dangerous around the machinery they were handling. Others had scarves tied up into turbans which hid the dinkie curlers in their hair, a sure sign that they had a date, although on Fridays it usually meant they were going dancing. They all wore goggles and were good workers, but as he walked to his own bench he was aware that they were discussing their dates of the previous evening with the American G.I.s based nearby. He cringed at their coarse laughter, and although he had often heard bad language on building sites he disliked to hear the women swearing the most awful obscenities, words he had never used himself no matter what. Often outspoken offers of sex were made to him, and some in the crudest form of gestures. Just the thought of kissing any of them with their ghastly, over bright lip-sticked mouths, made his mind and stomach churn in disgust. I hate the bloody lot, he thought.

All sorts of schemes were thought up to encourage people to part with their money to help the war effort. One such scheme was introduced into the factory and immediately won favour with the women. A coffin was brought into the building and on the lid was painted a full length picture of Hitler. For a copper or two everyone was allowed to hammer a nail into the image. The coffin was to remain in the building for two days. On the second day, George could see that a group of women were giggling, one or two near hysterics, and he strolled over to see what was going on. The women stood back so that he could see the coffin and he was astounded by what he was confronted with. It seemed someone had brought in a lump of plasticine with colours of blue, red, and where they had run into each other, a hideous mauve shade. Someone had quite artfully shaped an outrageous, elongated male anatomy and stuck it between Hitler's legs. In the short time George stood there a hand quickly snatched the plasticine away, reformed it into another grotesque shape and put it back. Loud laughter erupted from the group, George allowed himself a hidden smile before saying, 'Back to your benches now before money is stopped from your wage packets.'

Good-heartedly, the girls began to return to work but as they sauntered away someone asked George, 'Can you match that

George?' and set them all off laughing again.

Listening to Workers Playtime on the radio being broadcast, 'From somewhere in Britain' said the announcer, at lunch time in the canteen, George realised that there were exceptions to his view of the female workers. Beryl touched his shoulder as she passed by, 'Alright George? Got enough to eat?' He nodded and smiled back at her. 'Me and Joyce and a few others are off to the flicks tonight. If you're not doing something why don't you come along? Alec and Doug are coming. Do you good to get out now and again. What do you say?' Lighting up a cigarette, he told her he'd think about it.

'We're off to see Lucille Ball in *Best Foot Forward*. She's an absolute scream. Anything for a laugh, eh George?' He'd heard of the film and remembered that Harry James, a very talented trumpeter, was also in the cast, and music still being one of his passions, decided that he would meet up with them that evening. Mind, he told himself, if there hadn't been other fellows going, he'd have given it a miss.

At seven o'clock, he found himself waiting outside the cinema and was surprised and pleased to see that the women had made an effort to dress up in renovated frocks, gloves and one or two wore a hat. He sat between Joyce and Beryl, who had her never ending supply of boiled sweets, that she generously handed around the group. They sat through Pathe News showing the American forces in Italy, two cartoons and a B film called *Crime Doctor* before the main film. The film was to be always in George's memory. Firstly, as Beryl had predicted it was funny. Best of all, he admitted to himself, he was enthralled by Harry James playing faultlessly, 'The Flight of the Bumble Bee'. George knew he was listening to a brilliant musician with his own orchestra 'The Music Makers' and wistfully thought back to his own musical ambitions.

Sitting in the dark engrossed in the film, he was surprised when he felt Beryl's small, light hand slip into his. For a split second only he felt he should take his away, but immediately decided against this as he found it comforting. Beryl's husband was in the army, posted Heaven only knew where. They were both lonely and so he happily curled his fingers around hers. After the film show George, with Beryl's arm tucked into his, walked her home. Little was said between them, he told her of his children and Eve's slow recovery. She told him of Jack, her husband, and her only child evacuated to an aunt in Devon. Arriving at her door he politely raised his trilby and wished her a 'Goodnight.'

Writing to Eve that night, he told her of his outing, telling her it was a crowd from work and being sure to mention the other men who were there, and outlined the plot of the film. He left out the innocent walk home with Beryl. Trips to the cinema became routine, always the same crowd went together, George and Beryl enjoyed each other's company on these occasions although in the factory it was if nothing had changed between them.

Without fail he visited Eve once a month, and he could see that the treatment she was getting was beginning to improve her. Eve had blossomed, her eyes brightened and a wide smile greeted him as he walked along the veranda.

He in turn, seeing her looking much better grinned widely and quickened his step. 'By, you're looking bonny lass,' George said when he reached her. 'Have you seen yourself? Lovely rosy cheeks and you definitely look stronger.'

Pleased that he had noticed she said, 'You think so?'

'I do. Why you're beginning to look like the girl I married. Let me see, how long ago was that?'

Laughing, she answered, 'Oh, George, you know full well it'll be eleven years next January.'

'Aye, and to look at you now, it seems like yesterday.'

'So how are you going to explain our four children?'

'They're too young to be told that yet. That reminds me, I had a letter from Belle. I've got it somewhere.' He patted his pockets and discovering it in his wallet, handed it over to Eve to read. 'Read it out loud love, she's such a clever little bairn.'

Eve unfolded the letter, 'She might be clever but…Well, just look at her handwriting. It's very scrawly, George.' She sighed, 'She can be such an untidy girl at times.'

'Let it be lass. The child's left handed. I've seen her struggle with all sorts.'

'You're right. Remember how she always put the cutlery on the table the wrong way round and one of us had to keep showing her?' They smiled together at the memory then after taking a sip of water, she began to read to him,

Dear Daddy,

Could you pleese send some pockit money. This is why. Me and Alice
was under the table when a farmer came to see Gran. He was called John.
Gran gave him some eggs for his breakfest. We heard her say no then he
said something like the Eyties couldn't help and he was asking everyone
to come and pick up potatoes. He said he would pay, so Gran said we
could go. We got very muddy and when Mr John paid up he gave it to
Gran who bought us new hats to go to church. Lydia keeps crying. Is
mummy getting better.

When are we cumming home?
Love from
Miss Belinda Carr

George put his arms around Evelyn and stroked her hair when he
saw the tears sliding slowly down her face. Choking back his own
emotions he said, 'Don't take on lass. It won't be so long now. Cheer
up.'

'I miss them George. They're all so far away. If they were a bit
closer perhaps it wouldn't be so hard but...' They were interrupted
at that moment by the rattle of the tea trolley.

Cheerfully he said, 'Now just look at that. Couldn't come at a better
time. Me throat's that parched.'

When he was leaving he said, 'You keep the letter Eve. I'll tell the
girls to write to you more often. I'll send them your address. In fact,
I think I might be able to get up to see them next weekend or maybe
the weekend after. All right?' She nodded and lifted her face for his
parting kiss, as he waved goodbye, he said, 'See you soon, kid.'

The following Friday evening he set out for Durham. There was not
a seat to be had as every coach was filled with soldiers. During the
long night's journey the train stopped each time there was enemy
aircraft about. There were a couple of sleeping children on board, and
they were passed from soldier to soldier and not once did either child
wake up. The soldiers took it in turns to sit and included George in
their rota. Fortunately he had brought his weekend supply of cigarettes with him and he was more than willing to share them with his
fellow travellers.

Early Saturday morning he arrived home just as his daughters were
having their breakfast. They rushed towards him squealing with
delight and he was amazed to see how they had grown. It was odd,

that once the girls had got over seeing him, they left him to go out to play as if he'd never been apart from them. In a way he was a little disappointed that they didn't cling to him, on the other hand, he reasoned it showed that they must be happy here with his parents. And why not, I always was he reflected.

Lying on the creaky leather sofa, he dozed and was fed intermittently with titbits. These were left over from the open house Hannah held every Friday evening for the boys from Catterick Camp. There were the soft milk rolls he loved and missed, teacakes, fruit cake and, it seemed to him, endless cups of tea. Joseph, he could no longer be called Baby Joseph as he was now fourteen years old and working in the local butcher's, came in laden with off cuts of meat. After some bantering with George, Joseph told him there was a dance on at the church hall. 'Shall we go?' he whispered. George didn't need asking twice and together they set off.

'Got yourself a lass then, our Joe?' asked George. 'Oh, I can see you have by the colour of you face. Bonny is she?'

Joe gave him a push and as he ran off towards a girl waiting on the corner he called over his shoulder, 'Aye, she is that. Enjoy yerself.' Both turned and waved to George as they entered the hall together.

George had enjoyed his evening, but wasn't expecting the berating he got from Hannah the next morning. Flouncing around her kitchen as she prepared the Sunday roast, and tight lipped, she said, 'I thought you came up here to see your bairns, our Joe. Not gallivanting out dancing when you could have spent time with them.'

'Well you had them in bed by eight mother. I can't see any harm in me dancing, especially on a Saturday night.'

'I would've kept them up for you if you'd stayed in, Joe.' George watched as she tested the joint before she added, 'and how long are you staying? 'Cos if you're staying for a day or two, you could take them to Redcar on the bus. They'd like that.'

'Right. I'll do that and I'll treat you and Alice too.' She smiled, artful biddy, he told himself, she wanted to go all along.

Although it was nearly the end of September the weather was perfect, sunny and warm. The girls were excused school on Monday after Hannah had seen the Headmistress, and they set off for the seaside. They sat on the top deck of the bus, and their excitement grew as they saw the sparkling sea in the distance. George and Hannah smiled, and encouraged the girls who were talking of paddling and sand castles. 'Good thing, I thought to bring some towels then,' Hannah said, 'and I found the spades and buckets all your aunts and uncles used to bring here.'

They hadn't brought a picnic, just a few teacakes, as George had said he would treat them all to a large helping of fish and chips. When the bus reached the end of the journey, still seated on the top deck all of them were aghast at what they saw. There was no way they could get near the water, let alone get on the beach. There was barbed wire as far as the eye could see. The bus was returning in half an hour, so quickly George purchased their fish and chips which they ate on the way home. Everyone was disappointed, but when Lydia said, 'Never mind daddy, we have had a lovely long bus ride and we did see the water didn't we?' It was then George realised that his family had never ever seen the sea before.

'When this lot is over, I mean the war and your mam back home, we'll go to the seaside every year I promise,' he told her.

Mid week found him back at work, and as he thought about the weekend he admitted to himself that he had enjoyed the Saturday dance, so that when a dance was arranged at the weekend for the factory hands, he made up his mind to go. What harm could there be in it he asked himself? Arriving a little late for the dance, he preferred it that way so that he could see and hear what was happening, he bought himself a slice of fruit cake and a cup of tea and sat down. It surprised him to see how some of the girls he thought were common tramps actually looked more than attractive in their dance frocks. Indeed he found it hard to recognise some of them, then smiled to himself when he realised that they only had to open their mouths and he could distinguish each by their shrill voice. The music was good and the tempo exact, but artfully he sat through a few dances before venturing on the floor himself. By sitting out he was able to see the best of the dancers, this one for the quickstep, another for the foxtrot and yet another for the tango. Once on his feet, he danced every dance but always the waltz with Beryl, who confessed that it was the only one she could manage. It was a good idea, he thought, that many of the dances were Lady's Excuse Me – whereby the ladies were able to ask the men to dance without embarrassment although he suffered inwardly when some of the women with no dancing skills whatsoever picked him. In fairness when writing to Evelyn he did mention that he had been to 'a couple of dances, dearest' and to his surprise her return letter made no mention of it.

On Christmas Eve, work stopped at noon in order to give the children of the workers a party in the afternoon. The canteen had been decorated and the women had, from nowhere it seemed, produced all sorts of jellies, cakes, sausage rolls and sandwiches. They had also been sewing rag dolls with dresses and knitting gloves, scarves and jumpers, anything small that could be salvaged from unpicked garments. Over the last few weeks, the men had been allowed a small amount of wood to make suitable presents for children of all ages. George had made a couple of engines turned on his lathe and painted black and green and had hitched on a wagon. He also made roll-top pencil boxes, glove boxes and spinning tops. Belle, Lydia and Alice were sent a pencil box and top and his sons a wooden engine each. That was the best he could do and promised, with all his heart, next year he hoped they would all be home and have a proper Christmas together.

After the children's party there was a dance, and towards the evening so that everyone could join in, ballroom dancing was abandoned and the old favourites like Lambeth Walk, Hokey Cokey and The Saint Bernard's Walt were danced. The evening ended with a rousing sing-along. George had enjoyed himself, and once away from the home going crowd, allowed Beryl to put her arm through his.

At her front door, she said, 'Why don't you come in for a cuppa George?'

She said this every time he walked her home and he had always refused, but this evening he cheerfully nodded, 'Aye, I could do with a cup of tea lass. Dancing's right thirsty work.' She laughed as she opened the front door. 'I daresay a piece of cake won't go amiss either.'

They sat side by side on the sofa sipping their drinks and generally chatting, mostly about their respective families, when out of the blue, she asked, 'How long is it since you had any fun George?' He looked at her not quite understanding what she meant. Patiently she said, 'I mean, you know, a bit of loving between the sheets?' He felt himself going hot and red in the face and seeing this she went on, 'Oh, George. We've been friends long enough to be able to talk about such things. My Jack has been away for over two years and I miss him a lot.' Lost in thought for a moment she said, 'I don't know where he is but when he writes he says he's missing me something terrible.'

George nodded in sympathy. 'Aye lass, I know what it's like to be lonely. No one since my Evelyn went away. Not mind, that I've been looking, but yes, the bed seems bigger and colder somehow without her there.'

They were silent for a few moments, then putting out her hand and pulling him to his feet she said quietly, 'Come with me George.'

A little bemused and thinking she was leading him into her kitchen, he was surprised and then experienced an unexpected thrill as she led him upstairs to her bedroom. At the doorway he hung back, 'I'm not sure about this Beryl. We're both married and...'

'And both bloody lonely.' Tugging at his arm she said softly, 'Who's to know? We're not daft. Just lonely.'

'But...'

'Just lay down beside me. Let's have cuddle and see what happens from there. What do you say?' George said nothing, left just his shirt on and climbed in beside her. It was if their memories had forsaken them at first as they fumbled around each other, until they finally succeeded. Next morning they were both smiling and relaxed.

'Now George, I'm not going to pretend I love you or anything like that. I love my Jack to pieces. Okay?'

George laughed, 'And I love my Evelyn, so no worries my girl.' Beryl lit cigarettes for them both,

'When the time comes it must end. Promise me George. As soon as your Eve or my Jack comes home. Agreed?'

Kissing her lightly on the cheek he nodded, 'Agreed.'

George left before it got light hoping that he was unobserved by her neighbours. There was a grin on his face and a feeling that somehow he was special, not loved exactly, but needed and what's more, he thought as he remembered the night, he hadn't lost his skills in that department. There were to be two more lovemaking evenings and after each time, George experienced a surge of guilt and yet managed to convinced himself that he done nothing wrong.

It was early in March when Beryl, a little agitated, had approached George in the works canteen. 'George,' she said quietly, looking around to see if they could be overheard.

'What is it, pet? What's up?'

'I've had a letter George. My Jack. He's been wounded.'

'Poor bloke,' exclaimed George. 'How bad?'

'Bad enough for him to be sent home. We've got to stop seeing each other.'

'Well, of course. I know that. Didn't we say we would? But I tell you pet, I'll never forget you and I thank you from the bottom of my heart.'

A few weeks later Evelyn had written to say that as she was so much better, the doctor had said she could have a weekend away from the sanatorium, 'So George, I have booked some rooms in the village for us. Get down here as early as you can and we can have a wonderful weekend together.' After telling the foreman he was away for the weekend, George caught the first train down to Kent to be with his true love on Saturday morning. It was indeed a lovely weekend. As soon as he arrived he could see Evelyn was excited.

'I'm almost bursting to tell you,' she said.

'I can see that.' he answered as he held her close. 'So, come on tell me.'

'I'm to have my interview on Tuesday.'

'Your interview? What interview?'

'It's like this. When the doctor thinks you are well, fit whatever, they have you in for an interview to see if you are ready to leave. Oh George, just think, if all goes well I could be home by the end of the month.'

'Crickey, pet. You mean I've got to get rid of the lodger and start washing up?' Happily they laughed together.

Evelyn had chosen wonderful rooms and they had walked the quiet lanes together, and had found a pub able to serve them a decent meal. Best of all was the pleasure they found at being together in bed after such a long absence. Arriving home late on Sunday evening he wrote to Evelyn,

My darling wife,

Just a few lines to let you know I got back safely. Had a nice journey –
first class but arrived home rather late. This wasn't the reason I wrote

*tonight though. It will be Tuesday by the time you get this so, kid, I wish
you all the luck in the world at your interview today. Good luck, darling,
I am with you and still love you like blazes. Just a simple thank you dear
for a lovely week-end.*

*You know how much I enjoyed it. Good luck again kid, and all my love
and kisses,*

Your ever loving hubby,

George

CHAPTER TWENTY-ONE

The family were reunited in September nineteen forty-four. George
and Evelyn were delighted to have their children home. The girls had
flourished and had become confident, although Lydia seemed to have
developed some of her mother's traits, quick tempered, spiteful and
sulky. Belle seemed to take everything in her stride as Evelyn, not yet
really back to full health, made more and more demands on her.

The same could not be said of the boys. Both were thin, almost
undernourished. Billy was shy, kept quiet and played for hours by
himself. Both George and Eve were upset when, at first Francis,
would have nothing to do with them. It was Billy he hid behind most
times when one of his parents tried to pick him up and they noticed
at mealtimes he had taught himself to eat, and eat everything rapidly
put in front of him. Carefully, Evelyn coaxed Billy to tell her why
Francis was eating in this manner, and was shocked at the answer.

'When we got our dinners, auntie sat in the front room and left us
to eat and then Paul and Terry used to try to pinch our dinners.' His
eyes filled with tears and as she cuddled him he said, 'I tried to help
him, I did. I tried and tried.'

When she told George he was angry but knew he could do little
except to say, 'Don't you ever have those boys here to visit, Eve.
They might be your sister's bairns but I'll thrash the little sods, and
starve them if I ever get me hands on them. Aye, that I would.'

'Things were hard in Wales, George.' Evelyn explained. 'Billy told me some days the only decent food they got was from the British Restaurant, and that wasn't all that wonderful.' The wheel of one of Billy's toy lorries came off one day when Francis tried to snatch it away, it could easily be put back on, but in a soft voice Evelyn said, 'Drwg babi'.

The boys' reactions were unbelievable. Francis's lower lip began to tremble and he wet himself, Billy rushed across to him and stood in front of him his arms and legs stretched out in defence and defiance.

'What in God's name has been going on?' roared George. It took a few moments to settle the lads and assure them that no harm was coming to them after Billy explained that usually they got a smack when they heard 'drwg'. They knew it meant naughty. George wasn't sure what he felt. Perhaps guilty, but of what he asked himself? Sorry, was more like it. Sorry Eve got ill, sorry that Eve and himself had abandoned the children, sorry he never saw the boys during the last eighteen months, and sorry he hadn't a clue of what went on in Wales. One thing he was sure of, never again was his family going to split up.

It was some weeks before Billy returned to his former sunny self, but it took months before Francis began to smile properly at them and let himself be spoilt. George realised that they were spoiling the child, but he was their baby, their last child who'd had a really tough time, but he was also very aware of the resentment building up with the other three children. Nevertheless, Belle remained his special love and despite lack of money, he ensured that she had a bicycle to go to the shops over a mile or so away. This was a daily chore for fresh bread and meat. George made sure Belle had a winter coat and strong shoes as well, and Evelyn protested that the others were in need too, but realised George was right.

'She deserves it,' he told Eve. 'She has to cope with the money and coupons and queuing. Everything so you can manage things at home.'

George was well aware that Evelyn favoured Lydia who truly looked like a doll, fair skinned, blonde Carr curly hair, the bluest of eyes and white straight teeth. Whereas his princess, as he still mentally called Belle, had dark straight hair, green eyes and uneven teeth, in fact, the image of her mother whom he loved passionately.

There were times though, when he wished the children were still away. Although the second front of the war had begun in June, it seemed as if the civilians left at home had an invasion of their own. Doodlebugs were aimed at the country and found their random mark. They throbbed pilotlessly across the sky until the engine cut out. It was as if the world stood still in the eerie silence that followed. That was when fear gripped him most. There was no whistle of the flying bomb's descent, just a few moments later a terrible explosion. Waiting for the explosion was the hardest to bear – the bombs just dropped out of the sky. Afterwards he suffered from mixed feelings of relief and shame, relief that it had missed them and shame of his gladness that it had passed over and knowing in his heart that someone else must have suffered terribly.

Tuesday May the eighth nineteen forty-five was finally declared Victory in Europe day. Rumours had been spreading for days before and at last the nation was free of conflict. Everyone at the factory was sent home early, as were the children from school. Church bells were ringing, red, white and blue bunting was hung everywhere. Everyone George met was smiling, laughing and shaking his hand, slapping him on the back and shouting as they moved on, 'At last.' Every newspaper headline was blazoned with 'Today is V.E. Day'. The celebrations at home for the Carrs were modest. Most things were still rationed, but Evelyn put up a scantily filled meat pudding with jam tart to follow.

During the war years, Hannah had written to George, telling him how his brothers and sisters were coping. Sometimes reading between the lines he felt all was not well. Not exactly sure why, he had a longing to go home to Durham, and decided to make the trip for his mother's birthday.

'You'll be alright with the kids for the weekend, Eve,' he said. 'It's me mam's birthday. I want to surprise her. What do you say? Go Saturday morning early and be back Sunday evening.'

'Leaving me with the kids again. It's enough George that you're working most weekends. I need a break too, from them.' The trip was not going to be easily won.

'Lydia and Belle will help out,' then as an after thought added, 'I'll take Billy with me. How's that. It'll help, won't it?'

Eve sighed as she nodded, 'You go then George. I'm missing my own folks as well and one of these days I'll get myself down to Coulsdon to see Vi.' Turning to the girls she said, 'We'll be fine, won't we girls?'

When he arrived at his mother's he was surprised to see Emily nursing a boy about three years old. 'Em. has come home with her lad, our Joe. Bruce, and isn't he a grand little fellow?' said Hannah.

To him, Emily looked so downcast and listless he immediately felt sorry for her. 'What's up our lass?' he asked softly. Immediately she began to weep quietly.

'I'm going to my room for a bit. Have a lie down. Mam will tell you,' she told him as she hurried away with a hankie to her eyes and the boy following her upstairs.

After they had left, George lit up a tab, and said, 'What's going on mam? What's happened to her? She's looking that poorly.'

Giving Alice a biscuit she shooed the child out of the room, 'Go and find your friends in the rec. there's a good girl,' she told her. 'Em, still has little to do with Alice and we believe that is for the best,' she whispered to George. She settled herself in her chair with a cup of tea then sighed. 'Em came home last Friday week. Oh, poor girl, in such a state she was.' She sat for a moment then, 'Eh Joe, It seems the fellow she has been living with these last seven years or so, used to give her a backhander now and then.'

'He what? What sort of man is he?'

Hannah held up her hand, 'Let me go on. Last week was the final straw as far as our Em was concerned. It seemed he did not come home with his wages at lunch time, so she went to look for him. The boss where he works said he was in a nearby pub, and when she found the scoundrel he had a brazen woman on his knee. Em. asked him for the housekeeping, the bairns were hungry she told him. So after he gave her some cash the dreadful woman followed her out, and would you believe? She gave our Em a hiding. Can you believe it our Joe?'

Angrily George demanded, 'Did the fellow not go to help Em? I mean she was virtually his wife.'

'There's more Joe.'

'What do you mean more?' Hannah wiped tears from her eyes. 'Aw mam, don't take on so. It can be sorted. You'll see.'

She sighed, 'She has another boy, Joe. A lad of seven and when she told Duncan, that's his name, Duncan Foster, he said she could go to hell as far as he was concerned but she couldn't take their eldest boy, Alexander.' George threw his cigarette butt into the fire, then stroked his chin thoughtfully. 'What else could she do Joe? She had to get away from him. It broke her heart to leave the lad behind, but,' she sighed again, 'but Em says he does love the boy, and she's pretty sure he'll be alright.' She stood up brushed her hands down her apron and sighed again, 'Eh Joe, what it is to be a mother.'

'Surely she has some rights?'

She turned on him fiercely, 'Rights? Rights you say. What rights our Joe? 'She's an unmarried mother, even married mothers can lose the right to their children if the husband wants. So what rights do you think she has? Answer me that.' For a moment or two they sat in silence.

Then George said, 'Have you got his address, mam? I'll go and give the bugger a good hiding he won't forget in a hurry.'

At that point his father walked into the room. 'No you bloody well won't,' he snapped. 'The problem's not yours. It's Emily's, not yours.' Moderating his tone he went on, 'Think on lad. You've a family to take care of. Suppose, just suppose you do him an injury…'

'I'd make damn sure I'd give him an injury da. He can't behave like that to our Em.'

'Aye, and you'd land yourself in a heap of trouble. I mean it, prison at the least for assault. It doesn't take much to put people inside these days.'

George was frustrated knowing that what his father said made sense but still felt he'd love to pulp the brute into the ground. After some thought, he said, 'Aye, maybe you're right, da, but what about our poor Em? She's in a right state.'

'Time boy, time will sort it out.' Joseph lit up his pipe and unfolded his newspaper, then suddenly said, 'Did your mam tell you Robert is getting married?'

'The cheeky beggar. Kept that a secret.'

'Aye, to the girl who nursed him. You know he was invalided out of the navy just before the end. He had pleurisy.'

Hannah butted in, 'Came home last weekend Joe. He's looking fit and well and she's a bonnie lass. You can see she loves him to bits. No doubt you'll get an invitation.'

'That you will,' a cheery voice called from the doorway.

'Girlfriend thrown you out?' asked George as he went across to shake his brother's hand and throw his arm around his shoulder.

'She wouldn't do that. Loves me more than all the birds in the sky, she does.'

As their mother began to bustle about her kitchen getting everyone some supper, Robert went on, 'I came to tell our Emily some news. I think she'll be pleased.'

'Come down, Em,' George called out. 'Robert's got some news for you.' George pulled out a chair for her and Robert sat beside her and held her hand. So, she might have been a sharp no nonsense sister in the past, but George admitted to himself she was family, poor and broken in spirit.

'It's like this Em,' Robert began. 'Remember you gave me your fellow's address? Duncan's?'

Em nodded, 'He's not my fellow any more Robert,' she said, 'I hate him.' Robert patted her hand,

'Well now, the other night as he stumbled out of the pub, you didn't say he was a drunkard. Anyways, I followed him and got hold of him in a gulley behind the houses and thrashed the life out of him.' He looked down at his hands, 'See? Look at those knuckles, all red and bruised.'

Hannah said, 'Oh, Robert. I don't like it, this idea of brutal revenge.'

Da tapped out his pipe on the fender before saying, 'I just told George not to do such a thing, Robert. The risk of imprisonment is too great.'

'Don't you worry da. I made sure no one was about so there's no witnesses.' He laughed, 'He'll have a job explaining his black eyes and bruises I can tell you. Bet he never tells anyone he lost the fight.'

When he had finished, Emily hugged him, 'I just wish I'd been a fellow meself to beat the hell out of him,' she said.

'I can see that's cheered you up,' laughed Robert.

Later in the evening George told Robert how he had opted to go in the navy, but Robert in a more serious mood said, 'Thank your lucky stars you didn't, Joe.' He was quiet for a second or two then said, 'It was hell on earth. Believe me.'

'I'm no fool, Rob. I was well aware of the dangers, enemy ships and aircraft and all that. I just thought there might be a chance of us being together.' Robert leaned towards him.

'It wasn't the enemy George. It was an enemy of a different kind.'

'How come?'

Robert offered the cigarette packet and after they had both lit up, he said, 'The weather, Joe. Cold. You've never known cold like it. We were far up in the north, and it was mid winter. Everything, everything was frozen solid.' He drew on his cigarette before going on, 'When you came off your watch, your clothes were stiff with ice. Your mates had to almost cut you out of your clothes.' He paused for a moment and looked at his bruised hands. Holding them out to George, he said, 'This is nothing, but there were days when I could have cried with the pain of thawing out me fingers and toes. Two or three lads actually got frostbite and lost their fingers.' He put out his cigarette and ran his hand over his head. 'There was snow and sleet and wind, wind that whipped up the waves to an unbelievable height. Thirty, forty feet some thought. Staying alive in those conditions was harder than having a go at the Germans, I can tell you.'

George looked at his brother. 'You're a bloody hero, our lad. A bloody hero and I'm going to buy you a pint. Come on.'

Robert grinned, 'Not really a hero Joe. I was that glad that I got ill and had to go to hospital, but all the while I felt guilty leaving me mates behind to go on yet another run to Russia.'

'Don't be daft man. I daresay every one of them would have gladly changed places with you. Come on get your jacket before the pub closes.'

The weekly letters from his mother continued. He laughed when he read that Jessie was expecting her third baby, but was shocked to learn that Hetti and Mary were getting divorces.

'I don't know what the world's coming to,' he said to Evelyn. 'Hetti getting a divorce. She told mam and da it was because now the war is over they have nothing in common. I mean to say, Eve, they aren't even trying.'

'Best now than later when there might have been kids,' Eve replied.

'And our Mary, poor lass, just twenty-two and says the bloke she married seems to prefer men friends.' Sheepishly he added, 'well, that's how mam put it but I think she means poofs.' Half laughing, and shaking his head, said, 'I really don't know what the world's coming to.'

'Bet that shocked your mam and da,' laughed Evelyn. 'I can almost hear them. Most likely whispering about it and not telling a soul outside the family.'

Arriving home one Saturday lunchtime, he was surprised to see the children seated at the table and instead of Evelyn dishing up the dinner it was Belle. 'Where's your mother, pet?' he asked as he hung up his jacket and cap.

Belle answered, 'She says to tell you that she's gone to Coulsdon to see Aunty Vi.'

George was fuming. 'Is that all she said to say?'

Belle pointed to the mantel shelf, 'There's a note up there for you.' Hurriedly he read the short letter,

Dear George,

I have to have a break. We never have holidays. You went off to Durham a few weeks ago and now I'm off to see my sisters.

Will be back Sunday evening.

Evelyn.

The line of kisses below her signature failed to mollify him. 'She shouldn't have left you all on your own. Anything could happen,' he muttered almost to himself.

Belle answered cheerfully, 'No daddy. She's just this minute gone.'

'But what if I'd been late? What then?'

'I had to wait outside until I saw you turn into the street on your bike, then when I told her you were coming she said she was going to Auntie Vi's, gave me a kiss and went across the field to the station.' All weekend he was angry and tried hard not to take it out on the children whose demands seemed relentless. When Eve finally put in an appearance late on Sunday evening, he turned his back on her and stomped off to bed.

Early the following year, George was fed up. Most of the girls had left the factory and gone back to being housewives or to their previous jobs. Now, house joinery, door and window frames, doors, cupboards anything to be made of wood was the main manufacture. These were destined for new houses replacing those destroyed in the war. Unfortunately, seasoned wood was in short supply. Using unseasoned wood was unsatisfactory and there were days when little or no work was done.

George found idleness did not suit him and began searching for a better job. Another reason for his discontent was that once a month now, Evelyn made her way to Coulsdon. Try as he might, he could not find out which Saturday she would take off. He thought if he knew in advance he could stay home that day, and hold her back. Ruefully he thought, she's as wise as me, it's as if she can read my mind. Thinking of Eve, he couldn't understand her reluctance in bed these days, it's as if even that is rationed, he told himself.

It was unbelievable, George whooped with joy and thrust the letter offering him a stonemason's manager job in Cornwall into her hand. 'Read that my love,' he said, 'just what I've been looking for.' Eve read the letter slowly, and dismayed by her slow answer, he said, 'Look, even a house with three bedrooms. We need that for the family. There's plenty of sunshine. You're always saying sunshine is good for them and it's close to the beach. What do you say?'

'Give me some time to think will you?'

'Yes, but…'

Eve handed the letter back to him. 'We can't go of course. Whatever made you go for such a job so far away?'

George was jolted for a moment out of his excitement before saying, 'It's a good opportunity for us all Eve. I can't understand why you're not as thrilled as I am.'

'I like it here. The kids like it here. They love their schools and they've all got friends here. I have too. I don't know what I'd do without Nellie.' She went quiet then added, 'Anyway it's too far. Too far from Vi and the others. I'd never get to see them.'

George made his way to his shed. He wanted some time on his own to think things over. Later that evening, he sat in his chair staring into space. When he did that, he'd told Eve early in their marriage, he was thinking things through, and she knew it was wiser to hold her tongue. Finally he stood up and announced, 'Well, Eve like it or not, I'm going. I'm taking that job. You can come or you can stay here on your own.'

Sharply she turned on him, 'On my own. Oh, like you were when I was away.'

'And what is that supposed to mean?'

'You know full well George. You don't think for a moment that I believe you went without some sort of goings on while I was away do you? I'm not daft you know.'

'You believe what you like. You know I care only about you and I want you to come with me to Cornwall.'

'Yes, and in Cornwall, you'll soon find someone else to care about, I'm sure, if you go on your own.' She snatched one of his cigarettes, she'd never done that before, he'd never seen her smoking, and lit up then choked on the first intake of smoke. There was a determined look on her face, 'No, George. We are not coming with you. Now let's hear no more about it please. I'm off to bed. Goodnight.' The door slammed behind her.

Over the next few days George gave a lot of thought to his dilemma. He wanted the job, and he made up his mind to go, but couldn't find a way of persuading her to move home. Finally, he would have a show down and give her an ultimatum. If she says yes I'll stay, if her answer is no, I'm off, he decided. As she came in from the garden, her arms full of flowers he said, 'Come and sit here a moment, Eve. I want to talk with you.'

Putting the flowers on the draining board, she replied, 'Hold on a moment while I put these in water.' She busied herself for a moment or two then said, 'There, aren't they lovely? You've really got green fingers I do declare.' Sitting down close beside him, she said, 'Now, what is it George? Something important by the look of you.'

Looking into her happy, serene face his heart asked how can I leave her, but his head told him he must get ahead, improve himself somehow. Bluntly he said, 'Cornwall.'

She jumped up. 'No George. Not again. I'm not going to discuss it anymore. Go if you wish but I'm staying.'

'Sit down will you and listen for once.' Lips compressed and giving a long sigh, she sat down again. 'It's a good job Eve. I want it and I'd be good at it, but…'

'Well go then. I'll not stop you,' she snapped.

Taking her hand he said, 'Hear me out. I'm prepared to stay Eve, but there will have to be a…well a few changes like.'

She looked closely at him not understanding, 'Changes? What

changes. I thought you were happy, George. Oh, I know you want to change your job, I can understand that but...'

'I mean changes between you and me, Eve.' He could see she was puzzled. Gently he kissed her on the mouth, 'Eve,' he said quietly, 'ever since you came back from the sanatorium it's as if you've stopped loving me.'

'I do. I...'

'Yes I know you do, but in bed lass, you're always drawing away from me. I don't understand. What have I done to put you off me?'

With her head down, barely audible she said, 'I'm afraid George.'

This puzzled him, 'Afraid? Afraid of what my love?'

'Of falling again. I just couldn't have another, George. It will kill me.'

He left his chair and went on his knees before her and looked up into her face. 'Eve, my love, my darling. You know I'll take the greatest care. I know how your body couldn't take another bairn. I'll look after you, but a man has needs Eve. I need you and to tell the truth I've been that desperate these last few months, what with no loving and not even knowing if you loved me.'

She stroked his hair, 'How could I not love you George Carr. I always have and always will. You and the children are my whole world.'

He sighed with relief. 'So, what do you say, do I stay or go? It's up to you now lass.'

She laughed, 'Not much of a choice is there George. Stay, but...'

'But? What now?'

'I wish you wouldn't make such a fuss when I go to Vi's. Just let me go now and then and I think we will both be satisfied.' It took no time to think this over.

'Right,' he said, 'but for God's sake tell me when you're going.'

'I can only go George, when I've saved enough for the fare to get there from the housekeeping, which takes about a month. Vi gives me the fare home, so it works out quite well.' So that's the answer he thought, I never thought of that.

It was a few weeks later that George was surprised to receive a letter offering him a full managerial job in Amersham. The letter was from Cyril Matthews who had started a new business in his local town. In his letter he offered George a small car and an excellent salary, and suggested they meet up for a talk. You're the man for the job, he'd written. Nothing in the letter referred to their past differences.

The job was all he imagined well within his experiences. The car was a small Ford, and at weekends he folded his family into it and took them for rides. The extra money meant some new furniture including a radio and with much laughter everyone, including Lydia who sang off key, joined in singing the popular songs of the day, their favourite being Mairzy Doats.

George had a minor accident at work one day and when he reached home, he limped into the kitchen and slumped into a chair by the door. Well, he thought, no one took a blind bit of notice, so giving a pitiful moan he feebly made his way to his armchair. Everyone stopped what they were doing and watched him struggle, then all began asking questions,

'Dad, what did you do?'

'Does it hurt so much?'

'What's happened?'

George gave himself a secret hug. Got you, he thought, got the lot of you. He stood up, limped across the room again, turned to face them then said, 'I've cut me finger,' and held it out for inspection. It was to remain a family joke for many years, anyone with a minor injury always stated that they had 'cut their finger'.

One evening as they were all sitting around the table finishing their meal, George said, 'You know what? Something funny happened today.' They continued eating, but George had finished, and lent back in his chair and said, 'Yes, something very strange.'

After a few moments, Evelyn said, 'Well go on. We're waiting.'

George had his audience and began. 'Yesterday, when the men were digging a hole for a new drain as soon as they'd got, oh, about two feet down, the hole began to fill with water, but they went on digging. By the time they'd got to where the connection had to be made, the hole was full.' He stopped and asked, 'Any pudding to-night?' Evelyn went to get the stewed apples and custard while Belle collected the plates.

As she sat down Evelyn said, 'We're not laughing yet, George. Is that it?' Emptying his mouth quickly he said, 'No, no. I said to the lads it looks more like a fishpond than a manhole.' He looked across to the children. 'And do you know what, as we were having our morning break this morning, those scones went down a treat, Eve, one of the labourers called me over to the hole and said,' George mimicked a strong Irish brogue, 'Take a look at that will you.' George had cleared his dish and lit up a cigarette before going on. 'And there in the water, would you believe, were two goldfish. I stood looking down into that hole, took off my cap and scratched my head. I just couldn't work it out. Thought maybe a heron or some other large bird had dropped them in. I could see the men working on a wall close by, were having a quiet laugh amongst themselves, and then the penny dropped, the blighters had put the fish in the water earlier.' He drew on his cigarette, 'The devils caught me out nicely.'

There was laughter all round the table, and Lydia asked, 'What happened to the fish, daddy?'

'Oh, they had a lovely time. A big pond all to themselves for the day, someone christened them Fish and Chips, then one of the men took them home.'

CHAPTER TWENTY–TWO

Belle was to be fourteen in June and leaving school in July. Evelyn and George couldn't agree on what sort of work Belle should be looking for. 'I'll tell you one thing, Eve. There's no way she's going into a factory. No way. The women there are far too coarse. Not the sort for our Belle. I won't have it.'

Eve agreed with him and shuddered at the thought. 'And I'll put my foot down before she goes into service. Work, work, work. No time for herself, at everyone's beck and call. She'll be worn out.' Eve was sewing and George reading the paper.

'I'll look at the adverts,' he said. 'See if we can get any ideas.' The paper rustled as he put it aside. 'Nothing in there, just domestic help.'

'That's even worse than service,' said Eve, horrified at the idea.

'Or shop assistant,' he added.

Eve snorted, 'Varicose veins before she has a family if she goes into that. Anyway, she'd want her own shop that one.'

'We haven't asked her what she wants to do have we?' They were unprepared for Belle's answer.

Belle's face beamed as she announced, 'I want to be a nurse like Aunt Mary.' George glanced at Evelyn who was wide eyed and had gasped with surprise. The child's answer dismayed him as he remembered, in letters from his mother, that Mary had been working over eighteen hours a day sometimes and was often crying with exhaustion. This wasn't what he wanted for his daughter and without hesitation, brutally, snapped, 'No. That's not the life for you.' He could see the questioning look on Belle's face. 'Now don't take on. Listen to me. I'm your father and I'm telling you straight. Nursing is not for you.'

'George, you've got to give the child a reason. No good going off like that. It's not fair.' George glowered at the pair of them.

'Yes daddy. I think it's a lovely job. Looking after people who are poorly.'

'Don't you have enough looking after your mother, girl? Fetching and carrying all hours God made. In real life you get little thanks for that I can tell you. Believe me Belle it is very tiring. You write and ask your aunt. She'll tell you.' He stood up and then said, 'I'm going up the garden and let that be the end of the matter.' As he left he saw Belle pouting with disappointment, then, he wasn't quite sure, perhaps a look of defiance?

During the school Easter holidays an official letter arrived and when George returned from his day's work, he was very much aware of some excitement in the air.

'So, what's going on?' he asked cheerily. 'Won the pools have I?'

'Something better than that George,' Evelyn replied as she thrust the envelope into his hand. He frowned as he could see it had been opened, but as it had been addressed to Mr and Mrs Carr he said nothing. Quickly he read the letter, then slowly for the second time. Belinda, he could see, had placed herself behind her mother. Why, he wondered? Was she afraid of his reaction? A number of thoughts crossed his mind as he carefully folded the letter and wondered where to begin.

'There's a few things to be said here Belle,' he began. 'Firstly, I'll tell you that I'm that proud of you winning a scholarship. To the Nursing or Commercial Department I see. You realise that you can't go don't you?' He looked at her downcast face and knew exactly how she was feeling. Hadn't his own da said exactly the same to him all those years ago when he passed the eleven plus scholarship?

'But…' Belle started to say.

'We don't have the money. You should be spending your time this holiday, looking for something more suitable.'

'But daddy…' Belle tried again.

That's an end to it, I say.'

Belle fled the room in tears loudly calling back, 'I hate you.'

George was getting more angry and shouted after her, 'I should tan your hide girl. Being deceitful like that, going behind my back.' He turned to Evelyn and demanded, 'Or did you know about it?'

But she shook her head and quietly said, 'No, George. I did not.'

A routine they'd developed over the years was a drink of tea, sometimes cocoa before going to bed. On this particular evening as they sat together, both brooding over the letter, Evelyn turned to him and said, 'George, it's a good chance for her.' She held up her hand as he quickly put his cup down and before he could utter a word, 'All right, so you don't want her to be a nurse. I can understand that, and I can make her see sense over it too.' Taking a sip out of her cup, he could see her gauging his mood before she went on, 'Why not let her take up a place in the Commercial Department. Shorthand and typewriting could lead to all sorts of things. Didn't you start that once?'

George grunted. 'She's not going Eve. We get along nicely now on what I earn, but it won't stretch to keeping her out of work for another two years.' Eve took the letter out of the envelope and asked him, 'Did you read all of the letter George? Where it says grants are available?'

George took a deep breath then burst out, 'I'll not have charity woman. Never in my whole life have I had to take handouts.'

'Don't lose your temper with me George Carr. The grant is there to give the children a chance, children who have missed out a lot because of the war, and our kids have missed out, George. Toys, sweets, parents, pocket money and they've had to live with a fear for something they didn't understand.'

George noticed she was out of breath. 'No Eve. No charity.'

Eve screamed at him, 'It's not charity, George! It's a chance for her to work for something a little better.' She was quiet for a moment and taking a deep breath said, 'Let her go George.'

'No,' was his curt answer. For a few minutes they sat silently together then he rinsed the cups before washing himself down ready for bed. Glancing at Eve he could almost hear her thinking, but she said nothing.

No, artfully she said nothing, until they were in bed then she said, 'Some few months ago George, you gave me a choice remember?' He grunted his reply as he settled himself down beside and slipped his arm over her body. He felt her wriggle away from him. 'You said you'd stay here with me and the kids if,' she hesitated, 'if I let you have your own way more often. Right?'

George was tired and wearily asked, 'Where's this going Eve? I'm tired so get on with it.'

'Right,' she briskly, 'it's like this George. Either that girl goes to college or you can forget everything about bedroom favours.'

He couldn't believe his ears and smartly sat bolt upright. 'You what?' he exclaimed.

Calmly she answered, 'You heard me. I mean it. I'll not have her or Lydia slaving away when a little more time in school will get them on in life.' No more was said that night. After a week of loveless nights, George gave in and signed the consent forms for acceptance of a place and for a grant. The grant, he was pleased to note when it arrived, covered all. He was also relieved that everything was back to normal in the bedroom and Evelyn her loving self.

September saw Belinda, arrayed in her new school uniform, begin college. The pride and joy of seeing their eldest child on the way to what they hoped would be her chance of a good life, was marred. It was also the month that Evelyn had an abortion. George had sworn to her that he had been careful and was deeply sorry for the mistake. They were both surprised and shocked at the pregnancy and George was heartbroken to lose the child. Together they had visited the doctor who turned to George and said, 'Mr Carr,' George noted his serious tone, 'If you decide that your wife must go ahead with this pregnancy,' he broke off and seemed embarrassed then he coughed, 'well, there is a risk to your wife's life or at best she could be an invalid for the rest of her days.' George was horrified. 'I already have the signature of a colleague confirming this and you must seriously consider a termination,' the doctor said. In his heart, he knew that life would be unbearable without Eve. He knew too that he had to sign a paper giving his permission. The night before the operation he wrote to Eve,

My Dearest,

Just a few lines to let you know how we are getting on and to wish you good luck. Belle told me you may have your op. on Tuesday.

I hope so, the sooner it is over the better, don't you think? Ann gave the children a bag of monkey nuts and sweets. We gave Francis some and he was eating the outside shell and throwing the middle away. Poor kid, didn't know what they were. I do not know of anymore news to say at this time, dear, except of course, that I still love you and always will. Believe me, kid, I do mean this. I will come down Wed. night, and see if I can persuade the Sister to let me see you. Lots of luck and love to you darling,

Your ever loving hubby,

Geo.

Two years later Evelyn was once again in hospital. When asked, George really didn't know and answered to all enquiries, 'Women's problem,' which always ended the conversations. Although George sympathised with her ill health, he realised, it was only a coincidence that Eve was in hospital when Belle started college and two years later a job in London as a shorthand typist. Once again, the burden of household duties fell to the child, and Belle would come home, and set about the evening meal, although he made sure Lydia did her share by setting the table and washing and wiping the dishes. Financially, things were looking up. At last, George thought, we are keeping our heads above water as far as finances were concerned. Belle and Lydia got Saturday jobs in Woolworths, and he continued with his weekend work.

Nineteen fifty and George was still enjoying his role as manager. He realised there were gaps in his knowledge, and decided that it was time he got himself some qualifications. The opportunity was there locally. He enrolled at the college for two nights a week, and most Saturday mornings for two years. He bought books to study, wrote dissertations and designed and drew a variety of buildings to scale. Although the work covered most of what he had been doing all his working life, he was surprised and delighted at the new technology being introduced.

He continued to enjoy the weekend private work mostly on Sundays. There was a fashion among the wealthier people to enlarge their fireplaces with a wood, granite or marble surround. The most popular and expensive was for marble. George knew a supplier who had ready prepared marble blocks and so it was no hardship to design and build what was required. One day, turning over a dressed block he noticed an inscription. Quickly he glanced around to make sure the client wasn't nearby and checked over what he had already cemented in.

Quietly, he said to the boy, who was helping him, 'Be sure to place the good side uppermost, there's a good lad.'

It wouldn't do, thought George, for the customer to see what he had seen. '...dear departed. 1805' or Reginald Conn...' or 'mother of Isabe...' or '...eparted this life 1857' on the reverse side. Good, God, thought George, marble headstones from graveyards. Should he ask the supplier where he was getting his material from or should he keep quiet? In the end he decided, what you don't know won't hurt, and after all, he was earning good money with his work. He decided not to ask questions.

There were changes in his home life. Belle was courting. John, a nice enough lad, thought George, got a good, pensionable job on the Great Western Railway. Thrifty, hadn't the boy bought his own motorcycle? He didn't like to think of Belle being a pillion passenger, but the lad seemed sensible enough. He was not one of those mad blokes who roared around the streets and whizzed past at ridiculous speeds. What had really impressed George was that one evening John had called to take Belle to the pictures, but instead the boy had got interested in what he was doing in the shed and instead of taking Belle out had stayed, watched and helped George make a theodolite for his surveying work.

Belle seemed to accept that John was no dancer, whereas she had inherited her father's love for the music and dance. The United States

Fourth Military Unit base was less than a mile away, and George had dreaded that Belle might meet some American boy, and clear off to the States. So strong was this fear, he forbade her to go to the base dances, but relented one Saturday evening and took her there himself. Each time Belle was asked to dance, a young man with a strong accent asked his permission and when she was escorted back by the partner, the boy would say, 'Thank you, sir,' and salute. Good God, thought George, they think I'm old and I'm still in me thirties, just.

Both George and John were upset when Belle was rushed into hospital with a grumbling appendix. George's heart went cold as he remembered how the same operation was too late to save his sister. To celebrate Belle's homecoming and his relief, he bought her a wristwatch. Evelyn did not approve. 'George, you spoil that girl. I would have thought if you had that sort of money, you would have bought me one first.'

'You shall have one my pet. Next weekend maybe when I get paid for the work. All right?'

'And what about Lydia?'

Grinning at her he said, 'Aye, as soon as she has her appendix out.'

News from his mother was of a general nature, but one letter informed him that Jessie was expecting twins which would bring her family up to five. George laughed out loud. Well, she always said she wanted a large family and by golly she's on her way, he told himself.

What pleased George was that, his father so near retiring age, had been given the task of looking after the pit ponies underground. Both he and his father had a soft spot for the ponies, and he smiled as he remembered them. Da would have his work cut out. Each pony had its own personality. Some were so gentle it seemed unfair to make them work, others bad tempered, and one or two who were down-right lazy. George knew that the ponies were better looked after than the miners, well fed besides treats brought down by the workers, and what's more they had their own vet. Best of all, was to see them in the two weeks they were above ground when they were able to race around the field. Yes, he was certain that his father was more than satisfied with his last job at the mines.

CHAPTER TWENTY–THREE

June nineteen fifty-three and Belinda married to 'a decent man' as George told Evelyn. Belle seemed happy, although her wedding reception was smaller than the bride intended. George was able to meet the modest cost of the wedding. Evelyn made the cake because she wanted to and George insisted that he iced it. Using his best cement trowel, the cake, 'had the smoothest coating ever seen,' he bragged. Belle was delighted when her father took out a second mortgage on his house to help the couple purchase their own. Everything was just grand, he told himself. Until, for some unfathomable reason, he had an urge to visit his sister Jessie. It was a feeling that just wouldn't go away and on the Saturday he drove down to Jessie's taking Evelyn along for the ride.

Jessie and Ron had been allocated a four bedroom council house in Hampshire, well within a day's visit. When they arrived George was surprised to see Emily was there too. At first he didn't recognise her, sitting with her hands twisting and twisting in her lap, head down, and not answering when he said her name. Baffled, he said softly, 'What's up our Em? Something's happened I can see that.'

Jessie answered, 'It's that swine, Duncan. Done the dirty on her again he has,' then turning to Emily 'hasn't he pet?' Emily lifted her head, her eyelids red and swollen and her eyes dull as she looked up to George and nodded.

Evelyn and George sat one each side of her, Eve took her hand and George said, 'Tell us what's happened then perhaps we can sort it out.'

Full of misery Emily said, 'There's nothing anyone can do. They've gone,' and she broke into fresh tears. George turned to Jessie, 'Jessie, you know what this is about. The lass is not up to it. What's been going on?'

Jessie wiped her floury hands down her apron, pushed back a strand of hair from her face and said, 'Well our Joe, seems that bugger…'

George frowned his disapproval of her swearing, 'Aye, well wait till you hear, then by God Joe you'll be swearing too, I'll guarantee it.'

Hoarsely Emily said, 'You tell them Jess. Just as I told you.'

'Give us one of your ciggies Joe and you might like one yourself to keep you calm. How about you Eve?' Evelyn shook her head, and after they had lit up, she said, 'It's a long story. Remember Em left the eldest boy with Duncan when she ran back to mam's? Told her he wanted the boy Alexander to have a Catholic upbringing. Well, a few months ago he turned up and asked if Bruce could come to London for a couple weeks' holiday with his brother.'

Emily broke in, 'Oh Joe, I never gave it a thought. I mean it would be so nice for the boys to be together, get know each other so I...I...said, yes he could go and...' she started silently weeping again. George was relieved to see that for once, Eve put aside her practical, sometimes hard self, and put her arms gently around Emily, trying to soothe her shaking body.

Jessie and he exchanged glances before she went on, 'After two weeks, Em waited and waited. No letter, no word on the telephone. The Wilsons have one now and they said mam could give the number for messages.' She paused, 'So you can imagine when an official letter came for her, Em. was a bit puzzled.'

'It was awful, Joe. Just awful,' Emily gasped through her tears.

'What did it say? I can tell it must have been pretty grim to get you all in this state.'

Carefully and deliberately Jessie said, 'It asked her to sign the enclosed documents to release Alexander and Bruce Foster from the orphanages, separate ones Joe, not together, so that they could be sent to Australia for a new life.'

Bewildered, George said, 'But I don't understand. I mean I thought you said he had the eldest, Em. That he loved the boy and you trusted him. That everything would be alright.'

Emily sat up straight and said sharply, 'Yes, our Joe, that's what I truly believed but it seemed his new lady friend didn't like kids and so my poor Alex was put into an orphanage almost as soon as I left.'

'The swine! So how come he wanted your Bruce?'

Jessie answered, 'We, well I think he was trying to get even with our Em. But God knows what he must have been thinking. I mean, she never did him any harm and why has he waited so long?'

Evelyn sighed and said, 'To think someone could do such wickedness to another. I hope he rots in hell when his time comes.'

George turning quickly to Emily, asked, 'You didn't sign, did you?'

'Not for days. It broke my heart but what could I do?'

Holding on to his temper, he said, 'Oh Em. You should've come to one of us sooner. Maybe we could have got the boys back. Even if I had to have the boys meself, be their guardian like. You could have seen them, even had them with you probably. Isn't that right Eve? We would have taken them in.'

Without hesitation, Eve said, 'Yes, and welcome at that.'

It was Jessie who sadly finished the awful news, 'It was all too late, Joe, the boys were well out to sea when Jessie got the letter. That bugger, and you'll not stop me calling him that, made sure they were gone before Em had a chance to think about it at all.'

George sat for a long time thinking, feeling impotent knowing there was little he could do. 'Where's the sod now?' he asked bitterly.

'Nobody knows for sure, but he won't stray far from his favourite pub, you can bet on that.'

'What he's done takes some beating. Is there any way we can get the lads back? I mean if you explain all this to the authorities surely they can help. Be a bit sympathetic?'

'Mam and da have tried. But even though the form was late going back, seems Em had given her consent. And that's that.'

George could offer few words of comfort, he couldn't explain to anyone nor indeed to himself, the dreadful loss he felt in his heart. Two of our family spirited away, he whispered to himself. So what if our Em is a bit wayward, she was their mother and he remembered the heart wrenching days when his own children were sent away, all be it in different circumstances. As he and Evelyn were leaving, he did his best to give her some hope, 'They won't forget you, our Em. As soon as they're able they'll come back to you, even if they have to wait until they're grown up. You'll see them again one day.'

The whole affair seemed to have a gloomy effect on both George and Evelyn. Eve more so than George. Nothing seemed to raise her spirits, indeed George couldn't be sure, but he thought that quite often she was near to tears or had been crying.

One Friday afternoon Cyril called him into his office. As he entered he could see Cyril fiddling with a ruler on his desk. Something's up, thought George.

'Sit down George,' said Cyril quietly. George was not usually nervous but told himself that something's definitely wrong. 'I need to speak to you on something and now's a good time.' He leaned back in his chair and George heard him sigh. 'We go back a long way, don't we?' George nodded. 'You've been very loyal and truly hard working over the years I've known you. No doubt about that and you've been truly valued.' Well whatever Cyril was going to say he was taking the long way round to get to it, George mused.

Cyril reached for the packet of cigarettes on the table and offered George one who shook his head. Cyril blew a thin blue line of smoke into the air. Then making up his mind, said briskly, 'It's like this George. My brother is coming back to England. There's too much trouble in Kenya. Not the same since the Mau Mau uprising. He says it's no longer safe to be out there.'

George ran his calloused hand across his mouth and round his jaw and wondered what was coming next. 'Aye, well I can understand that,' he said.

Cyril stubbed out his cigarette and walked round the desk and put his hand on George's shoulder. 'I'm sorry George, but I promised him a job if he came back and well…'

George knew what was coming next and tried to keep the resentment out of his voice. 'You want me to go?' he growled.

Cyril pursed his lips and said, 'Frankly, yes. Think of it as a new challenge. A chance to do all those things you've dreamed about. You should do well in your exams that will help you find somewhere.' George realised the interview was hard for Cyril as he watched him shuffle some papers. 'Won't happen for a couple of weeks, but time enough for you to make plans.' Running his finger down a column of figures in front of him, he went on, 'Naturally, you won't be out of pocket. There's a pension, not much but if you should have difficulty getting a job it'll serve until you're settled.' Then lifting his head he smiled and continued, 'and I will be adding a generous bonus.' George grunted an acknowledgement. Money side of things was more promising than he'd hoped. 'Oh, and by the way, I shall need the car for my brother.'

White faced and angry, George, almost unable to speak for a moment said, 'I'm shattered, but if that's the way it's got to be…' He stood up to leave but didn't offer to shake hands, wisely keeping them in his pockets. He squared his shoulders and said, 'That's it then, I suppose,' and left the room quickly.

When he told Evelyn that evening, she said, 'Everything happens in threes George. First, there was your poor Em's troubles, now you've lost your job. I wonder what's next?'

In no time at all, he found another job. Not very challenging but, as he told Evelyn, it paid enough. Shortly before starting this new job, he bought a second-hand car, and, with John's help, soon had a road worthy vehicle, better really than the last one which frequently let him down, especially in the winter months.

'Well George, as I expected the third piece of bad news has come,' was the greeting he got one evening when he returned from work.

Sighing, he said, 'What is it now?'

Looking at Billy across the dinner table, he could see the lad was quite excited, 'I've got me papers. Call up papers to do me National Service,' he announced proudly.

George turned to Eve, 'You knew that was bound to happen, love. All the lads have to do a bit of soldiering.'

'Yes, but what about me?' she wailed. Billy and George looked at each other and shrugged. 'I mean what am I going to do with myself all day long here, alone. Belle married and gone, Lydia courting and never in. She'll be wed next you see and now our Billy is taken from us.' She burst into tears.

George was exasperated. 'It'll do him good, get discipline, not that he needs it, and make a man of him.'

'And I'll get to go overseas if I'm lucky. Travel for free mum. Can't be bad now can it?' Billy said.

Impatiently, George said, 'He'll be back after six weeks training and back for good after two years woman. What's up with you for God's sake?'

'I'll be lonely, the house will be empty and quiet. It's alright for you. You've got your job, someone to talk to all day. You come home and don't talk to me though.'

'Don't be so daft. It's what life is all about. Having a family, bringing them up as best you know how, then letting them go. We've done our best for ours, but that's how it is for every family, Eve. Think about it.'

'But they're all so young, George. They won't manage without us.'

George laughed, 'Well we did.'

She sniffed, 'That was different.' George laughed again. 'And another thing, our Belle never telephones, or writes or visits for all of that. I would have thought she would be asking me for help or something now she's expecting.'

'Well, if you keep going on at her making her feel guilty, she won't will she? Now pull yourself together woman. What say we go for a walk around the field, it's a lovely evening and I could do with stretching my legs.' Looking into her eyes he said mischievously, 'Like we did when we was courting, girl.'

George hadn't forgotten Duncan Foster, he knew the moment Em and Jessie told him of the kidnap of the two boys, my nephews he told himself, that a time would come when he would confront the man. Not then, as he knew his temper would lead him into possible danger and regrets. So it was one Friday many weeks later when he made his way to the east end of London to The White Hart pub he knew Duncan often frequented according to Emily. It was just on noon when he arrived. Friday had been chosen as it was pay day and too many men in his opinion, once they had their wage packet in their hands made immediately for a public house. From all accounts Duncan ran true to form.

Entering the premises he asked the barman, 'Do you know Duncan Foster?'

The man's answer didn't surprise him, 'You must be a stranger around here. Everybody knows that bastard.' He hesitated, afraid of what he had just said, 'Sorry, sorry. Is he a mate of yours?'

George smiled, and was surprised how coolly detached he felt, yet somewhat excited. 'Not exactly,' he answered, 'I am hoping to catch up with him.'

The barman looked up at the clock. 'Well, I reckon you're in luck. It's Friday and he'll be bursting through that door any moment, I wouldn't wonder.'

George gave his thanks and ordered a half. 'I'll wait,' he said, 'I'd be obliged if you'll point him out.'

Rubbing a glass on a grubby cloth, the man answered, 'He's a nasty bit of work, mate. Best not get on the wrong side of him, if you take my meaning. He'll land one on you as soon as look. Just watch your step, is all I'm saying.'

'Ah! Well, we'll see,' George answered.

The barman leaned across the counter and said, 'I hope you ain't here to make trouble guv. This place has been smashed up, mostly by 'im, more times than I've had 'ot dinners.'

Nodding, George said, 'I'll remember that.' The door swung open and a large man stood in the doorway, blocking the light, then reached behind him and dragged in a young woman who stumbled on her high heels. George saw she could be no more than twenty and by her darting eyes and demeanour, guessed she was nervous of the man she was with.

'That's him,' whispered the barman, then turned his back. Immediately, George felt his long suppressed anger begin to surface. The girl reminded him of a younger Emily. Emily, that's why I'm here, he reminded himself.

Foster, still near the door, turned and called out some obscenity to someone behind him, laughed, then turning back, came face to face with George. 'Move over, you silly sod,' he growled at George. George held his ground.

'You Duncan Foster?' he asked.

'Who the hell's asking?'

George straightened up, pulled back his shoulders and stood level with Foster. 'Are you Duncan Foster?' he repeated.

Foster shoved the girl quickly away from him. 'Get over there and keep your gob shut,' he snarled at her. Then, turning to George he said, 'I am. What's your business mate?'

'My business, and believe me I'm not your mate, is Emily, Alexander and Bruce.' Foster's eyes widened. 'Yep, I see you remember.'

Rubbing his hands together Foster smirked, 'Christ, another bloody hero.' Then as more memories became apparent, George watched as the man's body seemed to swell, and his face reddened with anger before he burst out. 'The last bugger didn't do me much harm, but by God, I'll thrash him if he ever get's near me again.' George waited, then Foster laughed, 'Yer, 'e said somefink abart his sister. Snivelling little bitch she was. Egging me on and teasing, then once she'd got into me bed, started demanding dosh for her kids.' He narrowed his eyes as he looked at George, 'Whose bloody kids, I'd like to know. Met sluts like her before. Always trying it on.'

George had heard enough and catching Foster unawares took his hands out of his pockets, said a silent 'sorry' to his old teacher and pushed him backwards out of the pub's swing doors, onto the pavement, with fists at the ready.

Foster threw off his coat. 'Going to try your luck as well are you me old sparrer? Your mate only got away with it 'cos I was a blind drunk. But for you me laddo, I'm bloody, cold sober,' and with that swung a punch at George, who staggered back. 'Not so bloody cocky now, eh mate?'

The anger that came over George then, was something like he had never experienced before, he was dangerous, and he knew it. Foster didn't have a chance. With fists flying George punctuated each blow with, 'That's for Emily.' 'That's for Alex.' 'That's for Bruce.' 'That's for the lass inside.' Punch after punch found its mark. A crowd had quickly gathered shouting out to George:

'Kill the bastard.'

'He got it coming.'

'Keep it up mate.'

'Serves the sod right.'

Foster swung his fists back, some landing on George, many wildly striking the air. George was relentless, 'That's for Em's misery.' 'That's for Eve's misery.' Punch, punch. It was when he thought, 'That's for me losing me job,' and seeing Foster bloodied, staggering and nearly dropping, he knew he had gone too far. A cry went up from the crowd, 'Rozzers! Cops!'

Someone grabbed George. 'Run for it mate or you'll find yerself inside.' George ran along with the fleeing men, and one dragged him into the gents of another pub. 'Get yerself cleaned up mate quick, then scarper,' the man said, as he left.

Half an hour later when it seemed the fuss was over, George made his way back to The White Hart. As he entered, the barman winked at him, shook his hand and offered him a beer on the house. 'Cops took him orf, mate. They arrested him for affray and disorder in the street. They also found some knuckle dusters in his pocket. So they got him for armed possession too. By, God you was lucky. See you got a split lip though.' George grinned, and took a careful sip of his drink, the outcome was far better than he hoped for.

The final qualifying exam was in May, and he was overwhelmed when his family had clubbed together to buy him a new fountain pen for his birthday, to bring him luck, they told him. It was late August, when Evelyn put into his hands, an official brown envelope. Immediately he knew it was the exam results. Thoughtfully he turned it over, lifted it to the light as if he could see inside. Eve and Francis watched as he opened then read it, and waited. George looked at them and then a silly grin appeared on his face.

'You passed, George?' Grabbing her first he danced her around the room then picked up Francis and swung him round and round, all the while shouting, 'I've passed, I've passed.' Falling into a chair and panting, he pointed to himself, 'Me,' he said, 'George Carr. C. of W. Clerk of Works. That's me. Letters after me name at last.'

Armed with recognised qualifications, he answered and got the position of Clerk of Works on a large council housing scheme. It was, to be truthful he told himself, much more prestigious and demanding than anything he'd done before. Clerk of Works, in sole charge of a large building project where his word was law, and, he admitted, he enjoyed the respect shown to him by the client, tradesmen and labourers, though he hoped he came across to everyone as a friendly, but firm gaffer.

Talking to Evelyn one morning later, he said, 'Now then my girl, you keep saying good and bad luck always comes in threes. I've got me qualifications, and a really good job, so now I'm waiting for the third bit of good luck to happen.'

Looking over the top of her glasses she said, 'Oh, it will. You'll see.'

He wandered down the garden, saw the now neglected swing, and thought about his children playing with the toys he'd made them over the years, toys which their friends had envied and begged for the same. In his mind's eye he could see their childish picnics of biscuits and pop, and it seemed, in those days, the garden was always filled with children's laughter. George splayed his fingers, gazed at them for a second, wishing to feel the familiar tools and wood between them. There was a sadness about him as he thrust them into his pockets in search of his ciggies. The dangers of smoking hadn't touch him yet, and me da is still smoking and he's near on eighty, George told himself. His daydreaming was broken into when he heard, 'George, George.' Evelyn was calling him urgently, beckoning him to hurry. Breathlessly he reached her side. She was crying and laughing at the same time.

Concerned he put his arm around her. 'What's up love? What's got you in this state?' he queried. She was unable to answer, but pointed towards the sitting-room. And there in the doorway was his heart's delight, his eldest, Belinda with her own son in her arms.

Belle was beaming. 'Here dad, meet your grandson. We've called him Derek.' George threw away his unlit cigarette, 'Damn things make me cough, anyway,' he muttered as he took the child in his arms. Gently he peeled back the blanket then gazed down at his grandson looking, he thought, so much like his mother when she was born.

George's heart was captured all over again. 'Be good to have another fellow about the house,' he said huskily. 'Isn't he just a perfect wee bairn, Eve? Our first grandchild.'

Eve laughed. 'Of course he is. Any baby in this family is never less than perfect.'

Talking softly to the child he said, 'Let's leave the ladies to their gossip,' he whispered to the child. Both women smiled then hugged each other, as they watched him stride off with the child down the garden. 'Come on little man, let me tell you something about women. They come into your life, and once there, you've not got a chance.' He looked back at his wife and daughter, 'but by God, you can't live without them.'

Already in his mind, George had begun to plan a junior wheelbarrow, maybe an ark, a racetrack. Who knows? 'You know what, Derek, your grandmother was right. She said things happen in threes, and you've proved her right. Only don't tell her. Keep it between you and me, or we'll never hear the end of it.' Was it his imagination, or did this little imp grin at him? Of one thing he was certain, a new chapter was about to begin in his life.

L - #0061 - 170522 - C0 - 210/148/13 - PB - DID3314055